DARK SIEGE

She whirled around to see it raise the club. Ducking low, she sidearmed a flat beam and it traveled along the ground and caught the beast's ankle. The blast tore through flesh and bone, severing the foot, and the creature wobbled and fell to its knee. It shrieked.

She darted past, and it swiped at her, the blow missing.

From behind, she heard its wings beat the air and now she was closer to the turret. "Hey! Over here! Hey!" she yelled.

She saw the moonlight reflect on a face that peeked between the battlements. *God, I hope they see me coming.*

Jenny was aware of something bearing down on her. The hairs on the back of her neck stood at attention. She wouldn't have time to turn and fire at the beast. In the distance, more of them swooped down, attacking the turret where she was headed. She thought she heard someone say, "It's Chen!"

And then she saw the bolt of light flash from the turret, rising above her, and a pop-sizzle sound as it connected with the target, the screech of the demon ringing in her ears, and someone yelling "Come on," before the weight of it flopped on her and she was pinned to the rooftop with the creature on top of her legs.

It lay perpendicular to her, on its side. There was a smoking hole in its midsection. A rotting, burning smell rose from it, and its hot-coal eyes had gone dim. She shoved it, but it wouldn't budge. She felt like an animal caught in a bear trap. *If I have to gnaw off my own leg to escape, that's really going to ruin my day.*

She looked overhead and saw more of them begin to swoop down toward the roof. Toward her.

Books by Anthony Izzo

CRUEL WINTER

EVIL HARVEST

THE DARK ONES

ANTHONY IZZO

PINNACLE BOOKS
KENSINGTON PUBLISHING CORP.
www.kensingtonbooks.com

PINNACLE BOOKS are published by

Kensington Publishing Corp.
850 Third Avenue
New York, NY 10022

All Kensington titles, imprints, and distributed lines are available at special quantity discounts for bulk purchases for sales promotions, premiums, fund-raising, educational, or institutional use. Special book excerpts or customized printings can also be created to fit specific needs. For details, write or phone the office of the Kensington special sales manager: Kensington Publishing Corp., 850 Third Avenue, New York, NY 10022, attn: Special Sales Department; phone 1-800-221-2647.

PINNACLE BOOKS and the Pinnacle logo Reg. U.S. Pat. & TM Off.

ISBN-13: 978-0-7860-1876-5
ISBN-10: 0-7860-1876-3

First Printing: June 2008

10 9 8 7 6 5 4 3 2 1

Printed in the United States of America

For Tony
Because heroes come in all sizes.

AUTHOR'S NOTE

The geography in this book is based on the City of Buffalo. Where applicable, I have changed some of the locations to suit my fiction. The Bethlehem Steel plant is long gone, and as of this writing, the former Iroquois brewery is still standing.

CHAPTER 1

Engel awoke in the darkness. Moist earth pressed against his nostrils. He breathed no more, so he had no fear of suffocating, even though he felt the dirt packed into his nose. The wet feel of the grave dirt weighed on his eyelids. The darkness was all encompassing, and he could not move his arms, which were folded across his chest and held in place.

He was back, ready to walk the earth again. The Light had diminished and now he was awake. He only needed something to free him from the grave.

His taste for blood and death was immediate, like an itch he could not scratch. It had been the same during the Dark Ages, when they would bring a cowering maiden before him and tie her down. In a frenzy, sometimes breathing like an aroused lover, he would swing the hammer, breaking shoulders, elbows, kneecaps, but never vital areas of the body. The crowd would mostly cheer. Some would cry, others would vomit on the cobblestone square. When the victim's body was nothing more than a tangle of broken limbs, he would weave the broken arms and legs through the spokes and hoist the wretch onto a pole, wheel and all. The crows would take care of the rest.

He had felt no pity for his victims. When he was a child, his mother told him his eyes were like two stones, cold and hard. His father, watching him butcher the family livestock, commented, "That boy, he enjoys spilling blood." It was no surprise to anyone, then, the path he took in life.

Now, he wished to bring that same pain on the ones who put him in the grave. The Light, which kept him prisoner, was extinguished, and he knew soon he would be free.

My Dark Master, set loose my children. Find those who wronged your servant. Bring slaughter upon them. This I ask of you.

His Dark Master. Satan, the Devil. Known by many different names on earth, the Devil himself had chosen Engel to lead his army. *You have a thirst for blood and no pity in your heart. You will bring darkness to the earth. A legion of angels could not stop you. You will rule beside me, and the earth will belong to hell and its Dark Ones.* So the master had told him upon his descent into hell.

In his tomb, he waited. Eager to please the Master.

Laura Pennington awoke in a fit. She had had the dream again, the one about Megan. Around her the covers were twisted and her pillow hung half off the bed. She had been thrashing in her sleep. She looked at the sleeping pills on the nightstand and shook her head. There was no way she was downing them again, even if they did help her sleep. *Sleep* was not the accurate term. The pills had practically put her in a coma, one from which she awoke with heavy limbs and fuzzy thoughts. A night's sleep wasn't worth the sluggishness induced by the pills.

Besides, she had to be sharp. Being an ER doc meant having little or no time to think. If it came down to deciding which drug to administer or needing steady hands to perform an intubation, she did not need sleeping pills slowing her down. The dream this past night was the same. Megan was asleep in her cradle and it squeaked gently as Laura rocked it back and forth. Sixteen years ago, as a nineteen-year-old mother, she had set the cradle next to the bed for fear of SIDS, and she awoke fitfully at every yawn or quickened breath the baby took. In the dream, she heard Megan gurgle, looked over, and watched the baby smile her toothless grin. It seemed terribly real, and if there were smells in dreams, she would have smelled the scent of powders and lotions and the baby shampoo she had used on Megan.

Now, lying awake, the fitfulness of her sleep seemed to contrast with the pleasantness of the dream. The dream itself was not bad, it was the urge that came over her when she awoke. *I won't do it,* she thought. *Won't.*

The baby seemed so real, so concrete. In Laura's first few minutes of waking, she fought the desire to get up and look. She rolled over, hoping to doze off, not having to get up for another half an hour. She pulled the sheets up tight to her ear and listened to the soft tick of the wall clock in the apartment's living room.

Do it, you fool. Go ahead, torture yourself.

She threw the covers aside, slipped into her robe, and padded out to the living room. There was no cradle. Only the sofa, her television, and an apothecary-style coffee table. What did she expect? Megan was sixteen years gone, and only a fool believed that she would be there, that the abduction never happened and a cooing baby girl would be waiting in a cradle for her mother to pick her up.

Maybe I need a psych consult, she thought.

The Megan dream was a version of one of Laura's childhood dreams. Every so often, she'd dreamed of Christmas presents under the tree. Barbie dolls, Strawberry Shortcake, and an E-Z Bake Oven, all new and unwrapped, just waiting. She had gone so far as to sneak downstairs at six a.m. before her father awoke to go to the office. She was always crushed when it wasn't actually Christmas. But the images of presents had been so vivid, as were the emotions that came with

Christmas morning, that she had to check. She was always disappointed. The dream of her long-gone baby daughter brought the same disappointment. That feeling like it should be real, like she had been cheated, upon waking and finding that the strong memory had vaporized into nothing.

Thinking too much again. About Megan, about things she couldn't change. After Megan's disappearance, medical school had offered a refuge for her, someplace she couldn't think about Megan, with nonstop studying, popping uppers to stay awake, professors who told you you were crap and couldn't cut it, and later on residents who treated you like a subhuman species. The ER had been a good place for her. You thought on your feet, no time to dwell on a long-gone little girl when the medics brought in a blood-soaked gangbanger or a kid practically turning blue from an asthma attack.

She decided to get moving. She showered and shaved her legs, thinking in the shower about Dad and his wacky behavior lately. He'd been on a quest to save the Iroquois brewery from demolition, and the old building was nearing its date with the excavator, with no pardon coming from the Common Council. It was like he was possessed. He'd been featured on Channel 2, interrupted numerous Common Council meetings, and nearly been arrested twice for seeking a private audience with the mayor. She hoped when the building was nothing but bricks and dust his lunacy would subside and he would go back to playing eighteen holes at Byrncliff twice a week and bitching about the greens fees.

After her shower, she got dressed and threw her scrubs in a small duffel bag. She then fixed herself a bowl of oatmeal and washed it down with cranberry juice. Time to get to the hospital, another day among the sick and the hurt. But it beat the alternative, which was dwelling on the wound Megan's disappearance had left in her.

She threw on a leather jacket, grabbed her bag and keys, and left the apartment.

* * *

David Dresser hurried toward Lexington Christian Church, a newspaper tucked under his right arm. It was early fall, and leaves whirled around his feet, stirred by a chilly breeze. He turned right into the church parking lot and spotted Reverend Frank's white Escort. As he approached the rear door of the parsonage, he peered back over his shoulder. He was not a nervous man by nature. In his early twenties, he had spent days camping in the most isolated wilderness with little more than a tent and a buck knife. Once a black bear had come within ten feet of his campsite and Dave had squatted by the fire, watching the bear until it lost interest and ambled back into the woods. He fancied himself a cool customer, not prone to ragged nerves or bad sensations, but he couldn't deny the feeling of dread that tickled his spine. He expected to whirl around and see a dark shape duck behind a tree, trying to remain unseen.

The parsonage was a gray Dutch Colonial, and next to the back door was a redwood deck. Reverend Frank had left his Adirondack chair out. On a warm day you could spot him from the street, arms hanging over the edges, a magazine flopped across his belly. David was never so anxious to see the man as he was now.

He knocked on the door.

Reverend Frank appeared, his gray hair spilling out from underneath the familiar Baltimore Orioles cap. Thankfully he took it off before service, although David suspected if the good Reverend had his way, the cap would go with him to the pulpit.

"Did you run over? You're sweating," the Reverend said.

"The meeting room. Now."

The Reverend took a key ring from a peg hanging near the door. David followed him to the church, and while he unlocked the door, David kept watch on the street. They had always been safe in the daytime, but after seeing the newspaper article, David wasn't so sure.

They entered the church lobby and descended the steps. David could smell the faint aroma of garlic and onion, left over from the spaghetti dinner two nights before. The two men went through the church meeting hall, where rows of steel chairs and tables were still set up from the previous night's dinner.

Reverend Frank took out his key ring and opened a door off the kitchen. He and David slipped inside, David noticing the metallic, dusty smell and the soft hum of the church's furnaces. Behind the furnaces were a card table and four chairs. He still felt safe in this room, and he remembered suggesting it for their meetings. Mainly because it lacked windows.

The Reverend sat down, and David sat opposite him. Dave set the newspaper on the table and unfolded it. Then he pointed to an article midway down the front page. The headline read, IOWA FAMILY BRUTALLY MURDERED.

The Reverend took a pair of reading glasses from his front pocket, scrunched up his nose, and picked up the newspaper. David watched him, trying to gauge the man's reaction.

The news had been a hell of a welcome back for Dave, who had spent the last two days on a drywall job in Bixby. A woman named Eleanor Cade had paid him a grand to gut her living room and drywall and mud it. No finish work. He had taken the job. It was easy money, and Mrs. Cade had kept a steady supply of sweet iced tea and turkey sandwiches coming. After roofing work had dried up, he had needed the money, and was willing to travel to find work. Leaving town meant leaving Sara behind, which was not a problem, because unlike other sixteen-year-olds, he could leave her alone and not find the house trashed from some wild party. Reading the article had made him fear for her. She would not be left alone in the future.

The Rev set the paper down, removed his glasses. "You go home yet?"

"I stopped at a convenience store on the way into town. I spotted that at the counter."

"The whole Little family. Murdered. You're sure it's Them that did it?"

"Frank, there's some sick people out there, but this?"

"Then it's a warning," the Reverend said. "They're coming."

"Will the Everlight keep Engel in the grave?"

David had never seen the Everlight, which Frank had described to him as a black, smooth stone. It could ward off the Dark Ones by emitting pure white light, and it had also kept Engel sealed in his tomb. There were two left in the world, one with Engel, and the other in a small Pennsylvania town.

Frank said, "If the Dark Ones are loose, the power of the Everlight holding Engel may be diminishing."

Officer Rollie McPherson popped a stick of Black Jack gum in his mouth and chewed, hoping to work up some saliva. Ever since he had gotten the call to investigate strange noises out at the Little farm last night, the inside of his mouth had tasted like he'd chewed dust for dinner. He had known Harold Little, seen him at the farmers' market in the town square on Saturdays. Little's girls, Maura and Tina, had often come up and asked questions ("What's that on your belt? Is that a real gun? You ever shoot anyone?") when he stopped at the stand to buy corn.

So when it had come over the radio, he had gone out there with a sick feeling in his belly. It wasn't cop instinct or anything like that. He didn't think he possessed that skill (if it existed), and he would most likely spend his days writing out speeding tickets. Instinct was for detectives and maybe Bureau guys. But that was okay. Instinct or not, a part of him hadn't wanted to go to the farm. He had pulled up to the driveway, and through the open car window, he heard the dry cornstalks rustle.

The Littles had a Lab named Sharkie that usually made its home on the porch, but as he approached there had been no barking. It had been just after two a.m. and he had crept up on the house with the cruiser's lights off.

The front window was dark, the curtains drawn. He climbed out of the cruiser, hand on the butt of his revolver. Somewhere out back, a loose board clapped in the breeze, maybe a plank on the barn. He stepped onto the wraparound porch, where two pink bikes with streamers on the handles lay against the house. Everything looked normal so far.

He rang the bell, and when no one answered, he started getting nervous. He went around back, shining his Maglite so he didn't step in a rut and bust an ankle. In the back of the house he found trouble. The screen door flapped back and forth in the breeze, and its center looked as if someone had punched a hole in it. The inside door was also open, the glass broken in a spiderweb pattern.

Now, he pulled his sidearm and crept into the house. In the kitchen, he found two chairs tipped over, and sugar from a dumped canister had scattered across the counter. He listened, and heard only the drip of water from the kitchen sink faucet.

Rollie assumed the bedrooms were upstairs, and he ascended the steps, where he found the spilled contents of a trash can, mostly tissues. He guessed it had been dragged out from a bedroom or bathroom.

At the top of the steps he got a whiff of something like spoiled meat. He looked in the first bedroom on the left. This one was done up in Powerpuff Girls decorations. The bedclothes were in a heap on the floor. There was no sign of the girls.

He found the other two bedrooms in similar disarray and began to think that the Little family had been taken somewhere against their will.

He was about to go and radio for help when he heard a scream. From the pitch, he thought it was a woman's scream, but could not be sure. It sounded like someone was tearing the guts out of the screamer.

He ran downstairs. He flew out the back door and in the darkness could see the outline of the barn silhouetted against the sky.

Rollie stopped about ten feet from the doors. One of them creaked open, and all of the sudden he felt like that scared ten-year-old boy who was too afraid to fetch his father's jig-saw from the basement. His insides seemed to curl up on themselves.

He looked at the opening as if the blackness might eat him up and make him disappear like the Littles. If someone was on the other side of that door . . .

Glock in hand, he made himself move ahead. He took out the flashlight with his free hand. He opened the barn door. A small dust cloud kicked up. He looked inside and pointed the beam.

He saw the girl's face, looking at him upside down. Bruised and bloody, the mouth open, the eyes bulging, he couldn't tell if it was Tina or Maura. The girl's back arched where the sharpened stick jutted from her belly. There were others. He trained the light on each of them. The other Lit-tles had been impaled on spears, slick fluid running down the poles accompanied by the smells of blood and shit.

He ran to his car and got on the radio. As he sat in the car and called into headquarters, he saw the cloud. Black as the sky around it, rolling backward across the cornfield behind the barn. *Never seen anything like that before.*

Now, he leaned on his patrol car, which was parked at the end of the Littles' driveway. He crossed his arms and watched the assortment of news vans parked across the road.

A good looking, dark-haired woman, whose last name he thought was Olivencia, a TV reporter, crossed the road and came toward him. Her skirt was just short enough to give you a glimpse of thigh, and she took long strides on long legs.

"Excuse me, Officer . . ."

"McPherson. And you need to go back across the road."

"Just one question."

"Please go back."

She stepped in close to him. She had on some good-smelling perfume, that was for sure.

"If I could just ask one question."

"You can try."

"Is it true what the papers are printing? About the way they died?"

Rollie stooped down low, until his head was right at her ear level. "You didn't hear this from me. They were all impaled, even the family dog, and Ms. Olivencia? If I live to be ninety-eight, I'll never forget the sight of those little girls with their mouths in a permanent scream." He stood upright, and glancing at the reporter, he noticed her pretty brown skin had turned a shade lighter.

Dave got up and shut the door to the furnace room. He wished he had his Smith & Wesson with him, but it was at home in his dresser drawer.

The Reverend took off his glasses and hung them on his shirt pocket. "You should get home and check on Sara."

"But you agree, it was the Dark Ones."

Reverend Frank stroked his mustache. "It was Them, and yes, they are sending us a message. We have to get to Buffalo. I'll contact Charles."

"What will you tell the congregation?"

"Sabbatical. Us ministers work other days but Sunday, you know. We need our rest."

"I thought that was the greatest job in the world, work one day a week. That and the garbageman."

Reverend Frank stood up. "We'll need to notify the others."

"The Dark Ones will be looking for Sara," Dave said.

"I've got the .357 at home, and I could pick up a shotgun for some extra pop."

Reverend Frank grinned. "You think that will do much good?"

"It will slow them down, draw less attention than the Light."

"You have any loose ends to tie up?" the Reverend asked.

David thought for a moment. He was so used to moving Sara around the country that he never really had any obligation to anyone but her. Packing up and leaving would not be a problem. "I told Mrs. Hannity I'd replace the trap on her sink, but she'll have to wait."

"We could be gone . . . a long time."

"How will Sandra react?"

"Probably worry. She still thinks we have poker games down here and I don't want the parishioners seeing."

"She's never even gotten a hint of what we're up to?"

Reverend Frank shook his head.

Frank had concealed the true nature of the meetings. David had managed to keep Sara in the dark as well until recently, when Sara had started asking questions about her mother; David told Sara her mother died in childbirth. He kept photos around of Janine Coldgrass, one of his old girlfriends. She had dark hair and blue eyes like Sara, and it wasn't too far of a stretch to imagine her as Sara's mom.

"We can take my truck. Meet you here in an hour?" Dave asked.

CHAPTER 2

"When will you be back?" Robbie asked.

Sara Dresser looked at her boyfriend and smiled. She loved the way his hair spiked up in back, the way his varsity football jacket slouched on his frame, the way he kept pushing his glasses up onto his nose. She loved holding his hand and driving in his beat-up Escort, the White Stripes blasting on the stereo. And she hated that she had to leave him.

"Don't know." She picked up her bag and exited the glass doors of the bus terminal. Outside, several Greyhound buses were parked at an angle, engines rumbling. She smelled diesel fumes in the air, and every once in a while, air brakes hissed and one of them pulled out.

"What will I tell your dad?"

"Tell him I'm on a bus headed toward Buffalo. By the time he catches up to me, maybe I'll find what I'm looking for."

"Sara, I mean, Jesus. It's dangerous out there. What if some creep on the bus takes an interest in you?"

She cocked an eyebrow. "And why would they do that?"

He smiled and said, "Because you're so fine."

She wanted to grab him and plant a kiss on him right now,

but it would make things harder. It might make her decide to get in his Escort and drive back home and tell Dad what a mistake she made. "Wouldn't you want to find your mom if you could?"

"I'll miss you."

"Do you care if I find her?" Sara asked.

"I didn't say I didn't."

"Then you'll let me go. And try holding off on telling my dad. He'll call you, though, soon enough."

Robbie slipped up beside her and put his arm around her. She put his arm around his waist, slid it under the jacket and his shirt, and rubbed his lower back.

"I can't believe you talked me into this," Robbie said.

Thank God I could. And I love you for it, she thought. Sometimes she loved him so bad it ached. "Thanks for bringing me."

He kissed the top of her head. "You know where to find this woman?"

"Got the name and address in my bag."

A bus rolled into the terminal parking lot and Sara saw BUFFALO on the sign over the windshield. She and Robbie stepped back and the bus pulled into the space. Now, more passengers had crowded around them, among them a tall elderly man with a cane and a heavyset woman who held the hand of a little girl with pigtails. The bus driver, clad in a blue cable-knit sweater and brown slacks, stepped down from the bus. "We board now for Buffalo, folks."

He proceeded to the side of the bus, where he opened up the luggage storage compartments. Sara rolled her suitcase over and placed it in a pile with other bags. She kept a carry-on duffel that had her cash, some CDs, an iPod, and most important, the printouts and articles she had found on Laura Pennington.

She returned from setting the bag down and now she looked at Robbie, who stood with his hands in his pockets. God, she loved him. It filled her up, ate her up. She thought about him in the shower, before bed, at the breakfast table, and especially in Mr. Montoya's social studies class, or the vortex of eternal damnation, as she liked to think of it.

She moved in close to him and said, "Thanks for the ticket, too."

"Be careful. And call me when you can."

She kissed Robbie quickly and then wrapped her arms around him and pressed her cheek to his chest. The wool letterman's jacket scratched her cheek, but she wanted to stay there. A moment later, she let go and stepped back from him.

"Miss you," he said.

"Miss you, too," she said.

She turned around, afraid that she might lose her courage. The bus driver had loaded up the bags and now stood at the door to the bus. Sara handed him her ticket; he looked it over, nodded, and gave it back to her.

She boarded the bus and took a window seat halfway down on the right. She set her bag on the seat and took off the suede jacket she was wearing. Looking up, she saw Robbie, who gave her a forlorn wave and then walked toward the bus terminal looking like he had a cannonball on each shoulder.

Poor Robbie. I'll be back. But Robbie didn't seem convinced.

Sara settled in to her seat, clutching her bag. So far, only four others had gotten on the bus: the old guy with the cane, the heavyset woman and her pigtailed daughter, and a young black guy in chinos and a Duke T-shirt. They all took seats to the rear of hers, and for that she was relieved. She didn't want company.

The bus backed out, and she watched the terminal roll away. She had twelve hours of watching brown and green farmland ahead of her, so she decided to try sleeping, but after leaning her head against the window, all she got was a stiff neck. Instead she unzipped her bag and pulled out a newspaper clipping. The headline read: LOCAL DOCTOR OFFERS SUMMER SAFETY TIPS FOR KIDS. She looked at Dr. Pennington's picture. *That* was a beautiful woman. If the boys at Lexington Senior High could see Dr. Pennington, they would forget chasing slutty Gina Trask. They'd probably all willingly get in line for hernia exams if Dr. Pennington was the school doctor.

She supposed she had some of the doctor's good looks. The blue eyes, the kind of shiny black hair that only seemed to exist in shampoo commercials—although Sara always kept hers in a ratty ponytail. She liked comfortable and casual. Today, she had thrown on a pink T-shirt and olive drab cargo pants. Robbie was always pointing out clothes that he thought would look good, but usually required showing more cleavage than a Pam Anderson poster.

No, she could not completely match Dr. Pennington's good looks. She tucked the article back in the bag.

It was more than the article, though. it was the letter, folded in thirds and written on yellow stationery. That was what drove her to head for Buffalo. The words in the letter echoed in her mind: *Laura must never know that Sara is her daughter.*

After locking up the church and bidding David farewell, Reverend Frank hurried through the parsonage. In his bedroom he took out a black suitcase and stuffed in pants, shirts, underwear, socks, deodorant, his toothbrush, his Bible with the gold leaf on the front, and a spare ball cap. He zipped the bag up and set it next to the bed.

The weight of his duty began to hit him. Guardian. Of the earth and God's kingdom. They had a mission to fulfill: Use the Everlight to kill Engel and prevent the forces of hell from claiming the earth. But could they do it? The Everlight gave the Guardians their power, and it was a formidable weapon, but he still felt small compared with the size of the task ahead. It was a task better suited to angels, but unlike Christ, Frank could not call down twelve legions of them to fight the Dark Ones. It was the duty of the Guardians alone.

He proceeded to dial the number for the Disciples' Church in Hooverville, one town over.

Samuel Mansfield, the pastor at Hooverville, picked up.

"Sam, Frank Heatly here."

"How are you?"

"I need a favor."

Mansfield chuckled. "You ever call me any other time?"

"Can you cover my ten o'clock service?"

"Next Sunday?"

"I was thinking the next four Sundays."

"Everything okay?"

"It's a bit of an emergency, family thing."

"June's cancer come back? Anything I can do?"

"Nah, Junie's fine. Back to being a big sister, nagging me about my weight and all. So what do you say?"

"Can I go over the limit, say fifteen minutes?"

Rule breaker. Any more than ten minutes at the pulpit and you're giving a sermon to zombies. "At your own risk, my friend."

"I'll chance it."

"Thanks, Sam."

"Let me know if there's anything I can do."

I wish there was. "Appreciate it."

He said good-bye and hung up the phone. When he turned, Sandra stood in the doorway, arms crossed. She eyed the bag, and then Frank. "What's this?"

"That's a suitcase, my dear."

"I know that," she said. "Where are you going with it?"

"I have to leave."

"You won a cruise and didn't tell me?"

Frank took a steno pad and pen from the nightstand, flipped open the pad, and sat on the bed. "Wish that were the case."

He began writing a general letter to the parish, which he had composed in his head while on the phone with Sam.

"Come on, Frank, what is it?"

"You'll need to tell the parish I'm taking a sabbatical."

Sandra stepped forward. She peered over, trying to get a look at what he was writing. "They have to vote on that. Your sabbatical."

"It's for emergency reasons. I'm sure they'll understand."

"Are you wearing that hat too tight?" she asked.

"My mental state is undiminished, I assure you."

"What about services?"

"Mansfield is covering for me. Hopefully he won't put them to sleep with his sermon."

Sandra nodded. "He has been known to be a bit dry."

"Dear, the Gobi Desert is dry. That man is parched and cracked."

She sat on the bed next to him. "Is it June? Is she sick?"

Frank shook his head.

"Are you sick, do you not want to tell me?"

"Fit as a fiddle."

"Your cholesterol is two hundred and thirty."

"Cholesterol is a state of mind."

"Not according to your last blood test," Sandra said.

He signed his name at the bottom of the note, tore the sheet from the pad, and handed it to her. She took it reluctantly and read it over. Then she said, "What will I tell people?"

"Just as the note says. Something urgent has come up and hopefully I will return to worship with them as soon as possible. The church is in good hands. The Elders will take care of things."

"You still haven't told me what this is about."

And I'm not going to, he thought. If he showed her that article about the massacre in Iowa, and then told her it was somehow related to his trip, she would put a padlock on the front door. "Urgent business."

"You're not gambling, are you?" Sandra said. "Have you gone beyond poker? You can tell me."

Frank turned to her. He placed his hands on her bony shoulders. He saw moisture in her eyes and it felt like hell seeing tears and knowing he caused them.

"You're coming back, aren't you?"

He leaned forward and smacked a kiss on her cheek. "I love you. And I hope so."

"Frank?"

Had to be honest, didn't you? "I have every intention of coming back."

"What if something breaks, the hot water tank goes, or that roof starts leaking again, you know, near the chimney?"

He patted her on the leg. "Millard's number is in the black phone book in the drawer. For you, he'll be here at a moment's notice."

"If he answers his phone."

"Be nice."

"Will you at least tell me where you're going to be?"

No harm in telling her that. "Buffalo, New York."

Her face twisted up, and seeing that stung him. He may as well have said one of the moons of Jupiter.

"What's in Buffalo?"

He could tell her everything. About the Enemy, about the murders in Iowa and how it connected, about David and the other Guardians, and the girl, but it was too late and he had a long road ahead. Besides, she wouldn't believe him. She'd think he had seen it on the *X-Files* and chalk it up to his overactive imagination.

"I hear they have good chicken wings," he said, and stood up.

Sandra stood, too. She placed her hand in the center of his chest. "Is there—is there someone else?"

Frank shook his head. He was ripping her apart. He had to get out of here. She had that worried look again, the same one that had stayed etched on her face the time his appendix burst and the resulting infection and fever burned through him. But she had never left his hospital bed, and here he was, ducking out with almost no explanation.

"No one else. Just something I have to do."

With that, he leaned forward and kissed her, and to his surprise, she wrapped her arms around his neck and pressed her lips against his and kissed him long and hard. He tasted apple cinnamon tea on her lips; as she drew away, she said, "I'm scared."

She worried too much. Every plane trip was sure to end with a 747 going into the Atlantic, every road trip to a neighboring church might turn into a fiery wreck. He needed to reassure her. "I'll be home before you know it."

"And that will be?" Sandra said.

"Just as soon as I can."

Mike O'Donnell took a drag on his Kool and blew smoke into the air. From his Monte Carlo, he looked up at the Hark Company's warehouse. A forklift was parked out front, and next to it was a stack of pallets. He watched the big roll-up door, now sprayed with green and pink graffiti. He glanced at his watch. He was early for the meeting with Hark. If he'd showed up late, Hark wouldn't have seen him.

He rolled down the window, tapped ash from the cigarette. The fishy smell from the lake wafted into the car.

The mechanical whirr of an unseen motor sounded, and with a creak the warehouse door was raised. The tallest guy Mike had ever seen stood in the doorway. He stretched, revealing a wingspan like a cargo plane. He approached the car, his slick bald head gleaming. Hark must've started hiring movie monsters.

The man reached the driver's side, and Mike was eyelevel with the guy's waist. The man crouched down. Mike looked into pale gray eyes, as flat and dull as a razor blade.

"Mr. O'Donnell?"

"Yeah."

"Step out of the car," he said in a flat tone.

Mike got out of the car, wishing he had his .45 on him, but the piece was in the glove box. Hark would have him patted down anyway.

Mike stood chest high on the guy. Right now he was looking at the man's red tie. The rest of his outfit was black: suit, shirt, and shoes. Mike looked up and said, "You going to a funeral or something?"

The guy smiled and said, "My job is to create a need for funerals, not attend them."

The guy indicated Mike to follow, and Mike hurried to keep up with the man's loping strides. His stomach fluttered as he approached the gaping door of the warehouse. It was like being an explorer in a newly found cave. He knew that Hark had a violent temper and little patience for mistakes. He wasn't sure what to expect.

Rumor had it he had taken a pickax to the last guy who screwed up one of his assignments. He had no trouble imagining the ghoul who escorted Mike into the warehouse using said pickax on an unfortunate victim.

They passed rows of crates and cardboard boxes, until they reached a door at the far end of the warehouse. It had a sign on it marked PRIVATE. As expected, the man patted him down, and, apparently satisfied, gave a grunt. They stepped through the door. Mike expected to find an old desk and scuffed furniture, but he was surprised. A dark hardwood floor stretched across the room, and on it rested an Oriental rug. The walls were paneled in a rich cherry and a leather couch and chair were arranged in front of a desk. Behind the desk, between two bookshelves, brightly colored tropical fish swam in an aquarium. The hum of the filter filled the room.

"Sit down," the man said.

"Don't mind if I do," Mike said, and plopped on the couch. The leather smelled new.

From behind him, the door opened. Hark rounded the

sofa. Mike caught a glimpse of his outfit: pink polo shirt, blue track pants, and sandals. He took a seat behind the desk and folded his hands as if he were a CEO preparing to address the board.

"So you know why you're here?" Hark asked. "You got the note."

He had. A week ago he'd been out at Cozumel getting some Mexican food and trying to talk Lisa McCready out of her panties. After dinner, he'd found a note in the pocket of his leather jacket. Someone was a crafty son of a bitch. It had said to meet Hark at the warehouse, with the date and time. "Got here early."

"That's good. Guy shows up late, I show him the fuckin' road. That's how it is." He opened a desk drawer, rummaged around. Mike studied him. A solid build starting to go to flab. Probably busted a few skulls in his day. Thick calluses on the hands, scuffed knuckles. You could hammer nails with those fists.

Hark pulled out a bag of jelly beans from the drawer. He took out a handful and popped them in his mouth. Chewing, he held out the bag. "Want some?"

Mike didn't want to be rude. "Sure," he said, and took a handful.

"I eat these things by the bagful. My dentist fucking loves me."

Mike popped the jelly beans in his mouth. They were way too sweet, but he managed to get them down.

"I hear you're good," Hark said.

"Who says?"

"It gets around. Heard you pulled that Peckham job. Nice score."

"How'd you know?"

"You think I'm a cop or something? We're in the same business."

"Makes me jumpy, is all."

Hark put the jelly beans away. "I don't need jumpy."

"Don't worry about it," Mike said. "So what've you got?"

Hark smiled. He was going to enjoy this.

"Like to get down to business, huh?"

"My time's valuable," Mike said.

Hark laughed, a short bark, like a blast from a machine gun. "Your time's valuable. What the fuck? This guy." Still laughing, he said, "You familiar with those condos going up over off Furman?"

"Near the old Iron Works?"

Hark nodded. "They're half done. The builder comes to me for a loan. Needs sixty grand go keep things going. I say fine. I tell him what the vig's going to be, he tells me to go fuck myself. I tell him get the hell out. Before he leaves, he tells me he might go to the attorney general regarding some of my . . . business dealings."

"And you want me to . . . ?"

"Burn the fucking things to the ground."

"I don't do arson."

"The price is good."

It had better be damned good. "I'm listening."

"Fifteen grand."

Mike could keep Mom's chemo treatments going for a while with that money, maybe have enough to fix the leak in the roof. "Why so much?"

"I want to nail this fuck, teach him a lesson. And you're good. You'll keep your mouth shut."

Mike leaned forward. "I'll need twenty. It's high risk."

"I got the fire marshal in my pocket, low risk."

"Twenty."

"Sixteen or get out."

Something told him it would be wise to accept the offer. "Okay. I'm in. What if I get caught, though?"

"You don't want to think about that," Hark said. "Concentrate on the job."

"Consider them toast."

* * *

Mike pulled into the driveway. He killed the Monte's engine and sat with his hands on the wheel. What if the job went wrong? He could wind up at the bottom of Lake Erie. But what if it went right? The money would be nice. But arson. That was a new one for him. He risked putting his ass in the fire—literally—but you didn't turn down Hark. The guy had connections, and if this job went well, there might be more. That could lead to more cash and better care for Mom.

He got out of the car and climbed the steps. He paused for a moment, looking at the peeling blue paint on the house. Forty years in the Valley and his mother wouldn't move. The McCrearys and the O'Laughlins were dead or living in the burbs. The Hoolihans remained next door. The Irish had moved out and the junkies and gangbangers had moved in. The Purina mill was long gone, and when it had been demolished, Mike had watched the rats in a veritable conga line leave the place. The Valley had begun a slow decline, like an aging movie star losing her looks. Except there was no facelift or Botox for a neighborhood.

He entered the house, inhaling the aroma of cigarette smoke and bacon grease. He slipped through the house, stopping at the photo on the dining room wall. In it, he kneeled, dressed in pads and uniform, his helmet at his feet. That had been sophomore year and he had started at free safety. He was All Western New York that year, but that was before he met Mickey Schuler, and according to his mother, before he had flushed his life down the toilet.

Schuler had been team manager. A wiry kid prone to wearing heavy metal T-shirts and studded belts, he had a whistling asthmatic wheeze. That alone had kept him off the team, and it was probably best, because half the team would've cheerfully snapped Schuler's leg. Mickey had a knack for irritating, slipping tacks in a set of cleats or juicing the water bottles with Dave's Insanity Sauce. The hot sauce in the water had left him on the verge of getting fired.

One day after practice, Schuler approached Mike. "I'm thinking of robbing a store. Maybe that place on the corner of your street."

"You nuts?" Mike had said, still dressed in full pads.

"It would be easy. Especially with two of us. I'm not talking using guns or nothing."

"Why you telling me this?"

Shuler leaned against the bleachers, arms crossed. The blue-and-white-clad Bulldogs jogged off the field, red faced and sweaty.

"You're smart, Mike. Not like those shitheads," he said. "I'll split it with you."

After going back and forth, something inside Mike clicked. It was like a switch turning on, some internal machinery that had been dormant. His body hummed. He liked the idea. Loved it.

Three days later, while Schuler distracted the clerk by breaking a bottle of grape Crush, Mike had slipped behind the counter, hit the cash button on the register, and grabbed a wad of bills. He slid the drawer shut and darted out of the store. Somehow he felt jazzed, smooth, and liquid. He floated home.

They had split $176 and were in court a week later. The crime spree had ended and because they were nice Irish Catholic boys they had only to pay back the money and perform community service. They wouldn't pull another job until after graduation.

It was Schuler he would call to help with the Hark job.

Now, Mike entered the back bedroom. Agnes O'Donnell was on the bed, dressed in a pale green nightgown, her veiny legs poking out from underneath. She had a white scarf over her head to cover her now hairless scalp. The skin on her face seemed to sag a bit more with each day.

"Where you been?" she asked.

"Out on business." He pulled up a chair at the side of the bed. He kissed her cheek and she rewarded him with a weak smile.

"Been gone a while, haven't you?"

"Don't worry."

"Hand me my smokes."

"C'mon, Ma."

"They can't do any more damage, Michael. It's like bailing water on the *Titanic*. Hand them over."

Reluctantly, he handed her the pack of cigarettes and a lighter. She took one out and lit it. The harsh smoke filled his nostrils. The tumor that had began in her right breast had metastasized in her lungs and liver. The doctors were giving her a month. He didn't like to think about that.

"Word's getting around Michael."

"About?"

"Your good deeds."

"I ain't no Boy Scout."

"Mrs. Torrez said you gave her a hundred bucks toward her cable bill. And you bought Mr. Galpin a motorized scooter. Ann Driscol told me. You hit the lottery?"

Yeah. The money. He kept a little tucked away from each job he pulled, selling stolen goods or using cash taken from a heist and spreading it around the neighborhood. Spreading money around was the least he could do, help out the neighbors.

"Well?" she said, through a curtain of smoke.

"I've been doing some odd jobs."

"For?"

"People."

"Ann said she saw you talking to Gino the Wop over chicken parm at Chef's"

"Ann Driscol needs some duct tape for that mouth of hers. Gino needed someone to run some errands."

She blew smoke overhead. "People say he sells hash out of that garage of his. Car repairs, my asshole."

"Mom, don't talk like that."

She cuffed him one across the side of the head. "Ow!"

"I'm still your mother," she said. "You and Schuler up to something?"

He pushed out the chair and stood up. "I'm going to take care of you, Mom."

She gripped his wrist, her skin warm against his. With a pleading look on her face, she said, "Don't lie to me. Are you pulling burglary jobs?"

He looked into her eyes, formerly full of hellfire, able to extract confessions from the heartiest of souls. Now, they were watery and red rimmed, the eyes of someone who had felt more than their share of pain. Eyes that were looking for the referee to call the fight. "Never, Mom."

"Okay, Michael."

He went upstairs, to the flat where he stayed, his guts feeling like a mess of knotted ropes. He had looked into the eyes of his dying mother and told the worst lie of his entire life. Taking a Heineken from the fridge, he unscrewed the cap and it gave a little pop. He took a swig. Right now it tasted like cigarette ashes in dirty dishwater. He set it down.

Just a few more jobs, then that was it. No more stealing. Or lying.

CHAPTER 3

"Chief, got a problem," Laura said, and watched Dr. Lawrence McGiver as he looked over the contents of a manila folder. The comb-over that he effectively plastered to his head hung down onto his forehead, and his rimless glasses were on the end of his nose. His narrow face seemed even more pinched than usual. He looked like a man in perpetual pain.

"Pennington, what is it? I'm going over the DiLeo case here. Busy busy." He snapped off his glasses and said, "Come in. Make it quick."

Laura hurried into the office. The smell of McGiver's cologne hung in the air, and under that, a whiff of the cigars she knew he snuck in here. The window to the office was cracked open, and she wondered if he had been sneaking one recently. She had an image of her boss bent over, craning his neck sideways and blowing smoke through the barely open window. She had to stifle a laugh at the thought.

"Well?"

"I have to leave."

"You sick?"

"No."

"What then?"

"It's my father."

"He sick?"

"I got a phone call." One of the ER nurses had come running in while Laura was looking over a kid with an ankle sprain. At first she had thought someone was dead or hurt, but the nurse had only said, "Your dad's in trouble."

"What is it?" MacGiver asked.

Here goes. "He's trying to stop the old Iroquois brewery from being torn down."

"And that's an emergency because?"

She felt her face get hot. Why did she always feel like such an ass explaining this to people? She wasn't the one acting crazy. "He's holed himself up inside the building. The machines are outside waiting to tear it down. He had the foreman on the job call me to come down. They're going to arrest him."

"Well, there's something you don't see every day."

"No, you don't."

"Can we spare you?"

"Ostrow and Sampson are here."

McGiver let out a long sigh.

"The brewery's only five minutes from here."

He put his glasses back on and picked up a pink form from the folder. She knew the DiLeo case was wearing on the boss. One of the docs had missed an irregularity on an EKG and sent a patient home. The patient had stroked out later that day and now the family had hired a billboard attorney to sue the hospital.

"Make it quick," he said.

She left him to his reports and hurried for the parking ramp.

* * *

Laura turned right at the street sign marked Iroquois Alley, taking note of the bullet hole punched in it. The alley, a stretch of rut-marked dirt, led to an L-shaped brick building. It was four stories tall. Around it was an array of construction equipment: dozers, excavators, and dump trucks. The old brewery was close to becoming rubble. Iroquois had been popular when her dad was a young man. Outside of brewpubs, Buffalo had no breweries left.

She parked the car near a rusted red dump truck and got out. She still had her scrubs on, and she drew stares from some of the workers as she approached a man in a yellow hard hat. He had a stubbly face and thick jowls. He spoke into a cell phone. He appeared to be someone in charge, perhaps the foreman.

She looked at the building. A large doorway, one meant for trucks, was open. The smell of oil and diesel fuel hung in the air. Darkness filled the opening, and she could only see a few feet into the building. That made sense, for they would have shut the power off years ago. But somehow the darkness inside seemed more complete, total, than any darkness she had ever witnessed. She didn't envy any of the demolition workers who may have to set foot in the old brewery.

Behind her, she heard one of the men say, "Hey, we got a nurse in case someone gets hurt."

Laura turned around to see a lanky guy with bushy hair leaning against the cab of the dump truck. A cigarette dangled from his lip. He held a Styrofoam coffee cup in one hand.

"I'm a doctor. And if someone drops a brick on that pointy head of yours while I'm here, yes, I can help you."

He took a drag off his cigarette and blew out smoke. "Okay, doc. Don't have to be so touchy."

She bit his head off. Maybe not necessary, but she was losing patience.

Now, the guy on the cell phone finished his call and

folded the phone shut. He stuck it in a holder clipped to his belt.

Laura tapped him on the shoulder and said, "Laura Pennington. I'm looking for my father, Charles. Got a call he was here."

"You're the crazy dude's daughter, huh?"

"He's not crazy."

"If you say so. Hang on a sec." He walked over to a beige pickup truck, opened the driver's side door, and took out a flashlight and a hard hat. He came back and handed her the hard hat. "Put it on. There's some crumbling bricks in there. Don't want you to get bopped on the melon."

She put the hard hat on. It was loose and wobbly, but it would keep said melon intact.

"Pirrone," he said, introducing himself.

He waved, indicating her to follow.

She followed him under the doorway to a set of stairs in a narrow case. In front of her, the flashlight bobbed and the stairs creaked underneath them. If not for the flashlight, the building would have been as dark and dank as a cavern. She wanted very badly to find her father and get back into the sunlight.

Pirrone stopped at the landing. Laura wound up next to him. In front of them, on the wall, was a wooden hatch with rusted steel strapping across its front.

"He's in there," Pirrone said.

"What is it?"

"When this place was a brewery, they had rollers in there, used them to slide the cases where they needed to go, I suppose." He crouched down and opened the hatch.

Laura crouched next to him, taking in the odor of cigarettes and aftershave. He handed her a flashlight, which she shone in the opening. Ten feet inside, she saw her father, dressed like he was going to play eighteen at the muni golf course. He wore a dark cardigan with a polo underneath it, and khakis, which were now stained with grease at the knees. He gripped a flashlight whose beam sputtered in the darkness.

What have you done now, Dad?

"Hello, Laura."

"Interesting place you're spending your free time these days."

"They won't listen any other way. Not the councilmen, not the planning board, nobody. This will get their attention."

Pirrone stood up, his knee popping. "The cops are on the way, you know."

Laura looked up at Pirrone. "Did you really have to do that?"

Pirrone tilted his hard hat back with his finger. "I've got machines sitting idle, and idle machines don't make my bosses any money. I need him out of here. Yesterday."

She looked back down the tunnel. Hopefully she could talk him out before the cops got here. "Dad, the cops are coming."

"I need to save this building."

"You can't fight it from jail," Laura said.

"As soon as they pull me out of here, this place will be rubble. I can't get the city to stay the demolition. And even though that moose standing next to you would probably like to bust my schnoz right about now, I don't think they'll tear the building down around me."

"Don't be so sure," Pirrone said.

Laura stood up. "That's my father you're talking about."

"Yeah?"

"You remove one brick while he's in there and I'll find the most rabid pit bull of a lawyer I can and sic him on you."

"That old man is trespassing and you know it."

"His name is Charles," Laura said.

"*Charles* is trespassing, then."

"Let me talk to him," she said, and crouched down again. "Dad, you have to come out."

"You have no idea what's riding on this, Laura. None."

"They don't let you golf from jail, you know."

Dad made a disgusted noise. "They're not sending me to jail."

"That cardigan won't match with a prison jumpsuit."

The creases in his forehead unfolded and a smile crossed his face, and then disappeared. He didn't want to give in, but she had gotten a quick smile. Perhaps she was breaking through.

"Let them move me."

Laura heard footsteps. She looked around and saw two Buffalo cops, both roughly the size of refrigerators, climbing the steps. The one in the lead was sliding a baton into his belt. The one behind him had a flashlight.

"Glad you guys are here," Pirrone said.

"Where is he?" The first cop said.

Pirrone pointed to the opening.

"Who are you, ma'am?" The cop said. Laura stood up, looked at his name tag. It read: Slowinski.

"I'm the trespasser's daughter," Laura said. "I'm trying to talk him out of there."

"What's he doing in there?" Slowinski said.

"He's trying to save this building from demolition."

Slowinski raised his eyebrows. "Better ways to do that."

"The Common Council didn't listen to him."

"I'll give him a chance to come out, but if he doesn't, and I have to go in after him, he's getting arrested."

Her dad wouldn't last half a day in jail.

Laura started to speak and stopped in midsentence when she saw her father emerge from the tunnel. Cobwebs littered the back of his sweater, and his fine gray hair stood askew.

"You going to leave now?" Slowinski said.

"I can't fight from jail, can I?"

Can't fight what, Dad?

"I suppose not," Slowinski said. "We're out."

The two cops felt their way down the stairs. Pirrone muttered something under his breath and motioned for them to follow. At the bottom of the stairs, Laura gave him back the hard hat and he gave her a thumbs-up as a big engine coughed to life.

Laura looked back at the building. Even the rats might stay out of a place that dark and dreary.

She walked toward her car, her dad next to her. She put her arm around him, gave him a squeeze. "You had me worried."

He gave a quick smile, then turned and looked at the building with a measure of sadness. No, not sadness, it was more like worry. The same look he used to get before she left on a date with a new guy, as if Dad feared she had brought home the Boston Strangler.

"What is it about this place?" she said.

"They don't know that they're doing. The only reason I came out was because in jail, I can't do any more."

"Do any more of what?" Laura said.

"Getting ready."

"For?"

"Honey, can you get out of here, pack up, leave?"

The question caught her off guard. She felt as if she'd been rocked back a bit. "There's this little thing called the hospital, and they like me to show up now and then."

"Don't get smart, girl. I'm not kidding. Can you?"

"Why would I leave?"

He placed his hands on her shoulders. "Things are going to get bad, Laura, and it all starts with this building coming down. That's all I can tell you, but very soon you won't want to be in the city. Not if I think what's going to happen does happen."

Was he drifting into the early stages of dementia or

Alzheimer's? Or maybe the stress of fighting to keep the brewery open had cracked Dad. Either way, the prospect of him slipping into some sort of mental abyss was disturbing.

"Dad, maybe you should get checked out. We've got a real good psychiatrist at the hospital, Dr. Pham, or maybe start you out with a physical."

"Always the doctor, aren't you?" He dropped his hands. Behind them, metal squealed as an excavator rolled to the building. The operator raised the boom and the metal claw bit into the brick and sent up a puff of dust. Again, Dad looked back at the building, his face taking on a pinched look.

"It's not just for historical value, is it?" Laura asked.

Dad turned and faced her. "I wish I could explain, Laura, but not now. There's too much to do."

"You can tell me anything. That's what *you* always told *me*."

"If you can't leave town, stay buttoned up in your house for a while. Please?"

"So the building is going to release a dust cloud, set off my allergies?"

Dad frowned. "Just listen to me, Laura." He looked down at his sweater and brushed off a bit of gray dust.

"I'll be careful."

"You'll need to be more than careful. Walk me to my car?"

He was being cryptic, which didn't surprise her, but his considering the demolition of an abandoned building to be a threat to her left her unnerved. Not because she thought his warning had any validity, but because the cheese may have slipped off Dad's cracker.

They passed through a cloud of dust and around them the shouting of men and the whining of metal on metal filled Iroquois Alley. They reached Dad's car, a white Caddy, and he opened the door.

"I hate shrinks, you know."

"I'm sorry, but you've got me worried."

Dad leaned over and kissed her on the cheek. "Stay safe, Laura. Hopefully things will be fine and I can keep it in check. And don't worry about me."

But I do, she thought. *Oh, how I do*.

CHAPTER 4

Upon entering the house, the first thing Dave noticed was the lack of noise, specifically the White Stripes or The Ramones pumping through the stereo speakers. The lack of noise left him on edge, and although he knew he hadn't been followed and the house appeared untouched, he wished for his revolver right now.

"Sara?"

He slipped through the kitchen and the living room and climbed the stairs. He entered her room. The blue comforter was neatly tucked under the pillow, the stereo off, her closet and dresser drawers closed. She wasn't working at Cook's Records today, and on days she didn't work, Sara came home and started on geometry, one of her least favorite subjects. She should've been here.

A quick call to Lori Packer, Sara's best friend, confirmed she wasn't there. He tried the school and Mrs. Davenport, the school secretary, confirmed that Sara had been by the office before leaving at three p.m.

Where the hell was she?

He checked the rest of the house, calling her name, and

when he got no answer, he decided to pack up, lock up, and try Robbie's house.

He threw together some clothes in a leather satchel, along with the Magnum and a box of shells. From under the mattress, he pulled out eighteen hundred dollars in cash, mostly saved from his drywall and carpentry work. He stuck his hand back underneath the mattress, unable to find what he wanted. The articles about Laura Pennington were gone, as was the letter.

It didn't matter now. What mattered was finding Sara.

He took the cash and his bag and went to the kitchen, where he counted off fifteen hundred dollars, the next three months' rent, and stuffed it in a number ten envelope. Then he called Vera Peterson, his landlady, and left her a message saying he had to leave for a few months and the rent was on the counter. Harris Roofing had laid him off, so there was no need to call in sick to a job.

He got in the pickup truck and threw the satchel on the passenger side floor. The Magnum went in the glove compartment. As he drove over to Robbie's, his worry about being followed had subsided. The sunshine came in the truck, warm on his face, and it seemed unlikely that an attack would occur on such a day. The breeze had died, and a bleached-out fall day had given way to the golden hues of Indian summer. He felt slightly better.

He pulled into Robbie's driveway, where he heard the hum of a weed whacker coming from behind the house. He killed the engine and got out and strolled through the side yard, past a row of neatly planted hostas and a blue storage shed.

He rounded the corner and saw Robbie swinging the trimmer like a scythe. Robbie looked up, aware that someone was watching, and he cut the engine, which puttered out.

David approached him and Robbie took a step back. He was a good kid, and an honest one, but he had one failing: Sara. If Sara had suggested they construct a life-size replica of the Eiffel Tower out of Popsicle sticks and Krazy Glue, Robbie would have cheerfully agreed to it. David had no doubt he knew where she had gone.

"Hi, Mr. Dresser."

"I'll be brief. Where is she?"

"Not at home?"

"Do you think I'd be asking if she was home?"

Robbie ran a thumb along the weed whacker's trigger guard, looked at the grass. "You going to hit me or something?"

Dave stifled a snicker. "That depends. You didn't do anything that would make her suddenly vomit in the mornings or gain inordinate amounts of weight, did you?"

Robbie looked up at him. "Hell, no. Sara wouldn't even let me—"

"That's enough info right there. Now where is she? It's important."

"I took her to the bus station."

"For a tour?"

"She got on a bus."

"Where to?"

"Buffalo, New York."

"Why?"

"She found some pictures of her real mom."

The pictures hadn't been with his stash of money, had they? He'd been in such a hurry he hadn't noticed them missing. "When did she leave?"

"About an hour and a half ago."

David scowled. "Whose idea was it?"

"Uh . . . Mine?"

"You sure about that?"

"Hers."

He felt a sick little cramp in his belly, and things around him seemed to spin and lose focus. She was heading right into the thick of things.

David thanked Robbie and ran for the truck.

* * *

Reverend Frank opened the door of the Trailblazer, threw in his bag, and sank into the passenger seat. He shut the door, taking in the artificial strawberry smell from the air freshener that dangled from the rearview mirror.

He checked his watch. He had enough time to make a phone call to Charles in Buffalo. He leaned to one side and dug his cell phone out of his pocket, flipped it open, and dialed Charles's phone number. Charles picked up on the third ring.

"Charles Pennington."

"Charles, Frank Heatly."

"Thank goodness."

"You sound out of breath," Frank said.

"I just got home. Bad news."

Why had he thought it would be anything different? "Shoot."

"They've torn down the brewery. I tried to stop it, but they called the cops and Laura showed up and I'd be no good to us in jail."

That was bad news. The worst. "You fought a good fight, Charles. Did you see the news about Little and his family?"

"Brutal. And it was Them, no question."

Frank looked out the windshield and saw no one. He didn't need Sandra poking around asking questions. "David and I are on our way there. I'm going to call Chen in Routersville and see what the situation is there."

Routersville was one of the last strongholds, and if things were going to get bad in Buffalo, they would need the Guardians in Routersville to help. Chen was always up for a fight. She would be rallying the troops by the time he and David arrived.

"Do you think it can still contain him?"

Charles coughed. "With the building down, I don't know.

And I'm not sure about the strength of the Stone. And the Dark Ones are probably on the move already."

"So this is it," Frank said.

"I'm afraid so."

Frank wished him well and hung up. He took his bag and got out of the truck. He looked at the Adirondack chair out on the deck of the parsonage and lamented that he might not be back (despite what he had told Sandra). Spending a lazy Saturday afternoon with a book and a glass of loganberry might be a thing of the past. All of this might be gone, the church, the town, all of it. All of America and maybe the rest of the world, too, if that brewery didn't hold its prisoner.

He wished for David to get here. Ordinarily, he despised a long car ride, but he never felt more anxious to get on the road than now. He checked his watch and waited for the ride that would eventually lead him to the Enemy.

Milo Gruder worked the excavator's foot pedals and joysticks and swung the arm around and over the red dump truck. He'd missed the excitement at the brewery, having spent half the day on another job, where he sheared apart abandoned oil tanks. Apparently some nut had crawled inside and the cops were called. Figures he would miss it.

He released the load from the machine's grapple bucket, and it thudded into the dump with a clang, giving up a cloud of brown dust. The machine's controls were like arms and legs, second nature to him. He was the best guy Eastern Wrecking had, an ace with a bucket or a shear, and he knew it. He didn't mind the heat in the summer, the cold in the winter, the dust, the mud, any of it. The only complaint he had was the stabbing pain that radiated down his right leg. Sciatica, the doctor had told him, an inevitable condition arising from spending fifty hours a week seated in the same position. But the pay was good, and in another two years he planned on retiring to a place in Boca Raton.

He finished loading the truck, the last one to go out. He shut down the machine and stepped down from the cab. The air was crisp and had taken on a dry, dusty smell. Nearby, half of the old brewery lay in a heap of bricks and twisted metal, and the dilapidated houses beyond the building were now visible.

Milo took off his hard hat and wiped his brow with the back of his hand. A chill washed over him. It had been warm in the cab of the machine, but damned if it wasn't getting downright nippy.

He gathered up his lunch box from the cab of the machine, as well as his quilted flannel jacket. He put the jacket on, remembering it as a present from Vera. She had bought it for him two Christmases ago, five months before the aneurysm dropped her to the kitchen floor and he had found her slack jawed and drooling. She had died during emergency brain surgery. He would keep the coat until it was rags. It had a rip in the sleeve and a tattered hole in the front pocket, but it had come from her and he was loath to throw it out. She would have sewn it and patched it if she were here. God, he missed her.

He started past the loading door, then the pile of rubble. The sky had started to go dark purple, and he hurried a bit to his truck. The East Side didn't have a good reputation. Just last week two rival drug gangs had a shoot-out on Swan Street, just a few blocks in the other direction. Milo had enough holes in his head already without needing an artificial one.

As he neared the truck, he heard the clink of brick on brick and he turned to look at the pile. A small cloud of dust had risen, as if the pile had stirred. It may have been a rat, although before they could start demolition, an exterminator had been brought in and poison bait set out. The city insisted on it before they issued a permit.

The pile shifted again and a few bricks tumbled from the top of a four-foot pile. *That's one big rat*, Milo thought.

"Anybody there?" He realized how feeble his voice sounded, but he couldn't deny his racing heartbeat and the stab of fear that went through him.

He popped open the door of his truck and slid inside. After starting it up, he backed out and pulled down the alley. As he drove farther from the wreckage, he felt a little silly jumping at what amounted to nothing more than a rat in a pile of bricks.

He reached Broadway and signaled left. The cell phone clipped to his belt rang. He unclipped it, opened the phone and said, "Yeah?"

"Milo. Drenker here. You still on the site?"

Great, a call from the boss when all he wanted was to get home.

"Just pulling out," Milo said.

"Do me a favor. Bill Holly called me up. He left a chop saw sitting by the big loading door. If it isn't already gone, grab it, will you? It won't be there in the morning if we don't."

He wanted to think of an excuse, but couldn't come up with one. *Don't really want to drive back there, do you?* Damn Holly for leaving a seven-hundred-dollar saw on the site. At least maybe Drenker chewed his ass for forgetting the tool.

"All right."

"You're solid, Milo."

He didn't feel particularly solid as he hung up the phone. Milo swung the truck around, kicking up a dust cloud. The suspension bounced and the joints whined as he steered the truck back down the rutted alley.

He stopped the truck within twenty feet of the brick pile. Leaving the headlights on and the engine running, he climbed out. *Wish I had a flashlight*, he thought.

He stood at the side of the truck for a moment, listening, and when he heard no more scraping noises, he started forward. Near the roll-up door, Drenker had said. Just grab it, throw it in the pickup bed, and scoot. That's all.

Approaching the loading door, Milo squinted. There it was, one of the new Bosch saws Eastern had bought for this project. Man, Bill Holly was going to get it for leaving the saw on-site. He gripped the saw by the handle and hoisted it. So far, so good.

It was when he turned back toward the truck that the hairs on his arms shot up. He was being watched. He had felt that same thing in a thicket of jungle near Da Nang, that prickly sensation, and he had looked over and saw a VC raising his AK, ready to blow Milo into the next life. One of his squad-mates, Ricky Piper, turned the VC into red mist and had saved Milo's life.

He turned slowly. Between the main building and the brewery's garage, the alley continued. At the far end of the alley stood a silhouette in the darkness. Milo guessed him to be about six-and-a-half to seven feet tall. He had long stringy hair and was dressed in a tattered trench coat. The moonlight reflected in the guy's eyes like they were shiny quarters. Milo felt afraid, more so than when Charlie had nearly capped him in the jungle. There was something wrong with this fucker. He stood perfectly still, and Milo knew it wasn't some bum or junkie looking for cash, but someone bad, someone who would hurt Milo, maybe just for sport.

Still holding the saw, Milo backed toward the truck, not taking his eyes off the guy. The figure stood and watched. Milo expected him to come charging down the alley any-time, but instead he stood still, which somehow made it more disconcerting.

He bumped into the front fender, then felt his way to the door handle. Watching the alley, he set the saw on the pas-senger seat. Then he climbed inside, shut the door, and pressed the lock button. He smelled his own cold, sour sweat.

He watched the guy for a second, the big dude standing, watching. From inside the truck, he thought he heard a raspy chuckle coming from the guy. Once again his arm hairs stood on end.

He backed the truck down the alley, thinking it would be a big mistake to turn the truck around and leave his back exposed. He fully expected if he turned around he would see the guy charging down the alley after him. As he reached Iroquois and Broadway, he backed onto the street, turned, and floored the gas. The tires gave a screech as he peeled away.

CHAPTER 5

Sara awoke, her face pressed against her duffel bag, which she had propped between herself and the window as a makeshift pillow.

A quick look at her watch told her it was eleven thirty.

She sat up and immediately noticed the sour smell of vomit. It made her stomach roll. She scooted over and peered back down the aisle and saw a green puddle with chunks of food in it. She also heard the soft sobs of a little girl and the woman's attempts to soothe her daughter. Poor thing must have gotten sick and not made it to the john.

She turned back around and held her hand over her nose and mouth. The bus was slowing and the gears whined as they pulled off an exit on I-80. The driver turned right. They passed a white farmhouse and then about a mile down the road they pulled into a gas station/convenience store. The driver parked next to the building and announced they would take a ten-minute break.

The heavyset woman got off, the little girl in tow, and as the little girl passed, she looked at Sara, her turtleneck spattered with food. Sara waved to her, and to her surprise the girl smiled and waved back. Little kids were tough. Puking one minute and smiling the next. If that happened to her, Sara would have been curled up in a ball, wishing she were home.

The guy in the Duke T-shirt got off next, and Sara followed. She needed to pee, and the prospect of bouncing around on a bus toilet and the subsequent cleanup it required did not thrill her.

She stepped off the bus and under a pole-mounted sodium vapor light. The fluorescents from the canopy over the gas pumps provided the only other lighting. She looked around and to each side of the store saw only the ribbon of highway and an expanse of shadow-shrouded fields. To the rear were woods, maybe fifty yards from the parking lot.

Sara entered the store behind the others and asked the clerk where the bathroom was. The clerk pointed to the rear of the store and said, "Through those double doors."

She saw the bus driver approach the counter with two rolls of paper towels, a package of yellow cleaning gloves, and a can of Lysol. She didn't envy the guy and he gave a shrug and said, "Comes with the territory, I guess."

The guy in the Duke T-shirt bought a sixteen-ounce cola and a bag of pretzels and went outside. Sara reached the double doors just as the woman and her daughter came out.

"She okay?" Sara said.

"Next time she's going to tell mommy when her stomach gets flopsy, right?"

Flopsy?

The girl nodded, her pigtails bouncing.

Sara used the restroom and exited the store. The bus was the only vehicle in the lot, and she watched the highway for a moment, but not one car passed. It was as if they had docked at a remote space station on a distant planet. She felt small out here and longed for the protection of the bus.

From around the corner, she heard a voice say, "Lookit that."

She rounded the corner, where the young guy in the Duke

T-shirt stood sipping from his giant soft drink, the bag of pretzels tucked under his arm. He was looking at the woods.

"What is it?" Sara asked.

He looked down at her. "Those branches, look how they're whipping around. I'm Ritchie, by the way," he added.

Sara introduced herself, but she didn't look at Ritchie. She watched the woods, the low branches on the pine trees brushing back and forth, as if pushed by wind. Except there was no wind tonight, and the tops of the trees stood still.

"You think it's some deer? Or maybe a bear. Hell, I grew up in Gary, never seen anything like that," Ritchie said, and took a swig of his cola.

She didn't want to get that close to a bear. "We should get back on the bus."

Now, in the woods, branches rustled across a thirty-yard front, and she could hear whispering. The branches whipped back and forth. A sparrow shot out of the trees, as if fleeing from an unseen predator.

Ritchie stood transfixed, watching the woods. Sara gripped him by the elbow and said, "Ritchie, get your ass back on the bus."

He gave her a quizzical look and said, "Yeah, yeah, probably should." He strode across the lot, sipping his drink.

She had a gnawing feeling that this is what Dad and Reverend Frank had talked about. She had laughed at the idea of the Dark Ones, but now she wasn't so sure, and she wasn't going to risk others' lives if Dad and the Rev were right. Had something been following her?

She jogged back toward the bus. The driver stepped off the bus, a bunch of paper towels in his hand, his face twisted in a look of disgust. Sara said, "Where you going?"

"I thought I'd keep these for my collection, along with my kids' shitty diapers. I'm throwing them out, what do you think?"

"Hurry up," she said. "Please."

He walked toward the trash can shaking his head and muttering. Sara climbed the bus's three steps and peered inside. The old guy was on board, as was Ritchie. The heavyset woman walked down the aisle, checking seats as she went, and said to herself, "When I find that girl . . ."

"Where's your daughter?" Sara asked.

"I told her to go out to the bus and I'd be right there. I thought maybe she's playing tricks and hiding, but she must be back in the store."

"What's her name?"

"What business of that is yours?"

"Ma'am, what is her name?"

The woman rolled her eyes. "It's Melanie, why?"

"I'll find her."

Sara turned and descended the bus steps. She hurried across the lot, walking under the canopies and stopping at the building's corner. She peeked around. A mist, black as spilled oil, rolled from the woods. It approached the store, swallowing up moonlight. So thick, it looked like you could punch it and your hand would disappear inside.

Got to find the girl.

She entered the store. The clerk had the phone to her ear and she looked over at Sara and said, "I can't get anyone on this line."

"Come with me. Now."

"I ain't going nowhere. I leave the store, Caesar's going to have my job."

"Then find somewhere to hide."

Sara moved down the first aisle, past rows of chips and pretzels and cans of fake nacho cheese. The girl was not in the first aisle, nor the second, which contained automotive supplies.

"Melanie? Melanie!"

She jogged up and down the aisles, but there was no sign of Melanie. She glanced at the front windows, which now looked as if someone had draped a black cloth over them.

The clerk, sensing something wrong, ducked down behind the counter.

Maybe the girl had gone in back, through the silver doors.

Sara pushed through the double doors. To the left was a doorway and she peeked in and saw a desk with a heap of pink and yellow papers stacked on it. A filing cabinet was the only other piece of furniture in the room. Farther down the hall was a receiving area, where cases of soda, canned goods, and cases of dry goods were stacked. She scanned the area and saw the white toe of the girl's sneaker poking out from behind a stack of cases.

Sara knelt in front of her. The girl recoiled. "It's dark," she said. "I want Mommy." She sniffled, and wiped a trickle of clear snot away from her nose with her sleeve. "I forgot my doll."

"I'm going to take you back to the bus, but we have to go now."

Sara reached out her hand and the girl's arm crept out, as if Sara were a dangerous animal. Sara gripped the girl's hand and pulled her to her feet. They went back through the double doors and into the store. The front doors were chocked open. The cool night air rushed in and brought with it the scent of something old and rotten.

She stopped and Melanie halted with her. Shapes formed in the darkness. One of them, the size of a large man, stood in the doorway. From the front of the store, Sara heard the hidden clerk whimper.

"What's that?" Melanie asked. "What is that? Where's the bus?"

What would happen if the unnatural darkness engulfed them? The thought of being shrouded in the oily dark sent a chill through Sara. She had to do something. The little girl clung to her. Sara hugged Melanie close to her hip.

Now the mist seeped inside, engulfing the walls, blocking out the hanging beer posters and the lotto sign above the counter. The clerk popped up from her hiding spot, threw the phone at the coming shadow, and ran back through the double doors.

Sara had to use the Light. It would be only the second time. How had she done it before? By thinking of the sunlight. It had been a cool, dark night and she was walking home from the library. She had taken a back road to get home quicker. Shoulder-high weeds surrounded the road, and she had heard rustling, most likely a deer. But fear had gripped her and she wanted to be home in bed. She thought of how the sunlight slanted in her bedroom window in the morning. The bubble of Light surrounded her, and she walked the rest of the way inside it.

Now she closed her eyes. She pressed the girl closer to her and thought of the sun's rays warming her face and hearing gulls in the background at Stoney Point.

The Light speared from her with a FOOMP! She felt good and warm and she stood in a bubble of white-gold glow. It surrounded her and the girl and now she could see the enemy backing up into the darkness. The pools of blackness that had clung to the walls like sludge receded, and she started forward, toward the doors.

As she reached the doors, the wave of blackness parted around her. She saw the bus and thought it best to keep the Light glowing until she reached it. She walked with Melanie in the bubble of light until they reached the bus door. Sara nudged the girl forward and she climbed the steps. Sara followed, and when she stood on the step, she turned and faced the store. The fog receded from where it had originated, rolling back over the grass and into the woods.

The bus driver closed the doors behind her, and she thought *done* and the Light dimmed around her and faded. She felt warm and tired. Melanie ran to her mother.

The bus driver said, "You do this all the time?"

"Only the second time I've done it."

"What was it?"

"I just want to sit down now," Sara said.

"Fine by me. I'm getting this rig the hell out of here."

Sara moved down the aisle. She saw Melanie sitting on her mother's lap, chattering away about Sara's "wizard powers." Ritchie and the old man gave her wary glances. She slumped into her seat and closed her eyes.

Sara awoke. It was still dark. She stretched, yawned. The only sounds on the bus were the roll of the big tires on blacktop and the soft snoring of one of the passengers. She felt tired and her neck was stiff. She wondered if the mist still followed her and if she was putting the other passengers in danger. *They would have attacked by now, wouldn't they?*

Ritchie sat down across from her. He took his earbuds out and set them on his lap. The iPod cord snaked down into his pants pocket. "That was something, at the gas station."

She didn't know what to say to him.

"Where did you learn to do that?"

"It's nothing."

"Seemed like more than nothing to me."

"Only the second time it's ever happened."

"What was that dark stuff? It was almost alive."

Sara crossed her arms. "Look, I really don't want to talk about it."

Richie shrugged. "She's not talking," he said to someone in the back of the bus.

The driver, hearing the exchange, turned and said, "No more trouble from you, got that?"

She didn't favor him with a response.

She wished now that she had waited for her father to come home, but when she had found the pictures of Dr. Pennington, she had nearly started shaking. How could he lie to her all these years? Part of her had wanted a little revenge, to put the dagger in him and twist. Leaving unannounced would make him worry, and she wanted to hurt him, just a little. She felt rotten about it. And she missed him. But the pull of meeting

Laura Pennington was strong and drew her farther east. She hoped Dad would understand.

Milo pulled into the driveway of his house. It was modest, a beige Cape Cod with a row of arborvitae planted beneath the bay window in front. White trim, white front door. Ordinarily it wasn't much to look at, but now, staring at the black expanse of the bay window, Milo wished he had left a light on. Normally, he wasn't afraid to be alone in the house, but the solid darkness unnerved him.

He had considered stopping at Mulvaney's for a beef on weck but realized that would only delay the inevitable. He was a grown man, so why was he afraid of his own house? The sight of the man in the alley had left him shaken, but the prospect of the stranger beating him home (and even knowing where he lived) was remote.

He killed the engine, got out, and grabbed the chop saw from the bed of the pickup. His gaze on the bay window, he approached the front door. Did the curtain move? His guts felt tingly. *Stop it*, he told himself.

After setting the saw down, he located the house key and opened the door. He hauled the saw inside and set it in the front hall. He then flipped on the lights and found no mysterious intruder waiting to jump him.

To be safe, he strode through the house and turned on all the lights. Then he locked the front door and checked the rear one. Satisfied he was alone in the house—and having no reason to think otherwise—he decided on a snack.

He whipped up some nachos with salsa and shredded cheese and popped them in the microwave. He complemented his snack with a cold root beer. As he plopped on the sofa, which faced the bay window, the tingle returned to his guts. The darkness seemed blacker to him, and wouldn't that shadowy creep from the alley find it easy to skulk around out there?

Feeling uneasy, he rose and closed the drapes.

I don't want to look out there, and I don't even know why.

He flipped on the television and watched an old movie, but as he watched, his thoughts repeatedly returned to the unseen window and the darkness beyond.

CHAPTER 6

The day of the job, Mike found a manila envelope tucked in his door. Inside was a note that read: Two gas cans by Dumpster. Car in lot on Fuhrman. Burn this note.

Before leaving the house that evening, he checked on Mom, who was still, head lolled to one side. Her mouth had been open and soft gurgles escaped her throat. At first he had panicked, thinking she had passed, but when he heard her breathing he relaxed a bit. The home health aide he had hired would be here shortly to take care of her.

He took the Metro to Fuhrman and Tift, and walked past a Gas N'Go. Beyond the gas station was a weed-lined road. No cars passed him, and for that he was glad.

He approached the old Donner Hanna site. The bases of old blast furnaces, rusted steel legs, and huge metal rings stood in a field. A low concrete wall ran in front of them. They were to be torn down after the condos were complete.

He slogged through the weeds, stepping over the occasional rusted beam. To his right, unseen, a frog croaked. Watching the road, he saw it remained dark—no sign of headlights. Nevertheless, he crouched, as if trying to shrink himself.

Up ahead, Schuler slipped out from behind the remnants of a blast furnace. Mike approached him, letting his eyes adjust to the darkness. Schuler had his hair pulled back in a ponytail. He wore a black T-shirt, black jeans, and over it a beat-up brown jacket. If it had been 1985 again, Mickey Schuler would have been right at home.

"Where are they?" Mike asked.

Schuler turned and pointed. "Over that ridge."

Some genius had decided to turn an industrial wasteland into high-priced condos. He wondered if the yards came with optional slag heaps.

They climbed the ridge, and descending, came upon the condos, one building at each corner of the property. Two of them were furnished with gray-green siding and the others were wrapped in white Tyvek board. A dirt road wound between the condos, one that Mike imagined would eventually be paved. In Mike's estimation this was another Love Canal waiting to happen. He didn't want to linger down here.

"We doing them all?" Schuler asked.

Mike nodded.

They wound through the weeds under a bright October moon.

Mike found the gas cans near a Dumpster. They were under a paint-splattered tarp. He took one of the cans and Schuler grabbed the other. Mike also grabbed the tarp and would burn that along with everything else.

They pried off a piece of plywood that covered the door to the first building and went inside. They climbed the stairs and entered the upper unit. A toolbox and cordless drill had been left on the unfinished floor. There was another door in the room, this one wide open. It led to a small balcony.

"Start at the far wall," Mike said. "We'll work backward so we don't step in gas."

"Okay, chief."

Schuler lugged the can to the porch door and set it on the floor. It made a small *thunk* when he set it down, and to Mike it sounded like a sledgehammer striking an anvil. He was sure any little noise would get them caught.

Schuler went onto the porch. Christ, but he was wasting time. "Schuler," he whispered. Mike set his gas can down, thinking they'd already been here too long.

"Hey Mike?" Schuler called from the balcony. "There's someone down there."

"Get down."

Schuler squatted below the half wall of the balcony. Mike ducked low and joined him. He sniffed, taking in a sour smell on the air that he had first attributed to the lake. But no, that wasn't the lake, but something else, something that had rotted.

"Who is it?" Mike asked. That was all they needed, someone nosing around while they were trying to work. If they spotted him and Schuler, that left two choices: cap them, or scare them off and ditch the job. Neither option was preferable. Letting Hark down would have dire consequences, to say the least.

"Don't know. He's walking around the building."

Mike pulled his .45 from the holster in his jacket. He joined Schuler on the balcony, keeping low. He peered over the railing. He got a glimpse of the guy, who rounded the building and headed up the ridge near the old ironworks. He took the hill with long strides and paused at the top. In the darkness, Mike could make out stringy hair and a linebacker's build. That was it. The stranger turned at the top of the ridge and stood watching.

"What's he doing?" Schuler asked.

"I don't know. I'll go ask him."

"Really?"

"What the fuck do you think?"

"Oh, yeah."

"Let's go," Mike said. "This whole thing's going bad."

"What about Hark?"

"We get spotted and jammed up, the cops show? We're dead. We'll come back, do it right. No witnesses."

Schuler paused, frowning, the internal gears of thought working. "We came here to light this place up."

"Listen to me."

Schuler grinned. "Okay, yeah, you're right."

They crawled away from the railing and grabbed the gas cans. The inside of the condo had filled with fumes, and Mike's eyes watered. His piece in one hand and the gas can in another, he went first down the stairs, Schuler following and muttering the whole time about how they should have set it off, anyway.

Outside, even the dead-fish smell of the lake was refreshing compared with the stale air and gasoline odors in the condo. Mike gathered his thoughts. They needed to ditch the gas cans where they wouldn't be found, and then get to the getaway car. Hark would be pissed the job wasn't done, but maybe Mike could talk to him. Hell, he had been smart not to light it up with witnesses around. And it wasn't his fault someone showed up to ruin things. At least he hoped that's how Hark would see things.

"To the car?" Schuler asked.

"That way. Bring the can with you."

They inched along the side of the condo, the building blocking the sight line between them and the ridge. At the corner of the building, Mike peered at the ridge.

The visitor had company. Along the ridge were dark shapes, some of them men with twisted limbs, others hunched over, and one that had wings. *Wings?* Mike counted twelve, not including the guy they saw first. They stood still. A breeze blew, carrying the scent of something sour and stale at the same time. The way his grandfather Shawn had smelled in the weeks before his death, when cancer ate him from the inside out. Rot. That was it.

"Schuler, you got to see this," Mike said, and turned. But

Schuler was gone, and from around the corner, Mike heard gentle lapping sounds and gas fumes drifted to him. That crazy fucker's going to—

There was a noise like WHOOMPF! Mike looked in the window to see the glow of fire and flames eating up the plywood subfloor. Schuler came back around and said, "I told you I thought we should torch it!"

"You stupid bastard," Mike said. "Come here." Mike grabbed him by the shirt and yanked him along. "Look," he said, and pointed to the ridge.

Schuler poked his head around, kept it there for a moment, and ducked back behind the condo. A worried look crossed his face. One eyelid twitched. "Who are they?"

"Homeowners' association? We need to get gone."

Behind him, the flames began to hiss and then crackle. He smelled burning wood. Mike sincerely hoped the fire wouldn't bring the men on the ridge down here. He didn't like the looks of them, and the one with the wings really freaked him out. What kind of moron went around in a giant bat costume? You could only get away with that if your last name was Wayne.

The heat from the fire began to bake the back of Mike's neck. They had to move and there was no way to torch the other buildings—at least not without the Halloween people on the ridge seeing them. That left getting to the stolen car and beating it out of here. He would decide his next move after that.

Besides, it wouldn't be long before someone called the cops.

He motioned for Schuler to follow him. They set out, Mike watching the people on the ridge, waiting for them to come down. But they stood still. The others, including the one with the bat costume, stood a few feet behind old tall, long, and stringy, as if he were the leader of the freak show.

Behind Mike, the fire crackled and popped and he turned to see a gout of smoke rising into the air.

They continued past the far condo and came upon a parking lot with cracked, jagged asphalt. Mike stepped over a pile of hypodermics and wrinkled his nose in disgust. Damned junkies. He saw a tangle of bushes and branches at the far end of the lot, and knew this is where Hark's people had hidden the car.

As they reached the car and began pulling away the branches used for camouflage, Mike looked around again. Silhouetted against the black sky was a winged form, big as a man. It climbed high, flapping its wings, and then dove like a Spitfire, whooshing over the ridge and disappearing.

He didn't know what he just witnessed, only that they needed to drive away fast.

"What were you thinking?" Mike asked. He gripped the steering wheel, his knuckles most likely white under the black gloves he wore.

"We had a job to do." Schuler shrugged his shoulders.

He wanted to scream, but in the vacant scrap yard among the heaps of cars, his would be the only sound ringing through the night. They had pulled up to Brown Recycling, slid the busted gate open, and parked the car between two rows of junked Fords and Chryslers. Mike needed to think, plan his next move, because when Hark found out what happened, *his* next move would be to serve up Mike's balls on a platter.

"We should get going," Schuler said.

"Why? Nobody here but the cars."

"Still think we should go."

"That so? We wouldn't be sitting here with our thumbs in our asses if you did what I said."

"You backed out. I expected better."

"Yeah, I backed out. 'Case you didn't notice, we had an audience."

"I tried, Mike. Hark will respect that."

Mike rolled his eyes. "The job's not done, the cops are all over the place, and they'll be watching the condos. If we walked away without torching anything, we could've gone back another day, maybe tomorrow. Now we're fucked."

"Enjoying your new television? How's Mom's medicine?"

"What's that got to do with anything?"

Schuler pointed a long finger at him. "You're in this business because of me. Your ma gets her medicine because you're in the life. She'd be dead right now, Mikey, remember that. I brought you in."

Schuler was acting like he'd just given Mike a kidney. "Leave her out of this."

"Why? She looks at me like I'm a cockroach."

"Cool it."

"Half a cockroach."

"Schuler."

"The crap on half a cockroach's ass."

Now Mike felt the buildup, a hot anger spreading through his torso, up into his cheeks. He had a vision of pounding Schuler's head against the window to see how many whacks it would take to bust glass. "I swear to God—"

Schuler raised his voice into a high falsetto and affected a brogue. "Oh, now ya wouldn't be hanging around with that piece of shite Schuler, now would ya, Mikey boy? That Schuler boy is not fit to wipe yer arse."

"You want me to kiss your ass because we robbed a corner store together?"

"Naw, not kiss my ass. Just a little respect. That's all."

"You fucked up."

Schuler crossed his arms, looked out the passenger's window. Beyond him, the dead cars rose like relics from a past industrial age. "I tried, you ran."

There was no winning this argument. "Take back what you said about my mom."

"She does hate me."

"Don't give you the right to rag on her."

Schuler turned back toward Mike. The moonlight coming in the window gave his already pale skin an even milkier tint. "I take it back. So what do we do?"

"You need to leave town for a while," Mike said.

"And you?"

"I can't leave Mom," Mike said. "I'll just have to watch my back."

"You better have eyes in your ass," Schuler said.

"Eyes in my ass?"

"Yeah, instead of the back of your head?"

"So I can watch myself take a shit?" Mike asked.

"You know what I meant."

"Just makes no sense, that's all."

"Clever, okay. Trying to be clever. I like it," Schuler said.

"Try harder."

Schuler waved him off. "Just drive the car."

"Fine." He would need an extra set of eyes, especially when Hark got word of the botched arson job. Just not in his ass. Fucking Schuler.

CHAPTER 7

Sara's sleep was fitful and while in the throes of a light sleep, she felt the bus slowing down. She knew the other passengers were in danger while she rode the bus, but perhaps she could use the Light to drive off her pursuers again. Every so often, she caught one of the passengers creeping up to peek at her. The heavyset lady, the older man, and Ritchie. As if she were some sort of circus freak.

You expected them not to be curious?

She saw the bus driver swing the Greyhound into a rest stop. There was a pickup truck and a motorcycle parked in the slanted spots. A single sodium vapor light cast its beam on the lot. There was a squat brick building with bathrooms and a few park benches in a wooded area. Why the hell were they stopping?

The brakes hissed and Sara sat up. The driver left his seat, stood, and turned.

"What was that you did back on I-81?" he said.

"Where are we?"

"I-90." he said.

"So, what was it? You got some sort of weird flashlight?"

"Something like that."

"What was that? I saw men in the fog. You wanted by someone, the cops?"

"I'm on the FBI's Most Wanted List."

"Smart-ass," he said. "Who were they?"

"I don't know."

"And that little light show you put on?"

"Can we just get moving? It's important I get to Buffalo."

"I'm not taking you any farther. The other folks on this bus are nervous as a canary in a coal mine, and it's because of you. You're going to have to leave the bus," he said, and pointed to the door.

"You can't just leave me here."

"You're disrupting the other passengers."

"By snoring too loud? I've been asleep."

He started toward her. Sara gripped her bag, ready to swing it into his gut. "Don't touch me."

"You getting off the bus or not?"

Sara stood up and turned, looked at the other passengers. The heavyset woman looked down, playing with her hands. Ritchie caught her gaze and then quickly looked out the window. The old guy was sleeping. "You're all just going to sit there, then?"

The bus was as silent as an empty church.

"I can call the state police, you know."

"You're a real gentleman."

"Maybe you can hitch a ride."

She picked up her bag and brushed past him. She paused on the bus steps and looked back at the passengers, none of whom would look at her. "Cowards."

Sara stepped into the night.

She sat on the bench, arms wrapped around herself. She had buttoned the jacket up to her neck, but it provided little warmth against the breeze. After kicking her off the bus, the driver had retrieved her suitcase from underneath. Sara had tried getting his name, but he would not give it, and she imagined the other passengers would corroborate his story if she complained to Greyhound. One pain-in-the-ass passenger removed from the bus. Yea for the bus driver.

Leaving home was beginning to seem like a horrible mistake. Hitching a ride didn't seem like a great idea. The driver of the pickup truck, a bearded man in hunting camouflage, gave her a glance and drove off. The motorcycle rider was a white-haired guy, maybe in his sixties, who had stuffed himself into a set of leathers. It looked like a Halloween costume. The prospect of hitting either one of them up for a ride didn't thrill her.

After ten minutes on the bench, she decided to move to the alcove outside the restroom. A glass wall partially deflected the breeze, and she felt some warmth creep back into her body. Beyond the rest stop, she watched the cars zip past, making lonely humming noises on the asphalt, all of them unaware of her. Every so often, she heard a branch snap or grass rustle and worried that her pursuers had found her. Since she had not been attacked, she assumed it was a raccoon or deer.

She thought of calling home, having David (thinking of him as Dad didn't seem to fit at the moment) come and get her, but that would prevent her from finding Laura Pennington. She wanted to see the woman, touch her, embrace her. Her supposed mother. Who had been taken from her. But could she build a relationship with a complete stranger? She wasn't a little girl anymore, and would Laura Pennington even be interested?

She suddenly felt even more miserable. Her gut hurt and a lump formed in her throat. She told herself to be tough.

A car pulled into the rest stop, and as it approached, Sara saw it was a midnight-blue BMW. It swung into a parking spot and the driver got out. The driver was a blond woman, striking in her features. Long hair, pale eyes. She wore a long leather coat, and underneath that a turtleneck and knee-length skirt. The ensemble was topped off with knee-high black boots. She looked as if she belonged on a runway in Milan.

Sara shrank against the brick wall. The woman approached, her boots clicking on the pavement. Sara smelled perfume and under it, a whiff of cigarette smoke. The woman nearly passed her, then paused.

"Oh, didn't see you there."

"Didn't mean to startle you," Sara said.

"You didn't. Are you here by yourself? I didn't see any cars in the parking lot."

"My bus pulled away without me."

"You poor dear," the woman said, and placed her hand on Sara's arm. "I live nearby. Can I give you a ride?" She smiled, revealing small, perfect teeth.

She didn't know the woman, but at this point, she couldn't be choosy about a ride. "Okay. I'm Sara, by the way."

"Joanne," she said. "Let me just use the bathroom and we'll hit the road. 'Kay?"

Sara nodded. She expected the woman to have an exotic name, like Nadia or Eva, but she was just plain old Joanne. Not that she *looked* plain.

Joanne swung the bathroom door open, and the odor of disinfectant and old urine wafted out. "Come on," she said and got ahead of Sara, taking impossibly long strides. She had no idea what Joanne did for a living but if David saw her, he would no doubt categorize her as a "nut buster."

Sara grabbed her suitcase and followed Joanne, who took the luggage from her, popped the trunk, and tossed it in. Sara climbed in the car, keeping her travel bag on her lap. The car smelled of new leather and perfume.

Joanne climbed in and started up the car. They pulled out of the rest area parking lot and merged onto I-90. Joanne kept her foot steady on the gas and Sara watched the speedometer creep to seventy-five.

"Nervous?"

"Just that you're driving like Dale Earnhardt Jr."

Joanne gave a throaty laugh. "Speed limit's sixty-five. And I've never been stopped below eighty."

The car cruised along and when they reached the next exit, Joanne flipped on the blinker. They took the off-ramp, made a right and a left at the next exit, down a road called Cherry View Lane.

"So where were you headed?" Joanne asked.

"Buffalo."

"Any reason?"

"None that I want to discuss."

"Fair enough."

They reached a pair of green mailboxes and a driveway and Joanne turned up it. The drive wound up into the hills and there were lights planted in the ground about every twenty feet. They turned right around a bend and Sara saw the house, a huge colonial, all brick. A three-car garage jutted out from one side, and it looked as if they had built living space over the garage.

Joanne reached over and pressed the garage door remote, which was clipped to the visor on Sara's side. The door opened with a squeak and Joanne pulled the BMW into the garage. She killed the headlights and got out. Sara followed, clutching her bag so as not to scrape it against the car. God knew what a machine like this cost.

They entered the house through the garage and stepped into a large kitchen with an island and a Viking range against the wall. The countertops were done in black ceramic and the appliances were stainless steel. It was, to Sara, sterile but nice.

Joanne set her keys on the counter and removed her coat. "You can set your bag down. I'll get your luggage out of the trunk."

She disappeared into the garage and returned with Sara's suitcase.

There were stools around the island and Sara pulled one

out and sat down. Joanne opened the fridge and said, "Would you like a Coke, or lemonade? If you're hungry I have some Lean Cuisine in the freezer."

"No, thanks." A chill passed through her and she shivered.

"Would you like to go upstairs and take a hot bath? You look chilled."

"Actually, could I use your phone?"

"Sure can. But I bet you'd feel better if you warmed up first. I've got plenty of extra towels."

She felt strange taking a bath in a complete stranger's house, but it did sound good. Being out in the fall night had given her a good chill.

"I think I'll take you up on that," Sara said.

"I'll show you where it is and get you a towel."

The bathtub was a claw-foot and Sara took advantage, filling it with piping hot water to the brim. Joanne had told her to help herself to any of the bath beads or lotions in the medicine cabinet. Before she got in the tub, she locked the bathroom door. Her host seemed kind enough, but she felt the extra caution couldn't hurt.

She soaked for half an hour, and after toweling off and getting dressed, she went back downstairs. The warmth had crept back into her body and she was glad for taking Joanne up on the offer of a bath. Despite her physical comfort, she began to worry again. She was at a stranger's house in the middle of Pennsylvania and still had no way to get to Buffalo. David had no idea where she was, and what if this woman turned out to be a psycho?

She found Joanne in the kitchen hunched over a stack of papers, pen in hand. A briefcase rested on the floor next to her chair. She took a sip of red wine from the glass on the table and offered Sara a seat.

"What do you do?" Sara asked.

"I'm vice president of sales for Markson Industries. We make gears mostly."

"Sounds glamorous, gears and all."

Joanne laughed. "Not so much. The hours are long, my boss is a pit bull, but the pay's damn nice."

"I can tell by the house. It's nice," Sara said. "No offense."

"None taken."

"Why did you help me?"

"I'm sorry?"

"Why did you let me come here? I'm a total stranger to you."

"I saw someone who looked cold, tired, and wanting a ride. Why do you ask?"

"People aren't always so nice nowadays."

"There's kind people around. Just have to dig a little to find them, that's all."

Sara kept waiting for the hammer to fall. For Joanne to kick her out, or say something weird, or pull a knife from the butcher block and threaten her. But she simply read over the papers on the table, writing occasionally and sipping wine as she worked.

"Is there a bus or train station around?"

"There's an Amtrak terminal in Erie, or if you can wait a couple days, I'm going near Buffalo on business. I'd give you a ride."

"No, I really need to get there."

"How about I take you to the train station in the morning then? You can crash here, plenty of room."

She wondered if Joanne was lonely. The house was a good four thousand square feet, a lot of space for one person. Joanne's finger did not bear a wedding band, and she saw no pictures of a husband or boyfriend. And Joanne hadn't mentioned anyone.

"I guess I'll stay."

"Can I ask you something?"

"Sure."

"Did your bus really forget you?"

Here it comes, she's going to get weird. "Why do you want to know?"

Joanne cocked an eyebrow. "If I didn't know any better, I'd say you were running away from somewhere."

"They forgot me. I was too long in the john."

"Okay, then. I'll show you the spare room. Did you still want to use the phone?"

"Maybe in the morning."

Joanne led her through a family room and upstairs to the bedroom. The spare room had a queen-size bed with a thick white comforter. There was a dresser where she set her suitcase, and a color television in the corner. A row of windows looked out into the backyard and Sara took a look. In the darkness, she could make out maples that climbed the hill behind the house. She flicked the light off, not liking that she could be seen inside. She watched the woods and a few times she thought she saw the brush move, but then thought it was too hard to tell.

As a precaution, she checked each window, making sure the latch was in place, and then pulled down the shades. To think someone was watching from outside gave her an itchy, tingly feeling on the back of her neck. She changed into a pair of sweats and a Nike T-shirt and slipped under the covers. The first few moments in the bed were spent in nervous anticipation. Outside, the wind hissed, tossing leaves around the yard. A branch snapped. An owl cried out from the woods.

Soon the noises faded, her eyelids grew heavy, and sleep took her.

She awoke to the sound of a creaking floor. Sara sat up and looked at the alarm clock. Four fifteen in the morning. She squinted, made out the shape of the dresser and the television. *Where the hell am I?* It took a moment to come back to her: Joanne, the pretty blond woman. Big house, three-car garage. Kicked off the bus.

She took her glasses from the nightstand and put them on. Peering at the doorway, she saw only long shadows from the hallway, but again heard the footsteps downstairs. Had Joanne risen early?

Sara climbed out of bed and padded to the door. She passed through the hallway and stood at the railing, which overlooked a large family room with a sectional couch and a plasma television. The furniture took on odd shapes in the purplish dark, as if the room were filled with alien artifacts rather than everyday items. A wedge of light spilled out onto the hardwood, presumably from the kitchen.

It had to be Joanne. Sara descended the stairs and crossed the family room until she reached the door to the spacious kitchen. Joanne stood at the sink and flipped the light off. She was peering out the double-hung windows over the sink.

"What's the matter?" Sara asked.

"What are you doing up?"

"I could ask you the same question."

Something had awoken her, for she wore a short white robe and her feet were bare. Sara didn't like the fact that she was looking out the window in the middle of the night.

"So?" Sara said.

"I heard something out back. Probably just coons, but we had a black bear up here a few years ago."

Sara joined her at the sink. She peered into the yard and looked at the woods. Nothing moved, save for maple branches in the wind.

"What did it sound like?"

"Grunting. Whispering. Like an animal, but not. Does that make sense?"

"We'd better get upstairs. Are your doors locked?" Sara asked.

"They are, but it's probably just a coon, or maybe a coyote. But that whispering." She scratched her head.

Sara grasped Joanne's arm. Joanne gave her a puzzled look, her hair frizzy and sticking up in three places. "Don't worry, hon. We're crime free up here."

It wasn't criminals Sara was worried about. What if they had tracked her here?

"We should go upstairs, call for help," Sara said.

"To arrest some raccoons?"

"I think it's more than raccoons."

A thud-clang came from the rear of the house, and Sara flinched. Joanne didn't move, standing like a sentry at the window. She peered out again and this time instead of blaming the noises on raccoons, she gasped. The sound took the heart out of Sara and she was almost afraid to breathe.

"What is it?"

"Something moved around the side of the house. A man. We need to call the police."

"How close are they?"

"There's a state police barracks about fifteen miles from here."

That was not close enough, and the police might be helpless when they arrived, anyway.

"Get to the garage," Sara said. "Are your keys still on the counter?"

A loud thump came from the front of the house.

"Yeah. I have a gun upstairs. I'm going to try for it."

A gun might be as useful as a windbreaker in a hurricane. Besides, if they were surrounding the house, the two women would not have much time to beat it down the hill. "To the car, now."

"I'm trying for the gun."

Sara tugged on Joanne's robe, but the taller woman slipped away and urged Sara to follow her. She crossed the family room and took the stairs three at a time. Sara stopped at the bottom of the steps. Outside, she heard scraping noises, like tacks across a tin can. They were closing in and where was Joanne?

Another thump, this one against the front door.

An eternity seemed to pass, but in reality was probably no more than five minutes.

She waited. Deformed shadows danced across the front windows and she decided to scoot up the stairs, not wanting to remain alone. The whole time she climbed the stairs, she half expected someone to grab her from behind. She would feel a cold hand on her leg as she was dragged away screaming.

She entered the master bedroom to find Joanne sitting on the bed and fumbling to load shells into a revolver. Hands shaking, the woman loaded the last shell and clicked the cylinder home.

Downstairs, the front door gave with a thunderous crack and the wind whistled inside. The sound of a guttural voice speaking in a strange tongue drifted up the stairs. It sounded the way a man with a cut throat might speak.

Not wanting to be left without any clothes, Sara grabbed her duffel bag and rejoined Joanne.

Joanne slowly rose from the bed and motioned for Sara to get behind her. Sara did, feeling somewhat safe behind the taller woman and safer still because of the revolver. Whether it was because it could inflict real damage or due to the some weird talismanic power, she didn't know.

"We have to get to the garage," Sara whispered.

Joanne nodded. "If I can make my legs move."

Joanne managed to make them move and the two of them crept across the bedroom to the hallway. Sara didn't hear the voice, but the wind still barreled through the open door.

They listened at the top of the stairs and Sara heard only the wind. They had to try for the garage, for barricading themselves in a bedroom would only serve as a trap, and

Sara didn't know if she could hold them off again. At least going for the car, they had a chance.

Joanne crept out on to the landing and looked down into the family room. It was free of intruders. A line of muddy, misshapen footprints stained the rug. She didn't want to go down the stairs. If they were on fire behind her, she still might not move.

Behind her, from one of the bedrooms, glass broke.

The issue was decided and Joanne hurried down with Sara grabbing the tail of her robe. It was smooth and slick, tough to hold. Joanne continued, holding the gun in a shooter's grip, both hands on the handle. She moved it back and forth, sweeping the room. When no boogeymen popped out and scared her, she hit the bottom of the stairs and rounded them. The door was still open, the wind brushing in a mess of leaves.

The dirty footprints led to the kitchen, and Sara was loath to follow them. "Do you have any other car keys?"

"Just the set on the counter," Joanne said.

That ruled out the front door. From upstairs, a series of thuds and bumps shook the house. Glass broke, and the sound of heavy furniture being turned over shook the ceiling. *They're looking for me and they're angry*, Sara thought.

She urged Joanne to the garage and the taller woman went first, holding the revolver in front of her. The light was out in the kitchen, casting the room in shadows. Sara looked at the switch and saw a splash of mud on the wall. Someone had turned the light off. The kitchen was empty. Sara spied the keys still on the counter. She picked them up.

The footsteps led to the garage door and she didn't want to go that way, but the crashes behind them became louder and she heard footsteps on the stairs. And that horrible, gurgling chatter coming from the other room.

"Let's roll," Sara said.

"Get the door, fling it open. I'll hold the gun."

Sara moved into position, gripped the doorknob. She flung it open. Joanne aimed the gun, froze for a moment.

She looked to Sara and said, "Clear so far."

The last word came out in a gurgle. A black spear tore through Joanne and punched out the back of her robe. She looked at Sara with surprise, croaking noises coming from her mouth, and then she was dragged forward into the garage, the weapon still jutting from her blood-soaked back. Sara started to scream, then clamped a hand over her mouth. The woman who had taken her in, albeit for a short time, had been butchered.

Sara pressed her shoulder against the door, but someone on the other side countered and the door swung and threw her back into the counter. A sharp pain shot through her back where one of the knobs dug in. She landed on her rear end and quickly scrambled to her feet.

Now she could see into the garage, where Joanne's body lay facedown next to the Audi. Her attacker stepped into view and entered the kitchen.

He wore black tattered rags that stank of something old and sour. His face was a mess of charred skin and pink blisters. One eye revealed a milky white cornea. He reached out his clawed hand; a spear with barbs on its tip seemed to materialize from the darkness itself. The attacker grinned, revealing jagged yellow teeth.

"Time for pain," he growled.

He stepped closer, and Sara heard two more step behind her, but she was frozen and could not turn. *I'm going to die*, she thought.

The man who killed Joanne cocked the spear at his waist. She would have to use the Light.

She closed her eyes and took herself back to a good place in her mind, this time imagining a field of golden wheat and a sweet summer breeze ruffling the grain. And sun on her face. Warmth spread from her torso and through her shoulders, down her arms and into the palms of her hands, making them tingle.

She opened her eyes and saw the attacker had stopped. He lifted up a scarred arm as if warding off the glow coming from her palms. She suddenly hated this man, this deformed freak, who had cruelly murdered an innocent woman, someone who had shown a runaway kindness.

Die.

The Light whooshed from her hands, rocked her back. The twin beams sliced through the man's torso with a sound like bacon sizzling. The stench of burning flesh filled the kitchen. The deformed man howled and dropped to his knees. There were two scorch marks on his torso, and when he flopped forward, she saw the burn mark where her blast had exited his back.

The Light had exploded a hole in the wall, and the edges of the wallpaper smoldered. The thing on the ground let out a final shriek and then was still. Keys in hand, she took the opportunity to jump over the body, grab the door handle, and slam the garage door behind her.

She stepped around Joanne's body, trying not to look. If there were more time, she would have gone for the gun. She tried to ignore the sound of her sneakers squelching in the blood on the floor and the smell of loosed bowels. Unlocking the BMW's door, she climbed in and stuck the key in the ignition. A thud came from the door and then it was flung open. Time to put the pedal to the metal, she thought.

Sara pressed the garage door opener and the door rolled on its track.

Come on, come on.

One of the other intruders ducked through the doorway, squeezing a pair of leathery wings against its body. It approached the car, its head a mass of horns and spikes. From her vantage point, she saw its clawed hands and watched as it created a wicked-looking hammer, like something a Viking warrior would use, seemingly from the darkness. It swung the hammer back and hit the driver's-side window and glass stung her face. Sara started the car, threw it into reverse.

The creature let loose a series of grunts and growls as the hammer was pulled from the window. Sara gunned the engine and swerved, scraping the side of the BMW against the garage door frame. She whirled the car to the right and did a hasty three-point turn, the tires squealing on the asphalt.

Throwing the car in Drive, she sped forward, thinking her driver's ed teacher would be swallowing his tongue right now if he saw her. She popped the headlights on and started down the road as fast as she dared. She took a glance in the rearview mirror and with dread saw the creature trot from the garage, spread its wings, and with a huge flap, take flight.

If I can get back to the 90, I can get going fast enough to lose it. But try explaining to a state trooper why you were speeding. That should be good. *Oh, I'm sorry officer, I was being pursued by the forces of evil. Could you let me off with a warning?*

She whipped down the road. Occasionally she glanced upward through the windshield. She saw only the tops of the pines at first. Then a shadow shaped like an overgrown bat appeared on the hood.

The end of the road approached, and she was heading sharply downhill. She feathered the brakes, hoping to maintain control of the BMW and still make the turn without stopping. The shadow grew larger and the creature dipped in front of the windshield, giving Sara a view of its multi-jointed wing. It was enough to force a swerve. She jerked the wheel but the car veered right and she slammed on the brakes, the car going into a skid, the back end whipping around until she came to a screeching halt facing the opposite way. Her head thudded against the restraint and little black dots clouded her vision for a moment. She prayed she wouldn't pass out.

She didn't, instead opening the door and grabbing her bag. She knelt at the side of the car, scanning the sky for the winged creature, and when she saw only clouds, she scurried into the woods.

As she ran through the woods, the air cut through her. The sharp crackle of leaves underfoot and her ragged breathing were the only sounds she heard. She ducked through bushes, the branches scraping her face. At one point she hit a fallen pine tree and sprawled forward, tearing a hole in the knee of her pants. Knee throbbing, she came to a clearing and found a rotted log, perhaps four feet in diameter. It was big enough to hide in.

Checking both ways, she darted to the log and ducked inside. It smelled of moss and dust and was too dark for her liking. Something tickled the back of her hand and she flicked it away, glad the darkness at least concealed the bevy of creepy-crawlies lurking in the log.

She crouched down and her knee sang out in pain. It stung like hell, but she didn't think there was any real damage. She watched the woods for half an hour. Soon fatigue caught up with her, and she slipped into sleep.

The beating of wings awoke her. She clutched her bag to her chest, pressed herself against the side of the log. Turning her head slightly, she watched the clearing. And it was there, the winged creature, gray-green against the dark woods. Her heart beat so hard it hurt and she began to think ducking into the log wasn't the brightest move. It hadn't seen her, though. Yet.

I'll have to fry it, like the other one.

Now the other one, presumably the one from inside the house, joined it in the clearing. It was naked save for a loincloth, and the moonlight showed pale bluish skin. In its midsection was an open wound and a portion of meaty guts bulged from the wound, slick in the moonlight. Whether it had been a man at one time, she couldn't tell.

It trudged up next to the gargoyle-thing and craned its neck. Looking for me, the guest of honor, no doubt.

Beyond them, over the trees, the first rays of sun appeared and with it a deep pink sky. She must have slept longer than she thought, for they had pursued her until dawn. She guessed they hadn't seen her run to the woods and had gone looking down closer to the main road.

Now, hunched in the log, she watched them split and circle the outskirts of the clearing. If they had seen her, she imagined she would have been torn from her hiding spot already.

She listened. Brush and leaves scraped. Wood snapped. She heard that awful speech, like a foreign language spoken by a throat cancer patient. Then the footsteps sped up and there was a muffled whoosh as the flying creature took to the sky. The second one appeared and from her vantage point she saw its thickly muscled legs.

It stopped and she feared that at any moment it would peer inside the log, spot her, and come in for her. But instead, it turned away, let out a noise that sounded like *"Gat!"* and bounded back through the woods.

It was an hour later when she came out of hiding. The sun was brilliant and her breath plumed in the crisp air. She suspected the dawn drove her attackers off, but as she made her way back to the road, she still checked the sky every so often.

She neared the edge of the woods. Her stomach rumbled and a faint hunger pang rippled through her belly. Her knee was cold and sticky with blood and the scratches on her face burned. At least she still had transportation.

Or so she thought. She reached the car and found it had taken a heap of abuse. The windshield was smashed, and the hood lay at a cockeyed angle against a pine tree. Wires had been ripped and mangled and fluids pooled beneath the car.

Whether they did this before hunting her—so she couldn't escape—or after, she didn't know. The prospect of those things being intelligent enough to cut off her escape vehicle unnerved her. The physical deformities and their very presence was bad enough, but to think they were smart, too?

And what were they? The same ones that had attacked at the gas station? Were they the "Enemy" that Dad and Reverend Frank talked about every once in a while? They seemed especially keen on finding her.

The Light had saved her. That was only the second time she had fired a bolt like that. The other had come when a homeless man down by the Royal Theater had gotten aggressive with her. The man, reeking of booze and sweat, a filthy beard around his mouth, had grabbed her arm, looking for spare change. He managed to drag her into the alley between the Royal and the Vacuum Center. She had grown angry, and a bolt of brilliant white light flew from her hand and caught him in the shoulder. It had singed a hole in his raincoat. He had run screaming from the alley, shouting that "fucking bitch" had tried to kill him. Never mind what he had planned for her in the alley.

Did Dad know about her abilities? And did Reverend Frank? She would sometimes catch them watching her and then averting their gazes. Waiting for her to light something up?

She wished he were here, Dad. Or Robbie. Anybody.

She resigned herself to being alone for now and walked back to Cherry Hill Road. After she had been waiting forty-five minutes, a white semi rolled up and stopped. The driver leaned over and opened the door. He didn't look much older than her, but he sported a thin goatee and smiled. Cocking the ball cap on his head he said, "Need a lift?"

"You going to Buffalo?"

"Tonawanda, right nearby."

She climbed up into the cab. A *Hustler* magazine with a topless brunette on the cover rested on the dashboard. She had bright red lips and was pinching her nipples. The driver grabbed the magazine and flung it behind him, into the bunkhouse. "Sorry. Get a little lonely on the road."

"I understand."

"Randall Powers."

"Sara. I thought you guys weren't supposed to pick up hitchhikers?"

"I'm Randall Powers the second. Randall Powers the first owns the company. What Daddy don't know won't hurt him."

"Roll on, then."

They had driven a few miles and were rolling up the ramp to the 90 when it hit her. Joanne, dead in the garage. She hadn't thought of the woman while fleeing from the attackers, but now it pounded into her. Her throat tightened up and it let loose with a single tear and then more. She couldn't stop it. She put her hands over her face and the sound of her own whimpering disgusted her.

Randall said, "You okay?"

She wiped tears from her face with the sleeve of her jacket and crossed her arms. "I'll be okay."

Sara looked straight ahead at the long expanse of blacktop and had never felt more alone than she did now.

CHAPTER 8

Harry Hargrove didn't mind his job. Mostly it involved sitting in the guard shack at the former Gate 4 of the mill. He had a kerosene heater, a little TV and DVD player, a drawer full of snacks, and a stack of John D. MacDonald novels. The pay sucked, but for part-time it wasn't bad, and it got him away from six screaming kids and a wife intent on smashing his balls into jelly half the time. No pleasing that woman. Car not running right, Harry. Did you call the dentist, Harry? Jules Spender got a three-karat ring from her husband for Christmas.

No, he didn't mind at all. The Yanks were taking it to the competition on the tube, and he had a belly full of Slim Jims and Dr Pepper. Every hour or so, he got up, drove around in the patrol car, and made sure no kids had found their way into the mill buildings.

When they hired him, Flanders—his boss—said guys didn't last more than a few months. Sitting in the shadow of abandoned blast furnaces, their pipes spiraling up in the darkness, and the big rolling mill buildings, gave some the creeps. The mill had shut down in 1982, taking five thousand jobs with it. The furnaces were cold and not going to be hot again. Big steel was a thing of the past, at least in Buffalo. There was talk of tearing the whole thing down and putting up wind turbines, but he'd believe it when he saw it.

Now, peeling the wrapper off another Slim Jim, he looked out onto the property. The blast furnace stoves, some hundred and fifty feet high, almost seemed to block out the moonlight. He took a bite of the Slim Jim, relishing the greasy taste.

He heard sirens in the distance and the blat of fire engine horns. He set down his snack, and after taking a swig of pop, stepped outside the shack. He immediately wished he had thrown his jacket on. The cool air caused goose bumps to pop up on his bare arms. He looked across Route 5 and saw smoke spiraling against the sky and smelled the acrid tang of it on the air. The high whoop of a police siren joined the fire trucks. *Must be a pretty good blaze.*

He stepped back into the guard shack, rubbed his arms for warmth, and was ready to pick up his Slim Jim when he saw someone through the picture window. They were about a hundred feet away, loping across the ground. Damn it, they must have hopped the fence. He grabbed his jacket and keys and got into the truck. He started it up and was ready to put the car in gear when he saw more of them. Black shapes, some dressed in rags, others appearing to have bluish tinted skin, still others with hooks and spikes piercing their faces. All shapes and sizes, claws and horns and fangs and what was he seeing?

They moved toward the Ten Inch Rolling Mill, perhaps a hundred, maybe more. He looked down the length of the chain-link fence and saw them scaling the barrier in droves. Suddenly being visible didn't seem like such a great idea. He slid down in the seat, staying high enough to peer over the dashboard. The one he saw first, the tallest of the lot, stopped at the gaping door of the Ten Inch Mill. He raised his arms and the others filed past him, into the mill. It took maybe five minutes for them all to enter the building. When they had passed him, the apparent leader seemed to look right in the direction of Harry's truck. Harry ducked lower, face pressed against the vinyl seat.

I don't know who it is, but I hope it didn't see me.

He gave it a minute, then sat up. The guy was gone.

He didn't know what he just saw, or who they were. Maybe some sort of Satanic cult. Whoever they were, they looked dangerous. This was more than he could handle, and he planned on calling the real cops.

Harry opened the truck door and stepped out. His heart thudded in his chest. He reached up to adjust his cap and knocked it off his head. It fell to the ground and rimmed around like a coin dropped on a table. He picked up the hat, telling himself to calm down.

He smelled something bad. Something old and vaguely mildewy. From the roof of the guard shack came a scraping noise and Harry jerked his head up and saw the winged creature perched on the roof. He felt a whimper rise in the back of his throat and he started forward, but the creature pounced, its claws digging into his shoulders, the full weight of it pressing him down, and he felt his ankle break with a stunning pop and he shrieked. It dug into his shoulders and his nerves lit up with pain, sending hot tendrils down his arms. He heard the *thwip* of wings overhead and slowly his feet left the ground.

It felt like being on some crazy amusement-park ride. As they reached the open door of the mill, the claws left his shoulder with a wet sound, and he hit the ground and rolled into the mill. His ankle sang out again and for a moment things started spinning and he felt a wave of nausea. He came to rest against a steel column, and now he was aware of shapes surrounding him in the darkness. He looked up and one of them approached, this one with stringy long hair and wearing a ragged trench coat.

Around him, the circle closed. Through cracked lips, the stringy-haired one said, "Flay him."

He felt himself hoisted to his feet. Something tore open his shirt, gashing his chest in the process. His pants were shredded by claws. His shoes were pulled off, and something gave his broken ankle a vicious twist and he nearly blacked out from the pain. Something took him in a bear hug around the chest. Another pulled his arm and he felt a snap in his shoulder and more pain and the shoulder separated. Rough hands turned his head toward the outstretched arm. A blade, flat and dull in the darkness, started in the crook of his elbow and split the skin down to the wrist. As the skin was peeled back and the raw red muscle exposed to the air, he passed out.

Engel remembered seeing the mill from his last encounter here. Large buildings, capable of holding a small army. Perfect for them. Even better that it was empty. The man had been a nuisance, nothing more. His screams had been exquisite. Engel ordered the skinned corpse impaled on a spear. They would place it outside the gate, near the road, as a warning: The Dark Ones are coming.

After dropping Schuler off, Mike ditched the stolen car in a field near the old Cargill grain elevators. He walked home, holding his coat shut the whole time, hoping to ward off the ever-stiffening October wind. He moved through the old First Ward, occasionally peeking at the houses, wanting to shake his head. They were all pre–World War II, built long and tall and narrow, with eight or so feet between the homes. They were so close it seemed like you could reach over and snatch a morsel of corned beef from your neighbors' dinner table.

Now most of them had been turned into crack dens. One couple, Sandy and Deke Labin, had been raided by the DEA. Deke had set up a meth lab in his basement. Parrish, who lived across the street, ran a gang called the Seneca Crew. It was sad, and he wondered what the hell he was still doing here. He knew the answer to that: Mom. She was just like the old Polish living down on Memorial Drive, too proud to leave despite the rash of home invasions. Some of them had been tied up, pistol-whipped, and robbed, but still they stayed.

With Hark most likely after him, Mike had good reason to leave, but there was his mother. She wouldn't make it to the end of the driveway in her current condition. Her breathing was more labored and she had developed a nasty wet rattle in her chest over the past month. Moving her would mean the end. He would have to find a way to avoid Hark, lay low until the whole thing blew over. And there was the life, as Schuler called it. He was growing tired of looking over his shoulder, wondering if someone was waiting to pop him in the back. Wondering if the plain brown and gray cars passing the house were plainclothes or not. Even Schuler had grown old. Mike found himself forcing himself to laugh at the same jokes, feign interest in the same war stories, how they knocked over this place or that.

By now Hark had to have heard about the fire. It would have made the eleven o'clock news. He hoped Schuler got out of town, even if the dirty prick did insult Mike's mother. He had to admit, the kid did one hell of an Irish brogue, and if Mike's mom hadn't been the target of the joke, he would have been bent over the steering wheel laughing.

He turned the corner onto Smith, past Ricotta's, its windows covered by plywood. The little corner store had moved to Orchard Park. Good for them, Mike thought.

He came up on the house. The first thing he noticed was the dim front window. It struck him as unusual. Mom always left a light on until Mike got home. Maybe she had retired early. Then he started to worry, maybe she'd fallen, or maybe Jasmine, her nurse, hadn't shown and Mom had slipped into unconsciousness.

He quickened his pace until he reached the front step, which rattled, the one-by-six having loosened over the years. That porch probably hadn't been fixed since 1985, when his father had still been capable of walking ten feet without sucking from an oxygen mask.

Reaching the porch, he noticed the door cracked open. That was another thing. Mom insisted he lock the door, and in this neighborhood, it was the wise thing to do. He never left it unlocked.

He reached into his jacket and pulled out the .45. He pointed it at the door. It might be nothing. Or maybe he did get careless and leave it open. Or it might be a junkie on the prowl looking to swipe something.

He opened the door and looked inside. The furniture blended with the complete darkness. Mike wanted to call out, ask where Mom was, but he thought it better to remain silent.

Winding his way through the living room, he refrained from turning on any lights. He listened, hoping to hear the murmur of voices from the television, maybe a *Golden Girls* rerun, one of Mom's all-time favorite shows.

The dining room revealed a tipped-over oak chair. The picture of him taken sophomore year, the one with the mullet and the skinny tie, hung askew on the wall. Trouble had found the O'Donnell house. The question was what kind, Hark or random street crime.

He still hadn't heard any noise from the back bedroom. The house was still except for the furnace motor whirring in the basement.

In the kitchen, he smelled the remnants of lemon dish soap. A pile of clean dishes was stacked in the dish drain, which meant Jasmine had been here to clean up, but she wouldn't have left the lights off.

Only the hallway and the two back bedrooms were left. In the hallway, he saw the bathroom door was open. The closet door was closed. Outside, he thought he heard a car pull up and a door slam, but he dismissed it. He poked his head into the bathroom. The shower curtain was drawn, but he saw no shape behind it, and unless someone had found a way to cram themselves into a medicine cabinet, no one else could have hidden in the bathroom.

He left the bathroom, stared at the scarred bedroom door, gouged by their late bulldog, Max. From behind the door he smelled it, like meat gone bad. And under it, the smell of shit.

Dear God, I'm going to go in there and she's going to be dead, like a wax dummy, lying in her own filth. You weren't even here, you rotten fuck. Your mother was dying and you were out burning buildings.

He nudged the door open with his foot. Between the twin beds, he saw the body.

It wasn't his mother, but Jasmine. The comforter and sheet lay crumpled on her back, and a blotch of blood soaked the sheet. The rear of her pants were soiled brown, and one white Reebok lay next to her foot. He felt his dinner start to kick back up his throat. He clamped his hand over his mouth. She'd been a nice lady, quick to smile, and Mom was always glad to see her.

It wasn't Mom, but would he find her somewhere else? Maybe someone tossed her down the basement stairs and she broke her neck and he would find her in a heap, staring at him with glassy dead eyes.

Behind him, the closet door opened with a groan. He whirled around and saw a bullnecked guy with a crew cut standing half out of the closet. He had a mole the size of a dime on his cheek. He grinned at Mike.

Mike leveled the .45, intent on blasting the mole back through the guy's face. The guy laughed, a phlegmy chuckle that added to Mike's already considerable nausea.

"You aren't gonna shoot me."

"Try me."

"You fucked up that arson job, O'Donnell. It's all over the news."

"I'd stop talking if I were you," Mike said.

The guy closed the closet door. He brushed off the front of his sport coat. His casual manner made Mike want to pull the trigger even more.

"Hark's got a car waiting outside for you. He wants to talk."

"Suppose I don't feel like taking a ride."

"I think we can persuade you."

"How's that?"

"You'll see. Let's go."

"You kill her?" Mike said and nodded, indicating Jasmine.

Again that phleghmy laugh. "You think I'd tell you? Now let's fucking go."

He started to reach inside the sport coat and Mike stepped forward and raised the gun and brought it down on an arc, the butt of the handle cracking against the guy's cheek and crumpling him against the wall. Mike hammered the gun down again, striking the base of the skull, and the guy flopped to the floor.

Now he heard another voice, a deep base, coming from the front of the house, saying, "What the fuck's taking him so long?"

He had two options: charge out the front door and blast his way out, which would definitely bring the cops to Smith Street, or retreat to the bedroom and opt for climbing out a window. It would be the bedroom. It would also provide a better defensive position, for they couldn't attack from behind.

On the floor, the guy groaned, and Mike kicked him in the ribs. He grunted again. Mike retreated to the bedroom. He shoved the twin bed around Jasmine's body and jammed it up against the door, hoping it would at least slow down Hark's men.

The bedroom had two windows, the one on the right looking over their dirt patch of a yard, and the left one looking over the Hoolihans' driveway next door. He looked out the right window and saw one of them, tall as a smokestack, rounding the rear of the house. He went to the opposite window and saw a shorter, skinnier one in a leather jacket coming up the Hoolihans' driveway. Both exits were blocked, and soon they would figure out he was in the bedroom and come knocking at the door.

No sooner did he think that when someone smacked the door. The twin bed screeched on the floor, moved maybe three inches. Another few good hits and the bed would be across the room.

He would take his chances with short and skinny. He went back to the driveway window. The dimness of the room provided him cover from the outside. Another whack at the door.

He reached over and unlatched the window lock. The guy was looking down the driveway, toward the backyard. The death smell in the room grew thick. Mike lifted the window. Now the guy in the driveway turned. He opened his mouth to yell and reached inside his jacket and Mike shot him in the leg, just below the kneecap. He went down howling and holding his leg. *Shit. Didn't want to opt for gunplay, but it was me or him*, Mike thought. That would draw the Buffalo PD for sure. Maybe he could claim self-defense. And just try and explain having a loaded .45 and no permit.

He hoisted himself out the window and dropped to the ground. The guy in the leather jacket was now spinning around on the ground like a crazy break-dancer, holding his leg and moaning. Inside, he heard the bedroom door give with a crack.

He'd run for the Hoolihans' backyard, hop the fence, and

cut through St. Stephen's parking lot. Now the guy on the ground was yelling in a high shriek, "He's here! The driveway!"

Mike had no stomach for putting another bullet in the man, so he ran down the driveway, hurtling one of the Hoolihans' kids' bikes, a blue Huffy. He reached the end of the house. The gated picket fence was in view, and beyond that, St. Stephen's parking lot and freedom. He'd get away, then figure out how to find Mom.

From the corner of his eye he saw a blur and then the guy slammed into him. He flew sideways. The gun dropped to the ground. He hit the concrete, shoulder stinging, and rolled three times. He thought a small bus had taken a detour just to flatten him.

He looked up to see smokestack standing over him. No wonder he'd been flattened. The big man wore a skintight ribbed turtleneck that hugged his torso, the muscles looking like sculpted ivory with the sweater. No waist, V-shaped, wearing loose black pants and engineer boots.

"Those steroids work wonders," Mike said and sat up, his shoulder singing with pain.

"Shut the fuck up," big and ugly said. He stomped on Mike's toes and for a moment the pain was so bad Mike thought he might swallow his tongue. Mike pulled his foot away, his toes feeling hot and numb. Looking around, he saw the .45 on the ground, about ten feet away. The goon took out a chrome revolver and pointed it at Mike.

Mike put up his hands. "All right, I take back the steroid comment."

The goon cocked the hammer on the revolver. Mike thought it prudent to shut his mouth.

He looked at the Hoolihans' rear porch. No one out there, only a silver ashtray on the railing and a Schmidt's beer can. The lights were dim inside, which meant no help from them. The number of crimes that went unsolved in this neighborhood was a joke. People who watched from their front windows while kids were shot to death would say they didn't see anything. They didn't want their houses firebombed or their living rooms sprayed with bullets in reprisal.

Now, the goon looked down, face impassive. Mike began crab walking backward, hoping to reach the gun. The big guy followed, and when he got close enough, Mike flicked up a foot and kicked him in the crotch. The goon winced, giving Mike enough time to grab for the .45. He gripped it, swung around. If he could take big ugly out, he had a chance to get across the church parking lot.

He had the man in his sights. A look of surprise crossed the guy's face, as if to say this wasn't supposed to happen. Mike exerted pressure on the trigger. Could he do it again?

Something hard whacked against the side of his head. It felt like someone was pressing thumbtacks into his brain. He dropped the gun and covered his head with his arms, expecting another blow. Instead, he heard a familiar voice say, "Get up. Hark's waiting."

He uncovered his head. Standing over him was the monster from Hark's warehouse, still in a dark suit. He wore dark shoes, a dark shirt, and a dark tie. Keeping the undertaker look going, apparently. He held a leather sap in his hand, and now he tucked it back under his suit coat.

Now the other guy, the one in the turtleneck, limped over and stood next to Hark's main man. Mike hoped he at least gave the guy sore nuts for a few days. The one he had kicked pulled out a sleek automatic and pointed it at Mike.

"The car's waiting."

"Not much for joyrides," Mike said, but stood up. He could feel the spot where a lump would form on his head. The leather-jacketed thug shoved the gun into his ribs and jabbed. In the driveway, Mike saw two more of Hark's men with the one he had shot. They had his arms over their shoulders, like football players helping an injured teammate off the field. He heard soft whimpering coming from the guy. That probably didn't go over well with the other thugs.

They reached the end of the driveway. Two cars, Toyotas from the looks of them, were parked in front of the O'Donnell house. He heard rap music echoing faintly from a house down the street. He hoped to see someone walking the block, or sticking their head out a door, but the street was empty. Hark's men helped the wounded man into the backseat of the rear car.

The man who had hid in the closet exited the front door. Blood trickled down his head, and he had removed his sport coat and was pressing it against his skull. He, too, got in the rear vehicle.

Mike was led to the front car. One of them opened the rear passenger door and shoved Mike inside. He saw why they had leverage. His mother sat in the backseat, her hands bound by an extension cord. Her skin had gone waxy and white, and a wet rattle came from her mouth as she struggled to breathe. Eyes closed, she rested her head against the window.

"Mom?"

No answer.

"Mom, c'mon, it's Mike." He nudged her shoulder. She moaned. Then she lifted her head and opened her eyes. They were wet and bleary and damned if she didn't look like a re-animated corpse. He hated himself for thinking that, wanted to shoot himself in the guts for it.

"What'd you do, Michael?"

"I'm sorry, Ma."

"Who are they? Are they Schuler's friends?"

"I don't think these guys are anybody's friends."

The man from the warehouse climbed into the driver's seat. He was so big it looked as if he were at the wheel of a clown car. The one in the black turtleneck took the passenger seat.

"If my hands weren't tied, I'd give you a smack. Who are they?"

"Hark's people."

"The warehouse guy? Oh, Michael, tell me you didn't get caught up with them."

The driver started the car and they pulled away from the curb.

The guy in the passenger seat, the one Mike had kicked, said, "What's wrong with her?"

"None of your goddamned business," Mike said.

"No, really, she sick?"

"Why do you care?"

"I don't. But she put up a pretty good fight for an old sick broad."

"I should have shot you on sight," Mike said.

The guy laughed. "Yeah, you fucked that up, too, didn't ya?"

Mom leaned her head against the window. She closed her eyes and sighed. "What are you into, Michael? Is it drugs?"

"No drugs."

"Getting a lecture from his mother, some hard-ass. I thought this guy was good," Turtleneck said.

"He is, Ed," said the driver, his expression not changing.

"It took three of you to catch me, and I still almost got away."

Mom said, "You didn't answer my question."

Mike looked out the windshield. They were on South Park now, headed toward the city, passing the low brick structures that made up the Perry Street projects. Outside, at the curbs, were the rectangular garbage containers with CITY OF BUFFALO in white on the side. Mike saw a rat scurry between two of the containers. Apparently the garbage containers the city required weren't very effective.

"Michael?"

He didn't want to tell her. He thought just maybe if he did

right now, it would push her over the edge, in some crazy way accelerate the cancer and cause her to shrivel and die right before his eyes. His mother was no fool, and she had most likely known. The old Irish of the First Ward didn't keep secrets, and when they ran into each other at B-Kwik or Tops on Bailey, they would stop in the aisle, carts askew, hands waving and gesturing, sharing whose daughter was pregnant and whose son had reading problems in school, all of it discussed with the fervor of Mideast peace negotiations. "Not drugs. Burglary. This one was arson."

Please don't cry, he thought. Just don't fucking cry, because if you do, I might start.

"I'd hoped for better."

"This is what you got."

"I'm going to rest now," she said.

"Come on."

"Resting."

The guy in the passenger seat turned. His turtleneck looked as if it were trying to swallow his head. "Guess she don't want to talk, huh?"

"Mind your business."

They pulled up in a small parking lot near the rear of a brick building. A blue steel door was marked with a sign reading EMPLOYEES ONLY. There were no other cars in the lot and any hope Mike had of someone spotting them vanished. The second car pulled in behind them and Hark's men got out. Mike looked out the rear window to see two of the guys helping the one with the gunshot. His skin tone resembled a pale pea soup color. They dragged him past and one of them opened the steel door. The driver of Mike's vehicle got out and said, "Call Doc Li, and tell him to pack some morphine in his goody bag. Can't take our man to the hospital with a bullet in him."

Hark's men flung the doors open. One grabbed Mike by

the arm and for a brief moment he considered smacking the guy, but even if he overpowered the man, they still had Mom, and he couldn't very well wrestle her away from the other giant. They shoved him along, his mom behind him, and the one called Ed opened the door. Inside, a hallway filled with gray light caused Mike to squint, trying to adjust to the semidarkness. At the end of the hall he saw a pool table, and beyond it a bar that took up the center of the room. Somehow he didn't think his hosts brought him here to buy a round of martinis. Another door, this one a six panel, was to the right. Turtleneck Ed opened it and this time Mike was forced downstairs, someone jabbing a gun barrel hard into his back. He reached the bottom of the stairs and wound up in a room with a cracked concrete floor. Cases of beer had been stacked against the wall, brands ranging from Amstel to Tecate. On the opposite wall, another door. Someone flicked on fluorescent lights, and they hummed to life.

He waited for his mother to come down, but instead Ed lumbered down the stairs. He stopped on the bottom step, folded his arms.

"Where is she?"

"Your mom's sick, right?"

"Beyond sick."

"How beyond?"

"She has a couple months, at most."

"We're putting her in Mr. Hark's private office. She needs rest."

"What is this place?"

The man gave him a hard stare, one that indicated he thought Mike to be an idiot. "One of Mr. Hark's establishments."

Heavy thuds came from the stairs. The one in the black suit came down, the other guy stepping out of his way. He leaned on a stack of beer cases. "Mr. Hark will be here tomorrow. He told me not to hurt you, that he'll deal with it. He doesn't like disappointments."

Turtleneck Ed went back upstairs.

"That's the impression I'm getting," Mike said.

"You've caused him two messes tonight. He's coming down to meet with you personally."

"I'm sure the pleasure will be all his."

The dark-suited man went to the door and jiggling the knob said, "Let me show you something."

He opened the door, entered the darkened room, and a moment later someone stumbled out and flopped onto the concrete floor. The man looked up. One eye was black and swollen shut, the nose a mashed tomato. The front of his shirt was torn as if by animals, and sticky blood stained the shirt.

In wheezing, wet breaths, Schuler said, "Nice of you to show." He rested his head back on the concrete.

"By tomorrow night, you'll wish you had never signed on for this. Mr. Hark will see to it."

Got to get out of here, Mike thought. Even if he called the cops and they wound up charging him and shipping him to Attica or Clinton, Mom would be saved, and maybe Schuler. At least from whatever fate Hark had lined up for him.

Mike went over to Schuler, gripped his arm, and pulled him up. Wrapping Schuler's arm around his neck, Mike dragged Schuler to the wall, sat him down, and leaned him against the beer cases. Schuler stared at Mike through his good eye, and to Mike it seemed accusatory: *You got me into this*. He had. He had been the one to call Schuler, and he had been the one to bail out on the arson job. But try explaining to Hark that carnival freaks had shown up on the site and scared them off.

"So?" Schuler said.

"I feel like you look."

"That room, Mike? We're done."

He imagined a soundproof room where a bullet would be delivered into the backs of their skulls. There were probably blood and brains on the walls.

"At least it will be quick," Mike said.

"Who are you kidding?"

Mike looked up at the big man. He observed the conversation with a small smile on his face, as if he were watching actors in a play.

"What do you mean?"

"It's like the Spanish Inquisition in there, Mike." Schuler coughed, and air came out his nose in wet, snuffling gasps. "Know how my nose got like this?"

Mike wasn't sure he wanted to know.

"One of those meat-tenderizing hammers, that's how."

Mike winced. Hark's man started up the stairs, chuckling low. Mike thought he heard the guy whisper to himself, "This is gonna be good."

The door slammed shut and Mike heard the click of a lock.

"They were waiting in my house," Schuler said. "I'm standing at the bathroom sink and one of them slips in behind me and I see him and a big gun in the mirror and it's pointed at my head."

"They followed us."

"To the site?"

"I'm guessing they did. Or maybe saw it on the news."

"Whatever they did, we're screwed. We should have just torched the whole place. Fuck those costumed freaks."

Mike sat up, the rough wall digging into his back. "And have witnesses? How is that any better?"

"My whole face hurts."

"A lot more is going to hurt if we don't find a way out."

Mike stood up and looked around. No windows in the basement, only damp concrete walls. He tried the door to the other room, yanked on the handle, but it didn't budge. He climbed the stairs, thinking it useless to try, but he jiggled the knob anyway. The door held tight.

"Any luck?" Schuler asked from downstairs.

"Nothing."

Upstairs, he heard the slow thump of bass as someone had fired up a country tune, maybe Alan Jackson. The music seemed to make the floor joists shake and it annoyed Mike. The music would also provide another purpose when the time came. No one would hear their screams.

CHAPTER 9

In the early morning, David and Reverend Frank pulled into the parking lot of the Savings Motor Lodge. A steady sheet of rain fell around them, forcing the wipers to work overtime. Thunder and lightning echoed around them, and the center of the parking lot had pooled with brownish water. Fighting exhaustion and the storm, they had decided to take refuge for the night. It was only a hundred more miles to Routersville, but David's eyes felt grainy and heavy. Even the high-test coffee he picked up from the truck stop on 81 failed to keep him alert.

Frank had checked them in, and they followed a pink stucco wall past a pop machine, to their room. Number 190 in tarnished brass on the pink door. David had expected a fleabag, but to his surprise, a pleasant vanilla smell filled the room, and the thick carpet appeared new. Two single beds were neatly made and a quick peek in the bathroom showed sparkling tiles and toilet. It wasn't half bad.

They set their suitcases on the beds, David closer to the window, Frank closer to the door. "Best lock up tight," David said. The feeling of something closing in on him, the same one he'd had as he approached the church parking lot, crept over him again. Several times on the wooded highway that led up to the hotel he thought he saw movement in the brush. Then it would dart away. He removed the revolver from his suitcase and set it on the nightstand.

Frank locked the door. As he returned to his bed and unzipped the suitcase, he said, "You think the gun is necessary?"

"It makes me feel better."

"You may have to use the Light again, you know."

"Not until I have to."

"You will, Dave, or you're putting us both at risk."

"For now it's the gun," Dave said.

"You think they're following us?"

Wind spattered against the picture window. David got up and drew the curtain shut. "I couldn't be sure, but while you were driving, I kept seeing things in the woods. Moving quick and then out of my view."

"We'd better keep watch," Frank said.

"I'll go first."

Despite the weariness that had crept into his muscles, David felt wound up, spring-tight. If he went to bed now, he would toss and turn, stare at the ceiling. He thought of Sara. Were the Dark Ones on to her? Was she cold, hungry? He knew she probably had a little money saved, but it wouldn't go far. And how would she find her way in a strange city? No, sleep would not come easy.

"If they come, you have to use it. It's the only way to destroy them for sure," Frank said.

"We'll see," David said, and eyed the revolver.

David sat on the bed, flipped on the tube. A *Seinfeld* episode, then the local news. The storm had trailed off for a while, but now fresh thunderheads rumbled.

On the other bed, Frank lay stretched out in a pair of sweats and a T-shirt that proclaimed him WORLD'S GREATEST

GRANDPA. He held the Bible in front of him, reading glasses perched on his nose. "I talked to Charles."

"And?"

Frank told him how the brewery building had come down and Charles wasn't sure if it would hold its occupant.

"I also called Chen from that rest stop on 81. While you were in the bathroom."

"She making preparations?"

"She's calling together the rest of our people, figuring out how to warn the rest of the town. Thinks maybe we can all hole up in the old armory if need be."

Hopefully it wouldn't come to that. "Is Charles going to check the site?"

"Are you kidding?" Frank said.

"Right. The Gray Crusader. Of course he will."

Frank closed his Bible and turned off the light. They agreed to take two-hour shifts on watch. David got up and turned down the television. He eyed Frank's Bible and wished he were more of a reader, but he had always been good with his hands. Carpentry, electrical, and plumbing just came to him. It was good to know, and drywall jobs brought in extra money, but it would be nice to be a book-worm at times, too.

He took a seat at the table, ran his thumb over the handle of the revolver. He would have to use the Light if it came to it. But could he?

Dave had not seen battle the way Frank or Charles had. His sole experience with his power had come by accident. He remembered freshman year, Taft Senior High School. He had been a skinny kid whose backpack had seemed to out-weigh him. None of his friends from St. Edmund's had gone to Taft, and he felt a little like a new inmate arriving in the state pen. The summer before freshman year, he had begun to feel different. He found himself thinking of warm days at the beach, sun-kissed wheatfields, sunbeams cutting dust motes through the living room windows. Images of light, flooding his mind, a comforting warmth running through him and not from the eighty-five-degree heat. It wasn't unlike slipping into a warm bath and feeling calm and relaxed.

In the first week at Taft, navigating the green-tiled hallways, he had caught the attention of Garrett Garvey. Garvey, he came to find out, dealt hash and coke to select students at Taft. Garvey also had a connection that could get him beer, vodka, anything. For fifty bucks he'd score you a case of beer or a bottle of your choice. Apparently Dave's fellow freshmen made good use of Garvey's services, pooling paper-route and lawn-mowing money and getting drunk down at Cooley Field on the weekends. Dave preferred to stay away. One day he was approached by Garrett in the hall, offering him a small bag of weed. Dave turned it down. Garvey kept it up. He offered Dave a snootful of coke in the bathroom, told him he could score *Hustler* or *Cheri*, or if Dave wanted some freaky shit, he could get Japanese porn. Dave had turned him down.

This had gone on a couple times a week, from September up until mid-December. The week before break, Dave had excused himself from class, taking the wood block that functioned as a lav pass and hitting the bathroom. Upon entering, he saw Garvey, all six feet four inches of him, standing in the stall, door open. His nose was chafed and red. He rubbed his nose with a slim index finger, and Dave saw little white granules stuck to his upper lip. His eyes were glazed and he jittered out of the stall.

"Hey, Dresser," he said, sniffing. "You want to join me?" He held up a silver cylinder with a twist-off cap. "Blow your brains out?"

"I don't do that shit. You shouldn't, either."

This seemed to set Garvey off and in two quick strides he had grabbed Dave by the shirt and pressed him against the wall. The lav pass clattered on the floor.

"What's wrong with you, Dresser?"

"Nothing."

"Not what I heard. Must be a fag to pass up porn."

"Let me go."

"Take a hit. Come on."

Dave struggled and the grip grew tighter on his shirt. His bladder felt hot and full. He really needed to go. Garvey was creeping him out.

"Come on, pussy," Garvey said, and thunked Dave's head against the wall.

That had been it, a trigger for the release. Dave managed to slip one arm up and push, and when he pushed he felt a surge of heat race through his arm and a flash lit up the bathroom. Garvey screamed and turned away. He let go of Dave and dropped to one knee. One hand covered the side of his face. His white button-down had a scorch on the chest and Dave saw the side of Garvey's face. It had turned into a mess of pink skin and fresh blisters had popped up.

To his surprise, Garvey began to weep. "You burned me, why did you burn me? Oh God, it hurts, it hurts."

Garvey had run from the bathroom and in a matter of minutes, Dave had been sent to see Mr. Wiggins, the principal. After interrogating Dave, and calling in his parents, Wiggins arrived at the conclusion that Dave had burned Garvey with a lighter and some sort of chemical igniter. Never mind that they didn't find a lighter or any type of flammable material. Not on Dave's person, in his locker, in the john, or even in the bathroom garbage cans. He got suspended for a week, and Garvey wound up having plastic surgery, which left the side of his face a puckered pink mess. He never offered Dave drugs again, and gave Dave a wide berth in the halls. Last Dave heard, Garvey was serving a sentence up in Michigan City for dealing heroin.

So he hadn't wanted to use the Light, even with their enemy on the loose and the stories Frank and Charles had told him, how the Dark Ones preferred to capture and torture rather than kill outright. How they sometimes roasted captives alive and consumed the flesh. He hoped when the time came he could use his power on them.

Dave caught himself dozing off. His head snapped back and he awoke. The clock on the wall said two thirty. Time to turn in and get some sleep. He rubbed his neck, massaging out the kink that had settled in, stood up and stretched.

Outside, he heard a bang. Something being tipped over. Maybe just a cat or a wayward raccoon in the trash can, but maybe not.

Picking up the revolver, he slipped over to the door, killed the overhead light, and peeked out the curtain. Outside he saw only the rain-slicked pavement and a few lights burning outside each hotel room across the way. He watched, squinted, thinking that something might move, the very darkness itself, take form and move toward the window.

A moment later, he heard a scream. A man, but high pitched. It was with dread that he realized the Enemy was here. He could stop Them. The poor bastard outside could not.

He unlocked the door, hands shaking from the fear of something waiting just outside. Throwing open the door, he pointed the revolver and let in the rain-soaked air, which was bitter and acrid.

He heard Frank sit up, the rustle of sheets behind him, and then Frank saying, "Where are you going?"

David didn't stop, but instead went outside and looked around. To his left were a few parked SUVs and to his right the soda machine, maybe forty feet away. He heard the victim now, soft whimpers carrying down the alley, punctuated by crying and "Oh, Jesus."

Now David moved toward the sound of the whimpering man, his heart rabbiting in his chest, thinking he might get jumped at any second. He passed the soda machine and found a door bashed open. He moved inside and flipped on the light and saw the man staked to the wall.

He had been pinned like an insect on display for an entomologist, a black stake through his gut and a spreading stain on his pajamas. He looked at David with pleading, wet eyes and then lowered his head and tugged at the stake. David put a hand over his mouth and nose to block out the metallic smell of blood and the odor of ripe shit coming from the room. He stifled a gag.

David raised his hand. "Don't pull it out, you'll rip out your insides. I'll call for help."

The man responded with a hacking cough, a rope of blood coming from his mouth and spattering the bed. The brutality of the attack stunned David.

The Reverend came up behind, bumped into David, and David moved out of the way to give Frank a good look. Frank gasped, started forward, and then, perhaps realizing he could do nothing, stopped.

"I'll call the paramedics," Frank said. "God help him."

David approached the man, whose head sank down. The front of his pajama pants were saturated black, and the man's hands, which had gripped the stake, now hung at his side. David reached up, felt the man's neck, checking for a pulse, but found none. There was no helping this one, so he went to the door and scanned the parking lot. Something caught his eye on the opposite roof, something black and deformed, crawling along the ridgeline.

He raised the revolver to fire. He never heard Frank approach. The Reverend slapped his arm down and, frowning, said, "We've got to go."

David saw that Frank had dressed, or at least thrown on a pair of khakis with his T-shirt.

"But they're attacking the hotel. Look," David said, and pointed.

Frank looked over at the roof. "We'll do no good dead. We have to move. And if the cops come, we'll only be held up," Frank said.

"What about the rest of the people? And using the Light?"

"They're looking for us, David. The people will have to fend for themselves. This is too important."

He couldn't believe what he was hearing from the Reverend. What about all the people in those rooms? And what if some of them had kids? Would they all be gutted and hung on walls like some sick trophy?

"I can't believe you," David said.

Frank gripped him by the shoulders. "I know it's horrible, but this is one hotel, maybe thirty or forty people. If we don't get where we're going, it could be thirty or forty million. Probably more. Now I've called for help and an ambulance is on the way and the cops will follow. Okay?"

He didn't like Frank explaining things to him as if he were a thickheaded five-year-old who had attempted crossing the street on his own. But Frank was right. If they stayed, they would be questioned, and it was either fight this small battle now, or be around to fight the big one later. Hopefully once they left, the Enemy would follow and leave the innocents sleeping in rented beds alone. But damn it, he thought of that thing slinking over the roof, probably the one that impaled the unwary traveler in the other room. *I could have plugged him, taken one with me.*

"We'll go," David said. "Maybe they'll follow us, leave these people be."

Frank took his hands from David's shoulders. "I'm sorry."

David glanced over his shoulder. "Not half as sorry as I am."

He prayed Sara was faring better than the people at the motel.

They snatched their bags from the room and after piling into the truck, tore out of the parking lot. On the highway, a shroud of fog had fallen and misted in front of the headlights. David checked the rearview mirror and saw nothing. There were no cars in front, no comforting glow of taillights to ensure him that they were not the only car out here. He suddenly missed Sara very badly and wanted to give her a hug and know she was up in her room studying. Hell, right now the stereo blasting Danzig through the floor would be welcome. David would at least know she was safe and they were together. He wouldn't complain. And the night and the shadows would seem far away.

"He was dead. Right after you left the room, he died," David said.

"I'm not surprised. That was a horrific wound."

"Why that guy? Do you think they couldn't find us?"

"I'm guessing they decided to go room by room until they did."

David watched the road. Mile markers whizzed past. The fog rolled over the windshield. "How many you think there were?"

"May have just been the one you saw, maybe more."

"Frank?"

"Yes?"

"You hear the screaming? As we pulled away?"

Frank remained silent.

"You heard, right?"

"I did."

"I thought so."

CHAPTER 10

Sara persuaded Randall Powers to drop her off six blocks from the hospital. She began the walk, feeling like it was six miles instead.

Laura stood in the hospital cafeteria line, aware that she was going to zone out again. The tray she held felt distant, the BLT and apple on the plate seemed like someone else's. The low hiss of the fryer and the squeak of shoes on the tile floor were muffled. She had been thinking of Megan again, and the world around her seemed to exist through a filter of gauze.

A cold October day, she remembered. She wasn't quite twenty. She wore a heavy turtleneck and cords; the temperature was in the thirties. She had bundled Megan in a heavy snowsuit for their trip to the Great Pumpkin Farm. It had been one of their first official outings. Just Laura and her plump little six-month-old.

They strolled through rows of pumpkins, around kiddie roller coasters and miniature cars that whipped around and incited squeals of joy from the riders. The crisp smell of fall hung in the air and she was looking forward to starting some Christmas shopping. It was Megan's first, and she meant it to be the best.

They came up to a stand selling hot cider, and despite the bitter day, a throng of people in winter coats and long scarves and mittens crowded the table, their breath rising in plumes. She looked for an opening to reach the table. Stroller in front of her, she hoped to slip through and get herself a cider. No one budged, but she thought she could slip through by herself. The baby would be okay for a second, and she was only a few feet away.

She put the brakes on the stroller, then bent down and tugged Megan's hat, making sure her ears were covered. Megan's cheeks were pink, and Laura pressed her hand to the skin. They wouldn't be able to stay out too much longer. She would get the cider, and she would head back to the car. Laura stroked her cheek and the baby giggled. That alone was enough to warm her.

"Be right back, sweetie."

Laura slipped between a heavyset woman in a parka and her teenage son. She asked for a cup of cider and the clerk served her and she paid. She turned back toward the stroller. The heavyset woman cut in front of her and Laura stopped. The woman gave her a frown.

The crowd had thickened and she brushed through, feeling the scrape of a tall man's wool scarf against her cheek, hearing a chorus of coughs and sniffles and wondering how many of these folks would be in bed with colds by next week.

She slipped through the crowd and Megan was gone. Maybe she had become disoriented in the crowd. She looked left, then right, started to make her way back into the crowd when someone plowed into her. She went down, banging her elbow on a rock. She scrambled to her feet, shoving and clawing to stand up and drawing angry looks from people.

Panic set in. The stroller and her daughter were not misplaced. She hadn't gone far. Her daughter was gone.

She had been nineteen, young, stupid. Guilty of turning her back for a moment, but in that moment, the absolute worst had happened. The state police and the FBI had found nothing, and Laura spent the next fifteen years wondering. They never found a body, and she never received a ransom note. Her only hope was that someone had given Megan a good life. God knew Laura hadn't. Or at least that was how she felt after the abduction.

She was jolted out of the memory by the clatter of a plastic tray on the floor. Over to her left, between a cooler and the food line, the cashier gripped a teenage girl by the arm. The girl had an apple in her opposite hand. She waved it in the air, playing keep-away with the cashier. The girl dug her feet in. The cashier pulled harder, then looked around for help. A nurse wearing a flowered shirt and blue scrubs ran out, presumably to fetch security.

Laura watched the girl. Her face was smeared with dirt and brambles filled her hair. The right knee of her pants was muddy and torn. A travel bag, slung around her back, bounced up and down as she struggled to keep the apple away.

Laura set her tray on a counter. She went and asked the cashier, "What's the problem?"

The cashier, who looked solid enough to take on The Rock in a cage match, said, "Caught her stealing this apple."

The girl's gaze flicked from the cashier to Laura.

"Let her go. I'll pay for the apple."

The cashier arched her eyebrows.

"I can't tolerate stealing."

"Let her be," Laura said. "I'll handle it. Now how much for the apple?"

"Fifty cents."

Laura dug two quarters from the pocket of her lab coat and handed them to the cashier. The cashier gave the girl a killer look and went back to her register.

The girl looked at Laura as if expecting to be rebuked.

"You're welcome," Laura said.

The nurse returned with a blue-clad security guard in tow. He approached, thumbs in his belt and said, "Problem here, Dr. Pennington?"

"I took care of it."

The security guard looked at the girl, shrugged, and walked away.

"Sorry," the girl said. "And thanks."

"Do you have a name?"

"My name's Sara."

"Are you seeing someone in the hospital?"

"I came looking for my mother."

"Is she a patient? Maybe I can help you locate her."

"She's a doctor," Sara said.

"What's her name?"

"Laura Pennington."

This was a joke, and a goddamned sick one at that. Who would do such a thing?

"Who put you up to this?"

Sara set down her duffel bag. She unzipped it and pulled out a pile of newspaper articles. They were the safety tips Laura had done for the *Buffalo News* two summers ago. "What is this supposed to prove?"

"Do you know a man named David Dresser?"

"Never heard of him."

"I thought he was my father, and now I'm not sure. I found these pictures. He kept another picture of my supposed real mother, but it's a fake. You're my mother."

"How old are you?" Laura asked.

"Sixteen."

She took a good hard look at the girl. She hadn't noticed before, but the eyes were the same light blue, the hair the same shiny black. Sixteen, the right age. There was one more test she could do, one that would seal the deal. It probably wouldn't amount to anything, and she was foolish for getting her hopes up.

Heart racing, she said to Sara, "Come with me."

She brought Sara to Room 4 in the ER and drew the curtain around them. Sara set her bag down and propped herself on the gurney. The sheets were fresh and white, and they crinkled as she sat.

"Did someone send you here to mess with me?" Laura asked.

The girl shook her head.

Maybe it was Callahan. He was the worst joker in the hospital, one time filling her locker with roughly a hundred Super Balls. She'd spent a half hour tracking them down and throwing them in the garbage for fear of someone slipping. But to play a joke like this was monstrous, cruel, even though it wasn't completely out of the question that her daughter might be alive somewhere. No body had been found, no suspects apprehended.

"So what's this test you're going to give me?" Sara asked.

"I had a daughter, but she was kidnapped as an infant. She had a birthmark on her lower back that we called 'Australia' because it was shaped like the continent."

"So you want me to show you my back."

Laura smiled. "You catch on quickly."

The curtain was yanked aside and Carol Wardinski, one of the nurses, told Laura a multiple gunshot wound was on the way in.

Laura looked at Sara, then back at the nurse. To Sara, she said, "Stay in the waiting room. Can you do that? I'll talk to you when my shift is up."

"I'm not going anywhere," Sara said.

* * *

Laura's muscles ached, her feet throbbed, and she wanted nothing more than to collapse into bed when her shift was up. The GSW had turned out to be a real hummer. Six people shot, all gangbangers. One of them had died while the trauma team worked on him; the guy had been riddled with slugs. The other five they had saved, although two of them would wind up paralyzed and one was nearly brain dead. There had been more gray matter on the gurney than in the guy's skull.

Now, as she strode into the waiting room, she found Sara curled up in a chair with her bag propped under her head for a pillow. She shook the girl's shoulder and Sara snored once and then snapped up to a seated position. She looked around, dazed, and then up at Laura.

She noticed Sara's bloody knee, and took her in back. After cleaning and bandaging the wound, she said, "Ready?"

Sara nodded and picked up her bag. They walked outside into dancing leaves and a stiff October breeze. Laura buttoned her coat, pulled the collar closed.

"Warm where you came from?" Laura asked.

"Indiana, gets cold there same as here."

"Where?"

"Little town called Lexington."

They walked for a while in silence. The girl didn't seem fully awake yet, and Laura didn't tell her, but she had risked losing her wallet and watch by falling asleep in the waiting room.

As they reached Laura's Honda, she said, "You can stay at my place for the night."

"I'd planned on it. Got nowhere else to go, right now."

Laura unlocked the doors and they got in. Laura pulled out. As they drove, she snuck glances at Sara, who didn't seem to notice. She looked at the hair, the eyes, the set of jaw and the more she looked, the more it seemed possible that

Sara could be hers. Or was it just the hope of a fool who wanted her child back?

It seemed she had heard if a kidnapped child were not recovered within twenty-four hours of abduction, then they were as good as gone. But still, she could hope for a miracle. They happened to other people, so why not her?

Twenty minutes later, they arrived at Laura's place. Laura parked and they got out. They took the elevator to the building's tenth floor and Laura took out her key and opened the apartment door. She flipped on the lights, hoping Sara wouldn't see her hands shaking.

"Something to drink?"

"No thanks. So what is it you're looking for. This proof?"

Laura exhaled. "A birthmark. Lower back. I thought it looked like Australia. I used to think of Megan as my 'Down Under' baby because of it. Corny, I know. But people can have birthmarks that are similar, right? I shouldn't get my hopes up."

"Well?"

"Let's see."

Sara set down her bag and turned around. Laura almost couldn't bear to look. What if it wasn't her daughter?

Sara lifted the back of her shirt up, and sure enough, a birthmark, roughly six inches by six, blotchy red, across the small of her back. And it was Australia, or at least that was how Laura perceived it. She heard herself gasp and the room began to tilt a bit as she staggered backward, her legs hitting the Queen Anne chair and forcing her to flop on her butt. *My God, she's found me.*

Sara lowered her shirt and sat on the couch, opposite Laura.

Laura said, "How?"

Sara shook her head. "I don't know."

"Tell me what you do know."

"My father, or the person who says he's my father, is

named David Dresser. I've been with him my whole life. I just found these photos the other day. He had them hidden."

"What possessed you?"

"I needed twenty bucks until payday. He keeps a stash under his mattress, which he thinks I don't know about. It's money from his drywall jobs, and I was going to pay him back, just a little light though. Anyway, this manila envelope is poking out, so I tug on it and it falls and out flops these newspaper articles with your picture," Sara said. "And a letter saying you can never find out I'm yours."

This was getting nuttier. "Your mother? What did he tell you?"

"That she died. Cancer of the ovaries. He kept a picture on his dresser, black hair, blue eyes. It could have been my mom, so I never questioned it."

"How could he conceal this?"

"We moved a lot. Fresno, Portland, El Paso. Every few years, he said he needed to find work, that the construction jobs were drying up. I've gone to a dozen different schools."

The poor girl. Here she had lived for years under the illusion that her mother was dead, and that the man she had known all along was her father. Why would someone do this?

"Who was my real father?"

Laura was still having trouble absorbing this. There were tests they could run, and she was already planning to contact the lab at the hospital in order to confirm it. But she had seen the birthmark, the pictures, the resemblance. "I'd like to say I knew him." She felt her face reddening. "But I met up with a guy after a Van Halen concert and we hooked up in the parking lot. I'd had too many wine coolers and he was higher than a satellite. His name was Rick."

"Don't be sorry," the girl said. She got off the couch and came to Laura and Laura stood up and embraced the girl, who returned her hug fiercely. This was her daughter, or at least that's what some form of maternal instinct told her. It felt right, like Sara was hers. She had heard theories about bonding and instinct but had never believed them until now. The hell with blood tests.

"I screwed up that night, or at least that's what I thought. But I got a beautiful little girl out of the deal. My father was nervous, scared, but not mad. He helped me out, paid for my schooling. Jesus, I don't know what to think. I did good until they snatched you from me. I just turned my back for a god-damned second."

Sara, her face pressed into Laura's shoulder, said, "I'm not leaving you again."

"I don't want you to leave." Laura gently pushed the girl away. "My next move is to find this Dresser jerk. I'm sure the FBI would like to have a word with him."

"No, please don't. I'm mad at him, too, but he's a good man. Besides, I have a feeling he'll come looking for me."

"Sara, he lied to you for years. He took you from me."

Laura went to the rolltop desk and took out a legal pad and red pen. "Did he mention anyone else? Give me some names."

"I can't. I don't want Dad—or Dave, arrested."

"He kidnapped you!"

Sara recoiled. "I've had a good life. I'm just confused. Shit, I'm fucking baffled, to be honest with you. This really rocked my world. But don't turn him in."

"That's an understatement. I need more names, information."

"Do you think I could get something to eat? It might help my memory."

What would it hurt? It had been a mystery for sixteen years. Another hour while they had a meal wouldn't hurt. But she would still find this Dresser, and when she did, he would be better off if they locked him in San Quentin.

Laura gave her a sly smile. "Let's eat."

They sat in the kitchen after finishing grilled cheese sand-wiches and tomato soup. Laura had garnished it with dill pickles and potato chips, and although it was far from gourmet cooking, in her book you couldn't beat grilled cheese and a pickle on the side. The meal reflected her style of living, as did the kitchen. It had a butcher-block table for two. The counter had a coffeemaker, toaster, and microwave. She owned four plates and four sets of silverware. There were no magnets on the fridge, no sunflower paintings or plaques with cutesy aphorisms on the walls. It was strictly functional. With most of her time spent at the hospital, she didn't see the need for clutter and fancy decorations.

Sara helped her wash and dry the dishes, and when they were in the drain, Sara asked if she could clean up. She still had smudges on her face and dirt under her nails. Laura hoped to hear her tale, but only if she was ready to tell. Laura got her out a white towel and a pair of blue sweats and a T-shirt that read PENN STATE. She then directed Sara to the bathroom.

Twenty minutes later, Sara came out looking freshly scrubbed and vital. With her glasses off, the resemblance to Laura was striking. They could have been sisters separated by a few years.

"Did your memory improve with that meal?" Laura asked.

Sara twirled her hair with her finger. "Yeah, there was one other thing they talk about sometimes."

"Who's they?"

"David and Reverend Frank. Once in a while when they don't think I'm listening, or when Dave's on the phone, I hear him talking to someone. More and more in the past few weeks."

"Why would that be suspicious?"

"A couple times, I enter the room, and if Reverend Frank is over, they get real quiet all of a sudden, like they were talking about me, but they're not. It's the guy."

"You get his name?"

"I think he's from Buffalo. First name is Charles. They call him Charlie, or the Gray Crusader, then laugh about it like it's the funniest damn thing in the world. Hey, you okay? Your face is as white as that wall."

She felt hot and sick all at once. It couldn't be. But hadn't Dad referred to himself as a "Gray Crusader" on more than one occasion? Usually when he was off to a Common Council meeting, charging off like some half-assed Don Quixote on a quest to save the brewery.

"Laura?"

"The man you just described," Laura said, "is my father."

Laura approached the phone. She stared at it as if it might jump from the table and bite her. The wall clock ticked in the background. It was like waiting for the chaplain and guards to enter your cell, waiting for that long walk to Old Sparky. Would calling her father clear up the mysteries that had plagued her for the past sixteen years? She wanted to know and she didn't.

"Are you going to call him?" Sara asked.

Laura reached out her hand, wiggled her fingers. There was no good excuse for not calling other than the fact she was completely terrified at the moment. She realized she might not know her own father completely, and while that scared her, the fact that he may have known the whereabouts of her little girl scared her more.

She picked up the phone and dialed. She let it ring nine times. His machine came on. "Dad, call me. As soon as you can, okay?" she said, voice cracking.

She hung up the phone and turned to Sara, who sat on the edge of the couch, arms crossed. "Well?"

"I'm off tomorrow. We'll go look for him."

In the spare bedroom, Sara turned down the sheets on the twin bed. There was a television in the room and she had flipped through the news stations and thought she might catch a story about Joanne's death. There had been nothing.

Laura entered the bedroom with a pink and white afghan. "It can get chilly in here. Keep this on the bed."

"Can I ask you something?" Sara said.

"Shoot."

"Why are you waiting to talk to your dad?"

"Another day won't make a difference. It's been this many years. I guess I'm just glad to have you back."

"I suppose we can find him tomorrow."

"Are you worried about it?"

Sara smoothed out the comforter. "The sooner, the better, I guess."

"Are you scared?"

She knows something, Sara thought. "Why?"

"I don't mind telling you I am."

Scared of what? "I don't follow."

"You. Back in my life after all these years. Don't get me wrong, I'm excited and happy and I feel like I could fly to the damned moon, but where do we go from here?"

Sara didn't have the answer to that. "I guess it's just important that we're together again."

"We'll take it slow, okay?"

"Get to the bottom of this."

"Starting with David."

Laura gave her a hug and whispered, "I am glad you're back; you have no idea. We'll find our way, won't we?"

"Together."

CHAPTER 11

Dave drove the truck over the last hill and Routersville came into view. As they dipped down the long hill, the rows of ranch houses at the edge of town spread before them. Beyond that was Main Street and the brick clock tower that marked town hall. The main road jogged again in the distance and led to an extruding plant and above it a hundred-foot-high smokestack that rose like a castle tower. As the road rose again on the far side of town, his eyes were drawn to it. The armory, constructed in 1911, had turrets and high walls and two massive steel doors that opened into an archway. It looked as if it had dropped in from a fairy tale. It had most recently housed National Guard units, but was now abandoned except for a minimal maintenance crew.

He had been through here one other time and guessed that it took a grand total of five minutes to travel Main Street end-to-end. That was Routersville, blink and you miss it.

"Doesn't look like much, does it?" Frank said.

"Not exactly the big city."

"But important, no doubt."

They started through the outskirts of town, where every house seemed to have a pickup truck in the driveway, many of them sporting stickers that said things like BUSH/CHENEY and I OWN A GUN AND I VOTE.

"Where does Chen live?"

"Off the main street. Near the clock tower," Frank said.

They entered the business district and passing through, David noticed all the buildings were the same neat red brick. The businesses, with names like Ruby's Diner and The All Niter Laundromat, had potted plants out front, mums or other brightly colored flowers. The moldings and doorways were all painted a clean white and the signs for the businesses were scripted in the same elegant gold on hunter green. David figured it must be a town ordinance, as many small towns liked to keep things uniform, especially if the buildings had historical significance.

They approached the clock tower, which cast a long shadow across Main Street, and Dave couldn't help feel a chill as the truck passed through the darkness, however brief. It made him think of last night at the hotel. Would they follow him and Frank right into town? There hadn't been any sign of them after the hotel.

"Up here. Greenview Lane."

Dave signaled right and turned down Greenview. Like the rest of Routersville, Greenview Lane was hilly, and many of the homes had driveways that wound upward from the road. As they drove, a sudden gust of wind rattled and shook the trees. It sounded almost like a hiss, and Dave had the urge to get inside. He knew it was silly, and it was only wind, but he felt bad things were coming down the road.

"There it is," Frank said, pointing to a blue mailbox with gold-foiled numbers. "Number eighty-six."

"We're not staying long," David said.

"Engel can't have found Sara this quickly, if that's what you're worried about."

"She's away from me, Frank. I have no idea how she is. She's a pretty girl, what if some pervert . . ."

"She's also smart enough to know who to avoid and when

to ask for help. She's on a bus with others. She won't go wandering off by herself."

"The sooner we go, the better."

Dave swung the truck up the driveway, and Chen's house, like many of Routersville's homes, was a nondescript ranch, white with powder-blue trim. A cornstalk was fastened to the porch, and a trio of pumpkins rested at the base of the stalk. Dave parked the truck next to a Ford Explorer and the two of them got out.

They approached the front door, which was decorated with a cardboard black cat, its back arched, its eyes pale green. At least Chen's Halloween spirit hadn't evaporated with all the news of coming trouble.

Frank rang the bell and footsteps sounded from behind the door. The door swung open and Jenny Chen appeared, a compact Asian woman with a set of brown eyes that could turn your heart to liquid. She wore a blue warm-up suit and matching Adidas sneakers. A fine sheen of sweat covered her forehead.

"Working out?" Frank asked.

"I've been cooking for you two all afternoon. Oven's hotter than, well, an oven," she said and smiled. Dave thought it was a particularly fine sight to see Jenny smile.

She welcomed them in, giving Dave and Frank each a hug and taking their coats, hanging them on a coatrack. The house smelled of warm bread. Dave felt his stomach rumble.

"Something smells good," Dave said.

"Homemade bread, roast chicken, mashed potatoes, and a pumpkin pie for dessert. Hope you're hungry."

"It won't go to waste," Frank said.

An hour later, they sat around the table, the chicken stripped to the bones and half-empty bowls of food surrounding the bird. Dave's stomach swelled and he felt the pull of sleep start to drag him under. Not wanting to doze off at the table, he said, "What do we know?"

Jenny leaned forward, rested her elbows on the table. "We know they slaughtered the Littles, kids and all."

"Nothing around here, though," Frank said.

"I've been sending out people to scout," Jenny said "They're definitely on the move, using the woods at night where they can."

"And as far as you can tell?" Frank asked.

"They're headed this way."

"How many?"

Jenny pursed her lips, thinking. "Hard to tell."

"How's that?" Dave asked.

"You haven't heard any news lately?"

Dave exhaled air out of his nostrils, realizing he was giving a snort of contempt, but then thinking Jenny had no way of knowing. She looked at him, puzzled. "Sorry. They almost caught up to us at a hotel."

Jenny's eyebrows went up. "And?"

"We got away," Frank said. "Some others weren't so lucky."

"How bad?"

"The one I saw was horrible. Not sure about the rest."

"It's worse than I thought, then," Jenny said. "That must've been terrible for you." She placed her hand over his and he couldn't deny a little jolt of excitement passing through him. A moment later, she removed her hand.

That man pinned to the wall wasn't so lucky. Dave could still see the horrified look on the man's face, hear the wet gurgling sounds that escaped him. "So what's this news?"

"They've been busy in a little town called Wickett's Corner, about a half hour from here."

"We have none of our people down there, right?" Frank said.

Jenny shook her head. "No, but it's close enough to us to send a message."

"Turn on the news, then," Dave said. "See if anything weird's been reported."

"Better yet," Frank said. "How about we see it for ourselves?"

"I was afraid you'd say that," Jenny said.

"We have to know what we're up against."

"It's getting close to dark."

"Dave, get your keys."

Jenny Chen approached the idling pickup truck. She had changed into a pair of jeans, sweater, and a denim jacket with a sheepskin collar. Since she was the smallest, they decided she would ride in the truck's extended cab, and she had quite a bit of room.

She gave them directions and as the truck wound down country roads, Dave watched every flickering shadow, expecting an attack. The trees seemed taller, cathedral-like, as if built as a monument to some dark god. The normally steady pickup swayed in the wind, and he tightened his grip on the steering wheel. The thought of being back in Jenny's living room grew more and more appealing.

They crested a hill and Jenny instructed them to pull over. Dave did, and after killing the engine, all three of them piled out of the truck. From the top of the hill, they saw a gray-brown gash in the earth surrounded by rusted machinery and piping that rose up into corrugated metal buildings. They would have to pass through Wickett's Corner to reach it.

"What's that?" Dave asked.

"Coal mine. Shut down ten years ago. By most accounts it's flooded. A few kids died in there, got curious and fell down the shaft."

This was getting better by the minute. "That end of town, near the mine, not a lot of lights on," Dave said.

"From what I gather, when the mine closed up, so did most of the town. The main drag's all boarded up."

"And the recent visitors didn't help."

Chen crouched down and sat on a rock. "Here's the thing, nobody killed or even hurt, right? But the people down there claim to see things at night, coming out of the mine, coming up to houses, looking in windows."

"And what do they take them for?"

"Costumes? Hallucinations? Who knows?"

David looked out onto the town. The houses nearest the abandoned mine were among the darkest, while the ones farthest from the mine had lights in the windows. What did they see, the people closest to the mines? The sight of the abominations were enough to make people pack up and leave town.

"I want to see the mine," Frank said.

"It's nearing dark," Jenny said.

"We have time," Frank said.

"It's too dangerous."

"Just a jaunt down there, get some idea of numbers, anything," Frank said.

"Let me send some of my people out," Jenny said. "We can't afford to lose you, Frank."

"She's right," Dave said. He had no doubt Chen would make a fierce and capable leader, but it was not the same as having the Reverend at the helm. He always seemed to know what to do and possessed a well of calm that knew no depths.

Frank was already on his way to the truck. "Start her up, Dresser. We're checking out that mine. And daylight's wasting."

They drove through town, down Veterans Memorial Boulevard. Many of the businesses sported plywood boards across their fronts, and others had the windows covered in soap. Most of them bore faded signs and David guessed they had last been freshly painted when Eisenhower was president.

No one strolled on the main boulevard and David saw no lights in the windows. He kept expecting to see the flash of headlights in front of him or in the rearview mirror, but they were the only car on the road. He supposed the residents had good reason to stay indoors at night, but it was still disconcerting. Wickett's Corner had a name that implied small-town charm, a place loaded with boutiques and quaint country shops, but instead it was a used-up corpse of a town. He wanted to turn and drive away, not out of fear, but out of the general sense of despair that had settled over him since entering the town.

As if reading his thoughts, Frank said, "Cheerful, huh?"

"About as cheerful as a field trip to the morgue."

"It wasn't always like this," Jenny said. "When the mine was open, it was a pretty bustling town. Builders couldn't put up homes fast enough and realtors couldn't keep houses listed. But then the mine shut down. Accidents, safety violations, rumors that it had been mined out. The town died."

"You've done your homework, Jenny," Frank said.

David looked in the rearview mirror. A wry smile crossed Jenny's face. "Talked to some of the old-timers, the ones who are either too stubborn or carrying false hope that this place will come alive again."

They passed through the township proper and arrived at the mine, which was now surrounded by a six-foot chain-link fence. Rolled barbed wire curled along the top of the fence, and a faded blue sign announced HARBEN MINING CO. MINE NO. 4. NO TRESPASSING. Beyond the fence David could make out the yawning mouth of the mine, framed with timbers and covered by a patchwork collection of beams in the hope of keeping adventurers out. He noticed with dismay that some of the beams had been snapped in two and cast away from the entrance.

"Kill the headlights," Frank said. "We don't want to draw attention to ourselves."

"But it's not dark yet."

"Better to be safe."

David pushed in a knob on the dashboard and the lights faded out.

"The gate, shouldn't it be locked?" Frank asked.

The tap on the window made David's heart jitterbug in his chest. He turned his head to see a flashlight beam hitting him in the face. Instinctively he put up his hand to block out the light.

He turned the key, preparing to lower the window, confident their adversaries had not begun carrying flashlights. He lowered the window and the man at the window lowered the flashlight.

Dave looked into the face of a man with a bushy white mustache and equally robust eyebrows. Dave saw the twinkle in the man's blue eyes and thought between that and the white hair, the man would have made a great Santa. He took a look at the silver name badge on the man's shirt. It read: B. MEYERS.

The guard said, "You're trespassing. This is mine property."

"Just checking it out," Dave said.

"Still trespassing," he said, and pulled a cell phone from his pocket.

That was all they needed was cops showing up. "That's not necessary," Dave said.

"I got a job to do, buddy," the guard said, and went to dial.

Dave reached up to snatch the phone, but the guard took a step back, moving out of Dave's reach. Dave started to open the truck door, intent on separating the guard from his phone. This whole thing was a bad idea, coming down here in the first place. He should have been on his way to Buffalo by now. Sara was out there alone and here he was messing around with a rent-a-cop. He said, "Give me that damn phone."

He felt a hand on his arm. It was Frank, now shaking his head. Frank leaned across the seat and said, "You seen anything strange up here, my friend? We've heard stories."

The guard held the phone away from his ear. At least Frank had gotten his attention.

"We came to see about things that go bump in the night. We mean no harm."

The guard paused, regarded the cell phone. Dave hadn't seen him dial the number yet.

"What can you tell us? There's a twenty in it for you." Frank pulled a twenty from his pocket and was waving it in the air. It had to work, because if the guard completed his call and they wound up in jail, the battle would be over before it started. The guard punched a button on the phone, and it made a warbling, beeping noise. He returned it to his pocket and approached the truck.

He held out his hand. "Let's see it."

Frank extended his arm, leaning over Dave. The guard snatched the bill and in one smooth motion tucked it in his shirt pocket. Dave had a bad moment where he thought the guard might laugh maniacally, whip out the cell phone, and summon the police. Instead, he grinned and said, "What do you want to know?"

"Is there somewhere we can go. Close?" Frank said. "We're in a hurry."

"The guard shack. This way."

They followed him, the man's ample rear end swaying in the headlights. He led them to a steel shack with rusty patches on its front. A dim light emanated from behind the curtained front window. The guard waved, indicating they should follow.

Once inside, the guard sat at a card table. On the table were a desk lamp, a travel mug, and a legal pad with messy handwriting scrawled on it. In the corner was a file cabinet with a dusty boom box on top. The closeness of the space made Dave feel as if the walls might press in and crush them. It was close enough to smell Jenny's spicy perfume. Not that it was a bad thing.

"Name's Bernie Myers, been with the mine thirty-eight years. Once a miner, now a rent-a-cop. What else you need to know?"

Dave cracked a grin. "Tell us about the mine."

They learned the mine had opened in 1919 with sixty employees on the payroll. By 1921 there were five hundred employees and they were mining coal as fast as the mine carts would move. The mine did well up through the Second World War, then things started going badly. In 1956 a cave-in killed nine miners. In 1961 an explosion killed eleven more. But the mine kept going, despite eleven more deaths between the last explosion and the fall of Saigon. By then the government started buzzing around, hitting the owners of Harben in the pocketbook with all types of violations.

"What about recently?" Frank asked.

"Strange things around."

"How strange?"

"You wouldn't believe me if I told ya."

Jenny said, "Try us."

"Those houses closest to the mine? All empty. People vacated them."

"Real estate market bad?" Dave asked.

"Boy, that's real funny," Bernie said, rolling his eyes. "They seen stuff."

"Dark's coming," Dave said. "He's told us nothing."

"Another twenty might loosen my lips."

David moved the curtain and looked out the window. The sun had nearly disappeared beneath the crest of the hills. If the mine was acting as a hiding place, its occupants would soon be coming out for the night. "I'll show you where to put a twenty," Dave said.

Frank intervened. "Hard times?"

"Why do you think I stay here? I worked in that mine twenty-nine years, made a decent living. Got bad lungs and a worse back, but I fed my family. I need all I can get."

"Yeah, can't make a living so extortion's the next best thing," Dave said.

Frank put up a hand. "Times are tough. How about another forty to help you remember?" He took out his wallet and handed Bernie two twenties.

Bernie took the money and muttered a quick thanks under his breath. He tucked the bills away in his pocket. "They come out of the mine at night. Started about a week ago. People seeing faces in their windows at night. Things that look like Halloween masks, only real. Half the folks around here have gone up to the Holiday Inn in Chancelorsville."

"And you?" Dave asked.

"I stay in the shed. That reminds me." He turned off the lamp and shut the curtain, cloaking the room in shadows. "They ain't bothered me, but I hear them stomping and muttering in the dark."

"But have you *seen* anything?" Dave asked.

"I peeked out the door one night. It was a clear night, all the stars out like little diamonds. One of them things flew over top of the hills, must have had a wingspan of eight or nine feet."

"I suggest you find a new line of work," Frank said.

"No other work around. I got the start of emphysema, need insurance."

The man had no idea how much danger he was in. Dave wanted to go, even though they had only been here a short time. He couldn't imagine spending a night alone with the Dark Ones roaming the desolate hills.

He went to the window again and looked out. To his dismay, the hilltops were now as dark as the sky. Night had fallen.

* * *

Frank, Chen, and Dave piled into the truck. From the cab of the truck, Dave watched the guard shut the door, blotting out the light. He pulled down the blinds and a moment later the light went off.

Dave backed the truck up, did a quick turn, and drove through the open gate and back down the road. Behind him, the steel machinery diminished in the rearview mirror. He realized he had the truck going fifty. It would be best to slow it down.

"Pull over," Frank said.

"You nuts?" Dave asked.

"We're a good distance away. Turn it around and pull over to the side. I want to see."

From the backseat, Chen said, "Frank, I don't know about that."

"Do it."

Dave looked at him. The bushy eyebrows had set themselves into a serious frown and when the Reverend got that look, there was no arguing. David eased the truck to the side of the road, checked the mirror, and turned it around. He parked on the opposite shoulder. The framework of the mining operation rose against the sky like an industrial leviathan.

"Frank, we can't stay."

"Just a moment. Look."

From the mine entrance at the foot of the mountain rose a cloud, blacker than the night. It swirled upward, curled on itself. It seemed velvety, thick. Dave imagined the deepest reaches of space would not be that dark. The cloud, perhaps a hundred feet wide and now two hundred feet tall, rose and corkscrewed above the hills.

"That's how they travel. That's how they can track us and keep up so fast," Frank said.

"Frank, let's go. It might head this way, then what?" Dave said.

Chen leaned forward and put a hand on Frank's shoulder.

Maybe he would listen to her. "We're outnumbered, Frank. No telling how many in that cloud."

"Why do you think they're coming out now?"

"To hunt," Frank said. "I've seen enough. Let's go."

The cloud dipped low and twisted, like a serpent. It spread across the hills, fanned out. David turned the truck back around, his tires spinning on the gravel shoulder. He thought for a moment that he couldn't get traction, but the tires dug in and the truck darted out onto the blacktop, back toward Routersville.

"You think they're coming now?" Dave said. If that were the case, Routersville would be the scene of a slaughter. They'd had no time to prepare defenses and the town would be overrun.

"No, I have a feeling they're waiting for something. Just not sure what."

They reached Jenny's house. The cloud had loomed in the rearview mirror for a few miles and then spread out to the east and west, among the hills. David pitied anyone living in the vicinity of the mine. He hoped they had the sense to move out, as the residents of the mining town did.

Frank had settled on the couch. He yawned enormously and removed his cap. His hair looked about as neat as a briar patch. Dave stifled a laugh.

Jenny came in with a ginger ale for the Reverend, and a Rolling Rock for herself and Dave. As she took a seat next to Dave on the love seat, she pressed her hand on his thigh, gave a little squeeze, presumably to steady herself.

"How fast can you organize a meeting? I'm thinking come daylight. We don't have much time," Frank said.

"We can go door to door. I've been stockpiling supplies at the armory, canned food, bottled water, guns, ammo, flashlights, crank radios," Jenny said.

Frank nodded his approval. "What will we tell them, the non-Guardians? They're not likely to believe us."

"Come to the armory or die a horrible death?" Dave asked.

"Subtlety is really not your specialty, is it, Dresser?" Jenny said, and favored him with a smile.

"It's the truth."

"I'm afraid he's right," Frank said. "We can mention the death of the Little family, imply that the same thing will happen here. It'll be difficult to persuade them."

Jenny took a swig of her Rolling Rock. "I can get some. They've seen us piling up goods at the armory, just not sure why."

"And the ones that don't?" Dave asked.

"There's nothing we can do," Frank said. "They'll perish."

"So that's it? Just like the hotel."

"Dave, think about it. Someone comes to your door and tells you the town is having a meeting. And the meeting's about a band of demons preparing to lay waste to the town. So just come on up to the armory so the good old Guardians can protect you."

Dave took a drink of beer. It was cold and good, and he could see himself downing this one in a hurry and then polishing off its brothers. "You're right. That answer sucks, but you're right."

"Most of the town owns guns. They can protect themselves," Jenny said.

David snorted out a laugh. "Hopeless, then. No one will come with us."

"You'd be surprised," Jenny said. "Like I said, they've seen the stockpiles at the armory. People are suspicious. If they think maybe the end is coming for some reason, and the prep at the armory fuels that belief, then maybe they'll join us. Paranoid enough to."

Frank swigged down the rest of his ginger ale. "So your people can start when, six, seven?"

"Seven. I'll get Hank Peters, Mickey McGill, and some of those guys to organize phone calls. They're retired, up with the roosters all of them."

Frank set his coaster on the end table. He picked up his hat, ran a hand through the tangle of hair, and placed the cap back on his head. "I'm turning in. You two?"

Jenny said, "We're going to stay up a while. 'Night."

Frank tipped his cap and walked down the hallway to the spare bedroom.

"I need to leave, first thing," Dave said. "I have to find Sara."

"She's a brave one, setting off on her own. But she's also smart and capable. I'm sure she got where she's going."

That was what frightened Dave. "It's what she's going in to that worries me."

"How bad do you think it will be?" Jenny said, and sipped her beer.

"Judging by the clouds we saw and the way they've pursued us, it'll be an all-out assault."

"Do you think we'll survive?"

"We have the other remaining Everlight stone here," Dave said. "That makes this a strong position."

"We'll see," Jenny said.

"I screwed up. I should have told Sara a long time ago what happened, about her real mother."

Jenny placed her hand on his. "She wouldn't have believed you." She drew little circles on the top of his hand with her finger. It made the hairs on his neck stand at attention.

"I miss her. I let her down."

Now Jenny set down her beer and took Dave's hand between both of hers. "You did what was best, what was asked of you. You protected her, gave her a good life."

"She'll need me. She'll have questions."

Jenny's hand went to the back of his head, and she stroked his hair. "You're tense." She began to massage the back of his neck. It felt wonderful. The muscles in his neck uncoiled.

"This could be one of our last nights," she said.

"Possibly," he said. Her strong fingers worked the muscles. Her other hand rested lightly on his chest. He felt himself start to stiffen and hoped she wouldn't notice. It had been a while since he had been with a woman.

"I haven't been with anyone in a long time, David."

He looked at her, the liquid brown eyes, thought of the gorgeous smile. "That's hard to believe."

"It's hard to hide what we are here, that we can't leave the town. There was one guy. We were serious. He wanted me to move to Seattle with him, help him run a car dealership. He was everything I wanted. Kind, strong, funny. I couldn't leave. The town needs me. The Guardians need me."

"He broke your heart?"

"Smashed it. Picked up and moved, said he loved me but he had to chase his dream. I'm not looking for anything long term."

She stopped massaging his neck and she started tracing the fabric on his chest with her finger. She was so close and he inhaled her perfume and it reminded him of a girl he had been with—what?—five years ago. Jasmine. Her name had been Jasmine, of all things. It had been five years since he'd kissed the soft skin on a woman's neck, felt the swell of breasts pressed against his bare chest. It could be nice with Chen. No, it *would* be nice with her. And only one night, a last bit of pleasure for both of them in advance of coming horrors.

"Love me, David, just for tonight."

"I will." He leaned in and kissed her, tasting the beer on her lips. He placed his hand on her side and then slid up and felt her breast. She broke off the kiss, buried her face in his chest, and moaned.

"Right here, on the couch. Make it last," she said.

"I will," he said, stroking her hair.

She leaned back and he leaned with her, kissing her on the neck, behind the ear, moving across her cheek to her lips. She reached back and clicked off the light, and they joined in the darkness.

Sara awoke in the middle of the night. She felt compelled to rise and go to the window. She slipped out of bed and tiptoed across the floor. Next to the window was a tall-backed rocker, and she sat in it. Eight floors down, she looked on the U-shaped courtyard, which was bathed in security lighting. She half-expected to see dark shapes converging on the courtyard, but since her escape at Joanne's, there had been no sign of her pursuers.

What were they waiting for?

She briefly considered leaving. Staying here put Laura at risk. But leaving might break Laura to the point where she wasn't fixable. Instead, Sara kept a silent vigil, rocking in the chair and watching for them.

It was three hours until dawn.

CHAPTER 12

Charles Pennington pulled down Iroquois Alley, now barely lit by the first rays of the sun. Half the brewery lay in a heap of bricks. Twisted metal beams lay in another pile. Dozers and excavators waited for their human masters to start them up and begin the process of destruction again. He saw no one on the site, so he pulled up and parked.

He picked up the folded copy of the *Buffalo News* that rested on the passenger seat. The article on the right of the front page read:

MURDER BAFFLES POLICE

Buffalo Police made a gruesome discovery on the site of the old Bethlehem Steel. A skinless corpse, impaled on a pole, was left near Gate 4 on Route 5. A passing motorist spotted the corpse and notified police immediately.

Police have not identified the body, and due to its condition, they must wait for the coroner to check dental records. Detective Joe Spignozzi says it's the worst murder he's

> ever seen: "This is bad. I've been on the force
> twenty-two years and never seen one like
> this. The Medical Examiner tells us the skin-
> ning was most likely done while the victim
> was still alive. Just awful."

Before arriving, Charles had watched *Daybreak* on Channel 2 and fortunately the police had taken the body down before the news crews could get to it. Although in today's
digital age, he was certain someone had snapped a picture
and would likely post it to the Net.

The article went on to say the police had no suspects. A
search of the security office found nothing, only a half-eaten
beef snack in the guard shack. There was speculation the
guy's name was Harry something or other, for he was the
guard on duty at the time and they couldn't find him. But
that still remained to be confirmed.

Charles knew who did it: Engel and his demons. He had
been turned loose, and Charles had come to the Alley to confirm what he already knew: Engel's grave would be empty.

He got out of the car, taking with him the flashlight he
rummaged from the junk drawer. The mud squelched under
his boots. He made his way to the main pile, stepping over
bricks and lengths of pipe twisted like pipe cleaners. The
rear right corner, that's where they had buried him.

Charles had figured the Iroquois would stand forever. The
city had a love affair with its past, and someone was bound
to put the brewery on a protected list. In its heyday, it was
one of the most popular brands in Buffalo. He remembered
drinking it at Molly's Tavern—the beer can with the Indian
chief on the side. The Anheuser-Busches and Millers of the
world had left no room for a local brewery.

He followed the jagged brick wall, now higher in some
places than in others. The air smelled of dust. He reached the
corner and stopped at a loose pile of bricks, some of them
lying in a hole. He crouched down and examined the hole. In

the clay were tracks about the width of fingers. Charles figured one of the machines had loosened the grave and Engel clawed his way out. He suddenly felt very uneasy here knowing Engel was loose.

The only thing left to do was find the stone, hope it was still on the site.

Milo awoke on the couch, the sun beaming in through a break in the curtains. When he finally fell asleep, it had been two a.m. With each creak of a board or hushed sound of water moving through a pipe, he had jumped. He hadn't been that scared of nighttime noises since he was nine years old. But he couldn't shake the irrational fear that every sound was the creep from the alley, and when he opened his eyes the ragged-looking man would be standing over him, butcher knife in hand.

He shook off the blanket, folded it, and fluffed the pillow. Since his wife had died, he could not sleep in their queen-size bed. It was the couch or nothing. In bed, he would roll over at night and go to put his arm around someone who wasn't there. Then he would lie awake, thinking about Vera. What if they had caught the cancer sooner? Or if they had gone to Sloan-Kettering or the Mayo Clinic? He didn't think like that on the couch, so that's where he stayed.

He showered and shaved. Then after a breakfast of grapefruit, bacon, and toast, he drove down to the job site. Low gray clouds had settled over the city, and although it wasn't the most cheerful of days, at least the night had receded. He parked his truck as close as possible to the pile of rubble. When the last truck had left, he would scoot to the truck and speed out of here. No hanging around and seeing Mr. Big and Ugly, if he were still in the vicinity.

His machine, a Liebherr 952, waited for him. Using the remote, he armed the truck alarm. He started toward the excavator. That was when he noticed the man standing in the rubble. He wore a red parka and blue watch cap. His dress pants were tucked into his boots, causing them to puff out like jodhpurs. Milo approached the man, who was holding a flashlight and was shining it at the base of the building. It was too early for a city inspector to be out here. Who was he?

Milo got within ten feet and recognized the old guy.

"What're you doing back here?"

The man twitched, almost dropping the flashlight. He looked up at Milo. "You scared the heart out of me."

"Pennington, right?"

"Who's asking?"

"Milo Gruber," Milo said. "You better get going before the foreman gets here. He bitched all day yesterday how you should have been arrested."

"Some things are more important than him."

"You put us two hours behind."

"Good."

"I was on another job half that day, missed your appearance," Milo said.

"Your loss."

Boy, this guy was a doozy. "What's so special about his place?"

"It held someone prisoner."

"Foreman shows up and sees you here, you'll be a prisoner, too."

"There was someone buried here. Look," he said, pointing to the ground.

Milo stepped closer. In the center of a ring of bricks was a hole. At its bottom was a small mound of dirt. It was approximately six feet deep with smooth sides. "Give me a break."

"Your demolishing this building set him free."

"So this guy's alive. Who is he, the Mummy or something?"

"Far worse than that. This one is real, and he's no mummy."

"So let's just say there is someone buried here," Milo said, and folded his arms. "How would you know?"

"I buried him."

Pennington belonged down at Elmwood and Forest, behind the walls of those nice brick buildings with the bars over the windows. "You killed someone?"

"You're not listening. He left the grave."

"Look, I'm going to start up my machine. I want to see you walk down the alley, get in your car, and take off."

Milo turned and started toward his machine.

"That's fine," Pennington said. "I found what I came to find."

Milo waved him off. "Just go."

"You haven't seen anyone suspicious, have you? The man I'm looking for would be about six and a half to seven feet tall. Long hair. Probably dressed in raggedy clothes."

It couldn't be. The creep he saw the other night matched that description, and as much as it had scared Milo, he refused to believe some zombie had crawled from the rubble and become one with the night.

"Nope."

Now he heard the ground crunch behind him—Pennington following him.

"Do you live nearby?"

"I'm not telling you where I live."

"In the city?"

"Yeah, the city."

"I suggest you leave," Pennington said.

"Sure, I'll be on the next plane to Tahiti."

Pennington caught up, clapped a hand on his shoulder. Milo stopped and turned. Pennington's eyes were wide, blue, and clear. His gaze seemed to go through Milo's eyes and out the back of his skull. "He's come back to destroy the city. Leave if you can. Take your family and go."

"It's just me and my daughter and we're not leaving. Especially based on something you said. Now do I have to call the cops?"

"One more thing. Where do you take your debris?"

"Why do you want to know?"

"I'm looking for a stone. It's black and smooth. It glows from time to time. And if its power hasn't faded, it will kill the man that stepped from the grave."

Milo was willing to tell him anything to get the old crackpot to leave. "AMD Recycling, on Seneca. How about getting your hand off me now?"

Pennington released his hand. He put his hands up as if to say "okay, okay." He backed up, then turned and got into his car and pulled away.

"Old guy is getting senile," Milo said to himself.

But what about the visitor to the alley? Long, stringy hair, build like a linebacker, raggedy clothes. Probably just a vagrant passing through, maybe thinking about asking Milo for a buck or two. Dug from the grave, what a load.

Still, he hurried to the cab of the Liebherr, wanting to get out of the darkness.

Charles drove from the alley. The brick, on which he had scratched an X, was gone, as was the Everlight. He had been looking for it when the construction worker pulled up. He would return home, have some scrambled eggs, and figure out how to gain access to the recycling center. He had little hope of finding the Everlight. Locating a stone that would fit in your palm at a dumpsite was like looking for a specific grain of sand in the ocean. He wondered how much time he had. Judging from the fact that Engel had already skinned a man alive, time was most likely short.

Twelve o'clock came, and Milo sat in his truck munching on a roast beef sandwich purchased from the food-service truck, otherwise known as the roach coach. He was halfway through the sandwich when his cell phone rang. He answered. It was Debbie.

"Hey, Dad."

"How are you, honey?"

"Good. Got some news for you."

"Well?" Milo asked.

"Can't tell you now."

"That's it, talk in riddles, just like your mother always did."

"Meet me for dinner tonight? I promise I'll tell then."

"You're holding out on me. This must be good."

"How about the Alligator, six o'clock?"

Milo set his sandwich on his lap. "That the place on Chippewa?"

"The one and only."

"I feel old in those places."

"You're not old, Dad. Besides, I've got news."

"I'll be there."

She said good-bye and he hit the End button. He hadn't seen her in a week or so. Debbie was busy with her social-work courses at Buffalo State. What could she possibly have to tell him? He was curious to find out, but also pleasantly surprised. He didn't get to spend much time with her these days. Debbie's time was divided among the Chippewa bar scene, her girlfriends, and Brian Penberthy, who was her current boyfriend.

Dinner with her would be nice.

CHAPTER 13

After making love on the couch, Dave and Jenny crept to her bedroom. She had slept, her head on his chest. The feel of her warm skin against his side, the delicacy of her hair spread on his chest, had been some comfort. He still hadn't slept well. Several times he heard the chatters and chitters of animals outside and he nearly held his breath, ready to spring out of bed, expecting an attack. When he wasn't worried about being attacked, he thought of Sara.

What if the Dark Ones had found her first? Or what if some predator with an eye for teenage girls offered her a ride? Maybe she was bound somewhere in a basement, held by some creep who would torture her for his own pleasure. When the morning came, Dave had never been so glad to see the rays of the sun.

He separated himself from Jenny. As he began to roll out of bed, she took his hand and whispered, "Thank you." Then she rolled over lazily and yawned.

Dave slipped into his jeans and T-shirt and went out to the kitchen. He heard the gurgle of the coffeemaker and smelled a nice French roast brewing. Frank was seated at the table, fully dressed and reading the newspaper. His Orioles cap rested on the table, next to a plate littered with toast crumbs.

"Sleep well?" Frank asked.

"Jumped at every little sound."

"We're well defended here."

"Still."

"Notice you didn't make it to the spare bedroom last night."

"You're grinning behind that paper, aren't you?"

"She's a lovely woman," Frank said. "Nothing to be ashamed of."

"Who's ashamed?"

Frank chuckled from behind the paper. David couldn't help but grin. "I'm getting some coffee before you drink it all, Reverend."

After his toast and coffee, and while Chen and David finished their breakfasts, Frank called home. Sandra picked up on the third ring.

"How are you?" Frank asked.

"Where are you? Are you okay?"

"I'm in a little town called Routersville, Pennsylvania."

"What in God's name are you doing there?"

"I can't explain."

"Try me," she said.

"Later."

"The parishioners didn't take your absence very well. Norma McCullough got up and stomped out of church."

Oh, boy. "Old Norma will get over it."

"You hope."

"I know."

"Really, Frank, why can't you tell me? Please?"

Her voice had the quality of a child pleading for a parent to reveal some awesome secret.

"Can you leave?" Frank asked.

"Leave where?"

"Lexington. Is your brother staying up at his cabin at all?"

"What does that have to do with anything?"

"Sandra, be quiet and listen."

From the silence on the other line, he knew he was over-stepping his bounds, but a lot depended on this. "Call your brother. You, him, Gertie, the kids, get up to that cabin. The mountains should be safe for now."

"Safe from what?"

"Trouble. It's coming, dear. That's all I can tell you. You might be able to avoid it up there, but not in the towns."

"What kind of trouble?"

"Can you do that for me?"

"You're not making sense."

"I understand I sound like a mental patient, but please trust me. I don't want anything bad to happen to you."

A long sigh came from the other end.

"What's going to happen?"

"If we don't take care of things in Buffalo, the whole country, maybe the world, is in danger."

"Frank Heatly, savior of mankind."

"Would you just go up there with Gertie. For me?"

"I suppose it wouldn't hurt to get away for a week. And it *is* awfully nice up there."

"I just want you to be safe. I love you," Frank said.

"I love you, too. I don't even pretend to understand you sometimes, but I love you."

They said good-bye and he hoped she would go to the cabin. He also hoped it wasn't the last time he would ever speak to her.

* * *

They agreed to meet at Ruby's Diner. Jenny had called McGill and Peters, who spread the word among the other Guardians. Dave walked into Ruby's, where a row of men in quilted flannels and camouflage jackets sat on red vinyl stools at a linoleum counter. The booths that lined the large picture window were full. More people crowded into a central dining area. A country song—Dave thought it was something by Kenny Chesney—rang out over speakers mounted in the corners. He smelled fresh-brewed coffee and the pleasantly greasy odor of bacon frying.

A petite woman in dark blue jeans and a flannel shirt approached them. She had hair that matched the red on a Campbell's soup can and large blue eyes. She looked as if she might have graduated high school in the past year. She walked up to Jenny, and they embraced.

She turned to Dave and said, "Well, good to see you all." Then she reached up and wrapped her arms around Dave and gave him a squeeze. She did the same to Frank. Friendly, this one.

"I'm Maggie Swain, but call me Ruby. Welcome to Ruby's. You guys want coffee? Got some good pancakes and waffles, too."

Dave said, "No thanks."

"You own this place?"

"That's right."

"I'm impressed," Frank said.

"You want to know how old I am, don't you? Twenty-three. I look about seventeen, right? This was my dad's place. Named it after me. Passed on two years ago. The MS finally got him."

"It's a fine establishment," Frank said. "Sorry about your dad."

"It's all right," Ruby said.

"Let's get down to business," Jenny said.

Over the next hour, Jenny shared what her scouts had

found out: The Dark Ones were moving closer. Frank then addressed the crowd about the group they had seen at the mine. Finally, Jenny spoke again and informed everyone of the provisions she had made at the armory. There was enough food, water, and ammunition for a two-week siege.

Jenny divided the diner into four groups. She strode back and forth like a Marine Corps DI. Dave was surprised she had never been in the military. Each group would cover a separate quadrant of town, making phone calls and going door to door. Red McCormick, owner of the Hobson Shoe Factory, was in attendance. He would call a meeting, tonight making them able to inform nearly three hundred people. They decided to meet at five. Most people would be home from work, and it was still a little before nightfall. Those who believed and wanted protection would remain at the armory. It was the general consensus that the attack was coming soon, and it would be best for people not to return to their homes.

"Let's go, then. No time to waste," Jenny said.

The crowd began to file out, a low murmur filling the diner.

"Didn't sleep well?"

Sara sucked in breath, startled. She'd been watching a morning news program called *Daybreak*. The cops had ID'd a skinned corpse found at the old Bethlehem Steel Mill. It was a night watchman named Harry Hargrove. They had no leads, but Sara knew who had done it.

"How can you tell?"

"Luggage under your eyes."

"Yeah, just thinking."

"Pretty gruesome find there," Laura said, nodding toward the television.

"People are sick."

"You don't have to tell me."

"Why's that?"

"I see it every day. Two weeks ago this guy brings his six-month-old in. Kid's got bruises from head to toe, black as a piece of licorice. Father says he couldn't take the crying anymore."

"What did you say?"

"I'm like, asshole, it's a baby, what do you expect?"

"You called him an asshole?"

"It fit, believe me," Laura said.

"What happened to him?"

"We called Social Services, they took the kid, cops came in, hauled Dad away. Sad thing is, he'll be out in a few years."

Sara immediately felt a pang of guilt for trying to hurt David by running away. Sure, he had deceived her, but he had also been a kind and gentle father who never laid a hand on her. She could have done a lot worse.

"What's your dad like, my grandfather?"

"Well, you'll meet him soon. He was a good father. Never panicked or threatened to kick me out when I got pregnant. Supported me all the way. The only thing, he would never let me take you out alone. If I was going to the mall or anywhere public, he insisted on going along. The one time I managed to escape, I lost you."

"The day of my kidnapping. That wasn't your fault."

Laura sat next to her on the couch. "You have kids someday, you'll understand. You'll hate to see them sick, in pain. You'll blame yourself for not watching them close enough, for letting them skin a knee or break a wrist."

Sara put an arm around her. "I'm just glad I found you."

"I am, too. We've got a long way to go, catching up. It won't happen overnight."

"But we're going to try, right?"

"Damn straight," Laura said. "How about I treat you to

breakfast? We'll go to Ambrosia, Greek place, great all-around food."

"Sounds good."

Laura went from the couch to the table and picked up the receiver. She dialed the phone and Sara noticed her chewing her nail while she waited for someone to pick up. After a few moments, she hung up.

"Calling your dad?"

"Strange. Still no answer. We'll have to drop in on him."

After leaving the brewery site, Charles drove through Niagara Square and over to South Elmwood. He passed City Hall and a little brick church called St. Anthony's. His parents had been married there. He jumped on the Skyway, then headed out Route 5. He spotted the sign for Gate 4 and pulled his car onto the shoulder. His stomach rumbled. Hopefully he could slam down some of those eggs pretty soon.

A web of police tape surrounded the gate. Tape in the shape of an X covered the door to the guard shack. Skinned alive, the poor bastard. People who crossed Engel's path usually got something unimaginable done to them. This guy had done nothing more than report for work.

Which meant Engel was likely hiding on the property of the mill. The rows of rolling mills and furnaces left places to hide, and since the mill was shut down, he could escape detection. How many of them were waiting among the abandoned buildings?

Charles got out of the car. Behind him, the cars hummed past on Route 5, and occasionally a gust of air blew at his back. He approached the fence. The wind rattled and blew a Styrofoam coffee cup along the ground, in front of the guard shack. The mill seemed desolate to him, eerie. Long gone were the heavy grinding sounds of industry, the hiss of steam, the roar of furnaces, the glow of molten steel being poured from huge ladles. He couldn't imagine a guard staying here at night, alone. Being here in the daytime left him with an uneasiness that manifested in chills up and down his arms.

The complex stretched for a mile in either direction. Engel could be anywhere. Charles considered going in to look for him, but without the power of one of the stones, it would be suicide. He would have to wait and hope that Reverend Frank would come through in Routersville. Or he would have to dig through tons of steel and other rubble at the recycling yard if they would even let him in. And the stone that had kept Engel buried was most likely burned out. For him to escape, its power must have diminished.

He walked the length of the fence, stepping over broken glass and rustling weeds as he went. He thought of Laura. She wouldn't leave. He would have to try and convince her somehow. Leave a good-paying doctor's job, a job she basically loved, because her crackpot father said the end was nigh? Doubtful.

The thought of leaving Laura's fate to others, to possibly be captured, enslaved, and tortured, twisted his guts. Engel was here, he knew it. That poor night watchman was not slaughtered by chance. The Lackawanna cops hadn't found him or the Dark Ones because they dissolved like so much black mist when they didn't want to be seen.

I have to try and stop this. I failed to keep him contained. It's my fault, mine alone. If I wait, the blood of thousands will be on my hands.

Charles looked up at the fence. He guessed it to be seven or eight feet tall. Back in his college days, he had run track and field, taken all kinds of meets. But now his knees ached and after a round of golf it felt as if someone were driving red-hot nails into his lower back. But he had to try.

Gripping the fence, he shoved a toe in between the links.

He pulled himself up, tendons in his wrist straining. The wind gusted again, shaking him. He clawed upward, one foot, one hand, until he reached the top of the fence. Luckily, Bethlehem—or whoever owned the mill these days—had seen fit to leave barbed wire off the fence. He swung one leg over, teetered, got his balance, then swung the other over. He scrambled down the other side, his foot catching in one of the links, and he stumbled at the bottom and hit the pavement. Wrist aching and a scrape on his palm, he stood up. He was in. *Were they watching him?*

He strode past the guard shack. Ahead were the blast furnaces, hundreds of feet of tubing and pipe running into the air. How the hell did you build something like that? Each was flanked by the equally impressive stoves that at one time had fed hot air to the furnaces. He continued past them, past the skeletal ore bridge, farther down until he reached the long, narrow rolling mills.

The opening to the one nearest him looked big enough to admit a cruise ship to its innards. The rolling equipment had been long since stripped and salvaged for scrap, but an impressive array of steel columns and jutting framework remained. Slats of light filtered in through high windows, but it would still be like entering a cave.

His heart sped up. His wrist ached and his palm stung. He had left his overcoat on the other side of the fence and each gust of October wind knifed through him and he shivered.

I can do this. I beat him before. He should fear me, the bastard. And after what he did to Lydia, I owe him another round of payback.

He mustered a little light, the warm glow spreading through his arm, and he held out his hand, palm up, and the white glow shone around him. He had been a Guardian so long he no longer had to think of light or goodness to make the light spring up. It had become as natural as walking or talking.

He stepped into the Ten Inch mill. The light showed a concrete floor smudged with grease. He smelled oil, the chemical pierce of solvents, and under that, something old and rotted.

He looked up at the catwalks that ran the length of the building, which seemed to stretch a mile in itself. A fine black mist swirled around the railings. It descended, curling and gathering at the floor. He turned and saw the cloud rising up over the entrance, making the daylight outside appear through a filmy black curtain. The mist rolled up and stopped in a circle around him, leaving him and the light untouched.

One of them materialized out of the mist, taking form as a shadow, then turning solid. Charles held up the light. The thing stepped closer. Charles recoiled. Its face was a mess of putrid, pockmarked flesh. The right eye had been sewn shut, and half the nose bitten off, leaving a ragged hole in the center of its face.

Charles backed up. He sensed something behind him. He peeked and out of the corner of his eye saw something big and winged and leathery.

The one in front of him said, "He wants to see you."

"Then let's go."

"Turn out the light or we'll tear you apart."

"I should fry your rotten hide where you stand."

He sensed the winged one behind him getting closer. More of them, grotesque forms in the darkness, crept toward the edge of the mist. He extinguished the light, and the darkness crept in around him.

"Follow me." The one in front turned, and the mist parted. "Don't let the mist touch you. Lest you want to lose your skin."

He started forward, the winged creature behind him thumping along. He flattened his arms at his sides and followed the path through the mist.

* * *

They led him through the mist. He guessed they walked a few hundred feet. His eyes adjusted to the slats of light filtering in the high windows, but it was still hard to see. The dark form in front of him stopped. It then stepped aside.

He saw the black mist part. Engel appeared. Dressed in a trench coat full of holes. Hair stringy and black. Face as white as porcelain.

"Interesting home you've chosen," Charles said.

The rotted, cracked voice said, "It suits me. Why did you come here?"

"To stop you."

"You couldn't stop me before."

"I buried you, didn't I?" Charles said.

"And I'm back. Where is the girl?"

"I'm old, not a fool."

"We caught up to her," Engel said. "She used the Light and drove off my children. Soon enough, I'll find her."

I should destroy you now, Charles thought. At least try.

"Did you really think you had a chance coming in here?" Engel asked.

"What are you planning?"

Engel chuckled. "Everything outside this mill," he said, with a wave of his hand, "will be gone. And if the girl has come here, as my Master has said, she will suffer and die."

Not this time. Not on my watch.

Charles flicked his hand and a bolt of white light streaked toward Engel. It hit him in the face and the force of the beam turned his head. Charles heard a sizzling noise. Then, he felt something heavy and dull strike the back of his head. He fell to his knees. He rubbed the back of his head. The winged beasts roughly grabbed his arms and hoisted him up.

Engel stepped forward, teeth clenched. The side of his face had been scorched. Smoke curled up from his skin.

Extending a pale hand, he gripped Charles's chin and tilted his head up. "Now you'll suffer. You'll tell us about the girl, whether you want to or not. You'll die like your bitch wife did."

If I fail, at least I tried something. God help us all.

CHAPTER 14

David watched Frank approach across the expanse of the armory's main hall. The tanks, most of them Vietnam-era, seem to dwarf the Reverend. He joined Dave, who sat on a bench next to one of the behemoths. They sat for a moment, watching men and women haul crates, load rifles, and stack boxes of supplies.

"I'm going," Dave said finally.

"We could use you," Frank said. "We could use everyone."

"Sara's on her own."

"If we fail here, it won't matter."

"You don't have kids, Frank."

"That's not fair," Frank said. "I care for Sara, too."

"Who's cared for her? Ripped her out of schools when people started asking too many questions? Worried that Engel and his freaks were looking for her?"

"We all have," Frank said.

"No one more than me. I shouldn't have come here. I should've kept going. I've wasted time."

"Know what?"

He felt his muscles tense. "What, Frank?"

"You've become a pretty damned good father," Frank said, and clapped him on the leg.

"I've lied to her all these years," David said.

"It was for her protection," Frank said."

"Still."

"Go find her."

"Good luck, Frank."

"We'll need it."

"I'm going to say good-bye to Jenny."

David crossed the main hall. He came up on heavyset guy in a hunting jacket, who was busy clicking shells into a shotgun. Dave tapped him on the arm. "You seen Jenny?"

The man pointed upward. "Roof. Go to the rear stairs, all the way up. There's an access ladder at the top of the stairwell."

Dave thanked him and proceeded through the building and up the stairs. His footsteps echoed as he walked. He found the ladder to the roof and saw an open hatch above.

He climbed the ladder. The roof was vast and black and spotted with bird droppings. Chen stood in one corner with a auburn-haired woman dressed in overalls. Chen was pointing off in the distance.

Dave crossed the roof, winding around air-conditioning units and ventilation stacks. He looked out over the valley. The hills were brown and the leaves yellow and orange.

He approached Chen and the other woman. They turned around. The woman with Chen was built like a baby bull and had an open, friendly face. Chen introduced her as Madeline. David shook her hand, feeling the callused palm and pegging her for a farmer.

"We were planning the defense of the roof. The winged ones will present the biggest problem. If they gain access to that hatch, we're in trouble," Jenny said.

"You think three dozen of us will be enough?" Madeline asked.

"They start swarming, it'll be like a shooting gallery for you."

Madeline nodded. "I'll go tell the others who'll be on the roof. Nice meeting ya."

"You, too," Dave said. Madeline walked across the roof and disappeared down the hatch.

"What's up?" Jenny asked.

"I'm leaving."

"We could use you," she said.

Don't lay a guilt trip on me, please. "I need to find Sara."

"Be careful?"

"As careful as I can, given the situation."

She stepped closer him, reached up, and wrapped her arms around his neck. He returned the embrace and she pressed against him. Last night had been wonderful, however brief.

"Thank you. For last night," she said.

"It was my pleasure, believe me."

She looked up at him. He kissed her wetly on the mouth.

"Good-bye, David."

With that, he let go of her and crossed the roof. He took one last look. Jenny Chen stood at the edge of the roof, hands on hips, as if daring all comers to knock her off. If the Guardians were to have any chance of victory, they would need her.

He stepped on to the ladder and climbed down.

Dave's car pulled away from Chen's house. When he arrived in Buffalo, he would look up Laura Pennington's address and start there. If she wasn't there, then it was on to Buffalo General Hospital, where Frank had told him she worked. He left Routersville with a sick stomach. It might be the last time he ever saw the Reverend, Chen, or any of them.

Reverend Frank climbed onto a tank, and Jenny followed him. He looked over the crowd, perhaps three hundred strong, not counting the hundred or so Guardians. A buzz rose from the crowd. He had expected—and hoped for—more people. The ones who didn't attend were dooming themselves.

Frank waved his arms to get the crowd's attention. Then, sticking his pinkies in the corners of his mouth, he whistled. That cut the crowd noise, and now most of them faced him.

"I'll say this quickly," he boomed. "I'm glad you've all come. How many of you read about the family slaughtered in Iowa, the Littles?"

A sea of hands shot up.

"The forces that were responsible for killing the Little family are on their way here. We've gathered at the armory because this is the best defensible position in town. We're expecting an attack at any time. We have enough food and water for two weeks. If we haven't driven them off by then, we never will. You'll be protected in here. Beyond those doors, you'll be slaughtered."

The murmur rose to a low roar. Heads shook, and people exchanged puzzled looks. A man wearing a leather jacket and a blue bandanna raised his hand.

Frank said, "Yes?"

"You expect us to believe this?"

"Believe what you want. Just know that you're safer in here."

"What is this, a cult?"

"Yes sir, it's the cult of save your own ass. That's the cult."

The man looked as if he'd been slapped. "What about this attack?"

He glanced at Chen, hoping for some suggestions. Chen shrugged her shoulders.

"Demons, sir. Demons that travel the night and look for flesh. They want some of us dead, and will kill anyone who gets in their way. If you go home, you'll be dragged from your houses. Some of you will be tortured. All of you killed."

"You're all crazy. Certifiably fuckin' nuts."

A woman in a dark overcoat raised her hand. "He might be right. My sister-in-law lives down in Wickett's Corner. There's been trouble, weird things moving around in the night."

"Yeah, right," the bandanna man said. "I'm out of here." He nudged his way through the crowd.

"What's your name, ma'am?" Frank asked.

"Agnes Bush. My sister-in-law saw something flying over her house a few nights ago. Man-sized, with wings."

An elderly man in a Caterpillar ball cap stepped up to the front of the crowd. "Just say we are under attack, how you going to help? And how you do you know about these things?"

"We have guns and ammo. And we have . . ."

Should he tell them? Give them a demonstration? People had already begun to file toward the main doors. He looked at Chen. She gave him a look that said "do something."

"They've been around for centuries, that's how we know. As for how we're going to defend ourselves, watch."

Frank raised his arms in a Y. He closed his eyes. Warmth surged through him and slowly brilliant white light appeared around him. He opened his eyes. A lone tank stood off to the side, away from the crowd. He flicked his wrist and a bolt of light streaked across the hall and struck the turret. It popped, leaving a scorch mark on the turret. The smell of burning metal filled the armory.

The woman named Agnes approached the tank. "How did you do that?"

The old man in the cap said, "How *did* you do that?"

Frank lowered his arms, and the light dimmed, then disappeared. The crowd had gone silent. Chen joined him on the rear of the tank. She said, "Time's running out. Stay with us and have a chance, or go back to your homes and die with the ones who didn't come here."

In the end, Frank estimated about half the crowd remained, Agnes Bush included. He heard talk among the departing crowd of a "fireworks show" and "trick lighting." After the crowd left, Chen ordered the steel doors shut and barred.

When the doors were shut, Frank asked her, "Now, let's see the Everlight. Who has the stone?"

"McGivens. Let's find him."

They found Digger McGivens in the armory's kitchen, stacking cases of canned fruit salad against the wall. He slung the cases with relative ease, his tattooed biceps flexing and pumping. Despite the apparent lack of exertion, sweat poured down the back of his neck and he cursed in a low voice.

"Digger," Jenny said.

He turned around, wiped his hand across his brow. Frank looked at him and thought *biker*. The man's wild gray hair was kept off his brow by a blue bandanna, and he had a beard that had never seen a razor.

"Oh, hey Jenny. Man, these cases is a bitch."

"This is Reverend Frank Heatly."

Frank extended his hand. Digger contemplated shaking for a moment, then quickly shook hands. "Meet ya. Not much on going to church, I'm afraid. I'm a lapsed Catholic."

"I'm not here to convert you, don't worry," Frank said.

"Is the light safe and sound?" Jenny asked. "We should go retrieve it."

Digger stroked his beard. "Yeah, my brother's still got it."

"Where exactly is it being kept?" Frank asked.

Jenny said, "At the Warlords' clubhouse. Digger's brother is club president."

Frank couldn't believe what he was hearing. "You let a bunch of *bikers* hold on to it?"

Digger took a step forward. Frank saw a fight brewing in Digger's eyes. "And what's wrong with bikers having it?"

"Oh, I'm sorry," Frank said. "I'm sure it's as safe as Fort Knox. Why would I ever question that strategy?"

"You making fun of me, Reverend?"

Jenny stepped between them. Digger backed off, sat on one of the cases.

"It's been safe there, Frank. First of all, the Enemy wouldn't think of looking for it there. Second, no one in their right mind would try and steal it from the Warlords. They've got a pretty bad rep in these parts."

Still, he didn't like this. Not one bit. "Let's go get it, then."

"Who's going with me, him?" Digger said.

"That's right."

"You'll need me. You walk up to that clubhouse door by yourself and they'll tear you apart."

"Do they know you're a Guardian, Digger?"

Digger stood up. With the front of his shirt, he wiped his brow. "Don't exactly go flaunting something like that, not even to your brother."

"Do you want me to send some of the others with you?" Jenny asked.

"You need all the help you can get here. Still prep work to do. Now why don't we get going?" Frank said.

Digger eyed Frank up. "Let me get my bike, and we'll go."

"I'll need a vehicle," Frank said.

"I'll round one up for you," Jenny said.

"They'd better have it, Digger."

"Let's just go."

*   *   *

Reverend Frank followed Digger in a borrowed pickup truck, the biker going hell-bent for leather. Frank pushed the truck to seventy-five and was still a hundred feet behind him. They drove about two miles out of Routersville. Digger turned right down a road cut out of the woods, and Frank followed. Digger slowed to a more reasonable speed. That allowed Frank to take a peek at his watch. It was two thirty, time enough to get the Everlight and return to Routersville before dark.

The road passed over a short wooden bridge, which led into a parking lot. Frank saw a row of motorcycles parked in front of a long two-story building with a covered front porch. The faded sign over the porch read JOHNSON'S INN. Frank guessed this place ran out of vacancies long ago.

Digger parked his bike, and Frank parked next to him. He got out of the truck. From inside, a southern rock band wailed on guitars. Frank thought it was Molly Hatchet. He'd spun a few of their tunes as a college DJ a lifetime ago.

Digger eyed the place. "Used to be a fancy joint, one time."

"What happened to it?"

"Owners went into bankruptcy. Building sat here. Warlords bought it cheap."

"Looks like they painted recently."

"Yeah, you surprised?"

"A little."

"We take care of the place, believe it or not."

"Are we ready now?" Frank asked.

Digger scratched his beard. "Stay close to me. Don't say nothing less I tell you, got it? They're not going to like that I brought you here."

Digger went up the front steps and in the door. Frank followed and found himself in a large foyer. An abandoned coat-check room and counter occupied one-half of the room. The counter had a film of dust on it.

They entered the inn; the main stairs were straight ahead. Around them was a great room, one end with a stone fireplace and the other end with a bar. Dirty-looking bikers in leather and denim sat at tables scattered around the room. Frank took a step and the floorboards groaned. He got dirty looks.

A biker came in from a doorway off the bar. He was a slimmer, clean-shaven version of Digger. As he approached, he eyed Frank with suspicion. He had the faraway stare of a convict in a mug shot.

"Hey, bro," the biker said. "Who's this?"

"Hey," Digger said. "This is the guy we're holding the stone for, Frank. Frank, this is my brother Ray."

"Call me Nitro."

"Okay, Nitro. And it's actually Reverend Frank."

"Reverend?" Nitro asked. "Digger, you go bringing a clergyman in here?" He looked at Frank. "You don't mess around with little kids like some of those priests, do you?"

That's a heck of an icebreaker. "No, do you?"

"I look like a queer to you?"

"Frank, shut your hole," Digger said. "Where is it, Ray? We need to take it."

"I don't have it."

"You don't have it?" Frank asked.

"Nope."

Digger said, "What the hell'd you do with it?"

"It's here, I just don't have it."

"Who does?" Frank asked.

"Roddy does. Came in yesterday from Pittsburgh."

"Shit," Digger muttered.

"Who's Roddy and why does he have the stone?" Frank asked.

Digger said, "Club president, mean as a wolverine."

Frank turned to Nitro and said, "Why on earth would you give it to Roddy?"

Nitro said, "Well, my bro here pulled that stone out and it starts to glow and doesn't he give us a little demonstration, making light glow from his fingertips. I called up Roddy and says you've got to come see this. Something like that's bound to be valuable."

Frank shot Digger a look designed to stop hearts. "I thought you didn't 'flaunt' your powers, didn't tell your brother."

"I didn't think he'd call Roddy, for Christ's sake!"

"Fool," Frank said. "Where's this Roddy?"

"Upstairs. First room on the right. But you can't go up there," Digger said.

"Why, is he up there studying calculus?" Frank asked.

"Frank, don't push it," Digger said.

"Smart-ass, why don't you get out and we'll keep the damned stone."

This called for action. Reasoning with them would do no good, and time was running short. Frank shoved off of Digger and bolted up the stairs. He heard Nitro yell, "Get him!" The stomp of boots followed him and he knew the bikers that had been at the tables were giving chase.

He reached the top of the stairs, huffing and puffing. He turned right down a corridor, found the first door, and entered. Frank saw a mustached man leaning back in an office chair, desk in front of him. His head was back, his eyes closed. A woman's head bobbed up and down from over the top of the desk. Needless to say, he looked like he was enjoying himself.

More importantly, Frank spotted the Everlight stone sitting on the desk. He barged into the room. The redhead stopped and picked her head up, a runner of saliva on her chin. The guy in the seat opened his eyes, saw Frank, and jumped up. He yanked up his pants and underwear and fumbled with his zipper. Frank grabbed the stone. The bikers plowed into his back. Two grabbed his arms and another wrenched the stone out of his hand, nails scratching his skin.

The recipient of the oral affection now had his pants zipped, a bulge still in his crotch. The redhead, dressed in cutoff jeans, black T-shirt, and cowboy boots, retreated to the corner.

Nitro stepped in front of Frank. Nitro had the stone in his hand, and he set it on the desk. The biker from behind the desk, presumably Roddy, said, "Who is he and how did he get in here?"

Someone stepped up next to Frank. It was Digger. "He's leaving."

Roddy came around the desk, maybe six-three or six-four of him, whip thin. The skin on his face was leathered and cracked. He had done long hours in the sun.

"Who are you?"

"Reverend Frank Heatly. And you have something of mine."

Roddy turned, looked at the stone. Then he faced Frank.

"That? That's gonna make me a fortune. Damn thing's magic. Genuine magic."

Digger said, "Just let him go."

Frank turned to Digger. "You know how important it is."

From the corner, the redhead said, "He walked in on us. I say cut the sumbitch open."

Roddy rolled his eyes. "Will you please shut the hell up, you skank?"

The woman in the corner lowered her eyes. She had bruises on her upper arm, just below the sleeve. Three guesses who put them there.

"No, you aren't leaving. You walked in on private property." Roddy leaned in close. He adjusted his crotch. Frank smelled cigar smoke on him. "Some sort of minister, huh? Jesus saves, and all?"

"Even people like you," Frank said.

The slap caught him on the right cheek and the side of his face immediately felt like it had blistered. His cap fell to the floor.

"Grab him," Roddy said.

Two of the bikers grabbed Frank's arms. Their body odor assaulted his nostrils. From his back pocket, Roddy pulled out a large folding knife. He clicked the blade open.

The woman in the corner said, "Yeah, cut him open, do it."

Roddy turned around and said, "Get the fuck out of here, will you?"

The redhead gave Roddy a dirty look, but complied with his request. As she strutted past Frank she said, "You're in a world of it now, aren't you?"

Charming woman, Frank thought. She left the room. He heard her footsteps echo down the stairs.

Roddy turned his attention back to Frank. He held the blade up, the tip an inch from Frank's nose. He might not even have to worry about the Enemy killing him. The bikers would be more than happy to oblige. Frank gave Digger a sideways glance. Digger looked ready to pounce.

"Hey, leave him be. You scared his ass, right?" Digger said.

"Shut up, Dig," Nitro said. "Let Roddy go to work."

With one quick stroke, Roddy whipped the knife downward, slicing a vertical cut in Frank's chest, right over the breastbone. Frank winced and sucked in a breath. Dear Lord, that hurt. There had to be a way out of this without hurting them. He had only one way to defend himself, and he didn't want to resort to it.

Digger grabbed Roddy's knife hand and Roddy looked at him with a measure of surprise and disgust. With his free hand, Roddy snapped a punch, catching Digger in the nose. Digger's head snapped back, and he staggered into the wall. Blood ran from his nose, and he knelt down, hands over his face.

"That's enough," Frank said. "Give me the stone if you want to live."

"I'm gonna give you a cross all your own, Reverend," Roddy said, and slashed a horizontal cut across the vertical, making a cross. Pain shot through Frank's chest.

Frank strained against his captors. He pulled one arm free, threw a wild elbow that missed. A sledgehammer blow caught him in the ribs and he doubled over. A boot shoved his rear end and he stumbled forward into the nearly empty hotel room. He crawled on the floor, sucking air hard. He heard the door slam.

"I'm going to cut you," Roddy said. "And when you think I can't cut anymore, I'm going to keep going."

Frank looked over his shoulder. Roddy stood there, blood-tinged blade in hand, looking like one of Satan's own imps. A group of dirty, tattered bikers stood behind him. Digger remained slumped against the wall. He covered his nose, blood dripping from under his hands.

Frank's chest hitched. The air began to return to his lungs, and he sucked in hard.

"Let's give the Reverend a Warlords welcome," Roddy said.

The bikers closed in around him. One kicked him in the leg. He grunted. Another rained punches on him. Frank managed to get his arm up. Some of the blows got past him, peppering his head and ear.

Roddy knelt down. Frank was on his hands and knees. Roddy held the knife in front of Frank's face.

They're going to kill me if I don't do something.

"You gonna die, 'cause I ain't afraid to kill someone, 'specially a preacher," Roddy said.

One of the bikers kicked him hard in the tailbone. The pain shooting up his spine was excruciating. He yelled. The bikers laughed.

"Why don't you say a little prayer for us?" Roddy asked.

"Yeah, preacher man, how about a prayer?" Nitro added.

"Let me go. Give me the stone. You'll regret it if you don't."

"Let you go? After we just kicked the hell out of you? I don't think so. I don't need the Staties coming up round here."

Frank, still on hands and knees, looked at the ground under his torso. Droplets of blood had collected on the floor from his chest wound.

"I think I'll cut you now," Roddy said.

Frank looked up, scanned the room. He saw Roddy, Nitro, and four others surrounding him. Behind Roddy, Digger was staggering to his feet. Lord, please do not make me do this, Frank prayed.

"Don't make me do it!" Frank said.

"Do what, bleed on the fucking floor?" Roddy asked.

"They'll die horribly," Frank said.

Roddy pressed the tip of the knife to the side of Frank's neck. Frank saw Digger approaching. Digger, like all Guardians, would not be harmed by a stray bolt of light.

"God gonna save you, preacher?"

"No. This is."

Frank looked at Roddy. In one motion, Frank rocked back on his knees, threw up his arms. A flash of light sizzled from his fingertips and slammed into Roddy's right shoulder. The knife flew from Roddy's hand. He stumbled backward. On his back, he looked at his shoulder, which was now a mass of blackened flesh and tattered fabric that had fused to the skin. He started to howl, then rolled back and forth on the floor, yelling, "What did you do to me? What did you do?"

Frank got to his feet. The other bikers in the circle stared, mouths open. That gave him a window. Digger, seeing what had transpired, grabbed the stone from the desk. Frank bounded over Roddy, outstretched on the floor. Digger went through the door first. Frank followed and slammed the door behind him.

From inside the room, he heard a muffled voice say, "Get his ass!"

Frank tore down the stairs with Digger at his side. He pressed his hand to his chest. The blood felt sticky and warm. His ass ached from being kicked and he considered himself lucky not to have a broken tailbone. As they ran down the steps, Frank jammed the stone in his pocket.

They reached the bottom of the stairs, then ran through the lobby and out the front door.

"Get in the truck, it'll be quicker."

"I'm not leaving my bike."

He stepped on to the blacktop, the truck in sight. From behind, he heard the thud of boots on the steps. If he could make it to the truck, they might outrun them to the armory. Frank heard the pop of rifle fire, and the truck's grille exploded. Water splashed from the radiator. Two more shots popped through the truck's hood with a *thunk*. So much for that, he thought.

Now, Frank turned and saw the bikers charge from the door. He spotted the rifle barrel sticking out from a second-floor window. The next—and last—sound would be a bullet exploding his skull.

Digger had stopped and was looking at the window. Digger raised his hand and fired a blast of light at the window. Glass exploded. The unseen gunman shrieked, and the rifle fell to the ground and bounced end over end. Small flames engulfed the window frame.

Frank looked at him. "Good shot."

The bikers came down the porch steps. In the doorway, Roddy staggered out, holding his wounded shoulder.

"Get back here, preacher. I'm gonna kill you," Roddy said in a pain-soaked voice.

Digger looked at Frank. "Don't like the odds. Take the stone and run for the woods."

Frank heard the rumble of motorcycles coming up the road. Their engines blatted and hummed. The cavalry was on the way, and unfortunately, the cavalry wasn't on Frank's side.

The bikers on the porch moved closer. Digger raised his arms over his head. Light crackled from one hand to another. The bikers began to back up. Behind him, Frank heard the engines cut out.

"They're backing off," Frank said. "Don't."

The light engulfed Digger's hands. The wide-eyed bikers continued to back onto the porch.

"Get to the woods."

The light fanned out in an arc from Digger's hands. Like a giant scythe, it slashed across the front of the porch, knocking the bikers backward. Frank heard a high-pitched scream. He saw Roddy fall backward through the doorway.

He turned and ran. Looking at the parking lot, he saw four more bikers approaching. One had a knife in his hand. Another drew a long-barreled revolver and aimed at Digger. Frank was about to shout a warning when the gun cracked and Digger's back exploded in blood. He flopped to the ground.

Frank whipped a blast of light at the four bikers in the lot. His shot went wide. It slammed into the asphalt like a mortar round and kicked up blacktop. The bikers instinctively ducked, covering their heads. Frank took the opportunity to run. If they came for him in the woods, he hoped for the advantage of an ambush.

He found a dirt trail and scampered down it. He raced through the woods. The rocks on the trail pounded the soles of his feet. His heartbeat throbbed in his ears. The front of his shirt was matted and sticky and his chest burned like hell.

Up ahead, Frank heard water gurgling. A stream?

Voices came from behind, maybe a few hundred feet

back. His initial blast with the light would have stunned them, left them perplexed. It had bought him time.

He came to a narrow stream. A shot cracked in the woods and Frank ducked. Another blast came from the gun, and Frank threw himself to the ground on the bank of the stream. He rolled over to see the stone dribble from his pocket and hit the water with a *plop*.

The stone settled to the bottom. It glowed yellow in the water. Not hard to find, but it would cost him time. He rolled into the water, flopped on his belly. The icy water was like knives jabbing him. He got on his hands and knees. A sharp rock poked him in the leg.

The stone was three feet from him. He jammed his hand into the water and picked up the stone. Then he shoved it in his pocket.

"Well, look what we got here," a voice said.

Frank straightened up so he was on his knees, hands resting on his thighs. The four bikers stood on the bank of the stream. They were a collection of denim and beards and strong body odor. The one in the front held the large revolver on Frank.

"What the hell are you up to?" the one with the revolver asked.

Instead of answering, Frank unleashed a beam of light. It hit the biker in the chest and blew him backward. The others jumped back. Two of them ran back down the trail. Their supposed leader was dead on his back, his chest looking like burnt spaghetti. One biker remained behind. He looked down at his dead friend, then at Frank.

"I don't know what you done to him, but you're going to pay."

The biker started down the bank.

"Stay back or you'll wind up like him."

"I'm gonna hurt you, bad. Maybe drown you in that stream."

Frank looked at the fallen one. The stench of burned flesh filled his nostrils. He had never meant to kill anyone. *I violated everything I stand for. Everything I preach on Sundays, I just did the opposite.*

The biker grinned, showing a row of greenish teeth. He moved down the stream bank. Frank readied himself, muscles tensing. The biker charged. Frank pushed up, driving his shoulder into the other man's stomach. They toppled sideways, the biker landing on top of Frank. Water splashed in his ears.

The other man wrapped his hands around Frank's throat. The water lapped against Frank's cheeks and he felt panic setting in. He wheezed, gasped for air, and clawed at the hands locked on his throat.

He would have to use the light one more time, no matter what the consequences. With his left hand, he conjured a ball of light. Then he swung it out of the water and bashed the biker in the head, the light and Frank's fist striking the skull. The biker's head exploded, the stump jetting blood and the torso slumping backward. Frank sat up, shoved the body off him.

He stood up, then looked down at the ruined body. He promptly spun around and vomited into the stream. When he was done puking, and his stomach continued to heave, he sat on the bank of the stream and wept.

The Light was never intended to be wielded against a human enemy, and the biker's corpse bore the horrible evidence of that fact. Frank walked downstream, knelt down, and washed his face with some handfuls of water. Shivers racked his body, and his chest felt raw. But he had the stone, and that was important.

He was ready to head back. A shot cracked. He ducked his head. He glanced down the trail and saw a denim-clad figure staggering down the trail. It was Roddy, apparently well enough to come and look for payback. Frank got to his feet, started up the bank. His foot caught a slick spot on the bank and he went down. Frank's head struck something hard, the world spun, and blackness took over.

CHAPTER 15

Sara watched out the front window. The shadows had lengthened across Charles Pennington's front lawn. There had been no sign of her pursuers, and although she was grateful for that, her nerves were still on edge.

"What are you looking at?" Laura said.

"Nothing."

"Where the hell are you, Dad?" Laura wondered aloud.

Sara turned around. Laura sat on the couch flipping through a leather address book.

"We tried the golf course, The Red Brick, his pal Eddie's, nothing. I'm getting worried."

"What's with the address book?" Sara asked.

"Thinking maybe there's another place I missed."

"I'm sure he'll show up. At least he left a spare key, right?"

"I suppose that's something."

"Mind if I turn on the TV?" Sara asked.

Laura shook her head.

Sara looked at the clock. It was five o'clock and there probably wasn't anything else on, so she would settle for the news. The television was a flat screen, mounted on a wall over a rich oak mantle. Sara turned it on, flipped to Channel 7.

A breaking-news graphic crawled across the bottom of the screen. The camera showed an industrial complex, maybe a steel mill, and over it, a black cloud that seemed to stretch for miles. The cloud swirled over the mill buildings. It appeared to be thick and covered the grounds of the mill in shadow.

"Laura, look at this."

Laura looked at the screen. "Holy crap."

A reporter's voice broke in, "*You're looking at a live shot of the former Bethlehem Steel plant. A strange cloud appeared over the mill shortly after four o'clock. Weather Team 7 is currently tracking the cloud on Doppler radar. It does not appear to be a tornado-forming cloud. More on this breaking development as it happens.*"

The screen switched back to a pretty blond anchor, who went into a story about a man who stabbed his wife and three children.

A heavy feeling of dread settled in Sara's chest. The cloud was similar to the ones her pursuers had used for cover. Could it be they hadn't attacked her because a larger attack was about to happen?

"We have to get out of the city," Sara said.

"Because of some funky cloud?"

"Bad things are going to happen."

"We're not going to get a tornado, if that's what you're worried about."

"It's worse than a tornado." She tugged on Laura's sleeve. "Let's go."

"I'm not going anywhere. If it storms, we'll take shelter somewhere."

"It's no storm."

"You're acting weird," Laura said. "Cut it out."

How can I convince her? "It is weird, but it's no storm."

"Then what is it? Alien invasion?"

That wasn't too far from the truth. "Not aliens, but not a storm."

"Sara, what's the worst that could happen?"

Should she tell Laura what happened? Maybe she wouldn't entirely believe the story, but hopefully she would recognize its urgency. Sara suddenly wanted to be back home, maybe sitting in the front row of the Royal, holding Robbie's hand. Away from all this. "I think a lot of people are going to die."

"How do you know that?"

"There's things in the cloud, things that tried to kill me. Let's find your dad and get the hell out. Go far away."

"Things in the cloud?"

"They killed a woman. I was at her house."

Laura placed her hands on Sara's shoulders. "Honey, are you okay? I understand you're scared, but c'mon."

Sara took a deep breath. She told Laura about the bus trip, the stop at the gas station, and the creatures tracking her down at Joanne's house. She left out the part about her firing beams of light at them.

"If someone was killed, we need to call the police."

"Not if. Was."

"Why didn't you call for help? It was probably guys in masks."

"Yeah, and a whole Hollywood special-effects crew?"

"You don't have to make things up. I believe something bad happened."

"I'm not making shit up, Laura."

"Watch your language."

Sara felt her face get hot. "I'm sorry. We're wasting time."

"We're not going anywhere without me finding my dad. Besides, we're probably safer indoors, anyway. No telling what that storm will bring."

"If only you knew," Sara said.

* * *

Enclosed in the darkness of the mill, Engel waited. The cloud had risen. When night fell, the cloud would descend, and the city would know pain.

Milo sat at the horseshoe-shaped bar in the Alligator Grill sipping a root beer and waiting for the only woman in his life. The bartender, bald as an egg and wearing a gold earring, flipped on the television over the bar. There was some weird-looking cloud hovering over the old Bethlehem site, and the weather people were saying they couldn't identify it.

Milo took another sip of root beer, the soda cool and sweet in his mouth. It did the job of ridding his throat of dust and tasted quite fine, to boot.

That was one weird-looking cloud. Not like anything he'd ever seen, but it *was* Buffalo. If you didn't like the weather, wait five minutes—it would change.

Debbie arrived five minutes later, coming up behind Milo and tapping him on the shoulder. He hugged her, kissed her cheek, looked at her for a moment. Every time he saw her he still got a little hitch in his chest, for she looked almost exactly like her mother. The graceful neck, the bright hazel eyes, the same shade of chestnut hair.

They took a table near the front window, and watched as the college crowd began to file in on Chippewa: guys in backward ball caps and girls in low-rise jeans strolling past the window. Milo took in the smell of fried onions coming from the kitchen. His stomach grumbled.

The waiter came, and they both ordered beef on weck and seasoned fries. Debbie also ordered an iced tea.

"So, what's new?" he asked.

"You believe that cloud over the mill?"

Milo turned, caught a glimpse of the television. The cloud seemed to have grown.

"That's some weird weather, all right."

"You think we'll get a tornado?"

"It's not unheard of, but I doubt it."

"So about my news," she said. "I got you in suspense?"

"I'm on the edge of my seat."

Please don't let it be that she's pregnant.

"I'm engaged."

"To Brian?"

She held out her hand. A small diamond occupied her ring finger. Milo looked it over. She had been dating Brian all of two months, and now an engagement?

"Of course, silly."

"Deb, you sure about this?"

"I know what I'm doing," Debbie said.

"It's not that, you're just so young. And Brian, he's a nice kid, but two months of dating?"

She withdrew her hand. A frown crossed her brow, then disappeared.

"You don't think I can handle it," she said.

"You're a junior in college. You've got plenty of time. You want to get your master's, right?"

"That's a given, Daddy."

"You set a date?"

"We're not setting any dates until I'm done with school."

"He treats you good, right? From what I've seen, he's a gentleman," Milo said. "What about when you're alone?"

"Couldn't be sweeter."

He leaned in, extended his hand. She placed her hand in his, and he put his other hand over the top. "Promise me you'll finish school. You don't want to end up like your old pops, running a machine the rest of your life."

"Somehow demolition doesn't suit me, Dad."

"You know what I mean," he said. "You happy?"

"Feel like I'm flying."

He remembered those days. When he'd first met his wife. Going home and smelling his shirt because it would smell like her perfume or soap where she had leaned her head on Milo's shoulder. Walking around in a daze, her name dancing through his mind.

"All right," Milo said. "Just take it slow." He patted Debbie's hand and she favored him with a smile. He let her hand go, thinking she had been about eight the last time he held her hand.

A waiter with spiky hair and an eyebrow ring brought their food and a bottle of Miller's horseradish. He set the plates in front of them and said, "Enjoy!" Then he bopped back toward the bar.

Milo took the top portion of the roll off and smothered his sandwich with horseradish. He put the roll back together and took a bite. The beef was tender, the roll salty, and the horseradish hot enough to clear the sinuses. Delicious.

After taking a bite of her sandwich, Debbie said, "That cloud's grown again."

In the weather department at Channel 7, Montgomery Felser watched a group of staff members stand around a bank of monitors. They watched the live feed of the cloud, eyes wide, some of them with mouths agape.

Felser was due to get on the air and give an update in five minutes.

As he looked over the Doppler, Rick Ferguson, the station manager, appeared at Felser's desk.

"That's some cloud," Ferguson said.

"If that's what it is."

"What do you mean?"

"I've been here thirty years, seen two blizzards, the October surprise storm. Some small tornadoes."

"That's why you're the best, you've seen it all."

"There's just one problem," Felser said. "I've been on the horn to the National Weather Service."

"So?"

"They don't have a clue what that thing is," Felser said. "And neither do I."

As David cruised down the 190, the elevated thruway that wound through the City of Buffalo, he kept looking at the cloud over Lake Erie. It rose up in a column, then fanned out, swirling blackness that darkened the horizon. The attack would come soon. Finding Sara became even more critical.

Using directions Frank had given him, David exited the 190 and wove his way through downtown Buffalo. It was early evening, the air just starting to take on a chill. Normally he loved this time of year and the crisp fall weather, but tonight it only chilled him. He turned on the truck's heater.

He parked on a ramp a block from Buffalo General. He untucked his flannel shirt and jammed the revolver in his waistband. Then he pulled the shirt down to conceal it.

He approached the hospital and found the ER entrance. He went down a corridor and found the ER waiting room. He approached the desk, where a pretty nurse with black-rimmed glasses sat. She had dark circles under her eyes.

"Excuse me," David said.

"You hurt?" she said, and yawned.

"I'm looking for a doctor."

"Okay sir, but do you need treatment?"

Did he look sick? "No, I need to speak to one of your doctors, Laura Pennington."

"It's her day off."

"Great."

"Who are you?"

"I've come a long way to find her. Did you notice her with a girl, sixteen years old, black hair?"

"I don't feel comfortable giving out information to strangers. Now do you have a medical issue?"

"I'm not a stranger, look."

The nurse craned her neck to look around David. "Our security guard will be making rounds. Do I need to call him over?"

He wasn't looking to harm anyone, but the nurse didn't know that. In today's day and age, he couldn't blame her for being suspicious. He could be a Ted Bundy clone for all she knew. "No, I'm sorry. I'm leaving."

She gave him a scowl and he turned and left the waiting room.

From the hospital, David drove to Laura's apartment building on Delaware Avenue. Charles had supplied them her address and apartment number. The hospital would have been the best place to find her; doctors were always working. Of course he caught Laura on her day off. He parked on the street and approached the building. A U-shaped courtyard with a faux marble statue faced the street. Beyond the statue was a set of double glass doors. David entered the courtyard and scurried across, bathed in yellow security lighting. He reached the double doors, looked around. Nothing had followed him. In fact, nothing had followed him all the way from Routersville.

He entered the building, passing through a marble-floored lobby dotted with potted palms and ferns. He saw a bank of elevators across the lobby. Luckily, it was deserted at the moment.

He pressed the button for the ninth floor. The elevator dinged and the doors opened.

He arrived on nine. Laura was in 903. The elevator doors opened. He stepped off, saw 901. Guessing, he turned right and found 903 on his right. He knocked on the door. Pressing his ear against the door, he listened for footsteps. No one answered, and a minute later, he knocked again.

"I help you?"

He turned to see a black man with curly white hair grinning at him. In his arm he held a brown grocery bag. In another gnarled hand he held a polished cane made of dark wood. He seemed kindly. "I'm looking for Laura Pennington." David said.

"How do you know her?"

"I went to high school with her. I've been out of town for a while."

"Don't know where she is. Saw her leave here with a teenage girl, though."

Sara was alive! And she had tracked down her mother. Try not to seem urgent, he told himself. He didn't want to seem like he was stalking them. "Do you have any idea where they might have gone? I'd really like to catch up with her."

"Naw," the man said, and shuffled past. His grocery bag gave a papery ruffling noise.

That left Charles's house. If they weren't there, then David had no idea where to look.

Mike sat in the basement of Hark's club listening to Schuler's snuffly breathing. From upstairs, bass throbbed through the floor. He hugged his knees in to his chest, trying to get warm. The damp air seemed to knife right through his clothing.

He looked at Schuler, who lay on his side against a stack of beer cases. Schuler moaned.

"How you doing?" Mike asked.

"Feel like shit. Wish they'd just kill me."

"We're not going to die," Mike said. "Don't suppose you have your cell on you?"

"They took it. You?"

More wet, bubbly breathing came from Schuler. Mike couldn't help but cringe.

"Left it on my dresser."

They had to do something. Mike stood up and went over

to the door where Schuler had been held. He turned the knob, found it locked. No surprise there. He searched the rows of beer and liquor cases, shifting and poking through them. Nothing to find, although he'd hoped for a stray tool, maybe a crowbar or hammer.

He needed a weapon, anything. Flipping open a case of Labatt's, he took out an empty. Holding it by the neck, he tapped it on the floor, and the bottom half broke, leaving a jagged edge. No one would hear him, for the music was too loud. He carefully picked up the broken glass and put it in the Labatt's case. Then he closed the lid.

He returned to his spot on the floor and left space between his rump and the beer cases. In the space he hid the bottle, neck facing his right side. That way he could reach back and grab it. It wasn't enough to kill a man, but if he could surprise one of them, he might be able to stab them and grab a weapon.

"That's no good, Mike."

"I don't see you doing anything to help us."

"Sorry, my nose is a little fucking broken."

"You got us here," Mike said. "Remember that."

Schuler propped himself up on an elbow. "I got us here? You should've never gotten involved with Hark. Never."

Before Mike could respond, he heard the cellar door open. Heavy footsteps thudded on the stairs. Hark, dressed in a black tracksuit with white piping, stood looking at them. The huge man from the warehouse, the one with the wingspan, was with him. Under his arm Hark held a package wrapped in clear plastic.

"Thought you were the best," Hark said.

"Even the best have bad days," Mike said.

"Which one of you started the fire?"

Mike and Schuler remained silent. The throb of bass pumped through the ceiling. There was really no chance of anyone hearing them.

"Don't want to talk? You will."

Hark shifted the package to his hand and began to unwrap it. He pulled it from the package. It was wrinkled and clear, with a hood. It became apparent what it was when he pulled it over his head: a clear plastic poncho. Disposable.

"This is for your benefit, O'Donnell," Hark said. "Actually, for mine. Things are bound to get messy."

"Wonderful," Mike said. "You know there were witnesses, that's why we took off early."

"Job not done. I hired you, you fucked it up. And you'll get the worst of it. Your buddy's getting off lucky."

With that, Hark nodded at the goon. The guy took a piece with a silencer from inside his coat. He aimed at Schuler. Mike watched his friend, whose eyes got big, and Mike wanted to scream, but the goon pulled the trigger. Schuler jerked, blood splashed against the beer cases, and that was it. His friend's chest looked like some weird red jelly. He was gone just like that.

The goon aimed at Mike.

Hark said, "We're going in that room now. If you don't squirm too bad, I might kill you early. Most people squirm, though."

"Where's my mother?"

"Resting comfortably in my office. Pretty sick, isn't she?"

"Cancer," Mike said.

"A shame," Hark said. "Though she's faring better than you are about to."

The goon motioned with the gun for Mike to follow. The broken bottle seemed useless now. They weren't going to get any closer. But he had to try something. He felt behind him and gripped the bottleneck.

"What you got there?" the big man asked.

"Nothing."

"Drop it or I'll shoot you in the nuts."

At least I'll die fighting, he thought.

Mike whooped and charged the gunman. He expected to see a muzzle flash and hear the *thwip* of the silenced gun. Instead, when he got within five feet, the gunman flicked his foot, catching Mike in the gut. He doubled over. The beer bottle fell to the floor and smashed. Then Mike fell to his knees, gasping and clutching his guts.

The gunman hauled Mike to his feet. Hark, now at the storage room door, chuckled. He took a key from his pocket and unlocked the door. Flipping a light switch, he entered the room. Fluorescent light spilled out. The gunman shoved Mike into the room. He fought the urge to gag. The room smelled like a butcher shop, the stench of meat and blood thick in the air.

He was still half doubled over but managed to scan the room. Against the far wall, a wooden armchair was bolted to the floor. He noticed padding on the wall; the room was soundproof.

The gunman nudged him over to the chair.

"Sit down."

Mike sat in the chair. To his left was a table with a variety of tools on it, each of them neatly in place. A row of pliers, a blowtorch, nails and a hammer, assorted knives, a bottle of drain cleaner (that one, for some reason, disturbed him most), and several pairs of handcuffs. He also saw the meat hammer they had used on Schuler. Brown splotches dotted the floor, no doubt the blood of Hark's victims. Mike's heartbeat shifted into overdrive.

The pain in his gut had settled to a low throb, and the air returned to his lungs.

"I'm going to cuff you to the chair," Hark said. "If you resist, I'll tell Mr. Sullivan here to shoot you in the kneecap."

I'd rather take a bullet, Mike thought. He shoved Hark, who moved back a few feet. Springing from the chair, Mike dove for the table, hoping to grab a weapon. Sullivan aimed the gun at Mike. Mike heard Hark say, "No, you'll kill him too quick."

Mike saw a couple of gleaming knives next to a container of what looked like salt. He reached for a knife. That's when he felt something hard smash the back of his skull and things went dark.

Water splashed in his face. Mike jerked his head back, whacking it against the wall. His arms were on fire, the forearms stinging. His upper arms had shooting pains that traveled up the side of his neck like electric shocks.

Where was he? Someone shot Schuler. His chest had exploded. He really was dead, wasn't he? Where was Mom? He shook his head as if to clear it. It hurt to think.

Hark stood in front of him, grinning. Bloody streaks covered the front of his poncho. He set a bucket on the floor at his feet.

Mike looked down at himself. He was shirtless, his chest hair matted with water and sweat. They had cuffed his wrists and ankles to the chair. There were shallow cuts on his forearms, raw and stinging. He looked again and saw the salt granules around the edges of the cuts.

Good Christ, that hurts.

The pain rocketed through his arms again. He turned his head to see long nails jutting from his upper arms.

"I see you've been busy," Mike said in a weak voice.

"We're just getting started," Hark said. "You know what happened to the last guy who screwed me the way you did?"

Mike managed to smirk. It made his head hurt. "Threw him a surprise party?"

Hark chuckled. "Two of my men held his head back. I poured drain cleaner down his throat."

"You're a sick fuck, you know that?"

CHAPTER 16

Engel stepped from the yawning door of the old steel mill. He looked above. The dark cloud swirled and whipped like a dust storm. It would soon carry his children to the city.

He looked at the host of trucks with their strange mechanical arms pointed in the air. He thought they were reporting the news. A throng of cameramen point their lenses to the sky, tracking the cloud.

Engel raised his arms in a Y. *Send the cloud upon them.*

The cloud began its descent. It dipped lower and moved toward the city like an alien fog, rolling across the grounds of the mill. There was nothing to stop it. *The cloud itself will eat flesh. Then it will roll back, leaving his army in the city to slaughter. It will surround the city, preventing escape.* If he were lucky, the cloud would kill the girl, or one of his children will bring her here. Either way, it was the end of the Guardians and the beginning of his Dark Master's reign on earth.

At the same time, another cloud was set to roll from the mine in Wickett's Corner and strike his enemy in Routersville. His army of demons would follow, taking out the last stronghold of the Guardians.

Engel watched the trucks and vans outside the mill gate. The people surrounding the vehicles pointed frantically. A woman screamed. Some ran, while others screeched away in vans and cars. It didn't matter, for there was no escape.

As the cloud whooshed forward, he grinned.

Jenny Chen was nervous. From the armory's eastern turret she scanned the town's main road with a set of binoculars. The lone ribbon of highway was empty. She hoped to see Frank coming down the road. A pair of headlights, anything.

The sun had dipped behind the hills, and she had been so caught up with preparing for the attack, she had not noticed the slippage of time. They had three dozen Guardians stationed on the armory's four turrets and roof. But the most important person was still missing: Reverend Frank.

Something has gone wrong.

She hung the binoculars around her neck. Then she climbed down the hatch that lead to the old commandant's quarters. She passed through the turret and found her way to the ornate oak staircase that lead to the hallway. She followed the hallway until she arrived in the main hall. The lights had been dimmed. Guardians and riflemen stood at the slitted windows.

She saw Ruby of Ruby's Diner fame at one of the windows. Ruby was a Guardian and carried no gun. Her weapon was the Light, more deadly to the Dark Ones than any firearm. Jenny crossed the hall and tapped Ruby on the shoulder.

"Frank's not back," Jenny said. "I need you to take a team and go find him."

Ruby covered her mouth with her hand. "Oh, dear. Such a nice man."

"Get some people together. You know where the Warlords clubhouse is?"

"Up at the old inn. He went by himself?"

"Digger was with him."

From behind her, Jenny heard heavy footsteps. She turned and found Dan Longo standing behind her. He gasped for breath. His ponytail, ridiculous on a man over fifty, hung askew. Sweat stains had formed on his T-shirt. The man wouldn't be running any marathons soon.

"What?" Jenny asked.

"Just ran from the roof," he gasped. "There's a cloud over in the direction of the mine. Spotted it with the binoculars. They're coming."

They had little time. Jenny turned to Ruby. "Get moving."

The tiny redhead gave her a salute and ran off to gather a search party.

Jenny turned back to Dan Longo. His breathing had settled down. "Alert everyone. The attack's started. I'm going to the roof."

Jenny had returned to the east turret. There were five other Guardians with her, two men and three women. She looked at each of them, bundled in Carhartt coats and turtlenecks and knit caps. They needed the warm clothing, for the wind began to snake through the battlements as if trying to force them off the roof.

She looked through the binoculars, again at the main road. The cloud, as black as the starry sky, rolled down the hill and had nearly reached the first houses at the edge of Routersville.

God help them. God help us. She'd had her chance to leave, take off with Derek to Seattle. He had been the best thing to come into her life. Smart, kind, and compassionate, he was the type she would have married. If not for being cursed—or was it gifted—with a strange power. If she were in Seattle, she would not have to face the attack and the blood and death it would bring. That was selfish. She was special, as were all the Guardians. And right now they were the last hope.

She peered through the lenses again.

One of the men, dressed in a brown Carhartt and matching bib overalls, said, "What do you see?"

The cloud had stopped short of the first houses. Now, shapes stepped out of the fog and spread out across the road. Dozens of winged beasts rocketed from the cloud and headed skyward, flying abominations from the bowels of hell. They rose higher and higher, circling over the town. They screeched and wailed, perhaps anticipating the killing to come.

Having seen the things emerge from the cloud, the man said, "God help them all."

"I'm not sure even He can," Jenny said.

"John, look at this," Helen Klump said.

John Klump rolled his eyes. He snapped his newspaper shut.

"What is it?"

"Just come look."

At forty-six, John Klump was the only dentist in Routersville, and by default, the most successful one. He had made enough money to build a four-thousand-square-foot home on the outskirts of the town proper. It was done in rustic style, the cathedral ceilings crossed by huge timbers. After a day filled with root canals, halitosis, and one nasty, pus-filled abscess, he wanted nothing more than to sit in front of the stone fireplace and read the paper. Now his crackling fire would have to wait as he got up to appease his wife.

She stood at the window seat, one knee propped on the red cushion. Hands cupped around her eyes, she pressed her face against the glass.

Klump joined her at the window. She took her face away from the glass.

"What did you want to show me?"

A worried look crossed her face. The muscles around her eyes twitched. The same thing happened when she got nervous before going to the doctor.

"I'm scared."

He didn't know what could be so frightening. The scariest thing in Routersville was the plaque on the residents' teeth. Nevertheless, he pressed his face to the window.

A dark mist hung in the air. It rolled down the main drag, uncurling like a huge rug. In the mist, a figure moved, short and squat; it carried what looked like a spear. Klump squinted, trying to improve his vision.

"Kill the light," Klump said.

Helen did, and the room matched the shadows outside.

Klump continued to watch, hands cupped around his face. More of them moved through the fog, some with limps, some impossibly large, all of them with weapons.

He was about to turn and tell Helen to call the cops. A large, dark shape appeared in front of the window. Klump gasped and backed away. Panic started to set in, gnawing at his brain. They needed to get to the van in the attached garage. That was all. Then they could drive out of this. The cops would handle it.

The form in the window cocked back its arm.

"What is it, John, what is it?" Helen asked.

Its fist punched through the glass with a *clink* and spat shards onto the window seat. The fist was fish-belly white and did not bleed. The hand should have been cut to shreds.

"Get to the van, Helen. We're getting out of here."

Jeannie Maldonado stepped out of a pool hall on Routersville's main drag. The crisp air was refreshing, for the pool hall had smelled of smoke, beer, and sweat. She found no takers in the pool joint. Tonight she wore a flannel shirt with the buttons opened to the chest. Under that, a tank top with a nice swell of cleavage showing. She'd squeezed into size eight jeans and tucked them into cowboy boots. At thirty-eight, hooking was getting old. But she still had it. Still knew how to make a man moan and twitch.

She dug into her oversized purse and pulled out a pack of cigarettes and a pink lighter. She flicked the lighter, stuck the smoke between her lips, and lit it. Leaning against the building, Jeannie pulled a drag from the cigarette, then blew a curl of smoke in the air.

Footsteps echoed from her left, down Main Street. She looked down the street. Across the width of the road, a line of men approached. They appeared to be armed. Was this some kind of gang? Routersville didn't have gangs, just the Warlords when they came through on their bikes. Behind the men a black cloud rolled backward, away from town.

She threw the cigarette on the ground and stomped it out. It would be smart to get moving the other way. She wished she had a car, especially since her apartment was ten blocks from the pool hall.

A screech, like a giant bird, filled the air. She looked up. Overhead a huge winged creature climbed high, turned in midair, and dove. Coming right for her. It was no bird, that was for sure.

Panicking, she looked around for an open store, an alley to duck in. The street offered no escape. The pool hall seemed a mile away.

She turned to run and the last sound she heard was the rush of air as something swooped upon her with terrible speed.

Jenny watched the cloud roll back. The Dark Ones advanced up Main Street, as if the cloud had been their mode of transportation and was now leaving. She heard the breaking of glass and the roar of a shotgun. Through the town, screams echoed up and down the street as the Dark Ones smashed in doors. Those unfortunate enough to be inside were dragged out and slaughtered. Above the town the winged ones dipped and dove toward street level. Jenny watched in horror as a woman was plucked from the sidewalk, carried upward, and ripped nearly in two by the clawed beast.

A van sped on Main Street. She thought it might be Doctor Klump's vehicle. It swerved, tires squealing, to avoid the throng of demons in the street. The driver lost control and the van rolled over, skidding into a lamppost with a loud CLANG! A group of Engel's soldiers scrabbled on top of the van and dragged its occupants from the now-shattered windows.

Jenny turned away. The sight of it was too much. More screams of agony rose up in the air. She wanted desperately to mount an assault, take the Guardians to the streets and meet the Dark Ones head-on. But their numbers were too great, and without the Stone, the attack would result in their defeat. They stood a better chance inside the armory, waiting for Frank to arrive.

If Frank arrived.

In her father's living room, Laura Pennington stood next to her daughter, gazing at the television screen. On the screen, the massive cloud that had hovered over the steel mill now rolled toward the camera. A reporter dressed in Channel 7's standard blue jacket eyed the cloud nervously. He looked as if he were deciding to continue reporting or run for his life. The cloud whirled across the lot and reached the fence. A voice off camera urged everyone to run. The cloud rolled closer. The reporter broke into a run, but the cloud overtook him. The camera dropped to the ground, giving an eye-level view of the blacktop. The audio continued for a moment, and a high scream—it could have been that of a man or woman—pierced the speakers. The feed then cut back to the blond anchorwoman, whose hands shook as she straightened her notes.

Laura put her arm around Sara and squeezed. "I'm turning it off." She stepped forward and hit the power button. The screen went black.

Laura glanced outside. It had gone as dark as the blank television screen. In the distance, a chorus of sirens wailed.

"I was going to call the police about the murder you described, but I think we have bigger problems right now."

Sara turned to her. Tears formed in her eyes. "We have to leave."

"We're safer here."

"They'll find us," Sara said.

"Who?"

"The ones who are looking for me."

Sara began to chew on her lower lip. Laura was beginning to worry that the girl might crack. "Who's looking for you, honey?"

"The ones in the cloud."

"There's no one in that cloud. It's freak weather."

"Then why did those people scream?"

That Laura didn't know. "They're scared."

Sara looked at the television screen, as if to confirm it were turned off. "That last scream was someone in pain."

Laura couldn't deny that. As an emergency room doctor, she had heard the screams of those in agony, and the scream on the television fell into the category of pain. "Even if we leave, we have no idea where that cloud is headed. We might drive right into it. We'll button up the house, go to the basement."

"They'll find me."

Laura gripped the girl's shoulders, hard at first, then relaxed her hold. Sara winced. "I'm sorry. No one's out to get you."

"You don't believe me," Sara said.

"What exactly are you trying to get me to believe?"

Sara backed up. Laura's hands slipped from her shoulders. "There are things in that cloud. I drove the cloud and the things inside it away at a rest stop in Ohio."

"What things?"

"Deformed men, creepy looking. It somehow ties in to my power, gift, whatever you want to call it."

Now Sara had gone from nervous to completely obtuse. "The boat left the dock, hon. I'm afraid I missed it."

Sara rolled her eyes, as if Laura were the thickest human being on the planet. "I'll show you. Back up."

Laura backed up, crossed her arms. Outside, a host of sirens had joined the initial cacophony. She flinched as a loud boom echoed in the distance. It sounded like an explosion. "Hurry up and show me. I'll feel better in the basement."

Sara closed her eyes and raised her left arm, hand open, palm up. At first, nothing happened, and then a tiny pinprick of white Light appeared in her palm. The Light grew in size, to a dime, then to a quarter, then to the size of a softball. Laura squinted. It didn't hurt her eyes, but it was certainly bright. The white glow filled the living room, and was reflected in the television screen. Sara's face was bathed in it, making her skin appear almost translucent. In the glow of the Light, she was beautiful. Laura heard herself gasp. She had never seen anything remotely like it.

Sara let the Light glow a moment longer, and it faded gradually, disappearing from her palm. Opening her eyes, Sara said, "Now do you believe me?"

"I don't know what I believe," Laura said. "What was that?"

"I'm not quite sure. I started to be able to do it about a

year ago. I think of light and warm places and it appears. That time I didn't have to think as much. I must be getting better."

Laura looked at Sara's arms. With a T-shirt on, there was no place to conceal any type of device. Her hands were empty, and she doubted there was any technology short of Hollywood special effects that could produce such a light. And Sara would have no reason for trying to fool Laura into thinking she possessed magical powers. "What else can you do with it?"

"The things—the men—that are after me? It will kill them. I can fire it like a gun."

"Anyone else know about this?"

"David, probably Reverend Frank. They've never approached me about it, though."

Laura's head spun. The light display was the most amazing thing she had ever seen. "Where did you get this power from?"

Sara shrugged. "We should get to shelter. They might be here soon."

Laura hoped her father was safe, holed up inside from the coming storm—or whatever it was. They had to make provisions to protect the house. She instructed Sara to check all the windows and doors on the first floor, make sure they were locked. Laura went upstairs, through the bedrooms and into the master bath, and did the same. Satisfied the windows and doors were locked, Laura went to the kitchen and found a flashlight in the drawer. Then they proceeded to the basement.

The basement was cool and dry. Her father had left it sparse. The only items, other than a washer and dryer, were a set of golf clubs and a rolled-up garden hose. Those, and a worn blue sofa set against the wall. The two women sat on the sofa. Sara moved close, and Laura put her arm around the girl, hoping to provide some comfort. She trembled slightly.

"We'll be okay," Laura said, and Sara responded with a weak smile.

She just wished the basement door had a lock. Sara's story of deformed men in the fog didn't seem so silly after the girl had displayed the ball of Light.

CHAPTER 17

Their meals finished, Milo and Debbie had joined the crowd at the bar. A throng of people packed around the Alligator's bar, necks craned to view the television. On the screen, the anchorwoman reported that the fast-moving cloud had reached the downtown area. Reports of screams, car accidents, and things seen moving in the fog were pouring in from reporters in the field. Milo was acutely aware of the silence in the bar. It was the only time he had heard such silence in a watering hole.

Debbie, standing at his side, tapped him on the arm. "Dad, should we go?"

Outside, he heard a shriek rise, hit an impossibly high pitch, and then die. "I think we're better off inside."

"What do you think it is?"

His first thought was terrorists, that Al Quaeda or some other group of maniacs had released a chemical attack. He didn't want to cause a panic by suggesting that option, so he said, "Don't know."

Outside the deep thrum of a car engine filled the air. Milo turned to see a green pickup truck swerve, jump the sidewalk, and smash into the bar across the street. Glass exploded onto the sidewalk. Smoke rose from the truck's hood. The driver stumbled out, holding his face. He staggered across the street, and now the crowd turned to watch from the Alligator's front window. The man barged through the door. He was sobbing. He took his hands away from his face. The skin came away, stuck to his hands in gummy strands. Ragged holes, surrounded by scorched skin, revealed white bone underneath. He looked as if he had washed his face in acid. Milo felt his stomach lurch. The crowd backed away; the man remained in the center of a loose circle of people.

"It's the fog, it huuurrtsss." The man fell to his knees. A stream of vomit shot from his mouth. He collapsed forward, and was still.

Milo scanned the faces of the crowd. A guy in a black T-shirt turned from white to green. Some of the girls covered their mouths. The bald bartender hurried away, presumably to the bathroom. He got ten feet from the bar and splashed vomit all over the plank floor.

Debbie moved closer to Milo. He slipped his arm around her shoulders. It reminded him of nights when she was little and ran into their bedroom, afraid of thunder and lightning.

"Dad?"

Milo had no idea. He shook his head. He took one more look at the dead man, then glanced at the door. It was open, and from outside came the smell of something rotting. Thinking it prudent to shut the door, he took his arm from around Debbie's shoulders and closed the door. He then clicked the brass dead bolt shut.

The bartender, who was bent over, hands on knees, breathed heavily. Milo called to him, "This place have a basement?"

Wiping his mouth with the back of his hand, the bartender straightened up. A green stain dotted the front of his T-shirt, but he didn't take notice. The man's bald head was the color of a lobster and a vein throbbed in his temple. "No way this crowd would fit."

"We'll bring a shoehorn," Milo said. The crowd remained mostly silent. Milo thought it a good time to address them and urge everyone to adjourn to the basement. They would have to be orderly. Didn't need anyone causing a panic.

He was about to speak when a cloud, darker than the surrounding night, rolled in front of the bar's windows. It didn't take a genius to figure out the cloud was deadly. Whether the mist was released by terrorists or from a chemical spill he didn't know, but venturing into the cloud would mean an awful death.

The crowd in the Alligator turned toward the windows. The bars on the other side of the street dissolved in the darkness. Milo squinted. A shape, roughly man-size, silhouetted in the fog, walked in front of the window, then stopped. Two more joined the first. The shape pulled back its arm, and something dark and heavy looking appeared in its hand. It was with sick dread Milo realized the man meant to smash out the glass.

Milo looked back over his shoulder. A hallway ran off the main bar. There were doors on either side of the hall. One of them was bound to be the basement door.

Returning to Debbie's side, he took her arm and said, "We're going to the basement."

Eyes wide, she nodded and said in a voice that broke his heart, "Whatever you say, Daddy."

They wound around the tables. Behind him, the glass was smashed, low cracking sounds followed by the higher ping of the shards being broken out. Someone screamed. Milo didn't look back. He gave Debbie a gentle nudge and urged her forward.

In the hallway, Milo twisted the knobs of the first two doors and found them locked. At the end of the hallway, a red exit sign glowed over a steel door. Next to that was the last door in the hall. If that wasn't the basement, they were in trouble, for the only other option was to return to the bar area. He didn't even want to think about going outside.

They reached the door. He pulled and it opened to a staircase.

As they began to descend the stairs, Milo saw two rough-looking guys emerge from one of the other doors. One of them had a shiny revolver in his hand. They seemed to pay Milo no notice, both of them streaking toward the bar area. Milo shut the basement door behind him, and they moved ahead, Debbie going first.

At the bottom of the stairs, they came to a storeroom with all manners of beer cases stacked against the walls. Blood stained some of the cases and the concrete. What the hell happened down here?

"Why is there blood? Why?" Debbie asked.

The tremor in her voice indicated the verge of panic.

Across the basement was another door. He would comfort her in a moment, but first he wanted to see where the door led. Before they had descended, Milo removed his flannel shirt and stuffed it under the door. It was possible the mist might eat through his shirt, but all he could do was hope to keep the fog out.

Above them, the floorboards thudded. He heard screams and squeals, as if the patrons of the Alligator had seen a rat. From the sound of the commotion, it would have to be a rat of epic proportions to inspire such panic.

Milo tried the other door. It was locked. He looked around the room. The walls were windowless, which would prevent the mist from seeping in that way. Not satisfied, he tugged on the doorknob again. To his surprise, a muffled voice on the other side said, "Go the fuck away!"

Now, from upstairs, Milo heard the distinct pop of gunshots. The crash of furniture reverberated against the floor. It sounded as if a group of rhinos were charging through the bar.

Encouraged by the presence of someone on the other side of the door, and hoping for an escape route, Milo kicked the paneled surface. To his surprise, the knob turned and he stepped back to avoid being hit with the door. It swung open, and he was nothing if not surprised. A tough-looking guy in a bloodstained poncho stood in the doorway, a claw hammer in his hand. Milo peered over the man's shoulder. Inside the mattress-lined room, another man sat handcuffed to a chair. His shirtless chest dripped blood.

The tough-looking guy said, "You're not Ed."

"And I'm guessing you're not the butler."

That seemed to set him off. The man raised the hammer to swing at Milo. Milo shoved the guy, who stumbled backward, but quickly regained his balance. The guy moved forward for another swing, raising his arm again. Milo lunged forward, hoping to close the distance and minimize the arc of the swing. The guy swung his arm.

Here it comes, Milo thought.

The hammer swung down and clipped him on the shoulder. Milo drove through it, plowed into the man, and wrapped his arms around the guy, pinning one arm to his side.

The man in the chair yelled, "Kill him!"

The guy shifted his weight. Milo shifted with him, the two of them partners in a crazy dance. They wound up on the floor, Milo taking in the coppery smell of blood on the poncho. They rolled around, Milo squeezing the man's arm and attempting to keep it at his side. The guy wound up on top of him.

From the corner of his eye, Milo saw Debbie hurry around the two combatants. She picked something up off the table of tools. Milo looked up at the man, who raised the hammer. With his blood-slicked poncho and his wild eyes, he looked as if he'd gone mad. Milo raised his arms to block the coming blow.

Instead of getting pummeled, he saw Debbie swing a handheld sledge that hit the guy's head with a *thwock*. The man's eyes glazed, he dropped his hammer, which fell to the ground, and he slumped over. Milo managed to shove the unconscious man off him. He stood up.

His daughter stood with the sledge gripped in two hands the way a samurai warrior might wield a sword. Tears rolled down her cheeks. Blood flecked the hammer's head.

"Deb, honey, put it down."

She looked at him and for a moment, she didn't seem to recognize Milo. Then the hammer slipped from her hands and banged on the concrete. Milo went to her, embraced her. She buried her head in his chest, sobbing. He stroked her hair and said, "You did the only thing you could've done. It's okay."

In a muffled voice she said, "I killed him, didn't I?"

Milo looked down at the man. His chest rose and fell in shallow breaths. "He's alive. Don't know what that shot to his melon did, but he's alive."

From behind Debbie, the guy chained to the chair said, "Can we have a family reunion some other time and get me out of here?"

"You going to be the next one that comes at me with a hammer?"

"I don't give two shits about you, buddy. Look at me. I need to get out of here and clean out these wounds."

Two nails jutted out from his shoulders, and a host of scratches and cuts leaked blood onto the man's arms. Milo eyed the tools spread out on the table and figured the man in the rain poncho had even worse things planned for his captive.

Milo gently pushed Debbie away. "I'm going to help this guy, okay?"

She wiped her runny nose with the back of her hand. Then she nodded, apparently satisfied that Milo was not going far.

"Who is he?" Milo asked.

"Name's Hark. Involved in some heavy shit. Once in a while grabs someone off the street, tortures them for sport."

Milo looked at the man in the chair. He had trouble believing Hark would snatch someone off the street at random. No doubt the man in the chair was a business partner, most likely in crime. He couldn't bear to leave the guy sitting there. Regardless of Hark's beef with the man, he didn't deserve to be tortured. It made Milo's stomach roll.

Deciding the man in the chair would not cause them harm, Milo said, "Keys?"

The man in the chair nodded, indicating Hark. "Check his pockets."

Milo crouched down and dug through Hark's pockets until he felt the key. He removed the key and unlocked the man's handcuffs, asking, "You have a name?"

"Mike," he said, not moving his arms. M ꞌ realized why he didn't move: nails still jutted out of his triceps.

Looking at the nails, and the blood that dribbled down, Milo said, "You must've really pissed this Hark guy off."

Mike winced. "You think?"

"Let's get those nails out of your arms. Hopefully they're not too deep."

Milo brushed past Debbie, who leaned against the table, arms crossed. She kept sneaking glances at Hark, as if he might jump up and yell boo. She had struck Hark in order to help Milo—self-defense if ever there was a case—but he could see the effect of her actions weighing on her. As he searched the table and found a pair of pliers, he patted her on the arm. "How you doing, kiddo?"

"Is he going to be okay?" Debbie asked, indicating Hark.

"Don't know," Milo said. "Give me a hand?"

She joined him at Mike's right side. Milo examined the nail. It didn't appear to be driven too far into the skin. It still must have hurt like hell, though. "Deb, hold his arm."

Mike turned his head away. Debbie pressed on Mike's arm and Milo squeezed the nail head with the pliers. He pulled and as it came out, Mike stifled a yelp. They did the other side, and Mike sprang from the chair, saying, "Bastard Hark, hope you killed him." He then snatched a short piece of pipe from the table and headed for the door.

Milo set the pliers back on the table. He didn't want to touch them any longer than he had to, for they felt tainted.

"Don't go up there," Milo said.

Still walking, Mike said, "They've got my mother up there. Thanks, but I'm going."

Debbie said, "All hell's broken loose up there."

That stopped Mike. Shirtless and pipe in hand, he looked like some crazed barbarian warrior off to storm the gates. "What do you mean?"

"There's a cloud—something toxic—sweeping through the city," Milo said. "And someone attacked the bar, smashed the windows. We ran down here."

Mike studied Milo for a moment, as if deciding whether or not to believe him. "Screw it. I've got to find her."

"Don't go," Debbie said, but he was already on his way upstairs.

After Mike disappeared upstairs, Milo ventured to where the beer cases were stored. He retrieved his shirt. Debbie followed him, and the two stood at the bottom of the stairs, Milo cocking his head as if it would help him hear. Floorboards creaked overhead. A dusky, rotten smell wafted down the stairs. Smelled like something died up there.

After Mike had been gone a few minutes, he reappeared in the doorway. His arms dripped blood. Milo was worried he might keel over from blood loss, so he climbed the stairs and stopped near the top. He watched Mike, prepared to catch him if he collapsed.

On closer inspection, Mike's face had gone gray. "You need to sit down," Milo said.

Debbie, who had joined Milo on the stairs said, "I think he's in shock."

"You will be, too," Mike said. "Come have a look."

Milo followed him and entered the hallway. What he saw made his heart kick against his ribs. Four bodies, piled on top of one another, some of them belly to back, lay on the floor. A puddle of blood soaked the floor beneath them. More blood had been splashed on the walls in gaudy strokes. The corpse on top, a woman in a white T-shirt, was the worst. Her throat was gashed and the head hung backward, as if someone had pushed it past its natural angle. The tipped-back head reminded Milo of a Pez dispenser. *Try selling that model in the stores.*

"Did you find your mom?" Milo asked.

"She's in the office," Mike said, jerking his head to indicate the door behind him. "She's alive, but I need to get her out of here. Her meds are at home and she's in wicked pain."

Behind Milo, Debbie said, "Who could have done this?"

Fighting the nausea increasing in his stomach, Milo moved closer to the bodies. He noticed more of them in the bar, but wasn't quite ready to venture in there just yet. He stood over the corpses. Tugging the collar of his shirt, he pulled it up over his nose and mouth, hoping to quell the stink of the dead.

Limbs twisted, sprawled over one another, they had run and been struck down. The fingers on one of the hands were bloody stumps. Another corpse had a bloodied nub where an ear had been taken off.

From behind a door, a woman moaned, deep and long. It was the sound of someone suffering. Suffering had been the order of the night. Milo glanced down the hallway. Another corpse was sprawled over a table. A plate of half-eaten chicken wings rested next to the corpse's head. Blood had mingled with the hot sauce that coated the wings. If they got out of here, Milo didn't think he would eat wings for a long time, if ever again.

The shirt over his mouth and nose provided little relief from the smell, so he lowered it.

"You got a vehicle?" Mike asked.

"My truck's out back."

"Give me a lift," Mike said. "Mom, too."

"We're not going out there," Milo said. "Not now."

"She needs to get home. Her meds are there."

"We don't know what's out there," Milo said, "so we should stay put."

"Give me your keys," Mike said.

Milo's blood pressure went up a notch. "Take it easy."

Mike took a step forward. He slowly raised the pipe. Milo balled up his fists. "Don't do it."

Debbie brushed past Milo. She got between the two men and spreading her hands apart said, "This gets us nowhere." Looking at Mike, she continued, "We saved your life down there. I may have killed someone because of you, so just take it easy and we'll find a way out. Your mother will get the help she needs."

"I'll say it again. We need to go."

Outside, another large bang sounded. It was followed by a chorus of screams. Mike turned his head in the direction of the noise. He seemed to ponder things for a moment. "Maybe we *should* at least take a look. I'm not exactly thinking straight."

"Your mom in there?" Debbie said, pointing to the cherry-stained door behind Mike.

Mike nodded.

Debbie said, "I'll look in on her. Why don't you two take a look up front? I'll try and find a first-aid kit somewhere, too."

Something told Milo Hark wouldn't keep first-aid supplies around for his intended victims, but it was kind of Deb to offer. They *did* need to get Mike patched up sooner or later.

Milo said to him, "How you feeling? Woozy at all?"

"My arms ache like hell, but I'll make it."

"What'd you do to piss this guy off so bad?"

Mike ignored the question. "Let's look up front."

Debbie went into the room to check on Mike's mother. Milo and Mike stepped around the pile of bodies and entered the main bar. Corpses lay everywhere, their blood staining the hardwood floor. One of them was draped across the bar, a solid black knife of a type Milo had never seen jutting from its chest. The front windows had been smashed out, and the broken glass had been scattered across the floor. Outside, the wrecked pickup truck remained across the street. The cloud that had rolled down the street appeared to have dissipated.

The knife in the chest of the victim on the bar intrigued Milo. He hated to get closer to the corpse, but he wanted to check out the knife. He went to the bar.

"What are you doing?"

"This knife," Milo said. "Never seen anything like it."

"What the hell happened here? They've been butchered."

Ignoring Mike's question, Milo approached the corpse. It was a college-age guy. He stared glassily at the ceiling, arms and legs draped over the edges of the bar. The poor bastard probably had nothing more in mind than slamming a few beers, maybe picking up a girl. Milo peered at the knife. It was as large as a short sword. Solid black, it didn't appear to be made of any metal Milo recognized. Wicked-looking serrated barbs were cut into the blade. The hilt likewise had sharp edges jutting from both ends. The tip of the handle curved into a point.

There were no markings. The blade reflected no light.

"Come look at this knife."

Mike joined him at the bar. He studied the knife for a moment and said, "Must be foreign. Looks old, too."

"It's solid, but it doesn't appear to be made of metal."

"Touch it."

"That's morbid."

"*He* won't mind."

Milo reached his hand out. With his index finger. He touched the flat side of the blade. He expected to feel something like cool metal. Instead, a wave of revulsion and nausea so severe swept over him, he immediately jerked his hand away. He turned from the body. Hands trembling, he bent over, stomach swirling, head now pounding. His heart kicked in his chest and a feeling of shame washed over him, as if he'd done something horribly wrong. He closed his eyes, and after a moment, the feeling subsided. It was as if he had touched something unclean, terrible.

"Hey man, you okay? What was it?"

"It made me feel horrible, touching it."

"It hurt your feelings? It's just a knife."

Milo shook his head. "Something's wrong with it. Like the damn thing is evil or something. Like it was somehow alive."

"Haunted knife. Right."

"Touch it, then, if you don't believe me."

Mike rolled his eyes. He still reached his hand out and instead of touching the blade, he grabbed the hilt. Almost immediately, he jerked his hand away. He stumbled sideways and leaned on the bar, head nearly against the rail. His breath came in shallow gasps.

"See?"

"What the fuck is that thing?" he asked, still hunched over the bar.

"Let's leave it be. You all right?"

Straightening up, Mike nodded. Milo went to the front door. Stepping outside seemed crazy at this point, but he wanted to get a quick view of the street. The black fog was gone, and it hadn't appeared to enter the bar. None of the victims seemed to have the skin trauma that the driver of the truck had displayed. Milo gripped the door handle.

Seeing this, Mike said, "I thought we were staying put."

"Just going to take a quick look outside. See what we're up against."

"Makes sense," Mike said, and joined him at the door.

Milo opened it and stepped outside. He was not prepared for what he saw.

CHAPTER 18

Frank heard a voice, far off, distant, say, "Frank, you okay? Frank? I think he's coming to."

He opened his eyes to see the red-haired woman—Ruby, wasn't it?—from the diner. She crouched beside him. A look of concern, as if she had just found a stray puppy, crossed her face. He sat up a bit, propped himself on his elbows. His head felt like glass had broken and splintered inside his skull. A greasy sensation arose in his stomach.

Don't let me puke in front of the pretty redhead.

After a moment, the nausea died down. It didn't go away, but at least it wasn't at volcanic-eruption level.

All he could think to say was, "Where's Roddy?"

Ruby said, "Who?"

"One of the bikers, he was chasing me. Where is he?"

Ruby, kneeling on the bank, looked over her shoulder. "I think we took care of him. Looks like you took out the others."

It came back to him. Taking the stone from the clubhouse. Running into the woods. Digger dying. Frying the rest of the bikers.

Frank sat all the way up. Ruby took his arm to steady

him. He saw the remains of the bikers near the streambed. Frank clasped a hand over his mouth. He hadn't wanted to kill them. What would be his punishment for this? Would God look upon him with fury or mercy? The Light had never been meant for this. It was a weapon designed to slay demons, not mortal men.

"Who else is here with you?"

As if on command, three men sauntered down the trail, all of them wearing some combination of blue jeans, work boots, and camouflage jackets. They formed a loose semicircle around Frank and Ruby. One of the men said, "We found Digger back there. The Warlords' place is empty."

"Frank, can you walk? The attack's begun."

"I most certainly can," he said, getting to his feet. Again, the stabbing pain radiated through his skull. He touched the side of his head. A nice size goose egg was forming near his hairline.

Frank felt in his pocket. He touched the smooth coolness of the Stone. He must have slipped it in there before blacking out. With it, they had a chance.

They started back down the trail. Roddy's corpse lay slumped in the bushes, and again Frank lamented using the Light on a human being. He pretended not to smell the scorched flesh and stink of blood as they left the stream bank.

It will be up for God to decide, he supposed.

Back in the parking lot, a row of bikes remained, along with the truck Frank had borrowed. A dark spot soiled the ground beneath the truck; vital fluids had seeped underneath from the gunshot wound. He spied Digger's body.

Removing the stone from his pocket, he stood over Digger.

Ruby joined him and said, "We really need to get going."

"I want to see something."

Frank crouched next to Digger. He placed the stone on Digger's blood-soaked chest. It glowed faintly, began to pulse, but after a moment, the Light dissolved and faded. Nothing.

There was something he hadn't told David about the stone, something only he and Charles knew.

Frank felt a tiny hand on his shoulder. "Frank, they need us. What is it?"

"The stone is capable of healing, at times, even mortal wounds. It won't work on everyone," he said, and removed the stone from Digger's chest. He placed it in his pocket.

"I'm sorry it didn't work."

In the distance, he heard rumbling, the sound of big Harleys or Indians chugging down the road. "We've got trouble."

"Let's get back to the truck," Ruby said. She turned to the group of men, who stood at the edge of the parking lot near the woods. "Y'all ready?"

Y'all. She was as charming as she was pretty. Ruby was bound to make some young man very happy someday.

If someday came.

They piled in the Ford SUV, Ruby behind the wheel, Frank in the passenger seat, and the other three in the back. He jerked his head toward the backseat and said to Ruby, "They Guardians?"

She nodded.

Ruby started up the truck and pulled to the edge of the lot, where the road came out of the woods. Frank looked in the rearview. A few of the dead bikers lay slumped on the former inn's porch. They looked like piles of dirty denim from here. God help him, he had helped kill them.

The bikes—five of them—cruised down the road. He guessed it was the last of the bikers that called the former inn their home. Their engines blatted in the night. Dust clouds kicked up around their bikes. They may have been mounted Tasmanian devils, whirling down the road like dervishes.

Seeing the Ford, they slowed, and the one in the lead raised his hand. The pack came to a halt.

"We can't wait for them," Frank said.

"What do you suggest?" Ruby asked.

"How about a game of chicken?"

He looked at Ruby and she looked back as if he just suggested she stroll down Routersville's main drag in the nude.

"Have you slipped a gear, honey?"

"My gears are intact. If they get too close, the truck will be surrounded. If we back up we'll be in the parking lot with no way out unless this is one hell of an off-road vehicle and I'm just not seeing it."

Down the road, the biker in the lead revved the bike's engine. He began to roll forward.

"They'll move," Frank said. "We're bigger."

Ruby eyed him wearily, then turned and said to the men in back, "Y'all strap in. You, too, Frank."

The bikers gained speed. There was perhaps a hundred yards separating the SUV and the bikes. On either side was a slight drop-off and beyond that trees and shrubs. Whoever went off the road would be feasting on a pine bark sandwich.

Frank reached back and pulled the seatbelt across his chest. Then he snapped it home.

Ruby accelerated. In the headlights, the truck seemed to chew up the ribbon of road at a terrifying speed. The bikers seemed up to the challenge, jetting down the road. They rode in a staggered formation, the hum-blat of their engines filling the night.

Ruby closed the gap. A hundred feet. Fifty.

Frank gripped the dashboard with both hands, realizing it would be fruitless and would not stop several hundred pounds of chrome and steel from smashing through the windshield. It was something, though.

At twenty-five feet, the lead biker lost his nerve. His front wheel wobbled. He turned the handlebars to his right and the bike skidded out of control and he went down, the bike on its side and flying around the side of the truck. The other bikers peeled off, the four of them managing not to dump their bikes.

Ruby hit the gas. In the side mirror, Frank saw one of them stop, climb off the bike, and help up the one who had wiped out. The other three turned around in the lot and were now speeding after the Ford.

If the bikers caught up to the SUV, he didn't know if he could use the Light on them again. He felt like a coward, but still hoped it wouldn't come down to a showdown. There had been enough death and blood spilled, with more to come in Routersville.

Ruby turned on to the road headed toward Routersville. When they were on the road for a moment, Frank looked in the side mirror and saw the bikers following.

"Had to run into them, didn't we?" a voice said from the backseat.

"They're speeding up," said another.

Frank peeked in the mirror. Sure enough, three headlights buzzed toward the truck. The bike's engines screamed louder as they neared the SUV.

Frank turned around. The three in the backseat had their heads craned, looking out the rear window.

"Get ready for a fight, guys," Frank said.

The one in the middle, a husky guy with a full beard, said, "They get close, we'll flash fry them." Apparently the man didn't share his reservations about using the Light on another person.

Ruby pressed on the gas. The Ford sped up, but soon denim-clad bikers flanked both sides of the vehicle, while the third lagged behind. The road was a two-lane, and the biker on the left danced with the yellow line, while the one on

Frank's side straddled the shoulder's white stripe. He waited. Let them make the first move. He could urge Ruby to swerve and run them off the road, but he wanted to avoid more bloodshed. On the road in the woods, he had guessed (correctly) that the bikers would blink. Here, it almost seemed too easy, running them off.

Frank looked at the biker to his right. He was fumbling with something on the other side of the bike, one hand still on the bars. He pulled up parallel to Frank's door. Glancing at the speedometer, Frank saw the truck was doing seventy. He looked back at the biker.

The biker whipped his arm across and something hit the window with a flat crack, leaving a jagged break in the glass. The biker pulled back again and Frank saw the chain uncoil like a snake and bust the glass. It gave and splintered into a mosaic of shards. Frank recoiled.

Ruby edged the SUV to the right, attempting to run the biker off the road. The biker dropped back, and the truck sped forward, but there was still one on the driver's side of the truck.

Frank heard the mechanical whine of the window lowering and turned to see the man behind Ruby getting ready to conjure a beam. He cocked his hand back, and his palm began to glow.

"Wait," Frank said.

Beyond the man in the backseat, the biker brought his arm around, across the handlebars. In the dark, Frank made out a shape. Gun. He squinted. Sawed-off shotgun. Double barrel. He jammed the barrel in the window and a blast erupted from the gun. It was as if someone set off an M-80 in the truck. Fire licked from the barrel and Frank watched with horror as the head of one of the Guardians exploded. Frank felt something warm and wet against his face. Flesh and brains now decorated the interior of the Ford. Ruby screamed.

The bearded man in the center of the backseat howled.

Frank looked at him. His arm was peppered with buckshot, and the smell of gunpowder and burned flesh filled the vehicle.

The victim of the shotgun blast—Frank never did learn his name—slumped forward, his ruined, smoking head leaning against the rear of the driver's seat. Frank thanked God at least the man's passing was quick.

Ruby hit the gas, edging forward and pulling slightly away from the biker with the shotgun. Mewls and moans came from the backseat. Frank turned around. The biker with the chain edged up to the window. He cracked the chain against it and this time the glass sprayed across Frank's lap. Through his beard, the biker grinned. The cool air knifed into the truck, making a mournful hissing sound.

Up ahead, about a mile in the distance, Frank made out the first of Routersville's homes. If they could make it into the town, the Dark Ones might actually act as an ally and slaughter the bikers.

"Faster, Ruby."

"I'm already going eighty-five!"

"Go ninety."

The truck accelerated and Frank expected at any moment to hear another wicked boom and this time it might be *his* head that was vaporized. He looked behind him. The wounded man slumped against the remaining live one in the back. The man who sat behind Frank was tall and gaunt. He wore a John Deere cap pushed back on his head, revealing a clump of black hair. His eyes were glazed over with shock. The man was on another planet.

The shotgun-wielding biker pulled parallel to the truck again. The double-barrel weapon would have another shell ready to fire.

If he tries again, I'm going to have to fry him.

"Almost there," Ruby said.

Frank turned to check their position and saw the biker on

the right whip ahead of the SUV. He cut across the bumper, maybe three feet from the front of the truck, sped over the yellow line, and stayed in the opposite lane. His maneuver caused Ruby to jerk the truck to the right. The Ford's tires kissed the rumble strip and it shook with a series of vibrations. Ruby pulled farther onto the shoulder, the truck juking and jiving like a dancer in a conga line.

She braked and the tires screeched. Frank put his hands on the dash. The truck hurtled forward for what seemed like an hour but was really no more than seconds before spinning around and coming to a halt on the shoulder. They were now facing the opposite way. The two bikes whizzed past. They would no doubt turn around and head back this way.

To his surprise, Ruby unfastened her seatbelt and got out of the car. Frank was more surprised when he followed suit. The two men in the back, the gaunt fellow and the one with the beard, stumbled out. The bearded one, leaking blood, leaned against the gaunt man. All four of them hunkered down in front of the truck's grille. The truck now shielded them from the bikers.

The bike's engines settled to a low hum. Frank guessed they had gone a mile or so down the road. Soon he would hear them accelerate, and the one with the shotgun had a shell left, assuming he didn't stop to reload the other barrel. Who knew what other weapons they carried?

Frank was vaguely aware of the blood and brains on his face. Lowering his head, he used his shirt to wipe off the carnage. Ruby did the same, although a streak of blood still decorated her cheek.

The wounded man leaned against the bumper, deep wheezes coming from inside him. The bike engines drew closer. Ruby stood up, peered over the hood. Coming fast, they whipped past and a blast echoed. Shotgun pellets struck the truck. Ruby ducked. The bikers tore down the road.

The truck would be damaged, if not useless. In the distance, the bikers stopped. Frank saw the silhouette of one reach into a saddlebag and pull something out. Then he opened the shotgun's breech. He was loading shells.

"They aren't getting another crack at us," Ruby said, and walked out in the road.

"Get back here!" Frank said.

The gaunt man said, "Ruby, you listen to him."

Now the bikers puttered forward, gaining speed. A gust of wind snuck under the truck tires and nipped Frank at the base of his spine.

Ruby flicked her hands toward the oncoming bikers. Twin streaks of Light crackled through the air. One biker—the one with the shotgun—flew backward off the bike. His Harley skidded, spitting sparks on the blacktop. The second one's gas tank erupted and he was blown forward, over the bars. He cartwheeled on the blacktop with a disturbing array of pops and splats. Neither one of them got up.

You did what I couldn't do, Frank thought.

Ruby passed the men in silence. She got in the truck. The engine coughed as she tried to start it, but would not turn over. It had suffered the same fate as the truck back at the Warlord's clubhouse. These guys really didn't like anything with four wheels.

Ruby climbed from the truck.

Frank went into the road. He heard the sounds of the attack in the distance: crying, screaming, things being smashed.

"What do we do now?" Ruby asked.

"We walk. You and me." He looked at the wounded man and his gaunt companion. "Stay here, in the truck. We'll send someone."

"You can't leave him here," Ruby said. "He's hurt."

"We need to get the Everlight there. We can't very well carry him."

"I don't like it."

"Time's wasting. We'll send help," he said, and started down the road.

The bearded man, the one who took the buckshot, said weakly, "Just a few pellets, honey. I'll be okay for a bit. Go take care of business."

"I still don't like it," she said, but followed Frank down the road.

Jenny watched from the tower. In the streets, the black mass fanned out. Two groups split off and headed down the side streets and moved among the houses. The winged creatures periodically swooped low and snatched people from the sidewalks.

The main force, one she counted as several thousand strong, shambled up Main Street. They smashed windows, broke streetlights, and hacked parked cars to pieces with their dark weapons. The pattern of destruction was mindless, savage. It was as if not having flesh to cleave, they chose the nearest target.

Now, the mass of them came within a hundred feet of the armory's front doors. Still no Frank. The group stopped. Overhead, Jenny heard the shrieks and whoops of the winged creatures. She looked up and saw dozens of them silhouetted against the clouds.

From her perch, she watched them. They held exotic-looking spears, axes, and swords, all forged from the darkness. One of them held a severed human arm over its head and shook it, as if in triumph. The ones around it grunted with pleasure.

Jenny turned to the others and said, "Get ready."

From above came an ear-piercing shriek and Jenny looked up to see the winged creatures spiraling toward the roof. On the ground, footsteps roared against the pavement as the Dark Ones charged the armory.

Gunfire erupted below. It would slow but not stop them. It had begun.

CHAPTER 19

David pulled away from Laura's apartment building. He hit Delaware Avenue, looked right, and saw a police car speed past, sirens blaring. The cop car turned down a side street, nearly going up on two wheels. David saw why. The cloud that hid the Dark Ones rolled down Delaware. It was blocking the way. He needed to get to Charles's house.

Realizing he had to outrun it, he turned left on Delaware. In the rearview mirror, the cloud rolled ahead like a wave breaking onshore. It was fast, and it dawned on him the cloud would overtake the truck.

He spotted a two-story commercial building. He pulled the truck over, grabbed the keys and his revolver, and got out. He tried the building's glass door and was not surprised to find it locked. He fired the gun. The glass blew out. Immediately an alarm blared from inside the building.

He kicked the remaining glass from the frame and, crouching low, moved into the lobby of the building. A reception desk was straight ahead, and to one side stood plush chairs and a coffee table covered with magazines. Next to the desk was a hallway and he hurried down it and found a door marked STAIRS. That door was unlocked, and he took the stairs to the second floor. The alarm howled, but he doubted any police would come. They would be busy with other emergencies.

He selected the first door he found and opened it. Inside was an office. Modest-size desk, two chairs in front of it. A large window behind the desk looked out at the cloud, which had thrown a curtain of darkness over Delaware Avenue. David shut the door behind him. It didn't have a lock.

He approached the desk, began moving pens, a stapler, a monitor and keyboard, setting them on the floor. A framed photo of an adorable blond girl stood on the corner. David picked it up, studied it for a moment, thinking of his own daughter. Where was she? How was she? With reverence, he set it in the corner. Its owner most likely wouldn't be back to claim it, but he felt he somehow owed the photo respect.

After moving the chairs and clearing off the desk, he pushed the desk against the door. He planned to ride things out until daylight, then resume his search for Sara. If he ventured into the street, he would be slaughtered. Even if he could fire beams nonstop, the Dark Ones would overwhelm him.

He crouched at the window. In the mist, he saw something fly past at eye level. The thumps and thuds of footsteps slapped against the street. How many of them were there?

Deciding it was best to stay away from the window, he sat in the corner. He curled his knees against his chest and waited.

It was perhaps twenty minutes later when he heard the crash. The alarm had gone silent. From downstairs, the sounds of heavy furniture being tossed reached David. He stood beside the door, trying to listen. He heard no voices, only the continuing clatter of heavy items being strewn around.

As quickly as it had begun, the crashing stopped. Were they coming upstairs?

He clutched the revolver at his side. The thought of using

the Light again, even on one of the demons, troubled him. If he concentrated hard, he could still smell that boy's scorched flesh in the high school bathroom all those years ago. *But demons are different, aren't they? And they want to tear your head off, David.*

In the hallway, a door opened and slammed. They must have found the stairs. David backed away from the door. He crouched on one knee, revolver pointed at the door.

The knob turned slowly.

They pushed on the door and it thumped against the desk. As if frustrated, they shoved harder. The desk skidded a bit. More shoves against the door.

Scooting across the floor, David sat and pressed his feet against the desk's side, attempting to get leverage and hold the door shut. They shoved again, but this time the desk held.

He pressed hard, and his quads began to burn. This wasn't a position he could hold for very long.

Another thud against the door.

David held the desk until his legs began to shake and he finally dropped them to the ground.

The door gave, and a wicked-looking ax, black as motor oil, splintered the wood. It was pulled back and thrust forward again and again, until a large hole was gouged in the door.

David stood up. Pressing his legs against the desk would be useless now. He leveled the gun, dropped into a shooter's stance.

One of the demons thrust its head through the opening in the door. It stared at him with pale gray eyes that matched the pallor of its skin. It had a wild-eyed, crazy stare, and it took David a moment to realize it had no eyelids. They had most likely been cut off.

David fired. The demon's head shattered, spraying black glop against the eggshell tinted walls. With half its head gone, it pulled back from the door, muttering and chattering

to itself. Soon another took its place, jamming an arm
through the hole, this one's pale skin laced with scars and
burn marks. Its clawed hand gripped the knob—at this point
David could see only arm—and turned. The door opened
and the desk skidded backward. The demon was thick in the
shoulders and the chest. It entered the room. Flaps of skin
hung from its chest, each piece pierced by a ring. A chain led
from each ring to another set of rings hooked into the upper
arms. That was a piercing you didn't bring home to show
Mom.

The pierced Dark One stepped through the door, a black
dagger in its hand. The other one carried an ax with a curved
edged and a spike protruding from the end of the handle.

David held the gun up. His hand shook. The one with the
half-ruined head seemed to take no notice of its injuries. The
gun was useless. It would come down to using the Light.

The larger one with the piercings spat out, "Guardian."

That's right, motherfucker.

David tucked the gun back in his belt.

The larger demon thrust forward and jammed the knife
into his upper arm. The demon twisted the blade. Nausea
flooded his stomach and his head throbbed, the blood seeming to gush through the vessels and the room swirled and a
feeling of something wrong, something dirty, filled him. He
looked at the knife and then back at the grinning demon.

With his good arm he backhanded a flash of Light across
the demon's face. The Light struck and seared the skin black.
The Dark One reeled back, pulling the dagger from David's
arm, and the sense of sickness and nausea immediately diminished. Still half-turned from David, it growled. Its partner, the one with the ax, glared at David with its wild eyes.
Not hesitating, David unleashed a bolt at its head, and this
time the remaining part of the skull disintegrated into a
black tarlike substance.

David surged ahead, shoving past the wounded demon.
The other one slumped across the desk, its soul returned to

whatever evil place spawned it. David was out the door and on the run.

We'll see what I find when I hit the street, he thought.

His shoulder cold and aching, he reached the front doors. The cloud had receded, and the interior of the building bore no sign of the intruding mist. The sidewalk and street were empty. His truck remained intact at the sidewalk.

He looked behind him. The two Dark Ones that attacked him must have been the only ones that entered the building. They had done a thorough job of trashing the place: papers were scattered and furniture was strewn across the lobby.

Still feeling weak from the wound, he staggered on to the sidewalk. Down Delaware, at Niagara Square, a troop of them rounded the McKinley monument. Perhaps a couple hundred, their steps booming like drums. Soon they would pass City Hall, which was empty at this time of night. The attack occurring at night had saved thousands. Downtown's businesses and government offices were closed, sparing the lives of workers.

He got in the truck and started it up. He made a U-turn on the deserted street and headed back toward Charles's house. The wound in his shoulder felt as if it were packed with ice. Strangely, there was little blood, and he found this troubling.

In the basement, huddled on the couch, Sara heard glass break. They were coming inside, and she couldn't bear sitting any longer, so she rose.

Laura moved to the edge of the couch. "What is it?"

"Just a storm, right?"

"I said I suspected."

"You were wrong."

She couldn't get too mad at Laura. The story of her pursuers was difficult for anyone to believe. Nevertheless, they were here and had to be dealt with.

"It could be the wind," Laura said.

"Wind doesn't break windows like that unless it's hurricane force."

The floorboards creaked. Multiple pairs of footsteps. Sara waited at the foot of the stairs. Looking at the door, she prayed they wouldn't come down here. That was a futile prayer.

The basement door swung open. A dark shape appeared.

Behind her, Laura gasped. "What is it?"

"They've come for me."

This time, she gave it very little thought. A quick image of a sunny beach flashed through her mind. She cast a beam up the stairs and it hit the shape at the top. A noise like meat frying filled the basement, followed by a baleful hissing noise. A pale body, naked save for a dirty loincloth, tumbled down the stairs. With it clattered a black dagger. Sara dodged the tumbling corpse. She had blown a hole through its gut, the flesh now crispy and black from the wound.

Laura stood up and said, "Oh my God. You were right. It's not a man, is it?"

"I don't know what they are."

"Can you do that again? Kill them like that?"

"I think so."

"I'm an idiot for bringing us down here. We have to leave."

But before they could move, two more entered the doorway. Sara fired, scoring two hits, and two more grotesque bodies fell down the stairs. How many would come? Enough to fill the stairway?

If Robbie were here, he wouldn't believe this. It would be a fuck-daddy of a thing, as he was fond of saying.

The two women joined hands, Laura stepping over the bodies and taking the lead up the steps. Sara tugged on her hand. Laura turned, an impatient look on her face and said, "What is it?"

"I can kill them. You can't. Let me take the lead."

Together they climbed the stairs, Sara prepared to face the darkness with her newfound mother.

Charles's house was built across the street from a children's hospital. The neighborhood had been prominent, even elegant in its day, and the houses remained impressive. Many were turreted Victorians or Tudors with lush gardens.

David did not like what he found. On the lawn outside the Tudor-style home, several demons had gathered, all of them armed. A winged creature perched at the peak of the roof. It looked like some horrible gargoyle statue come to life. He stopped the truck a hundred feet from Charles's place.

The tall windows were broken, and now more Dark Ones climbed inside. If Sara was in there, they would drag her out. Drag her out and deliver her to Engel. He would never see her again, never have the chance to explain. *I'm sorry I lied about your mother. Those false photos weren't too disappointing to you, were they sweetheart?* She would have every right to hate him, even more right to punch him in the nose, if that's what she felt like doing.

He stopped the truck. Leaving the keys in the ignition, he jumped out. A trio of the demons dragged a screaming woman from the house next to Charles's. Two of them held her arms. The third raised an ax above its head and with a swift stroke chopped off her arm. The woman slumped to the ground. The other demon let go of her remaining arm.

Move, Dresser. Or that's what'll happen to Sara.

As he approached the curb, the winged beast perched on the roof spotted him. It spread its wings and dove, gliding lazily off the roof. Without hesitation, David fired, striking its right wing. It screeched and angled off to one side, flapping the smoldering wing and trying to remain in the air, but the blast had left a hole and the demon dropped, landing on the driveway. It rose, shaking the bad wing. Now, the other demons turned and spotted him. They moved forward, a black mass of stinking, rotting flesh.

He considered his options: seek shelter in the hospital; get in the truck and run them down; grit his teeth, scream, and become a one-man banzai charge. He chose none of them, instead standing his ground. He fired two quick beams, turning two of them into smoking wrecks. There were too many, however.

They plowed into him and rough, cold hands seized his arms and legs. He was lifted off his feet and carried toward the house. Then they dumped him on the lawn, the host of them surrounding him in a circle. The crowd parted and the winged creature he had wounded stepped into the center. It planted a clawed foot on his chest. Drawing breath became an adventure.

It pressed harder, and he felt his ribs start to compress. The creature kept pressing. His sternum felt as if it were being forced out his back. He tried to draw breath, tried to make his chest move. His arms and legs flailed. A group of them broke from the circle and pinned his extremities to the ground.

He looked up. The demon, horned and leather faced, flicked out a pebbled tongue, as if mocking him.

Laura followed Sara to the top of the stairs. The house had taken on a stale odor. Laura became aware of the shapes all around, in the kitchen and blocking the doorways leading into other rooms. Pale-skinned shapes with all sort of deformities and wounds. Ones with split-open skulls and gray brain matter poking out, others missing lips and eyes, still more with incisions baring shriveled and rotting intestines. All of them carried exotic, dark weapons. Murder swirled in their silvery eyes.

"Get close to me," Sara said.

Laura moved in closer. As she did, something swung toward her from the right. She ducked and a blade bit into the basement doorjamb. She skidded down the steps, grabbing the railing to stop her slide. Now, Sara looked down at her. The girl retreated as the mutants filled the doorway.

Sara reached her and offered a hand. She pulled Laura to her feet. Her hip and leg ached, but she was grateful for the railing stopping her less-than-graceful descent. Looking up, she saw one of them coming, a short sword in its hand. Its chest and face were decorated with pink fleshy scars. It grinned and said, "Guardian."

Sara put her arm around Laura's waist. "Hang on."

They were instantly bathed in white light. It surrounded them in a globe and radiated from Sara's body, auralike. Outside the globe, the creature slunk back up the stairs. Sara might have been on to something, because it seemed afraid.

Despite the brilliant glow, Laura was able to see the stairs, and she moved upward. The creature backed up. Laura and Sara moved into the kitchen. Outside the glowing ball, she saw them backing up and as they moved through the house, the Light kept the creatures at bay. They reached the foyer and stepped outside.

Laura saw them gathered on the lawn, raising their weapons, stomping and grunting. They were in a loose circle and through the light Laura saw someone on the grass. A larger, winged creature towered over the others. The group of demons on the lawn continued to stomp and hiss and grunt.

"Stay close. We're getting that person out of here."

Moving forward, the demons closest to them backed away from the Light. Now, as they reached the circle, more of the mutants scattered. The outside sphere of light touched one of them and its skin popped and hissed. It fled back inside the house.

In the center of the circle, a man in a flannel shirt lay pinned beneath the winged creature's foot. Taking notice of the Light, the creature shielded its eyes and raised its leathery hands as if to block out the glow.

"David, I mean, Dad!" Sara said, and moved next to him, enfolding him in the Light.

So this was the son of a bitch she had to thank for holding her daughter all these years, Laura thought.

The man was sprawled on his back. A nasty gash was open in his upper arm. He got to his feet, kissed Sara on the cheek, and said, "You're alive."

"We need to go," Sara said. "I can't hold it much longer."

Now a weapon sliced into the Light. There was a *pop-hiss* and the weapon turned to dust.

"My truck's over there," David said, pointing to the street.

They made their way to the street, walking slowly, the sphere of Light protecting them. The ugly bastards outside the Light grew restless, and a throng of them followed, keeping a distance, but still agitated, stomping and growling.

They reached the driver's side of the truck. Laura didn't know how much longer she could hold off the demons. Behind the main group, the winged one took flight and circled above.

"Sara, I'll open the door," David said. "When I tell you, cut the Light and the two of you haul ass across the seat. I'll get in last."

David opened the door. The Light around them seemed to collapse and Sara crawled into the truck, Laura following. The Dark Ones advanced. David got in last and as he did a beam of hot white light shot from his hands and hit the ground in front of the horde. Chunks of asphalt flew up and tinkled against the windshield. The enemy advanced. David started the truck and backed up.

The mass of freaks charged. Some of them broke off and headed for the other houses, climbing front steps, smashing in doors and windows. Screams erupted from inside the houses. Laura could only hope that God would intervene and somehow they would ignore the children's hospital.

David managed to cut the wheel, back up, and get them

turned around. He pressed on the gas and the truck sped down the street.

In the rearview, the horde soon broke off. The truck proved too fast for them.

They drove through the deserted streets. Every so often Laura looked up but saw nothing flying in the sky. They were heading toward Laura's apartment building. They passed Millionaires' Row, a section of Delaware lined with pillared mansions left over from the Gilded Age. Most of them had been turned into offices. One of them was now a high-class hotel.

"Where do we go?" Sara asked.

"We need to find Charles. Did you look for him?"

"No, we just let him roam free among the freaks in the street. Of course we did," Laura said.

This drew a frown from David.

"When this is over, I'm turning you in," Laura said.

"To?"

"FBI, State Police, whoever will listen."

"I didn't kidnap her, if that's what you're implying."

"She didn't wander off on her own," Laura said. "You've been lying to this girl all her life."

"It can be explained," David said. "I know it doesn't make it any easier to take, but it can be explained."

"Explain away taking my child, leaving me with nothing."

"We have to get off the streets."

"Answer me," Laura said, and gripped David's arm. He pulled it away.

"I'm trying to drive, damn it."

Sara said, "Please stop."

Laura gave her a look that would melt steel. "Don't tell me to stop."

"He's hurt," Sara said. "His arm."

David glanced at his arm. Laura took a closer look. The shirt was torn and through a hole in the fabric she saw a gash in the skin, near the shoulder. *Why wasn't it bleeding more?*

"Pull over," Laura said.

David gave her a suspicious look. "We need to get away."

Laura looked behind her. For now, the street was empty. A fire glowed from somewhere past City Hall, oily smoke rising in the air. It would be safe to stop for a moment. She wanted another look at that wound.

"Do it," Laura said. "I want to look at your arm."

David pulled the truck to the curb. He left the engine running and his foot on the brake.

"Take off your shirt."

David put the truck in park. He pulled off the shirt, wincing as he did so. He had on a black T-shirt under the flannel. Very carefully, Laura pulled up the short sleeve to get a better look at the wound.

This was bad. The skin around the wound was an ugly red. An orange tributary branched out about two inches from the wound. "When did this happen?"

"Just before I got to the house. One of them stabbed me."

"You're going to the hospital."

"I'll be okay."

"You need treatment. Now."

"Why?"

"That wound's necrotic. We need to run a Gram stain, start debridement, get you on antibiotics."

"English, doctor," David said.

"The tissue around the wound is dead. And it looks as if it's spreading."

"That's some bedside manner you've got."

"I don't have time to screw around. The General's that way," she said, pointing.

David put the car in drive and they pulled away.

Chaos had paid a visit to Buffalo General Hospital.

David parked the truck a block away. They could not get closer because ambulances and police cars clogged the street outside the emergency room entrance. The wounded, some in bandages, others in blood-soaked clothing, staggered toward the doors.

After parking the truck, Laura, David, and Sara moved toward the doors. Laura kept watch on David. Sweat dotted his forehead, and his respiration had become shallow.

They weaved through the wounded and Laura led them through a set of double doors and into the ER's main corridor. Gurneys, all of them occupied, lined the walls. The smells of burned and putrid flesh hung in the corridor. From down the hall, a baby wailed. To either side, beds were full.

Laura spotted an orange plastic chair normally reserved for visitors. She grabbed it and set it against the wall. "David, sit down."

He did, muttering, "Don't feel so good."

"How does your arm feel?"

"It hurts bad."

Laura looked at Sara, who was looking at David and biting her lower lip.

Laura patted her on the arm. "Stay with him a minute. I'm going to see what I can do."

"Will he be okay?" Sara asked.

"I honestly don't know," she said, and began winding her way through the wounded and the dying.

Laura found Dr. Peter Ostrow, one of her fellow ER docs, in room twelve. He was tall, with gray hair and glasses, and wore a look of perpetual state of concentration. He would have been handsome if his mouth weren't set in a permanent grimace.

After stepping around the curtain, Laura found him standing at the bedside of a balding man with a face full of stubble. The man's eyes were closed. An IV drip hung on a pole. The beep of heart and pulse ox monitors filled the room. A sheet came up to the man's chest.

Ostrow stroked the arm of his glasses with his index finger. He glanced at Laura, then continued to study the patient.

"Peter, I've got a possible necrotic wound. What the hell is going on out there?"

Still not turning his head, Ostrow said, "All hell's broken loose. We're not equipped to handle all this."

"I need to run a Gram stain on someone. We'll need to start antibiotics, most likely, maybe get him to surgery."

"ORs are full. And don't bother."

"What do you mean?"

"You've got a strong stomach, right?"

"Peter, look at the line of work we're in," Laura said.

He grabbed a pair of latex gloves from a dispenser on the wall. Ostrow reached over and pulled back the sheet that covered the patient. Laura gasped. The man's right arm was devoid of skin from the shoulder to the elbow. The tissue underneath had turned a shade between black and gray. A stench of rot, thick and heavy, arose from the man's ruined arm. She had seen many horrible wounds—among them a toddler burned over 90 percent of his body—but this was the worst.

Ostrow gently placed the sheet back. "Michael Plant. Arrived three hours ago. Wound on his arm was the size of a quarter. Said one of the *freaks* stabbed him. I immediately took it to be a necrotic wound. Strange that it started so fast. Negative for strep and *E. coli*. Within an hour it ate almost to his elbow. Started him on antibiotics, heaviest stuff we've got. No effect whatsoever. We've got him on morphine to keep him comfortable."

"Others?"

"We've lost six this hour to it."

"Spreading fast," Laura said. "Have you seen them?"

Ostrow looked at her. "Who?"

"The *freaks*."

"Just their handiwork."

From the depths of his morphine-induced slumber, Plant moaned.

"Is it contagious?" Laura asked.

"Far as I can tell, it's not spreading. It's the rapidity that scares the hell out of me. And none of our heavy hitters—vanomyicin, mainly, are touching it."

That didn't bode well for David. As angry as she was, Laura had to treat him, had to find a way to cure him. It appeared to be a lost cause. "What if we amputate?"

Ostrow rubbed the bridge of his nose. "ORs are booked solid. They're taking the most critical first. We had an MVA with multiple cars come in. I've had three amputations come in the past hour, poor souls had their arms cut off. Lost two of them."

Laura imagined a conversation with the grim reaper would offer more hope than Peter Ostrow. Wishing him luck, she left the room to break the bad news to David.

She found him slumped in the plastic chair, moaning. Sara knelt at his side and was making small circles on his back with the palm of her hand. Trying to comfort him. What a good kid.

After telling them she'd be right back, she searched the corridors until she found an empty gurney. She wheeled it back to them and with Sara's help got David on the gurney. The two of them wheeled him down a corridor and, finding an empty spot against the peach-colored wall, rolled him against it.

He began to shiver, and Laura got him a blanket and spread it over him. She craned her neck, looking around for a nurse to come take his vitals, but they all buzzed around attending to the wounded, flashes of pink and blue pants and smocks.

It was Sara that asked first. "Will he be okay?"

Without answering, Laura pulled back the sheet and took a look at the arm. Hot-looking orange tributaries branched from the wound, running down his bicep and into his forearm. The area around the wound was beginning to turn black. "Let's get you something for pain. How much do you weigh?"

" 'Bout one ninety."

Laura went and tracked down a nurse. She ordered Demerol and a few moments later returned with the nurse, who administered a shot. The nurse buzzed away, on to her next patient.

"Mom, you never answered me."

Mom. That's the first time she's called me that, Laura noticed. Under different circumstances, it would have brought her to tears. Instead she gave Sara a quick smile. "The infection, if that's what it is, is spreading rapidly. It's eating the flesh. Antibiotics won't touch it, and even if they were, the hospital is out of the ones we need."

"So basically I'm screwed," David said.

"Is he going to die?"

She looked so sad and hopeful. Laura had seen that look on hundreds of faces, families of accident victims hoping for the best. It had always inspired pity in her, and this time it just about cracked her heart in half. "We can make you comfortable, David. I'm sorry."

David closed his eyes and sighed as if trying to absorb the force of the news she had just delivered. He opened his eyes and said, "I suppose I owe you an explanation, Laura."

"That might be the understatement of the century."

"How much time do I have?"

"Maybe a day, maybe less."

"Then I'll make it quick."

CHAPTER 20

Death had come to Chippewa Street.

Milo saw the dead everywhere. Bodies in the street, draped over cars. Headless bodies. Bodies with arms and legs missing. Bodies with jellied organs and guts hanging from opened bellies. Blood slicked the sidewalks and street. The raw smell of it all was overpowering.

"Who the hell could do this?" he asked Mike, who stood next to him.

"Have to be one hell of a terrorist attack. There's hundreds of bodies."

"They must've all ran from the bars when the attack hit," Milo said and noted a stack of bodies in the doorway of the bar across the street.

"What was it?"

"I-I don't know. They were weird looking. And you saw that knife inside the bar. They were carrying weapons like that," Milo said. "We ran downstairs. I didn't get a better look at them."

Mike kicked aside some broken glass. "We have to get my mother home. I need her medicine."

"We have to get out of the city."

"Not before we stop at my house."

Milo turned to face him. "There'll be help coming. The National Guard, someone. They'll have medical care."

Mike waved his arms around. "You see anybody? Have you heard anything, helicopters, trucks? I don't think anybody's coming. I'll take care of her."

"They'll come."

"Yeah, them and John fucking Wayne will arrive with the cavalry, and they'll all be blowing bugles out their asses."

"You're one bitter bastard, you know that?" Milo said.

"Almost being tortured to death does that to a guy."

"Spare me the pity party. I ask you something, Mike? If Hark grabbed you off the street, what's your mom doing here?"

Mike's face began to flush. Milo thought Mike might hit him with the pipe.

"I got involved with some bad shit with Hark. I won't say what. His people were waiting for me at my house. They grabbed her as leverage."

"You must have made him pretty angry."

Mike snorted. "You think?"

Milo took a look through the Alligator Bar's broken window. "We can't stay here. Wouldn't *want* to stay here with all the dead. Let's get out of the city. We'll get your mom help."

"They're not going to have what she needs. Our house isn't far from here. I also got some pieces stashed at the house. From the looks of things, we're going to need them. What say we get the guns, get the medicine, and then get the hell out?"

There was no telling what they would run into on the way out of Buffalo. Besides the strange things that had attacked the city, scores of criminals and looters would take advantage of the chaos and would be roaming the streets. Milo didn't want to become easy prey, and he shuddered to think of what might happen to Debbie. "Okay. We get the guns. Let's go help your mom into the truck. But then we get out of here."

"If we can."

Milo stepped over some stray bricks and went through the Alligator's ruined door.

Mike's mother looked one step away from death. The woman, who had been introduced as Agnes, lay on a sofa in the office. Her skin, gray and pale, was stretched over her cheekbones, and a red scarf adorned her head. Debbie sat next to the couch on an office chair, holding the woman's hand.

That was his good girl. When Milo's wife had been rushed to the ER, Debbie sat with him in the waiting room holding his hand the whole time. When the doctor, an Indian man named Bojedla, had come out of the OR and told them she didn't survive the surgery, it was Debbie who quietly slipped her arm around Milo's shoulder and squeezed. And it was Debbie who made the funeral arrangements when Milo couldn't bring himself to do it.

Now, Agnes let out a low moan.

Still holding the length of pipe, Mike said, "You okay, Mom?"

With a weak voice, she said, "You're stupid, Michael, you know that?"

"Yeah, been stupid," Mike said.

"She's burning up," Debbie said. "She needs to get to a hospital."

With her free hand, Agnes clawed at Debbie's shirt. "No hospital. I'm not dying in one of those places. Take me home."

"That's where we're going, Ma," Mike said.

"That's the first intelligent thing I've heard you say."

Agnes closed her eyes. She released her grip on Debbie's

shirt. To Milo, it didn't appear she would make the ride to the house. They would see.

"Let's get your mom to the truck," Milo said.

Together Mike and Milo lifted the frail woman from the couch and took her to the back door. Debbie, in the lead, opened the door and peered outside. There was no one in the parking lot, save for a woman's corpse. The dead woman had been wearing a miniskirt and now it was hiked up over her panty-clad buttocks. Milo looked away.

They got in the truck, Mike and Debbie in the back of the extended cab, Milo driving, and Agnes in the passenger seat, her head resting against the window.

Mike gave him directions to the house. Milo pulled out, hoping they would make it.

The ramp to the 190 had proved impassable. A tractor trailer lay on its side across the ramp, a host of cardboard boxes spilling from its opened doors. It may not have been wise to venture on the 190, anyway. When they had reached the ramp, Milo heard shrieking metal and more screaming coming from the direction where they wanted to go. He guessed those who had tried the thruway had not met with success.

They had seen columns of smoke rising in the sky and the hot orange glow of flames, as if the city were a giant furnace. In several places corpses had been impaled on oily black spears and left as grisly reminders of the attack. He remembered the Sabres had been scheduled to play tonight. There would have been eighteen thousand people in and around the Arena at the time of the attack. God help them.

Now, after backing the truck away from the 190 ramp, Milo pulled into a parking lot and stopped.

"Why you stopping?"

"I'm thinking."

"Think about finding another route. Go Seneca Street."

Debbie said, "Why don't you cool it?"

"Cool it? We're sitting ducks here."

Milo rubbed his temples. "Everybody stop. Let me think!"

That quieted them down for the moment. "I say we hole up for the night. It's dark, the roads are a wreck, and there's no telling what's out there. We could run right into the things that attacked us."

"Things?" Mike asked.

Milo turned around and looked at him. "You have a better word for them?" When Mike didn't answer, Milo said, "I didn't think so."

"Hotel," Mike said. "Maybe we could all sit in the Jacuzzi, too."

"Michael," Agnes said, her eyes still closed. "Listen to the man. Listen to someone for a change."

"Don't see what good it's going to do," Mike said.

"I could use a warm bed," she said.

"I think it's going to be decided for us," Milo said. Through the rear truck window, he saw a dozen of them emerge from a parking ramp across the street. Overhead, a winged creature looped in a circle. Milo got the truck going.

They pulled around, in front of the fountain, and Milo got out. The double glass doors were locked. Milo checked over his shoulder. The freaks hadn't seen them. Yet.

Kicking the door, Milo hoped to gain someone's attention. After a few seconds, a hotel employee dressed in a white button-down and black slacks came to the door. He was a small guy with a thin goatee. "Open up. I've got more people out here."

"No way," the guy said, raising his voice to be heard through the glass.

"Open the goddamned door!" Milo said, pounding on the glass.

Now Mike had climbed out of the truck and, standing at the passenger-side door, said, "What's the holdup?"

There was probably a service or side entrance for the

hotel, but they didn't have time to find it. Milo had an idea. "You see my friend there? You don't open this door, I'm going to have him get in the truck and drive the fucking thing through the doors."

"You wouldn't."

"Mike, he won't open up. Get in the truck, start it up, and drive through the doors. They're glass. They'll give."

Mike got a huge grin on his face. "You got it." He started around to the driver's side.

The clerk said, "You'll let them in. They'll get in here if I open up."

"Place is getting opened up with or without you, chief. It's your call."

The truck engine revved. It rolled forward. The clerk's eyes grew wide and he fumbled a moment before unlocking the door. Milo put his hand up, indicating Mike should stop.

Once the doors were opened, Milo went back to the truck and between him and Mike they brought Agnes inside the hotel. Debbie was the last one in and locked the door behind them.

Milo took a look across the street. The group that had exited the parking lot was headed in the opposite direction. He looked up and saw the winged thing—a grim silhouette against the dark sky—swoop behind City Hall and disappear. They had avoided trouble, for now.

Milo eyed the clerk. "You could've got us killed."

"I was just concerned for the safety of our guests."

"We're not paying customers, right?"

"You can be asked to leave, sir."

"I'm not leaving unless you throw me out," Milo said, looking the slim clerk up and down. "And I don't see that happening."

"If you want to stay, you'll have to behave," the clerk said, and stormed across the lobby.

Mike, propping up his mother, said, "What was his problem?"

"Didn't like our proposed method of entry, I guess."

Milo looked at Agnes, who was wilting. "I'll get a blanket and a pillow for your mom. Wait here."

Milo crossed the large lobby, which had a gurgling fountain at its center. The marble floors made everything echo. Near the front desk, a group of people surrounded a television set. He stopped and said, "What's the news?"

A balding man whose suit looked like it had been pulled from a packed suitcase said, "It's everywhere. Look." He pointed to the television, as if Milo didn't know where to cast his gaze.

The view on the screen was from a television camera at about waist level. It appeared the cameraman was crouching down, perhaps trying to stay out of sight. The camera showed the HSBC arena. On fire. Flames shot from the windows that overlooked the atrium. Curls of smoke snaked into the sky. That wasn't the worst. It was the dead, stacked and piled on top of one another. A tangle of arms and legs and blood and viscera. Around the stacks of corpses, the attackers (Milo had no better way to think of them) speared and hacked the dying. The grunts and shrieks of the things came through the television speakers, along with the ragged breathing of the cameraman. How many dead? How many had gone out for a night downtown, maybe hitting Hemingway's or the Pearl Street Grill before the game, never expecting?

Milo turned away from the set.

He went to the desk and asked for a pillow and blanket. A clerk was kind enough to bring him one.

When he returned, Mike's mom was stretched out on a sofa in the lobby. Mike crouched at her side. Milo handed him the pillow and he placed it behind her head. While he did this, Milo spread the blanket over the woman. She muttered a raspy "Thanks."

"What's on the tube?"

"The HSBC's up in flames. It's a slaughter outside there."

"Oh my gosh. The hockey game," Debbie said.

Milo said, "There were hundreds dead, and that's just what I saw on the TV."

Mike sprang up from his squatting position. "Where's the fucking National Guard in all this? Why aren't we blowing these fucks into the next dimension?"

Milo didn't know the answer to that. Given the strangeness of the attackers, he didn't even know if weapons would be effective. From what he had seen, they looked like Halloween creatures come to life. They weren't from this zip code, that was for sure.

"Get some Apache choppers in here, air support, tanks. Hell, dig up Hank Fonda and John fucking Wayne and get them in here, too!"

Now the other patrons in the lobby were staring at Mike, and with good reason. Jacket unzipped, chest bare, he ranted like a televangelist looking for donations.

"Why are we just sitting here? Why don't we go out and fight them? Tell me that."

"You've seen what's happened so far. Who says we can fight them? Look at the body count," Debbie said. "And what we've seen is probably just a fraction of it."

"Doesn't this piss you off? I'm angry!" he said, and kicked the couch.

"Really? I didn't notice," Milo said.

"It scares me," Debbie said. "*You* scare me."

"*I'm* not the one wasted a bunch of people on Chippewa Street, honey."

Milo intervened. "That's enough, Mike."

"Don't tell me it's enough—"

From the couch, a weak voice said, "Michael, shut your mouth. You're upsetting people."

"This is 9/11 all over again. Worse."

"This is nothing like 9/11," Milo said.

"How can you say that?"

"It's worse. We don't know what we're up against. And it appears to be citywide, not just a building or two."

Mike's gaze went to Debbie, then to Milo. "Still, where's the National Guard? Shouldn't we be fighting back?"

"I'm not sure we can," Milo said.

"What do you mean?"

"You saw what was across the street, didn't you? The things that came out of the parking ramp?"

"Quit calling them 'things.' "

"They're not men. You didn't see them smash through the windows at the Alligator."

"We'll see what a nine millimeter has to say about it. I'll find out if they're flesh and blood."

He could see Mike was intent on doing damage to those who besieged his city. Arguing with him further would serve no purpose. "Yeah, we'll see. Let's try and get some rest, okay?"

"Yeah, rest. Hopefully your 'things' won't show up here."

Milo sat in an overstuffed armchair across from the couch. His head was starting to hurt.

CHAPTER 21

The horde surged forward—grunting, yelling, screeching. They met the steel doors of the armory with a terrific thud. The clang of their weapons as they beat the door rang through the night. From below, Jenny heard gunfire pop. The guns wouldn't kill them, but might slow them down long enough for Frank to arrive.

The others in the tower joined her. She looked up at the sky. Could've had a nice apartment, maybe with a view of the Space Needle. Sipping Starbucks lattes and watching the rain go splat on the windows of a coffeehouse. Or whatever it was you did in Seattle. That would have been comfortable, nice. But no help to her fellow Guardians.

She looked up. One of the winged creatures dove at the far turret and a streak of Light shot up and caught it square. It whirled off to the side, flapping its wings, smoking and flaming. It spun off into some tall pines and disappeared. Score one for the good guys, she thought.

Down below, the Guardians who had taken up positions at the windows began to fire blasts of Light at the attacking horde. The beams flashed and popped and soon curls of smoke rose up from the smoking bodies. Jenny caught a whiff of the burnt, dead flesh and had to stifle a gag.

She heard shrieking, and now a dozen of the airborne creatures dove, wings pinned back, whipping through the sky. Two of them streaked toward Jenny's turret. Coming fast.

When they were about thirty feet overhead, she raised her arm and warmth went through it. A bolt of Light shot out and smoked one of the creatures. It hit the rooftop, smoldering, and lay still. The other swooped in low and swiped with a claw; Jenny felt the air whoosh past. She looked at the other Guardians, who had also ducked and were leaning against the brick wall of the turret. "A little help would be nice," she said.

Jenny looked up and saw the creature climb high, disappear into a cloud, and then return with rocket force. Now the others in the turret stood up. They fired a succession of beams that missed, flew past the approaching beast, and lit up the clouds like fireworks. Still the creature came, and when it seemed for sure it would crash into them, it pulled from its dive and lit out over the trees.

It took a moment before she realized what had happened. One of the men fell down hard on his rear end. Hands grasping his throat, blood poured over them and ran down his knuckles. A pleading look crossed his face, and he tried to speak, but nothing came out. The winged one had managed to slash his throat when it made the pass.

Now the blood came in a steady stream and Jenny started toward him, intent on getting him below. The blood pumped even harder and she suspected the creature hit something major in his neck. He fell sideways, still clutching his throat. Jenny knelt at his side. The other men and women stood watching.

"Open the trapdoor. We've got to get him downstairs," she said.

But it was too late. The man gave one last choked gurgle, twitched once, and stopped moving.

Jenny got to her feet. "Stay sharp. They'll be coming around again."

She ventured a look across the roof. She counted five dead creatures on the rooftop. A look to the sky showed dozens circling. Two more broke from the loose circle and began a descent toward the northwest tower. They seemed to prefer attacking in pairs.

From below, she heard the ping of metal on metal. *How long before they got through those doors?*

The wind kicked up, stinging her cheeks.

She was coiled tight, waiting for the one that had just attacked them to return. Looking to the skies, she didn't see it circling or preparing to dive, only its brethren and the purple clouds.

The woman with her said, "Where did it go, the one that killed him?" She nodded her head toward the dead man.

"That's what worries me," Jenny said.

A quick scraping sound came from below them. Jenny saw a clawed hand grab the battlement and then the creature was hoisting itself over the edge. It went right for the woman. Leathery wings and an impossibly wide back facing Jenny, the demon grabbed the woman. It threw its horned head back and brought it forward with tremendous force. There was a pop-crunch and a short scream before Jenny saw the woman's corpse fall to the ground. It had bitten off the top half of her skull and the pink-gray mush of her brains ran onto the stone. Jenny's stomach lurched.

The other two men backed away from the creature. With one swipe of a claw, it gutted the first, and he went to his knees, holding his exposed innards. The second man, seeing this, attempted to climb the battlement and escape down the roof ladder. Raising its hand to the sky, the demon closed its fist around a club-shaped object that had not been there a moment ago. It slammed the weapon on the Guardian's head. His skull caved in and the man fell to the floor.

Now it turned toward Jenny, club in hand. Its forked tail waved in the air behind the head, like a charmed snake. The eyes glowed like hot coals. She realized it was between her and the ladder that led to the roof. For a moment she considered the trapdoor, but the attacker would rip her to pieces before she could open it. If she made it across the roof to another turret, she may have a chance.

It stepped forward and she fired a short beam, catching it in the chest. The demon hissed and beat at the wound, smoke rising from where her bolt hit. She scrambled past it, climbed over the side, and found the ladder, which she took to the roof.

On the roof, she wove her way through air-conditioning and heating units, praying she wouldn't stumble in the dark and become an easy target. She heard its feet hit the roof and took a glance. It was coming, club in hand.

She picked up her pace. A quick glance showed it gaining. The turret parallel to the one she vacated was too far. The demon would close the gap before she could reach it. A boxy air-conditioning unit was ten feet ahead. She scrambled around it and ducked down, peeking just enough so that she could see her pursuer. It charged forward and she prepared to unleash a beam, but it beat its wings and launched into the air, going up and over and landing behind her.

She whirled around to see it raise the club. Ducking low, she sidearmed a flat beam and it traveled along the ground and caught the beast's ankle. The blast tore through flesh and bone, severing the foot, and the creature wobbled and fell to its knee. It shrieked.

She darted past, and it swiped at her, the blow missing.

From behind, she heard its wings beat the air and now she was closer to the turret. "Hey! Over here! Hey!" she yelled.

She saw the moonlight reflect on a face that peeked between the battlements. *God, I hope they see me coming.*

Jenny was aware of something bearing down on her. The hairs on the back of her neck stood at attention. She wouldn't have time to turn and fire at the beast. In the distance, more of them swooped down, attacking the turret where she was headed. She thought she heard someone say, "It's Chen!"

And then she saw the bolt of Light flash from the turret, rising above her, and she heard a pop-sizzle sound as it connected with the target, the screech of the demon ringing in her ears, and someone yelling "Come on," before the weight of it flopped on her and she was pinned to the rooftop with the creature on top of her legs.

It lay perpendicular to her, on its side. There was a smoking hole in its midsection. A rotting, burning smell rose from it, and its hot-coal eyes had gone dim. She shoved it, but it wouldn't budge. She felt like an animal caught in a bear trap. *If I have to gnaw off my own leg to escape, that's really going to ruin my day.*

She looked overhead and saw more of them begin to swoop down toward the roof. Toward her.

Now she saw them, oily shapes tearing out of the clouds, swooping toward the roof. Again she shoved the demon's corpse, but she still couldn't budge it.

She remembered Lily, her mother, also a Guardian, discussing the great responsibility that came with these powers. Jenny had come to her at eleven, distraught after being startled by a spider that climbed into her bed. She had panicked, and when she was shooing the spider away, a streak of brilliant white light had flown from her fingertips and incinerated the spider. It had also set her sheets on fire, and her screams brought Lily running. Her mother grabbed Jenny out of the bed, fetched a bucket of water, and doused the flames. In the aftermath, she had held Jenny close, rocking her and stroking her hair. She had whispered, "You have been chosen, my daughter. You have a gift. And someday you will do great things with it. But it will also come with a cost. Be careful."

Apparently it had come time to pay. Now she sat up, legs still pinned. Two of the demons pulled up and gently landed on the roof. Both of them formed spears, forging them from the darkness. Their black bodies glistened. The one on the right opened its mouth. A forked tongue rolled out, and it licked its lips. They were closing, perhaps fifty feet from her.

She cast a beam at the one on the right, but her shot only grazed its wing.

They sped up their pace, their leathery wings bouncing as they moved. This would be her last stand. She might be able to get one of them.

To her surprise, they blew right past her. Twisting her back, she turned around as far she could. Behind her, the Guardians who had been in the turret were coming. A blast rocked one of the demons, putting a hole in its wing. Two more beams cut down one of them. The other reached the group of Guardians, and Jenny watched with horror as it drove its spear through one of the men, lifted him up on it, and flung the screaming victim over the side of the building. The others quickly cut the beast down.

The group, four of them, reached Jenny. A man with a wild red beard and a ponytail—she thought his name was Myron—crouched next to her.

"You okay?" he asked.

"Uh, been better. How about getting this stinking thing off me?"

"You got it."

"Thanks for coming for me, Myron."

He gave her a wink. The other men, all looking as if they could play defensive line for the Steelers, grabbed the dead creature. She recognized a few of them from the construction site where a new First Penn Bank was being put up. They lifted the corpse and tossed it aside.

Myron, he of the wild beard, grabbed her arm and helped

her up. Pins and needles danced in her legs. She did a few quick jogging motions and then they all ran to the turret before anything else swooped from the sky.

Once behind the turret walls, Jenny saw the damage: two blood-slicked bodies, facedown.

Myron was watching her and said, "They came in real fast. Sliced them up and were gone cat-quick."

"I don't know how long we can hold the roof," Jenny said.

A thump came from below, on the trapdoor. Myron crouched and opened the door. It was the ruddy face of Emma Cloon, smudged and sweat-soaked. Emma hauled herself up and Myron shut the trap door.

"What is it?" Jenny asked.

"We need help. They're breaking through the front doors."

"Those doors are solid steel," Jenny said.

"Their weapons are cutting right through."

"We'll come," Jenny said. "Go to the northwest tower, from inside. Tell them I said to come down and help defend the doors."

Emma said, "You're going to leave the roof practically unguarded."

"Don't see much difference either way. Either we fight them up here or down there."

"That's not very optimistic," Emma said.

"I'm hoping the Reverend gets here quick. Otherwise, it doesn't matter where we fight. Follow me."

With that she opened the trapdoor and led them down the ladder.

Frank and Ruby reached the edge of town. The ribbon of highway that became Routersville's main drag was littered with bodies, wrecked cars, and broken glass. Frank saw the mass of Dark Ones at the armory doors. Their grunts and yells echoed down the road. Above the armory, winged creatures dipped and dove. He heard moans and screams coming from the town, as if it were undergoing one massive agony.

Those noises troubled him, but there was another that troubled him more at the moment. The *blat-blat* of a motorcycle engine. He turned and in the distance saw a lone headlight coming toward them. It was the last biker, the one who had stopped to help his wounded buddy back near the clubhouse.

Ruby turned and saw it, too. "He's coming fast."

"I don't think I can hit him moving that fast," Frank said. "I can't until he gets closer."

Along the road were drainage ditches, and that was their best chance for an ambush. Assuming the biker hadn't spotted them on the road. "Duck into the ditch," Frank said.

He led the way, scrambling down the bank. His chest burned and his head was a throbbing ache. He made his way into the ditch and Ruby followed. The headlight slowed. It came within a couple hundred feet. Frank and Ruby plastered themselves against the ditch wall, heads below road level.

The engine quieted and cut out. Frank heard boot heels clicking on the road.

"Oh, my," Ruby whispered.

"Stay still."

He tried desperately to press himself into the earth, make himself invisible.

The steps came closer. A voice said, "Come out of there. Now."

There was no sense trying to hide. The biker must have seen them on the road. Frank stood up, his pants now sopping and caked with mud. Ruby did the same.

The biker, his slick bald head gleaming in the moonlight, held a large revolver on them. He had a pointed goatee and thick black eyebrows. Frank could smell him from here, a combination of dirt and body odor.

"C'mon, hurry the fuck up," he said.

They climbed out of the ditch and stood on the shoulder.

The biker jerked his head toward the town and said, "What the hell's going on up there?"

"The end of the world."

The thug glanced down the road. "I don't know *what* it is. What I know is you two killed my buds."

Frank had the awful urge to laugh at his use of the word "buds." Something told him that would be a fatal mistake. He bit down on his lower lip. "We can't stay here. It's dangerous."

"You aren't going anywhere," the biker said.

Ruby spoke up. "Your 'buds' had something that belonged to us. See what's going on up there?" she pointed to the armory. "You had the one thing that can maybe stop it. And we had to get it back."

"Shut up," he said, and pointed the gun at Ruby.

"Now what's this about the apocalypse?"

"The bull chips are hitting the fan," Ruby said. "That explain it for you?"

The biker looked toward the town. "What are those things flying in the air?"

"I don't have time to explain this," Frank said. "Come on, Ruby."

The biker's eyes widened. "You aren't going anywhere." Nodding toward Ruby, he said, "She's coming with me."

"Like hell," Ruby said.

The biker angled the revolver so it pointed at Ruby's lower legs. A grin that would look comfortable on a crocodile crossed his face. "I'll blow yer knees out, then you won't be able to get away while I'm going about my business." He then said in an almost conversational tone, "What you do fella?"

"What I do?" Frank asked. Perhaps he could talk his way out of this. The biker hadn't shot anyone yet.

"For a living. You her daddy?"

"No, not her daddy. And I'm a pastor."

"Even better. Hey, I got an idea. This little redhead can come over here and get down on her knees in front of me. And she's gonna suck the old hog root while the Jesus lover watches. That's only fair, right? You killed my bros."

Frank like the word "bros" even less than the previous aphorism for friends, "buds."

"Anything you try and put in my mouth'll get bit off," Ruby said.

Could he get a shot off? The danger in that was the revolver discharging and taking out Ruby at the knees. Did this sick mother really think Ruby would service him while Frank stood here and watched?

"Get over here, or I shoot her in the knees."

Frank glanced at Ruby. She flicked her hand and a ray of Light shot out but flew over the biker's shoulder and disappeared into the pines. The biker's face contorted into a look of rage. He raised the gun and fired. The blast hit Ruby square in the chest and threw her into the ditch.

"Probably wasn't worth it, anyway. Don't look like she'd like the hog root much," the biker said.

Frank looked at Ruby. Legs up on the bank, her head in the ditch, arms splayed out, staring at the stars. The sweet, down-home country girl was dead. Because of this biker scum.

The biker started to turn the gun on Frank. Frank crouched, whipped his arm forward. A beam of Light shot out. It caught the biker in his gun arm. The gun fell to the ground and the biker spun around, clutching his arm and whimpering. Frank eyed him. That girl deserved better. Had a business to run, world by the tail. He fired at the biker's leg, striking the calf. The guy fell to his knees. Sweat beaded on his bald head.

"What the fuck did you do?"

Frank fired, hit him in the other arm, then the shoulder. The biker fell to his belly and then rolled onto his back.

Frank stood over him. A burned flesh smell rose up; his skin smoked. Frank fired a bolt into his chest, finishing him.

Bastard bastard. Fucking murdering bastard (do you mean him—or you—good Reverend?). I just tortured a man and Jesus Christ will you forgive me now? Can you forgive me now? Look at him, you burned him alive, Frank. Is that what you wanted? What about mercy?

"What's become of me?" he wondered aloud.

He wanted to believe he killed the man in the heat of battle. But what about him and the other bikers? The one by the stream's head had exploded. Suddenly being a Guardian seemed to carry a heavy weight. Something pressing on his shoulders, compressing him, driving him to the ground, and he still had work to do.

He took a last look at Ruby. For now, she would have to remain in the ditch. He said a quick prayer and turned to look at Routersville. A roar rose from near the armory. He had to get up there.

Trudging at first, then breaking into a jog, he continued down Main.

Routersville's main drag was a wreck. A van lay on its side. The rear doors were spotted with blood. As Frank progressed, glass broke under his feet and the heat from a burning house to his right warmed his face. Along the side streets he heard the tramping of feet, the occasional squeal of tires, and screaming.

He carried on. The main drag was free of Dark Ones for the moment. They seemed to be concentrating on the armory and the side streets.

Frank continued to jog. His chest began to burn. At least you can still draw breath. Unlike poor Ruby.

He was perhaps a half mile from the armory, going slightly uphill. As he came to the next side street, there was a large gray Victorian home surrounded by neatly clipped shrubbery. A swing hung from a huge oak limb, the tree taking up most of the front lawn, which was hemmed in by a front gate. Frank came even with the house. He heard a high-pitched squeal. It sounded like a child, of which sex he couldn't tell.

Should I keep going? He wondered.

Another squeal, this time louder. There was no way.

He passed through the gate and climbed the steps. The glass on the front door was smashed. He opened the door. In the foyer, a coatrack lay on the ground.

He passed through the foyer and saw a rumpled piece of fabric on the staircase. It was red and shiny and wet. A second glance told him it wasn't fabric, but human skin. Dear God.

More screaming. From upstairs. He needed to hurry.

He took the stairs, stepping over the skin and gripping the polished wood banister.

At the top of the stairs, a pair of French doors stood open, and inside the room stood the Dark Ones. Four of them, crouched over a girl of about ten. She wore pink pajamas and held a stuffed rabbit. The demons jabbed their weapons at her, apparently not drawing blood—yet. Tears streamed down her face and her breath came in hitches. They were doing a damned good job of scaring her.

"Away from her!"

They turned, pale, scarred faces scowling at him.

He couldn't unleash a beam without possibly hitting the girl. It was too close.

They started forward.

Frank reached into his pocket and took out the Everlight. It began to glow, softly at first, then the white light fragmented into beams and shone like a torch. The girl lifted an arm, shielded her eyes. The demons cowered. One of them tore past Frank and ran down the stairs. The others scrambled for other rooms.

"Begone! Back to the depths with you!" He'd always wanted to say something like that.

He held the Light at his side. It dimmed slightly, but still glowed. He approached the girl. She scooted back across the plush rug and sat against a canopied bed. Clutching her stuffed animal, she gave him a look of such ferocity that he nearly backed up a step. "Get away! Get away!"

He put his free hand up, in an "it's okay" gesture. He half turned toward the French doors, listening for the demons. Heavy steps fell on the hallway floor and he saw the three remaining ones in the house flee down the stairs and out the front door. It would keep them away, but for how long?

Frank knelt beside the girl. She started to scoot away.

"I'm not going to harm you."

"What is that in your hand?"

Frank held up the light in an open palm. "It's a very powerful weapon, but a good weapon. It protects the good people of the world against evil—against the things that came in your house."

"Is it magic?"

"You might say that," Frank said. "Are you hurt?"

"Just bruised, maybe. They kicked and hit me."

"It could have been worse."

"They killed my mother," she said. "I saw them do it. One of them stabbed her."

The child would never be the same after something like this. "I'm sorry," he said. "I'm Frank. What's your name?"

"Anna."

"Do you have any other family or friends in town, Anna?"

She nodded. "My aunt's up at the armory."

"Then I guess you're coming with me."

"You're a stranger."

"I won't hurt you. You're safer with me."

"Nuh-uh. I'll hide here."

He hated to try and scare her, but time was short. "If you stay here, they'll come back for you."

Her eyes grew wide and she began to pick at the stuffed animal. After a moment, eyes downcast, she said, "Okay."

Frank stood up and offered his hand. She shook her head, preferring to stand on her own. "Can you put some clothes on quick while I wait out here? We have to walk a bit."

"Okay."

Frank stepped into the hallway and the girl closed the curtained French doors. He stood ready, muscles coiled, waiting for a possible attack. The door opened and Anna came out wearing a pink sweatshirt, Capri-style jeans, and white sneakers. She had a blue bracelet around her bare ankle.

He didn't want the child to see what waited on the stairs. It was likely all that remained of her mother. "Anna, will you let me carry you down the stairs?"

"Why?"

"There might be some bad things down there. Things you shouldn't see."

The weight of his words seemed to penetrate and to his surprise, she said, "Okay."

He picked her up, straining. She probably weighed a good seventy pounds. Did his kids really feel this heavy when he picked them up? Of course that was thirty years ago when his muscles were bigger and his belly was smaller. "Don't look until I tell you, okay?"

She buried her head in his shoulder. Her legs came down past his knees. She trembled against him and gripped his neck tightly. "Here we go kiddo, okay?"

One arm around her back and the other carrying the Light, he padded downstairs, went through the foyer, and stepped on the porch. A breeze blew, bringing with it the smell of rotting things.

He set Anna down and closed the door behind them.

"It was my mom, right? You didn't want me to see her body."

"Best not think about that."

"I didn't want to see her like that."

"No child should. We have to go. Can you stay close to me? No lagging behind, no running off?"

"I can."

"Okay."

They stepped onto the street and Anna looked up toward the armory and she began to tremble. "We're not going there. Please. Look up there."

A great mass of them swarmed around the doors like flies on trash. The winged beasts zipped down, spread wings wide, and landed almost gracefully on the roof. The constant beating of steel echoed through the night. They were at the doors.

"I have this," he said, holding up the stone. "You're safer with me."

Together they started toward the armory.

CHAPTER 22

David groaned weakly. Laura had cut away his sleeve with surgical scissors and now the rot continued to spread, almost down to his wrist. According to Ostrow, it wasn't contagious, as far as they could tell. It had been inflicted by whatever weapons the attackers carried.

Growing impatient, Laura said, "So tell us."

"This whole thing dates back to the Middle Ages. There was a man named Engel, he was a torturer and executioner, one of the most sought after in Europe. He loved what he did, and was good at it. His specialty was breaking with the wheel. He put hundreds to death, but then he started freelancing on the side. Mostly women started disappearing in a little German village near what's now Berlin. The villagers found him with a woman tied up. He was burning her with hot pokers, had already taken out her eyes. So they sentenced him."

Laura said, "Let me guess, breaking with the wheel."

"They did him in. Buried his body in a pit outside the village. There were reports it didn't stay buried. Villagers saw him walking in the moonlight, limbs twisted and broken, naked and blood-soaked."

"What does this have to do with anything?"

"Let me finish. He descended into hell. He was remade, turned into a demon. Given the power of darkness. There came reports, two years after his death, of a man with twisted limbs and pale skin who walked the night. This was in Sicily. He had others with him, hundreds like him. They'd been tortured in the bowels of hell, given powers, turned into an army. Able to forge weapons from the darkness around them."

Laura would have thought this the ravings of a lunatic, except she had seen it firsthand. "What happened to him?"

"Why didn't you ever tell me this?" Sara asked.

"You wouldn't have believed me without seeing them. Engel and his army began to terrorize the countryside. Showing up as a black cloud and materializing out of the darkness. They disappeared into caves by daytime. Villagers locked doors, livestock were slaughtered, babies and children were snatched out of beds. Meetings were held. A strange man named Sanborn appeared. He had a group of followers, the first Guardians. Sent to counter Engel. They promised to dispatch Engel and his followers. They carried a stone that radiated powerful light.

"They battled up in the mountains. Engel was defeated with the stone. They buried him with it, sealing him a cave in the mountains. He got loose when a construction road crew was doing some blasting. This was around nineteen eighty-nine."

Sara clung to the steel gurney rail. David had a rapt audience in her.

"He showed up in the States. Looking, hunting."

"For who?" Laura said.

In one of the bays, a team of nurses and doctors rushed in. Someone wheeled in a crash cart. They threw the curtain around. Someone's ticket was about to get punched.

"You."

"Why me?" Laura said.

David nodded toward Sara. "Because of her."

Sara knew it. The sidelong glances Frank and David had given her. The way she could produce the Light. The whispered conversations between the two of them that would suddenly end when Sara entered the room. And the things that had followed her.

David continued, "You're a Guardian, Sara, a very strong one. Maybe stronger than Sanborn. Your grandparents were strong, strong enough to defeat Engel."

"Wait, my father?" Laura asked.

"Your father *and* mother. Engel was getting close. People started turning up dead in Buffalo. Tortured, bones broken before they died. The cops thought they had a serial killer, but it was Engel. Your father tracked him down."

"And?"

"He buried him."

Charles Pennington was in the dark. He saw only shadow. He was on his back, arms stretched over his head and hands bound to something. He was shirtless. His body ached and burned and in a small way he was glad for the darkness, for that meant he couldn't see the extent of his wounds.

Hisses and grunts came from the shadows, no doubt the Dark Ones. He remembered being kicked, slashed, feeling blood run freely over his skin. The damage had been delivered by Engel himself, who had gotten in Charles's face, his breath smelling of grave rot, mocking Charles, asking him where his pathetic God was now. Did the oppressors ever change? Hadn't that line been uttered before, albeit to someone much greater than Charles?

He had managed to kill a few of them before they bound his arms. The beams he fired at Engel did little or no damage. He needed the stone to properly battle hell's favorite demon. He'd been a fool to come here, hoping for a quick victory.

Putting Engel in the grave had seemed easier years ago.

Seventeen years ago. The Fruit Belt Killer—or at least who the police suspected was the Fruit Belt Killer—had taken a sixth victim. A prostitute, flayed, arms and legs broken, eyes gouged out, all while still alive, at least according to the coroner. The FBI came in, brought in profilers. They found no one.

Frank had come to town. Through the years since Engel's last appearance, the Guardians had been warned. Stories had been passed down. Be vigilant for killings like this. Investigate. Frank and Charles had watched the news, picked up a police scanner. When the fourth killing happened, they rushed to the crime scene. There had been a large crowd. Frank and Charles had gotten as close as the police would allow. As the crowd nudged and jostled, Charles had felt as if he'd been watched. He turned, and saw a man at the rear of the crowd. Tall, pale face visible under the hood of a sweatshirt. The man tugged his hood lower. The wrist on his arm was malformed, as if the bone had been broken and poorly set. Charles nudged Frank. When Charles turned back around, the man was gone. Charles was sure it had been Engel.

He had returned home. Charles, his wife Sylvia, and Frank had sat at the table near the window, watching ambulances come and go at the children's hospital. They had decided to find Engel and kill him. Frank had brought the stone and had it in his palm, rubbing it and working it around.

Their break came the following week. Sylvia caught a newspaper article about a Hickory Street resident seeing strange-looking men at the abandoned Iroquois brewery. The police investigated and found nothing. Charles guessed Engel and his demons had dissolved into a cloud, disappearing before the police could arrive.

On a cool September evening, the three of them drove to the brewery. Frank killed the headlights and they drove the length of the rutted alley in silence. They stopped, got out. Frank had the stone. Sylvia stood at Charles's side. She reached down, placed a small, warm hand in his, and squeezed. He looked at her, skin smooth and beautiful in the moonlight, wishing she were safe at home.

They had heard a rustle in the rear building, a one-story brick structure with a pile of old mattresses sitting near the door. One of the windows had been smashed out and a breeze blew, whistling through the opening.

The suddenness of it startled Frank. A thing with leathery skin and huge, papery wings swooped in from above. Sylvia fried that one. Three more demons broke from the building, smashing down the door and charging forward, the pile of mattresses falling over. Frank took out two, Charles one. Engel had followed, emerging from the doorway dressed in a trench coat and filthy khaki pants. He had taken them from a victim, no doubt.

They had chased him down the alley, through the side streets that bordered the brewery, eventually winding up back at the complex. It was Sylvia who had rounded the corner first. Engel had gotten ahead, had been waiting. With a slashing arc, he brought forth an axlike weapon and struck her in the chest. Her blood stained the dirt. She fell to the ground.

It was Charles who had killed Engel while Frank tended to Sylvia. Taking the stone from Frank, harnessing its power, he fried Engel in his tracks. Frank stayed and began the process of burying Engel. Charles had rushed Sylvia to the hospital. She bled out in the car. Her last words had been, "There's leftover mac and cheese, Charles, if you're hungry."

He had dealt with the cops, who had grilled him. They didn't particularly buy his story (she had been attacked by a mugger), but they didn't charge him with anything, either.

The following morning, he and Frank had returned to the brewery. Frank had buried Engel near the wall of the brewery, the Everlight keeping him in place. With one in Engel's grave, that left the remaining stone safe in Routersville. The demons they killed had been dragged by Frank (Charles still didn't know how he managed that) and shoved behind some type of industrial press.

He had left the brewery that day with Sylvia's funeral arrangements on his mind. And how he was going to tell Laura.

Now he didn't know how long they would let him live, or what was happening in the city.

He heard footsteps. Someone squatted down in front of him. Engel's pale, angular face appeared.

"The city is dying," Engel said.

"That's what you wanted, isn't it?"

"Do you hurt?"

"No."

"Liar. Why don't you pray? Maybe your God will save you, yes?"

"And who is it you pray to?"

"My Master is greater than your false God. He's promised me a place in the new kingdom. Can you say that of your God?"

The pain started to flare up in his wounds again. "It will do me good to see you die again."

"See, your prayers are useless."

"You won't win. There are others coming to stop you."

"I'll enjoy breaking your bones," Engel said, and slipped back into the darkness.

Sara watched the man who she believed was her father doze off. Either that, or he had passed out from pain.

Her life had been a lie, or a series of secrets. She was part of some secret order hundreds of years old. Her world had been rocked, shaken, and turned upside down. She feared for Robbie. Would the things in the city be victorious, and would they spread out from here?

Laura was pacing at the side of the gurney. More wounded

staggered in, some bleeding, some with burns and bruises, still others afflicted with the same rot that was now overtaking David's arm.

Sara reached out, smoothed David's hair. Thought of the time he had taken her to Cedar Point. They had ridden every coaster in the park, the two of them screaming and laughing. Then eating pizza and candy apples and David/Dad winning her a giant stuffed Garfield by knocking over milk cans. That had been good. That had been her and Dad. You wished the sun would never set on a day like that. Now he was dying. And he wasn't who she thought. But should that matter? Her real father had gotten a quickie from Laura and never been seen again. But David *had* lied. For good reason though, right?

Laura continued to pace.

"How are you?" Sara asked.

"Fine."

"No, you're not."

"Okay, not, then. You're really observant, huh?"

"Look, don't snap at me."

"I didn't snap," Laura said.

"Did, too."

Laura didn't answer. She stopped pacing and was watching David with a look that made Sara want to hide the sharp objects.

"He's a good man," Sara said.

"He took you from me. Any idea what that feels like?"

"What about me, Laura? I've been lied to for sixteen years. This whole thing is fucked up."

"Watch your mouth."

Sara rolled her eyes. "Okay, messed up. I'm not exactly loving him right now, either."

"I'm calling the cops."

"Think they're a little busy right now, don't you?"

"He belongs in jail."

"He's suffering enough. He tried to save me, Laura. Doesn't that count for something?"

Laura's eyes welled up. She covered her mouth. "I'm trying to help him, it's my job, but—" A sob escaped her. "I've had dreams. Two or three a week. You're there in my dream, and it's so real, and I wake up and you're gone. Oh, God you're right. It'll be bad for him." She backed against the wall opposite David's gurney and slumped to the floor, knees up to her chest.

Sara sat next to her, put her arm around Laura, who rested her head on her newfound daughter's shoulder and quietly sobbed.

Jenny and the others descended into the turret's upper room, which housed a pool table, leather sofa, and an old Defender video game. Jenny guessed it was some sort of officers' lounge at one time. Once inside, Jenny locked the hatch, then exited the room, locking that door, as well. She hoped the door would hold the winged creatures—if only temporarily.

She could hear the beating of metal and shouting. Rifle fire popped. A shotgun boomed and she heard high-pitched squealing.

Jenny, Myron, and the others wound their way through the armory's many corridors and stairways, winding up at the balcony that overlooked the main drill hall. Jenny pressed herself against the polished wood banister and looked at the battle.

She caught a whiff of cordite. That, and the stink of them burning. Through the film of smoke in the air she saw the main doors. A man-size hole had been cleaved in the steel. Pale arms, some of them clutching black spears and swords, jutted through the door. A host of Guardians opposed them at the doors, firing beams and driving at least some of them back.

It appeared to be too many, however.

The doors strained inward, the sheer mass of the demons making them buckle.

"We'll stay here, fire down on them when they break through."

"You mean *if* they break through?" Myron asked, scratching his beard.

"No, I meant when. Be ready."

Myron and the others positioned themselves along the railing.

The doors pressed inward with a hollow boom. She guessed the bulk of the Dark Ones were backing up, gaining momentum, then charging the doors with the hope of battering them open.

Jenny heard footsteps and looked to see someone approaching along the balcony. It was a woman. Jenny didn't recognize her. Blood streamed from her head. She staggered up to Jenny, who steadied the woman. Her face was ashen, her forehead slicked with sweat.

"The rest are dead," she said. "They've taken the roof."

The end was close, then.

Jenny helped the woman, helping her sit against the wall and taking off her jacket, instructing her to hold it against the cut on her head. Then she returned to the railing

The doors gave with a huge crash, and the wave of demons poured into the main hall. The line of Guardians attempting to hold the main door opened up, firing beams, cutting down the initial line of attackers and creating a small pile of bodies. The Guardians retreated, backing up and continuing to fire. Those at the windows, now behind the breaching demons, blasted away with rifles and shotguns. The bullets seemed to have little effect.

The Dark Ones surged ahead. Jenny took aim and fired at

a tall lurching demon with yellow eyes. She caught it in the chest and blew it off its feet.

That was one down, anyway.

Now they came forward, the ones with spears driving their weapons into the front line of Guardians. She saw one man impaled, and as his back arched and his arms flailed, more Dark Ones surrounded him and hacked off his hands.

Jenny kept firing, as did Myron and the Guardians who had been in the turret with her. She hit three more, but it was merely a few grains of sand removed from a beach.

There were just too many.

Anna remained quiet and looked straight ahead. She was avoiding the sight of bodies at the curb. Perhaps they were friends or relatives. She kept a fierce grip on Frank's hand and a few times he had to give her a gentle tug to keep her moving.

They moved down the main drag, passing bars, a barbershop, and Ruby's diner, its red neon sign dimmed. It seemed appropriate, for its owner was gone and would not be returning.

He heard shuffling noises in the road behind him. More of the Dark Ones arrived on Main Street. They were apparently done ravaging the neighborhoods. Many of them held grisly trophies: severed heads, arms, one item that he tried to convince himself was a doll but was most likely a dead baby. He picked up his pace, walking steadily, hoping they didn't see him. Anna moved along with him. She turned and saw them and opened her mouth, a piercing firebell of a shriek leaving her.

Frank turned. The scream had caught their attention. Frank kneeled, placed his hands on Anna's shoulders. "No more of those, okay?"

Staring blankly, she nodded.

Now the throng of them charged up the street. Frank and the girl broke into a run. He wanted to get close enough to the armory, then pull out the light and drive them off for good.

Jenny saw it coming, and it looked mad as hell.

The creature, jet black with glowing red orbs for eyes, tucked its wings back and stepped through the opening to the balcony. It was perhaps fifty feet away. Myron saw it, too, and exclaimed, "Jumpin' Jesus, we're getting it from both sides!"

Jenny decided to take the winged beast. Coming at her, it spread its wings, which were lined with tendons and grayish veins. It held a double-bladed ax.

She was quite sure she was going to die. Hopefully it would be quick, perhaps one quick stroke of the ax. That was all you could hope for at this point, wasn't it?

She raised her hand and a rope of white Light flew from her fingers. The demon raised the ax and with the blade deflected her beam. It ricocheted with a sizzle-hiss and bounced off the brick wall and faded. She fired twice more and both times the winged creature turned the blasts aside. Now it advanced, confident. She noticed two more coming up behind it.

She let it get closer. It raised the ax over its head, holding it two handed. Still it came closer. She tensed, crouched. If she timed this wrong she would be split in two.

The demon broke into a run, its wings beating against its back. As it closed in she flung herself to the side and flattened against the wall. The ax fell and embedded itself in the balcony's hardwood floor. It was now stuck and the creature struggled to free its weapon. Jenny moved in close, and with Light glowing from her fingertips, she thrust her hand into its flank and ripped across its gut. Its steaming gray innards tumbled out. It fell to its knees, trying to gather its guts. She finished it off with a blast to the head and it tottered sideways and died.

That left the other two, who were almost upon them. She yelled to Myron, who was preoccupied with the battle below. He turned, eyes wide. The demon was upon him. It picked him up, claws digging into his chest, and threw him over the balcony. His arms and legs flailed and Jenny was partially grateful for the din below, for she didn't hear Myron smack against the floor.

One of the other Guardians turned but was too late. The second demon ran her through with a spear and yanked it out. She fell to the ground, blood seeping into her sheepskin jacket. Jenny spied the woman who had told them the roof had fallen, the one with the gash on her head. She had curled up like a turtle and pressed herself against the wall. So far it had worked. She had remained invisible to the Dark Ones.

Jenny backed against the wall. There was nowhere to run. It was just her and the bricks. They approached her side by side, one of them holding a spear.

She raised her arm. The one on the right crouched. Jenny fired. Her shot glanced off the tip of its wing. The one on the left chugged ahead and before she could turn and fire, it plastered its full weight against her, driving Jenny almost through the wall. Her back smacked the bricks. For a moment the thick stench of the creature was overwhelming. It kept her pinned to the wall. She struggled, kicking and screaming.

A clawed hand closed around her waist and she got the sense it was strong enough to snap her spine. She saw a dagger with a jagged blade in its hand. There was nowhere to go.

"I've made a fool of myself," Laura said, wiping tears from her face with her sleeve.

"Nah," Sara said.

"I don't like him. I need to help him, but I want to hurt

him for what he did at the same time. Does that make sense?"

"I can see why you're mad."

David's head lolled back and forth, making a rustling noise on the pillow. A short moan escaped his lips. A light sweat had broken out across is forehead, making it shine. He opened his eyes, watching the two women.

"Do you want to hear the rest?" David asked.

Laura supposed she did. The two of them went to the gurney's side. Before David began, Laura flagged down a passing nurse, an African American woman in purple scrubs. The woman hugged a clipboard against her chest.

"Get some vitals on him. He's going to be staying."

"I'll get to him as soon as I can," she said, and hurried off.

If they got to David, Laura thought. She didn't like this man but the thought of him dying alone in a hospital corridor bothered her. He didn't deserve that.

"What are Guardians?" Sara asked.

"They're the answer to the Dark Ones. Are they sent from heaven? I don't know. It started with Sanborn and his wife. They had fourteen children. The line of Guardians continued to the present day, passing down their knowledge of Engel and the Dark Ones, always on guard for them."

"How do I fit?"

Laura interrupted. "She's one of these Guardians. My parents were. Why don't I have this ability?"

"It sometimes skips a generation. Not sure why. My parents didn't have it, either," David said.

"My mother was one, too, then," Laura said. How the hell did they keep that from her?

"Right."

"Why did you take Sara from me?"

"I didn't. But Engel was close. She wasn't safe. Your father suspected Sara might be like Sanborn—incredibly gifted, powerful. It wasn't until after Engel's death, when Sara was about two, that we knew. She showed powers at a very young age. Usually they don't manifest until the teen years."

"That *we* knew?" Laura asked.

"I didn't take Sara," David said."

"The boogeyman got her then, right?"

"I don't believe in the boogeyman," David said.

"Why did you do it?"

"She was brought to me, Laura," he said, and weakly cleared his throat.

What he had done to her was bad enough. Now he was being coy. "By who, FedEx?"

"By your father. He arranged the abduction. That letter you found under my mattress, Sara? It was from Charles. He typed it, didn't sign it. Told me to take good care of you and never let the truth out."

Laura had a moment where everything went silent. She didn't hear the moans of the injured, nor the shuffle of footsteps on the tiled hospital floor. It was like being in a vacuum. She looked at David's face, seeing every pore, a small mole on the cheek, his brown whiskers growing in. He looked back at her with something like pity. That news was like a train. You're standing on the tracks, unaware. And here it comes, the Amtrak special, and it hits you and sends you flying. All she could manage was a soft, "That son of a bitch."

"He did it to protect her."

"This Engel would have killed me?" Sara asked.

"Yes. We also think you're our only chance against him. Because of your abilities, you can use the Everlight as a weapon."

"The Ever-what?"

"The stone that gives the Guardians their powers. It can drive off the Dark Ones in the hands of regular Guardians. But there's people like you, who show the power as toddlers, who can use it to cut down the enemy. Engel included."

Laura felt a little dizzy, detached, as if she were watching herself and David and Sara have a conversation. Not unlike the sensation that followed a dose of cold medicine.

"The Everlight kept Engel in the grave. It was disturbed when the brewery was torn down."

That comment snapped Laura out of things. "That's why he was so adamant about that damned brewery. And why he told me to leave town."

"There's one other stone left, in Routersville, Pennsylvania, a Guardian stronghold. Reverend Frank Heatly is looking for it. Probably battling the Dark Ones right now."

"Then we need to leave," Sara said. "He's going to be looking for me, isn't he?"

"Yes, but you can't leave. You have to find the Everlight."

"And what if I do?"

"Use it to kill Engel."

That was crazy. "You want her to what?"

"The stone was hauled away when the brewery was demolished. The debris was taken to Brown Recycling near Elk Street. Your dad found that out. It's one of the last times we heard from him."

She had started off wanting to find Dad very badly. Now she wasn't sure she wanted to see his face at all. Or that she could look at him without wanting to slap his face. That was terrible, wasn't it?

"You have to go there, Sara," David said. "Find the stone. It will be glowing. Then track down Engel. Use it to kill him."

A panicked look crossed Sara's face. "I can't do this. How do I find him? How do I use it? Those things will kill me."

"They haven't killed you yet. You're our hope, Sara. If he succeeds, his army will move on. Killing until the only ones left are him and his demons. It will be the end of all things."

"I'm not risking losing her again. We're getting out of the city."

"Go at dawn. They can't come out in the light."

David's head lolled again and he went back into a Demerol-and pain-induced sleep.

The wall pressed hard against Sara's back. The emergency room corridor had grown stuffy and hot. Her face felt flushed, her ears hot. She looked at Laura, who sat next to her. Her hair, drawn in a ponytail, had gone frizzy on the sides. Even so, she was still beautiful.

Right after David had nodded off, Sara had watched Laura check his wound. The look on her face said everything; David's condition was dire.

A nurse's aide wheeled an X-ray machine past, and a pair of black-clad paramedics came down the main corridor with an elderly man on their gurney. He was wearing an oxygen mask; his shirt was spotted with blood.

So much suffering, Sara thought. And I can end it. Maybe it wasn't an accident she came to Buffalo when she did. Perhaps whatever force had created the Guardians had given her a little nudge in the right direction.

Laura started rubbing her temples.

"I think we should go find it," Sara said.

"Find what?" she asked, still rubbing.

"The Everlight."

"Are you crazy?"

"What other hope do we have?"

"Someone will come. The National Guard, the army."

"You really think so? Most of them are cleaning up Bush's folly in Iraq. Besides, what can they do? I doubt bullets are much good right now."

"And if we do find it?"

"We'll figure that out. Kill this Engel."

"We need to find my father and go."

Laura still wasn't looking at her. Her head was down and she was still massaging her temples, as if she had the world's worst headache. Maybe she did. But how would running help them? If this whole thing spread beyond Buffalo, as David had said it would, would they be safe? "And if they get out of Buffalo and continue across the country, then what?"

"We'd be going right into the lion's den, so to speak."

"They'll take over the city."

Now Laura stopped rubbing her temples and looked at Sara. Sara could see a storm brewing in her eyes, sensed she wouldn't budge on the issue.

"We're getting out," she said. "That's final."

"I'll go myself, then."

"You can't. You'll be with me."

"Don't you want to stop this from getting worse?"

Laura drew herself up on her knees. "Getting killed won't stop this."

"You heard David," Sara said. "I'm especially powerful."

Laura laughed, a harsh snort. "Especially powerful, huh? You see all this?" she held her hand out, palm up, indicating the emergency room. "Those things did all this. To a whole city. You think you can stop them?"

Laura looked at David, whose skin had taken on a milky shade of white. He had lied to her, yes. But he was also a father to her. And now he was dying and she felt helpless and scared and, except for Laura, alone. The past sixteen years had been lies. She had only Robbie in Indiana, and what did that mean? If she returned home, they would wait, watching the Dark Ones spread like cancer, marching across the country and swallowing towns and villages whole. No, she didn't want to go out like that.

"Well, do you?" Laura asked.

She stood up. "I'm going to wait here with him until dawn. Then I'm heading out to find the Everlight. If we wait, or we run, we're doomed."

"You don't even know where the recycling yard is."

"I'll ask."

Now Laura stood up. There was a gleam in her eyes that

Sara saw in a person one other time. It had been ninth grade, and Candace Summers, all two hundred pounds of her in a pink jogging suit, had insisted Sara get out of her cafeteria chair. Sara had stood up, looked her in the eye, seen that same angry gleam. Right before Candace had coldcocked her and she flopped to the cafeteria floor, the world spinning and her head feeling all syrupy. She didn't think Laura would deck her, but she was prepared for a fight.

"You won't go anywhere. I'll send the cops out after you."

"I think they've got better things to do than hunt down runaways."

"You're impossible, you know that. Stubborn thing."

"I'm going. Please come."

"You're just like me, you know that? Goddamn dig in and fortify your position, that's what you're doing."

"Will you come?"

"We're leaving. That's it. No heroics."

"How can we just stand by knowing we can change things?"

"It would kill me if it happened again," Laura said.

"I won't let it. I'll be careful."

Laura frowned. "It's not in your control. You saw what they did."

"I can drive them off, protect myself."

"You're staying put."

Sara didn't see any point in arguing any further. She got up and went over to the gurney. David had gotten worse. The blackness had crawled up his neck and overtaken his ear, which now appeared as a blackened lump. She watched it for a moment, careful not to touch, and swore it spread right before her eyes.

Just take him, Lord. Please. Stop his heart. Anything to make it stop.

But it wouldn't, would it? And she doubted the Good Lord could do such a thing. Or would do such a thing. But why make someone suffer, especially someone who had done good? And where was He right now? Why were the abominations allowed to torture and kill and pillage? She supposed smarter people than her had tried to answer those questions for ages. And those who were on the *Titanic*'s decks and faced drowning in the icy Atlantic, or those who were led into gas chambers in Treblinka and Auschwitz no doubt asked the same questions. But what was the answer? Would there ever be one?

For now she could only watch. And hope that it didn't hurt David too badly.

Laura said, "I know you want to do something, but I can't lose you again. Do you understand that?"

"I understand."

CHAPTER 23

When they'd been at the hotel for three hours, Mike had heard a boom that rattled the windows. It sounded like something big going up. Maybe a crashing airliner, or one of the refineries on River Road being blown to hell.

The number of wailing sirens had died down. Mike went to the front door, where they had piled up couches, tables, and chairs in a makeshift barrier. There was a small triangular opening where a sofa arm and an end table came together, and he peered outside. He saw only the fountain and Milo's truck. But he smelled the acrid tang of wood burning and knew it wasn't a campfire, but part of downtown Buffalo going up in flames.

He returned to find Debbie pulled up in a chair next to Agnes. She was holding Agnes's hand. The old woman's skin was as thin as tissue paper and her veins snaked across the tops of her hands.

"Hey," he said. "Thanks."

Debbie looked genuinely puzzled. "For?"

"Holding her hand like that. You didn't have to, but you did. I appreciate it."

"It's all right."

"No, it isn't. It isn't anywhere fucking near all right. Won't ever be again, either."

Milo, who sat in an overstuffed chair, said, "You don't know that."

"You hear the news? That TV's loud enough to wake Rip Van Winkle, so I know you must've. They're everywhere. Killing whatever gets in the way. That's why I know."

"Help will come," Milo said.

"Yeah, John Wayne and his merry bunch of Indian slayers, right? Ride right through that fountain."

"What's with you and John Wayne? That's the second time you referenced him."

"The whole cavalry come to the rescue thing, you know."

"They might come yet."

Mike waved him off. He didn't know if this was the apocalypse or if someone had forgotten to lock the gates to hell, but he'd wished he'd spent more time praying at St. Stephen's instead of robbing corner stores. In all likelihood they were finished. He didn't think they had much chance of reaching his house and getting Mom her medication. Hell, it might not even help her.

But he had to try. Had to. He'd screwed everything else up to this point. He was not one for irony, but he had to chuckle when he realized the condos they had been sent to burn were going to be destroyed anyway. So Schuler was dead and Mike had been tortured and here they sat waiting for the end of the world. If he didn't feel like crying so much, he'd laugh. A real belly buster, too.

"They've stayed away from here," Mike said. "What do you think that means?"

"Not enough victims in one place?"

"Long as they keep away," Milo said.

"We'll leave at dawn for my house. It can't be as bad during the day, right?"

Milo didn't answer him.

In Routersville, Frank removed the Light from his pocket. He held it up and the beams radiated out in points that seemed to go on for miles. Had he been as powerful as Sara, or perhaps the original Guardians, he could have turned it into a devastating weapon. As it was, the effectiveness would be measured in fear—on the faces of the demons.

The ones approaching from behind stopped. Some of them grunted and twisted in spasms. Others covered their eyes. Some dropped to their knees and crawled away. Another group fled, shrieking and howling in a language Frank couldn't even begin to understand.

Holding the girl close against his hip, he advanced toward the armory. She let out a soft mewling noise and he comforted her, saying, "It's okay."

The Dark Ones, now crowded in front of the armory's brick walls and trying to squeeze into the breached doors, began to take notice of the Light. Those at the rear turned and some went running off into the woods. More wailing rose from the horde. Frank continued, willing his legs to move against fear that wanted him rooted to the ground.

He advanced, and the throng before him parted, blotted out by the pure white beams from the Everlight. Ahead he could make out the gashed-open door and a pile of pale corpses. He made his way through, the girl at his side, and stepped over the bodies and into the armory's main hall.

In the flood of Light, he saw the dark shapes coming toward him, not to attack, but to get away from the Light and hurry out the door. "To hell with you all," he muttered.

Jenny was aware of a shift in the crowd below. A string of inhuman yells rose to the balcony. The winged beast, which a moment ago had been intent on running her through with its dagger, dropped her and turned its back toward the sounds of chaos.

She took the opportunity to aim between its wings and unleash a blast of Light. Its back arched and it fell to its knees, trying to reach around its back, as if to plug the hole the blast had caused. It fell aside, trickling yellowish fluid from the wound.

After she killed the demon, she saw the Light shining in the main hall. Spears of pure white, tinged with the slightest golden hues. It reminded her of the sunlight streaming through the stained-glass windows at Blessed Sacrament she had seen as a girl. She had never been so glad to see something in all her life.

The winged demons that were streaming onto the balcony saw the Light and retreated. Two of them hurdled over the balcony rail, flapped their wings, but not having enough space, fell to the floor. Jenny took the opportunity to fire at the ones retreating back to the turret and the safety of the roof. She caught one in the back, a glancing blow. It bellowed and kept going.

Now, she looked over the railing and saw Frank standing in a wash of Light. The demons that had breached the main hall were gone. Frank stood among hell's dead and fallen Guardians. When the hall was clear, Jenny helped the wounded woman, who was slumped against the wall. They took the stairs to the main hall and joined Frank.

He had lowered the Everlight and now the hanging lights in the main hall provided the only illumination.

Jenny helped the wounded woman, removing the woman's jacket, easing her to the floor, and placing the jacket under her head as a makeshift pillow. "We'll get you some help."

A crowd gathered around Frank. Jenny spotted Dottie Flores, who was a nurse at Dr. Masters's office. She motioned for Dottie to come over and attend to the woman. Dottie knelt at the woman's side and began tending to her wounds.

Jenny saw the girl at Frank's side. She was thin and blond and had a faded summer tan. "Who's your friend?"

Frank, his hair wild and sweaty, said, "I pulled her from a house on Main. She was the only one inside."

"What's your name, honey?"

"Anna."

"Nice to meet you, Anna, I'm Jenny."

The girl gave her a weak smile and crossed her arms.

"They'll come back," Frank said. "The Light will keep them away, but not for good."

"What are you thinking?"

"I need to go to Buffalo, and I could use backup. What do you think?"

"Who will stay here and lead? What about Ruby?"

Frank opened his mouth as if to speak, then closed it.

"What about Ruby?" she repeated.

"She's gone. One of the Warlords killed her. Shot her point-blank."

The Warlords had been allowed to ride and pillage unchecked. Aside from the occasional harassment from the local cops, they did as they pleased. Now they had killed a lovely person. Ruby had a smile for everyone who walked through the diner doors. Didn't matter if you were a lifelong Routersvillian or just passing through. She would be missed. "I'll find someone."

"We need to round up a search party, go down into the town, and bring back any survivors."

"And hole them up here."

Frank shook his head. "We need to leave. The Light is coming with me. I need to find Sara."

"Where did they go?"

Frank motioned for her to follow and she did. They looked out the main doors. The cloud that had brought them had retreated past the edge of town. The demons themselves had disappeared into the dark mist.

"They're waiting."

"Then let's get moving."

Frank and Jenny gathered the remaining people in the armory, Guardians and non-Guardians, and explained the need to rescue survivors and then leave town. Frank divided the town into four quadrants and assigned rescue parties to each. He gave them two hours to bring back as many as they could and advised them to let people know they had to get out of town. After what had just occurred, he didn't think that would be a hard sell.

The search parties dispatched, he and Jenny sat at a long rectangular table in the mess hall. Dottie Flores had dressed his chest wound and checked him for a concussion. He still had a mild throb pulsing through his head, but thought he would live. He and Jenny had dined on cans of microwaveable stew, washing them down with warm 7-UP.

Anna had been reunited with her Aunt Marcie, who had been one of the lucky ones who took refuge in the armory. Something had gone right this evening, anyway.

"How long do you think before they come back?" Jenny asked.

"No way to tell."

"Then the town will fall."

"It will."

"We worked so hard all these years to keep our secret. It was truly ours—I mean Routersville—right?"

"There was no standing up to that force without the Everlight."

"I wish we could've killed more."

"You did what you could."

They finished eating, and for the next two hours Frank helped out in the main hall, moving bodies and tending to the wounded as best he could. A few ambulance crews from town had arrived, and he informed one of the medics about Ruby and where to find her body. She should be given a decent burial and her family notified, Frank thought.

The wounded were taken up to the County General, the dead covered and laid outside the armory. Upon returning, the rescue crews informed Frank that most of the surviving residents were fleeing town, a convoy of cars snaking up the main road, headed away from where the cloud had originated.

Frank asked one of the Guardians, a moose of a man named Henry, to notify the state police as soon as Frank was gone. They could come down and figure out what to do with the bodies. Someone had to do it.

He and Jenny left the armory at five thirty in the morning in a borrowed GMC Yukon. They headed to her house in the pink glow of the early morning sunrise, where she packed a bag. He wolfed down some instant oatmeal and orange juice, showered and changed his clothes, and the two of them left, driving back through Routersville and heading for the thruway entrance.

On his way, Frank surveyed the destruction. Windows had been broken out of the restaurants and bars, most likely so the people inside could be dragged out. A crew of firefighters sprayed water on the burning East Towne Grill. There were about a dozen wrecked cars, either overturned or smashed into light poles. Frank felt an overwhelming sense of despair. If all this destruction came from an attack that had lasted hours, what would happen if They began to move across the country?

He thought of Sandra and hoped she had heeded his warning to leave for the mountains. The thought of her holed up, perhaps with the furniture stacked against the door as the murderous demons attempted to get in, broke his heart. She would die as so many others had, her last moments panicked and frenzied, perhaps wondering how this could all be happening.

Now, Frank pulled out of town.

From the passenger seat, Jenny said, "What are you thinking?"

"About my wife. If she'll be safe. I told her to head to a cabin in the mountains."

"Probably better off than in one of the cities."

"I don't want her to end up like the others."

"She won't."

"We'll see."

CHAPTER 24

Milo awoke, neck stiff, head lolled to one side. He had slept in the armchair all night and was paying the price. He massaged his neck, trying to work out the kink. He had a feeling it would be there all day. He saw Mike's mother asleep on the sofa. Her chest still rose and fell, which meant she had made it through the night. Mike lay on the floor next to the couch, a white pillow under his head. Apparently he had either swiped it or asked the staff for one. Milo would bet that he swiped it.

Debbie was curled up in a chair opposite Milo's. She had one arm tucked under her head. It reminded him of the way she had slept as a little girl. Until she was ten or eleven, he would always peek in on her before he went to bed. No matter if she was on her side or back, the one arm was always tucked under. He remembered thinking with her eyes closed, lips slightly parted, and her hair spread across the pillow, she had looked like one of heaven's own angels. He could have stood there and watched her sleep all night, his love for her swelling in his chest until he thought it would burst.

That little girl was now in college and engaged. When the

hell did that happen? She had played a dirty trick: She had gone and grown up.

Milo rose from the chair and looked around. Some of the other refugees in the hotel now rose, massaging their backs and stretching, no doubt sore from evenings spent on the floor. There had been no vacancy at the hotel—he'd checked.

Milo looked toward the front doors and saw a pretty Indian woman in a navy blue hotel uniform standing there. She had her hands wrapped around a Styrofoam cup. A stainless-steel carafe and stack of cups were on the ground at her feet.

Milo joined her at the door. "Morning."

She favored him with a radiant smile and said, "Good morning. Would you like some coffee?"

Coffee sounded fantastic. "You're officially my new best friend. Milo."

"Amala," she said. She picked up the carafe and a cup and poured Milo a coffee. Then she handed it to him. He sipped it and it was hot and strong.

Amala said, "The sky is strange."

"What do you mean?"

"Look through the opening."

Milo peered through the opening in the furniture barricade. The first thing he noticed was his truck was still in one piece, for which he was grateful. It was dim outside, the way it got before a bad thunderstorm. But the sky wasn't cloudy. Then he realized it was because he couldn't see any sky, only a dome of darkness that towered over the city.

"Can you help me move some of this?" Milo said. "I want to have a better look."

"Is that safe?"

"I think so. Something tells me these things operate in the dark."

Milo and Amala set down their cups and spent a few minutes moving the furniture. When the door was clear, Milo took a last look and stepped outside. Amala followed him.

He looked up and saw blackness. It was the mist that had

swept through the city last night, except now it hovered. The sun was barely visible through it, like a lightbulb through a piece of dark cloth. Looking across the street and to the south, he saw the same mist in the distance, a wall of it. Hundreds of feet high. It had effectively surrounded the city, blotting out most of the sun.

"Freaky," Milo said.

"Excuse me?"

"Strange."

"I'm going back in to serve coffee."

Across the way, a white pickup truck rolled down South Elmwood. In the bed were a group of people, most of them dirty and bloodstained. The truck stopped at a light. They were most likely going to head over the Skyway and into Lackawanna, maybe hoping for an escape route that way. He noticed the shell-shocked looks on their faces and wondered what horrors they had witnessed last evening.

He heard the *whap whap* of a chopper, faint and then louder, and he looked up and saw the outline of it through the mist. It was hard to tell, but he thought it was military. Perhaps Uncle Sam was coming to the rescue after all. It rumbled overhead and then flew off into the distance.

He stepped back inside and closed the doors. He picked up his cup and drank the last of his coffee. He then discarded the cup in a trash can. Across the lobby Amala cheerfully served coffee, that wonderful smile on her face. He hoped a woman that lovely had someone nice waiting for her at home. That was a feeling he missed: having someone to greet him when he came home from a day on the excavator.

Mike stirred and sat up. He ran a hand through his hair.

"What's up?"

"Sky's blotted out."

"What?"

"The mist that rolled through the city last night? It's covering us like a dome."

"So?"

"That stuff ate through one guy's skin, damned near melted him. Nobody's getting in or out as long as it's there."

"What about the freaks?"

"No sign of them yet."

"So what now?" Mike asked.

"We go to your place, arm ourselves, find a place to hunker down before dark."

They waited for the others to wake up. Debbie got up next, followed by Mike's mom. The hotel staff brought out croissants and muffins, along with orange juice and more coffee. After waiting in line, Mike and Milo brought back food. They all sat in the lobby and ate, nobody talking. In the background, Milo heard the television droning on. Apparently the National Guard was on the outskirts of the city at the old Ogden toll barriers. They were trying to figure out if they could penetrate the mist.

Milo felt sorry for the poor bastard who was going to be the guinea pig for that experiment.

The free food eaten, Mike and Milo helped his mother to the truck while Debbie went ahead and opened the door. Once in the truck they weaved through downtown, Milo driving. There was little traffic, but there were stragglers on the streets. He saw looters carrying computer monitors, a forlorn woman pushing what looked like a dead child in an umbrella stroller, a rag-clad homeless man with a shopping cart full of pop cans (he hoped the guy got his nickel's worth), and several people just walking around, blank looks on their faces, as if wondering where to go, what they should do. *Get the hell off the streets, that was what.*

They had to weave through some wrecks, and got held up on Seneca where an ambulance and fire truck had responded to an accident. There was a sheet-covered body in the road, and next to it the twisted remains of a red hatchback.

They arrived at Mike's house a half hour after the auto accident cleared out. Milo saw more corpses on the drive than he did in the hell that was Dak To. It was possible to disassociate a bit, because these weren't members of his unit, but it didn't make it any less disturbing. Most of the corpses he'd seen looked as if they'd been savaged. Limbs and noses and ears hacked off, bellies opened, and guts lying on their laps.

Milo and Mike stood on the front porch of Mike's house. Milo looked down the street at the stacks of cars and rusted steel in the scrapyard, thinking this was a hell of a place to grow up in. Kids were supposed to have green grass and playgrounds, not junkyards. Debbie and Agnes remained in the truck. Mike had asked Milo to come on the porch with him.

"There's a body in the house," Mike said.

"The freaks get it?"

"That guy Hark that was after me? They got here, offed my mom's aide."

"So you're saying?"

"We'll move her."

Milo scanned the street one more time. Other than a few parked cars, the street was deserted. It appeared the destruction that had taken place downtown had not come to the Valley.

The wind picked up, chilling the back of Milo's neck. He wanted to get inside, but didn't relish moving a corpse. "What about the neighbors, they home?"

"Now you're thinking. Let's try the Hoolihans'."

As they descended the steps, Milo heard a whoosh-roar overhead and looked up to see the outline of a fighter jet through the mist. "Think they'll bomb them?"

"At least someone's shown up."

"They won't get through the mist," Milo said.

"We'll see."

Mike and Milo climbed the porch steps at the Hoolihans'.

The front door was adorned with Indian corn. Mike rang the bell and they waited for someone to answer, but no one came. He rang it a second time and after no one answered, Mike said, "I'll go in." He slowly opened the door and went inside. Milo followed him. They went through the entire house and found no one. After finding it empty, they brought in Agnes and Debbie. They laid Agnes on the couch and covered her with a rainbow-colored afghan. Mike went next door to get her meds and his guns.

While Mike was gone, Debbie and Milo raided the fridge, finding bagels, cream cheese, and orange juice. They brought them into the living room. Agnes refused the food with a weak, "No thanks," so Milo and Debbie dug in.

Mike returned with two sleek handguns tucked under his arm and a plastic grocery bag filled with brown pill bottles. Mike gave Agnes the pills and she popped them. He went to the kitchen and got her a glass of water, which she used to wash them down. "You're a good boy when you want to be, Mike."

"Rest, Mom, okay?" Mike said.

When they had finished the bagels and juice, Milo said, "Where do we go now?"

"Help will be along. You saw that fighter," Mike said.

"They won't get through."

"How do you know?"

"It ate through someone," Milo said. "The shit actually melted some poor bastard's face."

"The army has chemical suits," Mike said.

Debbie gave a harsh laugh. "Lot of good it'll do them."

"They'll come for us," Mike said.

Maybe or maybe not. They seemed safe here for now. But what would happen when the sun went down? They couldn't fortify the house well enough to resist an attack. Even if they plastered plywood over the windows and nailed the doors shut, it wouldn't be enough.

"So what do you propose?" Mike asked.

"We get some supplies and get to a high building, like we said. Move during the day. Wait for help." Or forever, he thought. Help may or may not come, but they weren't getting out of the city and the house wasn't safe.

"What about my mom?" Mike asked.

Agnes said, "Let me rest a bit, then we'll go."

"I don't think we should move you," Mike said.

"We can't stay here, Michael."

Mike took her hand, squeezed, and let go. "So where then?"

Sara awoke to the sounds of someone wheezing. No, not wheezing, but gasping, bubbling, and choking for breath. She had been curled up on the emergency room floor using her jacket as a pillow. Head fuzzy, she stood up. Laura was gone.

The sounds came from David. His chest heaved, rising and falling with alarming rapidity. Mouth open, he strained for breath, but could make only liquidy gurgling noises. As if that weren't torture enough, the skin affliction had wound its way up the side of his neck and something black and crusted had taken over the side of his face. It seemed to pulse, bubbling up in skin blisters. He looked to her, eyes frantic.

Where the fuck was Laura when she needed her? "I'll get a doctor!"

She tore down the hallway, nearly bowling over an elderly woman in a gray hospital gown. She reached the nurses' station at the junction and found a sour-looking redhead behind the counter. The redhead was scribbling on a pink form.

"My father's dying. Help."

To Sara's surprise, the woman looked up, slapped her pen down, and said, "Show me."

They reached David and the nurse took one look and ran. A moment later she came back with a crash cart and an Asian doctor in green scrubs. Sara stepped back to let them work. Now David tried to sit up and Sara saw the frantic look in his widened eyes, knowing he was in trouble. He gave a heavy, wracking cough and yellowish phlegm splattered on the sheets. The blisters on his face blew up like tiny balloons and popped, each oozing more yellowish fluid. The smell hit Laura, a thick smell, almost sulfurous. She backed up and covered her nose and mouth.

There's nothing I can do, nothing at all. He's dying and I'm standing here with my back to the wall and thinking how horrible it must be.

Then Laura appeared at the junction near the nurses' station. She was carrying a Styrofoam cup and, seeing David, set the cup down and ran to help.

Now he was thrashing and a deep wet sob came from inside him. He turned his head and Laura thought how brilliant and blue his eyes looked against the scaly stuff that had overtaken his face.

He gave a choked moan and flopped on his back. His hands clenched and unclenched. She caught a sharp whiff of urine as his bladder let go. Laura prepared the paddles and the machine gave a high whine. They shocked his chest and his back arched but he remained still. They shocked him again. It seemed useless.

Laura turned to her. "Does he have a DNR?"

What was she asking? "Huh," she managed, feeling stupid.

"A do not resuscitate. A health-care proxy?"

"Not that I know of. He never told me."

He never told me a lot of things, she thought. Why the hell would he tell me that? She wondered.

They kept shocking him and did CPR and shot him up with a syringe. She lost track of how long they worked on David. It seemed like a long time. They finally gave up and draped the sheet over his head.

Sara moved toward the gurney, parting Laura and the

Asian doctor. She peeled back the sheet from his face, which had now gone slack, eyes closed. Sara reached out to touch his face. Laura gripped her wrist. "You shouldn't."

Sara calmly removed Laura's arm from hers and said, "I want to."

With the back of her hand she stroked his cheek on the side of his face that didn't bear the growth. It was hot and rough with stubble. How many times had she kissed that cheek as a little girl? Usually after he surprised her with a doll or a box of Lemonheads, her all-time favorite candy. It wasn't right that he was gone.

She took her hand away and then replaced the sheet. She felt an arm around her shoulder. Laura's.

"I'm sorry," Laura said.

She tried to speak but felt her throat start to close up. Instead she pressed her face against Laura's shoulder and Laura embraced her and she cried harder than she ever had before.

After she had cried herself dry, her throat hoarse and her eyes stinging, Sara decided she needed some fresh air. She wound her way through the sick and the injured, who clogged the hallway, most of them on gurneys and some in wheelchairs. As she passed, she smelled unwashed bodies and was glad to be nearing the emergency room's main door.

Outside she found a green bench. There were a slew of cars parked at crazy angles on the street. She hadn't noticed at first, but the day seemed gray. Almost black. She looked up at the sky and saw it: a dark, swirling mist that dimmed the sun and hovered like ashes. Was this Engel's doing?

A breeze blew down the street and she caught a chill.

A moment later Laura joined her on the bench.

"How are you holding up?"

At least she didn't ask the all-time dumbest question reserved for funerals and wakes: How are you doing? Were you supposed to say, Great! Love it when people die! Keep it coming.

"Not so good."

"I'm sorry I said bad things about him. Do you understand?"

"He was a good man. Good dad."

"I'm sure he was."

"You didn't like him."

"I didn't know him," Laura said. "Didn't like what he did."

Laura watched an elderly man wrapped in a blue blanket hobble past. He looked out at the tangle of cars on the street and said, "Jesus Christmas," then kept going.

"I'm leaving. To find Engel."

"You're safer here."

Sara didn't see the point in arguing. Laura wanted to protect her, and for that she was grateful. But her father—and yes, he was her father—was dead because of these *things*. If she sat here safe and sound knowing that she could have stopped something, the guilt might gnaw a hole in her. "You can come with me, or not. It would be better if you did. I don't exactly know the way. And you're a doctor if I get hurt."

"You're set on this, aren't you?"

"I'm going."

"Not without supplies we aren't."

Laura and Sara arrived in the cafeteria. It was empty save for a weary-looking doctor who was stirring a cup of coffee and staring into it as if it held the meaning of life. They crossed through the eating area to the food line. The cashier's station stood empty. Laura began handing food to Sara: bags of chips, cookies, some bottled waters, Slim Jims, a few bananas, and some cereal bars. Laura had no money left: she had spent her last dollar on the coffee. Given the circumstances and what they were about to undertake, the hospital could spot them a few snack items.

Their next stop was the locker room, where Laura found a knapsack. She emptied out the contents: a pair of running shoes, shorts, a shirt, and thong panties. Then she took the food from Sara and placed it in the bag.

They made one more stop in the supply room, where Laura grabbed gauze, tape, Band-Aids, a suture kit, rubbing alcohol, ointment, and some samples of amoxicillin. She stuffed those in the outside pocket of the knapsack. She felt more guilty about the knapsack than the other items. Stealing from a huge corporation that owned a dozen hospitals wasn't too terrible. Taking another doctor's belongings made her feel like she had a film of dirt on her skin. If they survived, she'd return it.

With their gear now slung over Sara's shoulder, they left the hospital and got in David's truck. In his haste to get inside, he had left the keys on the driver's seat.

Laura started it up and was able to back out of a spot only a foot wider than the truck (after three tries). The tangle of cars that took up High Street was bad, but someone had left her an opening.

"This is crazy."

"What will happen to him?"

"What do you mean?"

Sara looked out the passenger side window. "His, you know . . . body?"

That was a question she really didn't want to answer, but the kid was two years from official adulthood, so she supposed it wouldn't hurt if she wanted to know. "They're busy. While you were outside we declared time of death. They'll take him to the hospital morgue. Does he have family? Someone will be notified."

"Just me far as I know." A fresh tear trickled down her cheek.

Laura reached over, took her hand, and gave it a squeeze. "I'm here. Whatever you need."

Nodding and sniffling, Sara said, "Okay."

They wound through the streets in David's truck, bypassing wrecked vans and cars, steering around bodies and broken glass in the street. While they were at a red light, a dreadlocked homeless man in a paint-spattered raincoat came to the driver's side window and knocked. Laura sped away.

As they approached Seneca Street, she marveled how they had been left alone. The things that attacked the city most likely only came out at night. But it was like nighttime here, under an ashen dome, the sunlight seeming gray and dirty. Who the hell could conjure up something like that? It was huge, covering the city as far as she could see

An hour after leaving the General, Laura and Sara pulled up at the foot of Seneca Street. She had a vague idea where the scrap yard was located, having seen it from the I-190 on her trips out of the city.

The street itself was rundown. The houses had patches of lawns, maybe ten by ten feet. Almost all of them had peeling paint and sagging front porches. One home had a rectangular hole cut in the roof and Laura hoped no one was presently living there. She didn't see any bodies or the signs of destruction that the attack had brought. In fact, the street was deserted.

Here it goes, she thought.

She rolled forward. There it was at the end of the street. Double chain-link gates, six or seven feet high. An arched sign read: AMD RECYCLING. Beyond the sign and the gates were stacks of junked cars, some of them still with blue or red or white paint jobs and others with mottled rusty hides.

"We're going in there?" Laura asked.

"That's where it is."

She parked at the front gate and got out. She noticed something spray painted on the street: Seneca Crew. Gang territory.

"Wish we had a gun," Sara said.

"Probably no one in there but the rats."

"Gee, that's better."

"After what happened last night, be glad if it's only rats."

Laura walked up to the gate. A chain was looped through the posts and she saw a padlock lying on the ground. At least getting in wouldn't be a problem. As she started to swing the gate open, she heard the shuffle of footsteps behind her.

She turned around. A group of men wearing bandannas over their mouths and noses had surrounded the truck. Some of them carried handguns, others small automatic weapons. The tallest of them, who wore a black hoodie and had the hood up, raised a sawed-off shotgun and aimed it at Laura.

"You two are coming with us."

She supposed they didn't have much choice in the matter. The man in the hoodie waved the shotgun. Laura waved, indicating Sara should follow, and she put her arm around the girl.

It turned out they didn't go far. The men led them into a house across the street. As Laura entered she heard the wild thrashing of a group she thought was called Korn. The heavy sweet smell of marijuana hung in the house.

They entered the living room and found a tattooed man of about thirty sitting in a recliner. He wore a tank top and jeans. Presently he was smoking a cigar and he took a puff, Laura noticing the hoop piercing in his lower lip. He blew out the smoke and sat forward in the chair. The one with the hoodie directed them to sit on a sofa, which faced a flat-screen television of about fifty inches.

"Who are they, Tim?" the tattooed man said.

The gunmen fanned out around the room, some sitting in chairs, others leaning against walls.

The man in the hoodie said, "Caught them trying to get in the scrap yard."

"What are you two doing hanging around the scrap yard?"

"None of your goddamn business," Sara said.

"Sara, please," Laura said.

"Yeah, Sara, shut your hole," the tattooed man said, jabbing the cigar at them for emphasis.

"We're looking for something."

"And what's that?"

"A stone. It was lost. It's valuable."

"What kind of stone?"

"You wouldn't believe it."

The tattooed man took another puff and then exhaled bluish smoke. "This is my turf. The Seneca Crew, got it?"

"You have a name?" Laura asked.

"Parrish," he said. "You?"

"Laura Pennington. This is my daughter Sara."

He studied them over his cigar. "It ain't too smart being out with those things running around."

"We're trying to stop them," Sara said.

That drew a chorus of laughter from the rest of the room. Parrish put up his arm to silence the laugher. Laura noticed a shamrock tattoo that took up the better part of his forearm. "Yeah, we did that, too. When this all went down I rounded up my boys and went down to Allentown locked and loaded."

"What happened?"

"They killed three of my boys. Two more hurt. They're in the back of the house, one of them got some sort of shit growing all over him. Other one, Greg, got nicked by a bullet. Think it's infected."

This might get them some leverage. "You planning on letting us go?" Laura asked.

Tim, the one in the hoodie, said, "The younger one's cute. I say we keep her here."

Laura looked at Tim. Between the hood and the bandanna, his eyes were the only thing visible, and she didn't like the way his gaze fixed on Sara.

"Don't mind Tim. He likes 'em sort of young."

One of the other men, who wore a surplus army jacket and a red bandanna tied around his mouth, said, "Better if there's no grass on the ball field, right Tim?"

"Fuck you, Boz," Tim said.

"What's it matter?" Parrish said.

"I'm a doctor. You agree to let us go and I'll treat your friend. The other one with the skin problem, was he stabbed?"

"Yeah," Parrish said. "How'd you know?"

"This girl's father died of the same thing."

"Can you cure it?"

"I can't. Your friend with the infection? Him I can help."

"He's in the back room," Parrish said. "Then maybe we'll see about letting you go."

CHAPTER 25

They followed Parrish through a dining room, where a stack of ammunition clips and various machine guns and handguns rested on an oval table. In the kitchen, a pair of sullen teenage girls with heavy makeup leaned against the counter. They looked as if they'd claw your eyes out just for the fun of it.

As they approached the hallway to the back bedroom, Laura heard moaning. It was the sound of someone whose suffering could not be relieved, a bit of pleading, some begging God for help. She had heard it before and never quite got used to it.

"My boy's in this bedroom here."

Parrish opened a door on the left and they went inside. The room had a single bed, rolltop desk, and an office chair. The man in the bed was shirtless and well muscled. He wore shorts that came past the ankle and could have qualified as pants. Beads of sweat glistened on his chest and abdomen. His face seemed to glow with fever.

With the back of her hand, Laura touched the man's forehead. His skin was slick and hot and she knew immediately he had a fever. Laura told Parrish she needed the knapsack from the truck and he sent one of his gang members to fetch it.

The bullet had only skimmed the surface, which wasn't bad, but she worried about the infection. The skin around the wound was red, inflamed-looking. And the man was fighting a fever—a high one if she had to guess. "How did he get shot?"

Parrish said, "Friendly fire."

Laura cleaned the wound out using alcohol swabs and some soap, water, and a washcloth she asked Parrish to fetch. The kid's muscles tightened up and he bit his lower lip. He held up good. She put gauze and tape on the wound and instructed him on how often to change the dressing. Then she gave him an antibiotic pill and set some more on the nightstand for him to keep.

Laura felt someone standing over her. It was Parrish. She looked up to see him craning his neck, inspecting her handiwork. She hoped he was satisfied. She didn't want to wind up with a 9mm round in her anytime soon.

"Thanks, doc. Why don't you and your daughter have something to eat?"

She didn't know when their next meal would be coming. "Okay."

After Laura treated the gang member with the bullet wound, the one with the skin growth died. Sara heard him howl and moan from behind the closed bedroom door. After what had happened to David, she could only try and block out the man's pathetic cries for mercy. She couldn't bear to listen or see that again.

Laura had accepted Parrish's offer of lunch and was eating salami sandwiches and cream of mushroom soup in the kitchen. The food had not sounded appetizing to Sara. The heavy reek of marijuana and the funky smell of the house didn't help her appetite. She decided to step outside and get some air.

Leaning on the wrought-iron railing that surrounded the front porch, she saw the street was still empty. She smelled smoke on the air and the sweet aroma of baked Cheerios from General Mills.

She heard the door squeal behind her. Expecting to see Laura behind her, she instead saw Tim—the gang member in the hoodie—step onto the porch. For a moment he only stood there, hands in the front pockets of the sweatshirt. He still had the bandanna over his mouth and nose. *Did he think he was some sort of half-assed cattle rustler?*

"What do you want?"

"What you want in that scrap yard?"

"Something important."

He moved closer. She wished now she hadn't come out here.

"I'm going to see what Laura's doing," she said, and began to move around him.

He stepped sideways, blocking her exit. His hand came out of his pocket. In it was a small revolver. He pointed it at her. With a voice muffled by the bandanna, he said, "We're going in the scrap yard. I'm gonna give you a personal tour."

He was on her quick, wrenching her arm behind her back and forcing her to the steps. She grabbed the railing with her free hand, but he was too strong and pulled her away. He forced her down the steps and her ankle banged the lip of the last stair. She cried out in pain. He clamped his hand over her mouth. He was shoving her along, over the curb, on the street and toward the gates to the yard. "I won't hurt you, trust me."

She found a piece of skin and bit down on his hand.

"Ow, bitch." His wrapped his arm under her chin. He squeezed and she felt her throat get tight. She clawed at his arm, but he was too strong.

He managed to drag her to the gate and swing it open. Her only hope was that Laura or someone had seen something. She didn't come all this way to die in a junkyard.

Frank approached the toll barriers on the 190, and when they were about a half mile from them, easing around the exit ramp from the thruway, he was forced to stop. The road was blocked by a convoy of army vehicles. Hummers, troop carriers, and armored personnel carriers lined the road. Troops scurried around. A wasplike helicopter buzzed overhead. Frank noticed the full complement of missiles attached to its wings. That type of bird was designed to do serious damage. He also saw a white news copter with blue and orange piping on the tail circling around. Those weren't the most impressive sight, though.

A wall of black mist, seemingly hundreds of feet high, rose and curved over the city like a poison dome. He craned his neck, trying to see the top of it, but there was no end in sight. He wondered how far up it went. It appeared that the city was effectively sealed off.

Various brightly colored news vans were parked on the shoulder.

He was surprised at the lack of other traffic, then figured he was probably the only one crazy enough to be going *into* the city.

"Well boss, what's our next move?" Jenny said.

"We've got to get closer."

"We aren't doing it in this vehicle."

Frank pulled the Yukon over and found a spot on the shoulder. They got out and he motioned for Jenny to follow. They hopped the guardrail, drawing a curious look from a red-suited newswoman. The ground led downward sharply, and they moved through the short brown weeds until they reached flat ground.

They moved along the embankment that followed the

road above. So far, so good. Then they climbed a hill that led upward, near the toll booths. They reached the road again, remaining at the shoulder and guardrail, eye level with the road. He was peering under a truck and had a line of sight to the toll booths. The cloud began on the 190, perhaps twenty feet from the tolls.

Frank recoiled, feeling sick. Two soldiers in bulky chemical suits crept out from the toll booths toward the cloud.

"Good Lord, they're going to see if they can get through."

"I'm guessing they were volunteers."

The soldiers reached the swirling black mist. One of them put his hands up to his suit's helmet, as if listening for a radio transmission. They paused, looked at one another, and went into the mist.

At first, nothing happened. Then Frank heard a hissing noise like meat frying on a stove. It was followed by the most awful, warbling scream he had ever heard. The only other time he had heard a scream like that was when Betsy Morgan, eighty years old, was dying of bone cancer. Frank had sat at her bedside through every piercing wail.

A moment later the soldiers stumbled out of the mist. Their helmets and face shields had been eaten away. One of the men's gloves had dissolved, and his fingers resembled raw sausage. The other man's face was a sticky mess. His skin was bloody and hung from his face in steaming strips. They both collapsed on their knees. The one with the ruined faced fell forward, his face making a flat smack on the black top. They rolled and cried and twitched on the road.

Lord, please help them through this, Frank prayed.

Four more soldiers, in desert camouflage, M-16 rifles strapped across their shoulders, ran out to the men. They split in two groups and grabbed the wounded under the arms and dragged them back to the booths.

"Jenny, let's go. They're distracted."

"They'll gun us down."

"Not if they can't see us."

He thought about the possibility of having to fight by using the Light against the soldiers and it sickened him, but they needed to get through the cloud and into the city.

They would have to sprint across the open field and pass through the cloud parallel to the toll booths—all while hoping none of the soldiers spotted them.

"Now or never. Go."

Frank took off toward the wall of mist, running parallel to the thruway ramp and hoping the embankment would provide some cover. From behind him, he heard Jenny mutter, "You're impossible." But she followed. He heard her heavy breathing, her footsteps rustling in the grass.

They were within fifty feet of the wall when he heard someone yell, "Stop!" And then the roar of a helicopter engine and the *whup whup* of rotors. He looked up to see the black chopper coming in low and slow. In addition to missiles, it had a nasty-looking cannon sticking out of its snout. If they opened up with the cannon, they'd be able to fit his remains in a soup can.

"Frank?" Jenny asked.

He grabbed Jenny by the arm and they moved toward the wall. Now they were about twenty feet away. He looked at the exit ramp, where four soldiers had rifles pointed in their direction. So much for being stealthy. The helicopter continued to hover.

Now, three more soldiers moved down the embankment while their buddies provided cover. The soldiers coming down the embankment carried M-16s and wore flak jackets. A few of them had on sunglasses, making them appear vaguely insectlike.

He reached in his pocket and took out the Everlight. He held it in his closed fist. He could kill the soldiers with a beam of his own making, and they would escape. He briefly considered it, thinking that if they were captured, the city and possibly the rest of the world would be lost. But then he thought of the bikers he had killed, the stench of their burning hair and flesh. He had taken lives and the thought of doing it again made his hands start to shake.

"Whatever you've got planned, I'd do it now," Jenny said.

Blind them. Create a wall of light.

He raised the Everlight over his head, resting it in his open palm. He didn't have his hand up a second when he heard the pop of a rifle and then something like a bee stinging his wrist. He immediately lowered his hand, grasping at the wrist with the other hand. The stone fell to the ground. He fell to his knees, examining the wound. The bullet had nicked him. Someone was a damned good shot. Another inch and he would've been looking at a shattered wrist and shredded blood vessels.

It still stung like mad.

Jenny dropped to the ground and grabbed the stone. Frank looked up. The soldiers had come within twenty feet. Their rifles were aimed at Frank and Jenny. They stood in half crouches. One of them said, "Get on the ground. Now."

Frank decided to play things up. "My wrist, oh God." To Jenny, he mouthed, "Hand me the stone."

"Drop that. Drop it or I'll shoot," the soldier said, voice cracking.

"Afraid I can't do that."

Now his voice came in harsher tones, "Drop it! Damn it! Drop it!"

Jenny slipped the stone into Frank's good hand. Palm open, the Light glowed, faintly at first, growing brighter and whiter. Frank stuck his arm into the air (hoping it wouldn't get shot off), and a mass of white light filled the field and surrounded him and Jenny. He heard the soldiers gasp and imagined they would be shielding their faces from the glow. He heard the helicopter engine whine and hoped it would back off, but also hoped it wouldn't crash, either.

Together, they started toward the black wall. Frank hooked his arm around Jenny's so they wouldn't be separated.

He heard rifle fire and actually felt a few bullets thud

against the ground. Hopefully the shooters wouldn't get lucky.

The outer edges of the beam cut into the mist. Frank and Jenny were surrounded in a bubble of light. The mist parted in front of them as Frank and Jenny moved steadily up the hill. Around them, through the barrier of Light, he saw the faces, twisted, deformed, swirling in the mist. They pressed against the Light, then turned away, their shrieks muffled and distant. Engel's demons. *So that's where they go during daylight.*

After what seemed like an hour, but was likely five or six minutes, they passed through the other side of the mist and stepped clear of it. Frank extinguished the Light and placed it back in his pocket.

It had been sunny and clear on the other side. In here, the air took on a dull gray quality, the same way it got right before a thunderstorm. They were near a two-story brick motel that bore a red-and-white sign reading EXIT 53 MOTOR LODGE. A yellow Volkswagen was the lone car in the lot. There were two bodies on the ground near the motel's wall. They looked like a man and woman, both in blood-soaked pajamas.

"What now?"

"We find transportation," Frank said. "Then we look for Charles and David."

They approached the hotel's doors, which bore a large, jagged crack across the glass. Frank opened the door and stepped into the small lobby, which was furnished with a gray carpet and wicker furniture. He moved straight ahead to the counter. There was no clerk in sight, only a stack of brochures with the Motor Lodge's picture on the front. He reached his hand out to ring a desk bell for service when someone popped up from behind the counter. It was a stringy-haired woman in a faded flowered dress. There were scratches across her forehead and nose. In her left hand she held an aluminum baseball bat. Eyes wide and looking for a fight, she said, "What're you doing here, huh?"

"We were wondering if you had a phone book."

She looked at him as if he had just requested a block of Limburger cheese. "Phone book? I ain't got a phone book, just this bat, keeps things away. Keeps the crazy things away, things that came last night."

She waved the bat around as if warming up for batting practice.

Jenny said, "Can you put the bat down? We won't hurt you."

"No, no, no. They'll come again. I *need* this. You got that, you bitch of a bitch? *Need*," she said, and twisted her mouth into a toothy yellow grin.

He peered around her and on a table behind the counter he spotted a phone book. "Can I just use the phone book?"

"I told you I ain't got no damned phone book!" she said, and slammed the bat down on the counter. The brochures toppled over the side and landed on the floor. She lifted the bat over her shoulder. Breathing heavily, she eyed Frank and Jenny as if they might be her next targets.

Frank didn't have the time or inclination to battle the woman over a phone book. He had hoped to call for a cab, but given the state the city was in, one might not show up. The cell phone circuits might all be jammed up, anyway. "Okay, we don't want your phone book. We're just going to leave."

"I should split your heads," she said, eyes narrowed.

"What about the phone book?" Jenny asked.

"We'll find another way."

They backed out of the hotel, and the woman slunk back below the counter like some demented jack-in-the-box waiting to surprise the next visitor. He didn't know whether she had been touched in the head already or if yesterday's events pushed her over the edge.

They started past a Wilson Farms convenience store. It was dim inside and no clerk stood at the register near the window. Frank's hand still bled, so they stopped in the store and helped themselves to some tape and gauze. Outside the abandoned store Jenny bandaged his hand and he tucked the roll of tape and extra pads in his pocket. Then they started back down the road.

Frank had been to Buffalo numerous times and was trying to navigate in his head the way to Charles's house. They went a little farther up the road, past a lot filled with semitrucks, and he spotted the van maybe fifty yards ahead, pulled at an angle onto the sidewalk. "That could be our ticket."

"Hopefully there's no crazy bitch with a bat waiting in the passenger seat for us," Jenny said.

They approached the white van. The rear bumper bore a sticker proclaiming, PROUD PARENT OF AN HONOR STUDENT AT EAST AURORA HIGH SCHOOL. There was a bloody palm print across the sticker. Frank wondered what fate had befallen the honor student and the parent.

He walked around the driver's side and found the door open. There was more blood on the tan interior of the door. He poked his head in the van and found it unoccupied. A car seat in the rear. A soccer ball on the floor. A half bottle of Diet Pepsi in the cupholder. It appeared to be the standard vehicle of the suburban family. He leaned on the seat and checked the ignition. Bingo. A set of keys.

"Good news," Frank said. "We got wheels. They must've abandoned ship."

"If it starts."

"What do you mean?"

"That door's been open. Hopefully the interior lights being on didn't kill the battery."

"Let's try."

Frank got in the driver's seat and Jenny went around and sat shotgun. He turned the key and was rewarded with the engine coming to life. He shut the door and maneuvered the van back on the road.

They pulled up in front of Charles's Tudor home a short time later. Frank already didn't like what he saw. The Children's Hospital was across the street and a group of staff dressed in scrubs had gathered on the sidewalk. Most of them were crying. He saw one woman whose hands shook as she pointed to the building, explaining something to another staff member.

Frank and Jenny got out of the car. He hadn't noticed at first, but there were lumps covered with sheets on the sidewalk. Maybe a dozen of them.

"That can't be good," Jenny said.

"Hey! What happened here?" Frank called to the group.

A black nurse in a flowered scrub top said, "They got in the hospital. Bastards starting throwing patients out the windows. Look," she said, and pointed up.

Frank looked up at the ten-story building. Several windows were smashed out. His mind finally made the connection. The sheet-covered corpses were small. It was a children's hospital. He suddenly felt sick. Everything had gone wrong in the world. The innocent were not spared death. You had only to look no further than the television news to know that. Children abducted, raped, molested, beaten by parents, forced to live in filth. Death didn't discriminate when it came to age, and he knew that, but it still appalled him. How could this go on? How could his God allow it? And would God be angry with him for asking that question?

"That's the worst thing I've ever seen. Some of those are babies, Frank. Babies."

"Let's get inside. I can't look anymore."

Charles's kitchen was a wreck. The refrigerator door was open and the odor of spoiled food drifted through the room. The large island that dominated the room had its marble top cracked by something. The cabinets had been gouged and hacked. Broken dishes lay on the floor in front of opened cupboard doors. The rest of the house was in much of the same condition, upstairs and down. And they didn't find Charles.

Jenny leaned on the island. "Any idea where he could be?"

"I'm afraid the worst happened."

"They came for him."

"The lawn had been trampled when we came in. Did you notice? I'm guessing it wasn't the welcome-to-the-neighborhood committee."

"Do we know for sure it was the Dark Ones?"

"The cabinets bear their handiwork. Those were made by their swords, axes. It's unlikely that a roving gang broke down his door and trashed the house."

"You think Engel sent for him?"

"It's possible."

"Do you think David came here?"

He hoped they didn't have David, as well. "No way of knowing."

Jenny straightened herself up. "Charles's daughter might know where he is. Maybe we'll find David, too."

"Hard to know that."

"I'm just worried."

Frank nodded. He found his way into a room lined with cherry bookshelves. A massive desk in the same dark wood took up a corner of the room. After going through a few of the drawers, he found what he was looking for in the bottom one: the phone book.

He flipped through it and found Laura Pennington's address on Delaware Avenue, in the Park Apartments.

CHAPTER 26

"I still say we go downtown, hole up in a tall building," Mike said. He was pacing again, a gun in each hand.

Milo rolled his eyes. O'Donnell was certainly stubborn. "Again, trapped."

"Think about it. Those fucks would have to climb twenty, thirty flights of stairs to get us. I doubt they know about elevators. And most of the buildings are probably empty, anyway. The attack hit after business hours, right? So they're not going to be looking for people in there."

"We get trapped on the top floor, is someone going to send a chopper?" Milo asked.

"Dad, Mike's got a point," Debbie said. She was perched on the edge of the couch at Agnes's side. "We can't stay here."

"It looks like they didn't come down here last night," Milo said.

"And if they do tonight?" Debbie asked.

Milo sighed. They couldn't leave the city and staying here would leave them vulnerable to attack. "Okay, where then?"

"The HSBC building's the tallest in the city. Something

like thirty-five floors," Mike said. "And they have an underground garage. The truck would be safer down there."

"Good enough, I guess. We should start rounding up supplies."

"Let's—"

Mike was cut off in midsentence by voices coming from outside. It was a female and multiple male voices, and it sounded like tempers were getting hot. Milo went to the front window and saw a blond woman pointing toward the scrap yard and yelling. A tattooed man in a white tank top was flanked by two others who wore bandannas over their mouths and noses. She could be in trouble.

Mike joined him at the window, nudging Milo with his elbow. "Look at this."

"That piece of crap, going after a woman like that," Mike said. "Fucking Parrish."

"You know him?"

"Him and his boys are in a gang, call themselves the Seneca Crew. They ain't much. Just good for harassing locals."

They were doing a pretty good job of it from what Milo could see. "We need to help her."

But Mike had already passed him and was heading out the front door, a .45 in hand like some old-time gunslinger. Milo yelled for Debbie to wait inside and then followed Mike out the front door. The air hit him, brisk and chilly. He wished for a sweater.

He heard the woman saying something about taking her eye off her, then the tattooed guy saying he'd find her, then the woman saying if that piece of crap hurt the girl, she would kill all of them.

Mike led the way, Milo following.

Mike said, "Parrish, what's happening?"

"Stay out of this, O'Donnell."

"You okay, lady?" Mike asked.

The woman, who in Milo's opinion was good-looking enough to be a movie star, maybe not A-list, but close, turned and gave them a fierce look.

"One of them took my daughter in there," she said, pointing to the scrap yard. "I'm trying to stop her from getting raped."

"Who was it?" Mike asked.

Parrish raised his hands. "Not your fight, O'Donnell, okay? Go back and play nurse maid to your mother."

Milo noticed the guns in Mike's hands. He had been holding them at his sides, barrels to the ground. But now he raised them slowly and aimed at Parrish.

"Apologize."

The other two gang members, who were unarmed, glanced nervously at one another. Milo could only see their eyes over the bandannas, but they looked back and forth several times, twitchy looks.

"You're writing a check your ass can't cash," Parrish said.

"Say you're sorry," Mike said. "Then tell me who took the girl. It was Tim C, wasn't it?"

Milo considered putting a hand on Mike's shoulder, but thought it might set him off. Instead he said, "Put the guns down, okay, Mike?"

"Stay out of this. It was Tim, wasn't it?"

"Go inside."

The woman said, "It was someone named Tim."

"That's what I thought," Mike said. "I'll help you find her. And if I find Tim, too, even better."

Parrish said, "Remember you have to come back out this way, O'Donnell."

"I'll take my chances," Mike said, then turned to Milo and said, "You coming?"

Parrish said, "You really don't want to hang around here."

"I'll go."

The woman looked at Parrish and said, "So you're not

going to help? Don't you care? That girl is in trouble in there."

Parrish shrugged his shoulders. "I can't control him," he said, a grin spreading across his face.

The woman went ahead, saying, "If you're coming, let's go."

As Milo and Mike started for the scrap yard, Parrish called out, "Good luck," and broke into wild, high-pitched laughter.

They slipped through the gates and after they were inside made quick introductions. The woman's name was Laura. Milo felt dwarfed by the rows of rusted cars and piles of twisted steel that seemed to go on for miles. The ground was covered with crushed stone and it made crunching noises as they went forward. Milo guessed the place took up maybe a hundred acres. It was big. You got a sense of its size looking at it when driving on the 190. An expanse of rust, concrete, and gray-brown pathways zigzagged through the scrap.

Mike nudged him, handed him a gun. "You know how to use one of these?"

Hopefully he wouldn't have to use it. He'd killed two NVA soldiers during his tour in Vietnam. It was at a distance of a couple hundred yards. He couldn't imagine killing up close. "It's been awhile, but yeah."

"We'll find the girl and then get back to Mom and your daughter. They'll be fine. Parrish just hates my guts."

"After pointing a gun at him, why would you think that?"

Laura was stalking ahead of them. She stopped and turned. "You two waiting for a bus or something?"

Tim had hustled her down the first row of junked cars, gripping her arm and tugging. Sara had to fight to keep her balance, once falling to her knee. With one arm he dragged her along and with the other he held the gun on her.

They rounded the corner and for the first time she got a sense of the size of the place. Piles of scrap metal, some twenty or thirty feet high, carried on toward a distant elevated highway. There was a tall red crane in the distance and a track excavator with a shearlike attachment. Even if she were able to escape, the chances of finding the Everlight in all this were slim.

Now he wrapped his arm around her throat. The gun was pressed at her temple. His breathing was ragged through the handkerchief, and he stank of sweat and stale weed. He continued to drag her along and she figured the farther they got into the complex, the less chance she had to survive.

"This could be fun, you cooperate."

"Fuck off," she said.

He gave a twist on her neck and she grunted in pain.

"Quit fighting it."

"You're a piece of garbage."

They came to a pile of twisted I-beams and he dragged her around it and then shoved her. She flew forward and, arms out, braced herself before smacking the ground. Her palms stung. She rolled on the ground and got up on her knees.

He was pointing the gun at her. "Give me any more shit, I'll shoot your knees out, do you right here."

She felt hot, anger boiling up into her face. She could use the Light. But would it work on a person? And what effect would it have? It could mean burning someone horribly. She wasn't sure even someone like this deserved that fate, but if she could blind him, that might work.

"Get up. We're going farther in."

She began to stand, finding that she didn't have to conjure an image of warmth or light. The tingling sensation was in her fingers and she started to flick her hand, but he was quicker and leapt forward, pushing her over. She fell backward and he was standing over her and pulling on her shirt, forcing her to her feet. He stood Sara up and again wrapped his arm around her throat, this time squeezing hard. "I told you to move."

She found herself being dragged along again, deeper into the yard.

They neared the big red crane. For a moment she thought she heard voices in the distance. Tim must have heard them, too. "Move faster."

Near the crane stood a narrow corrugated outbuilding marked STORAGE. Tim corralled her toward the building. She tried prying his arm away from her throat, but his grip was viselike. He pressed the gun against her head again. "Stop struggling."

She couldn't use the Light right now. She had nowhere to aim, for he was behind her. But if she had the chance, she would. Just needed to get loose for a moment.

He brought her to the door and gave it a kick and it banged open. Dragging her inside, he kicked the door closed behind them. The room smelled of oil and gasoline and she got a whiff of the type of orange soap that David had sometimes used to get his hands clean after a dirty job. Now he shoved her to the ground and she wound up on her rump on the concrete floor.

Again he pointed the gun at her. "Take your clothes off."

"No."

"Take them off."

"Make me."

He kicked her in the ankle and the pain shot up her leg. "Do it or I'll hurt you worse."

She backed up, crawling on the floor, until she bumped up against a large tire. "You touch me and I'll make you pay."

"That's it," he said.

In one swift move he was on top of her, shoving her to the ground. He still had the gun, but was pinning her arms to the floor. She kicked her legs, thrashing her head back and forth. He ground his crotch against her and she tried to buck him off. The idiot still wore the bandanna. He sped up his grinding. "How's that feel?"

He slid up and down against her pelvis. Damn it but he was heavy and she tried to force him off by thrusting against him, hoping to separate herself from him. He began grunting and panting and raised his head up, eyes squinted shut. It was then that she saw her chance. His face was only a few inches from hers. The bandanna separated from his chin.

Raising her head, she bit down on his chin, clamping hard. She put every ounce of anger into the bite, pinching the skin between her front teeth until she tasted blood. Then she jerked her head to the side, tearing a strip of flesh from his face and spitting it out. Yelling, he rolled off her and she got to her feet. He was on his hands and knees, one hand examining the wound. She took the opportunity to kick him square in the face and he sagged sideways.

She considered stomping him more, hoping to incapacitate him, but that might give him a chance to grab her. She bolted out the door and darted down the first path she saw, heading back toward the gate.

Behind her, the door slammed and she heard him yell, "I'll find you, you fucking bitch!"

She wouldn't have much time. She sprinted, the rows of cars towering over her.

I need to hide. I can't outrun him, she thought.

Up ahead the tail end of a white Ford jutted out from the pile of cars. The trunk was open and she figured she could jump in and hold the lid closed and hopefully he would pass by her.

She reached the Ford and climbed in the trunk, which smelled of sweat and dirt. Luckily no critters had taken up residence in the trunk. Rats and pigeons made for lousy roommates. She lay down on her side, reached up, and held the trunk lid shut, leaving enough room to breathe and allowing a sliver of dirty light to enter the trunk.

She heard footsteps on the gravel, *crunch-crunch*. He wasn't running, as she had hoped. Her hands began to tremble, and she took a deep breath. *Stay still, stay still. He'll walk right by. If you move, and he sees you, you're dead.*

Now the trembling went up her arms and she hoped she wasn't jiggling the trunk lid. The footsteps came closer and stopped.

He began to whistle. Now his feet, clad in brown work boots, came into view. She closed her eyes and bit her lip. She was aware of the blood—his blood—on her mouth.

"Where did you go?" she heard him say. "Toward the gate, that's where I'd go if I were after me. Yes I would."

Not only is he a rapist, he holds bad conversations with himself.

He stood there a moment longer. Sara reminded herself to breathe.

She opened her eyes and saw the boot-clad feet walk away, slowly at first, then gaining momentum. She heard him yell, "I'm coming to get you!"

Sara waited in the trunk until she couldn't stand it any longer. Cramps began to form in her calves. The muscles in her back tightened. Something jagged dug into her back. She guessed she had stayed there for half an hour. When she thought he was gone, she raised the trunk lid and climbed out. She jogged in place for a few seconds to shake out the cramps.

She had to get back to the gate.

She started in the direction of the gate, snaking along the junked cars. She looked at her watch, surprised that it was midafternoon already. This was one place she wouldn't want to be trapped at night.

As she moved along, she heard voices in the distance, this time calling "Sara!" She stopped and listened. The call came again, a woman's voice. Laura had come for her. There were two other male voices. She hoped they weren't gang members.

Sara moved through the rows. A couple of times she heard tinks and pops in the metal, expecting Tim to come charging out at her, but finally she made it back to the pile of twisted I-beams where Tim had initially thrown her on the ground.

She could see the gate in the distance, and beyond that the street, cloaked in a gray haze created by the black mist.

She hunched down by the pile of steel. Her body ached from being cooped up in the trunk and thrown to the ground numerous times. The palms of her hands stung. But she was almost out. She scanned the yard between her and the gate, looking for him.

She was about to go when she noticed the glow. It came from her right side, and was warm and bright. Coming from the other side of the pile. She went around and saw it shining out from the rusted steel beams.

Kneeling down in the light, she could see the stone tucked away in the rubble. There was a gap where the I-beams leaned against one another, and perhaps ten feet into the rubble was the Everlight. The glow diminished somewhat, but there was no doubting it: The stone David described had been found. How had she miss it earlier? Being dragged around by a rapist didn't offer many opportunities for examining the surroundings, she supposed.

She began to crawl in the opening, on her belly, using her elbows to drag herself forward. Five feet to go. She reached out her hand.

Someone grabbed her ankle and she was dragged backward. She tried digging in for purchase, but he was too strong and she was out of the rubble and on her belly and being pinned to the ground. "Should've left while you could," Tim said. "Now I'm gonna take my time, see what's up that pretty little ass of yours." He slapped her on the rump.

How could I be so stupid?

He was straddling her and began to roll her over when she heard another voice say, "Get off her, Cunningham, or I'll pop you."

Tim stood up and the next thing she knew Laura was kneeling at her side and helping her up.

"Are you okay? He didn't, did he?"

Sara shook her head. "Almost. I fought him off one other time and got away."

"Good girl," Laura said, and hugged her tight. Sara buried her head in Laura's shoulder and the tears came.

"It's okay, it's okay," Laura said.

They stood up, Laura keeping her arm around Sara. She saw two guys with guns, one young and dark haired. His eyes were dark and intense and he was looking at Tim like pulling the trigger on that gun might make him real happy. The other man was fiftyish and wore a patched flannel coat. He held his gun at his side.

The younger guy said, "He hurt you?"

Sara wiped the tears from her cheeks. She felt like a fool. "No."

"I should do it," the young guy said.

"You do and Parrish will cut you down."

"Milo, go over and make sure he doesn't have anything in that sweatshirt pocket. I'll watch him."

Milo, the older one, went over and jammed his hand in the sweatshirt pocket. Tim didn't struggle. Milo pulled out the revolver and took it back over to the younger guy. "Piece of crap, going after a girl like that," Milo muttered.

"Find something to tie his ass up with," the younger one said.

Milo rummaged around the piles until he found a few

lengths of thin steel cable. They made Tim sit down and Milo bound his hands behind his back, then his feet, while the young one covered him with the gun.

"We're walking out of here. I don't want you going back and telling your boys we hurt you, maybe have an ambush waiting for us."

"You're a dead man, Mike."

"Go ahead. We'll be gone."

"We need to find the stone," Laura said.

"I did. It's in there," Sara said, and pointed to the pile of beams.

Milo and Mike exchanged puzzled looks.

Sara ignored them and got down on hands and knees. She crawled into the pile and managed to snag the Everlight, which now gave off a soft yellow glow. As she crawled back out, she examined it. The light in the stone appeared to be fading.

She rejoined the others.

"What's that?" Mike asked.

"It's not very bright," Sara said.

"You mind filling us in?" Milo asked.

She didn't feel like talking right now. Her eyes were puffy and raw from crying. "You tell them."

Sara listened as Laura gave them an abbreviated version of David's story regarding the Everlight and how they needed it to destroy Engel.

"So what does that thing do?"

Sara held the stone in her palm. Its glow had faded and it pulsed weakly. "It can destroy Engel."

"Demons, huh?" Milo said.

"I still say it's a terrorist thing," Mike said.

"You saw them, Mike. You see the cloud around the city. It's definitely not terrorists."

"Seems farfetched."

"I saw them. Down on Allen. Those things ain't from this world," Tim said.

"Shut up," Mike said. "Look, demons or not, we need to get out of here. We're going downtown, going to hole up in the top floor of the HSBC. You should come."

Milo added, "You don't want to be caught outside at night."

"Crazy story or not, you two seem okay," Mike said.

"Don't you believe your own eyes?" Laura asked. "You've seen them, right?

"At a distance. They could be anything, guys in costumes."

Sara rolled her eyes. She wasn't one to believe in the supernatural, but she didn't understand how anyone could deny the existence of the Dark Ones. Not after seeing them in action. "Then watch this."

She stuck the stone in her pocket and walked around Mike and Milo, who turned to watch. Raising her right hand, she fired a blast of light into a junked Jeep. It hit the fender with a pop-hiss and the Light sparked and left a scorch mark on the rusted paint.

"What did you just do?" Milo asked.

"That's some freaky shit," Mike said.

"It's part of being a Guardian, like she told you."

Sara removed the stone from her pocket. It was shiny and black. No light radiated from it at all now. "Look," she said, and held it up.

"We'll have to hope the Reverend finds us," Laura said. "Its power is gone, like Dave said."

"And hope he brings the other stone," Sara said, and placed the stone in her pocket.

What little hope she'd had for escaping this mess began to fade.

"We'll take shelter with you two. Based on what David said, we can't face Engel without the stone," Laura said. "And thank you both for helping."

"You're welcome," Milo said.

"Wasn't nothing," Mike said.

As they walked away, Sara took one last look at Tim, now on his side and straining against the cables to free himself. She was slightly ashamed of herself for having a vision of a wrecked car falling from the pile and crushing Tim into the gravel.

CHAPTER 27

When they reached the street, Parrish and two of his goons were waiting at the gate. Mike directed them where to find their buddy and told him he didn't want any shit, so Parrish and the other two had gone in looking for Tim. He must've caught Parrish in a somewhat charming mood. Parrish was a lowlife gangbanger, but Mike suspected even he didn't condone Tim trying to rape the girl, so he agreed to go in and get his boy and let it go for now.

They reached the Hoolihans' porch to find Debbie standing at the railing. "Mike, it's your mom."

"Keeping her warm?"

"Where were you?"

"Saving Sara here in the junkyard."

"She passed, Mike. I'm sorry."

"Did she . . . say anything?"

"Her breathing got real labored. She was hard to understand, but she said to tell you you're still a good boy."

Gone. And he was off on a half-assed adventure. He turned and faced the others. "I'm going in to be with her for a few minutes. Nobody come in."

He climbed the porch steps and went in the house. The

only sound was the ticking of a chime clock. He made his way into the living room. She was on the couch. The afghan came up to her chin. Her head lolled to one side and her mouth hung slack. She looked so pale. He pressed the back of his hand to her cheek and the skin was cool. Then he knelt at the couch and bowed his head. He reached under the afghan and took her hand. He sat that way for a while, watching and holding her hand.

Someone came up behind him. He looked around. It was Debbie. "How are you?"

"I told everyone to stay outside."

"You don't want anyone to see you like this."

"So what if I don't?"

"She seemed like a nice lady."

"She was good. Better than me. Better than the rotten shit son of a bitch she had for a son."

"You're being too hard on yourself."

"Should've been here, that's all."

"You did what you could. It was good of you to bring her back here, get her meds."

"Least I did something, huh?"

Debbie came and knelt beside him. "Is there anything I can do?"

She seemed like a sweet girl. He appreciated it. "There's one thing."

"Name it."

"Her rosary and cross. They're next door. Right rear bedroom. The rosary is on the long dresser. The cross is over the bed. Could you bring them?"

"You bet."

She left and came back a few minutes later with the glass rosary beads and the silver crucifix that seemed to weigh five pounds. It had been brought from the Old Country by his great-grandfather and had hung in every O'Donnell house since 1918. He took the items from her and removed the afghan. Then he folded her hands best he could and wrapped the beads around them. He set the crucifix on her chest.

He said the Our Father, a Hail Mary, and the Glory Be. It was the first time he had said those since he was eleven or twelve. Debbie stood silently behind him. Then he kissed his mother's forehead one more time. "I hate to leave her here."

"There's nothing else you can do."

"I suppose not."

"Not to totally change the subject, but I packed some grocery bags filled with food for the road. I hope your neighbors won't mind."

Mike cracked a grin. "They don't have much choice, do they?"

"I suppose not."

"It's getting late. We should go," he said.

He turned and took one last look at his mother's corpse, thinking he could have done better for her. When this was over, he would see she got a proper burial. And a mass. If they made it back.

Laura found herself squeezed in the extended cab's backseat between Sara and Debbie. They had put the grocery bags, along with some flashlights and candles, in the truck bed. Milo drove and Mike sat in the passenger seat, looking out the window.

They traveled in the late afternoon shadows, which were made darker by the mist surrounding the city. On the way to the 190 ramp, they passed a few houses that had plywood over the windows and doors, the residents hoping to ward off an attack. They got on the elevated highway and Laura watched the sun descend through the film of the cloud.

As they rolled along she looked out at the HSBC arena, which still smoldered. They passed the abandoned Mills Shoe Factory and she had to glance twice because she thought she saw a line of bodies impaled on spears outside the big loading door. It made goose bumps dance on her arms.

"How you doing?" she asked Sara.

The girl only shrugged her shoulders and looked out the window.

"We'll be safe for tonight. You can get some rest."

"I suppose."

"You want to talk about anything?"

"I miss Robbie."

"Robbie?"

"Boyfriend."

"Same grade as you?"

"I don't want to talk right now, okay?"

She left the girl alone with her thoughts. Hopefully that creep in the scrap yard hadn't damaged her. If he *had* managed to rape her, Laura would have taken Mike's gun and shot him between the eyes.

She watched the sun. It descended a few more notches in the sky. She craned her neck to see up and out through the windshield. The cloud seemed to be gaining speed, swirling. Parts of it were darker than others. It had been fairly static during the day and now there seemed to be activity within. They were getting ready to move. "Hey Milo, step on it. We don't have much time."

"It's not dark yet."

"I think it's close enough. Look at the mist."

Milo leaned forward a bit, head over the steering wheel. "It looks like it's moving around."

"Am I right?"

The truck lurched forward, Milo pressing it toward the exit ramp.

Engel stepped into the doorway of the mill and looked at the black mist that hung over the city. He waved his hand,

and from the mill, two of his soldiers dragged Charles outside.

"Bring him here."

Engel looked at the wretch. Mouth caked with dried blood. Shirtless and bruised. He was pathetic.

"Why don't you get it over with? Kill me. It's what you want, isn't it?"

"I want what's out there," Engel said, and swept his hand toward the city. "I want the girl."

"She's strong."

"The light went out in that stone you buried with me. That is why I'm free. There's nothing that can stop me."

"Then why kill her? Why not send your barbarians across the country, then the world?"

Engel turned his head. He clasped Charles's chin in his pale hand. "I want you to watch. She'll do her share of screaming before I'm done."

"I'll enjoy watching you die again," Charles said.

"She bears the mark, much like you, doesn't she?" Engel said, and pointed to the irregular birthmark on Charles's chest.

"That means she's strong enough to kill you."

Engel gave his head a shove. "My army is descending right now. The sun is low in the sky. You won't see another sunrise." To the two demons holding Charles he said, "Take him back inside. Bind him to the wall."

As they led Charles away, Engel watched the cloud.

He raised his arm again and summoned forth a soldier. Engel had personally seen to this one's torture in the depths. He had cut off the ears, slit gashes in the skull. "The girl will have a red mark on her skin. That's how you will know her."

The soldier grunted and fell back into the mill.

Go now, my children. Bring her to me.

* * *

Milo had pulled the truck off the 190 at the Elm Street Ramp. They made a few turns and wound up on Washington Street. It was on Washington that Laura saw they couldn't go that route. A blue Hummer and an SUV had collided. Both cars had met head-on and were now blocking the street. A third car, some sort of wagon, had flipped over. The windshield was smashed and shards of glass littered the asphalt.

She looked at the sky. The cloud swirled faster.

"Damn it, have to find another route," Milo said, and backed the truck up.

"Be quick," Laura said.

The truck rolled backward. Laura watched the sky. Milo began to swing the truck back onto Broadway, the street from where they had turned. Laura looked out the rear window and saw it. A black, funnel-like cloud descended from the mist above, extending like a bizarre finger. It swirled and churned soundlessly, touching down and remaining in contact with the ground for a moment. There were others, perhaps ten or twelve in different locations. The one she was watching dissipated, and in its wake left a group of the Dark Ones.

She heard screeching coming from above and saw winged things dipping and swooping from the clouds.

The second night of attacks was about to begin.

The horde of Dark Ones was about a hundred yards away.

"Look behind us," Laura said.

The others in the truck turned. Mike muttered, "Jesus Christ."

One of the demons pointed at the truck, and then they started forward, lurching, dragging limbs behind, others running.

"Gun it, Milo," Laura said.

Getting to the HSBC building would be tough. Straight ahead would take them to Court Street, then into Niagara Square. They could either flee into City Hall or the Statler Towers. She voiced these options to the rest of them.

"Either or," Milo said.

They drove ahead, hitting Niagara Square, a large traffic circle where the white obelisk dedicated as a monument to William McKinley stood. Milo drove a quarter way around and jogged off on a diagonal, onto Delaware Avenue. The Statler Towers, which had once been a grand hotel, stood right near the square. Milo double-parked and they all jumped out.

Laura could hear glass shattering and the voices of the demons, speaking in garbled tongues.

They grabbed the groceries and supplies from the truck bed, then found the doors locked. Mike took out his .45, blasted out the glass, then reached in and unlocked the door.

They hurried inside and went up a set of marble steps. The grand lobby, with its twenty-eight-foot ceilings and wealth of Botticino marble, had been designed to impress visitors. Done in a Renaissance-revival style, it had been Buffalo's grandest hotel. Now the lobby was occupied by retail shops, and across from the shops were the elevators, their doors gold.

Mike got to the elevators first. He hit the button.

Laura watched the elevator light with anticipation. If they were caught in the lobby, they were dead. A moment later the elevator arrived; the five of them hopped on and Mike hit the button for the top floor.

The elevator started up and Laura felt the little twinge in her gut that went along with elevators and roller coasters.

They got off on the top floor and stepped out into a beige-carpeted hallway. The hallway was dim, save for some moonlight that spilled in. A set of double wooden doors was directly ahead and on it a sign for an accountant's office. Laura tried the doors and found them locked. She guessed most of the places would have locked up for the night.

They spent a few minutes trying other doors on the floor and found them all locked. Laura supposed if the Dark Ones got up here, hiding behind a thin door wouldn't offer much protection anyway. She wondered if they would find the stairway doors or if they would roam mindlessly in the lobby, thinking their quarry had escaped. She hoped for the latter.

"Why don't we at least set these bags down?" Debbie asked.

They set the bags at the end of the hallway that branched off in two directions. One direction led to a dead end and a window. Laura saw a dull gray door to her right marked STAIRS. The hallway continued to the left, beyond the stairway door, wrapping around the corner. She had an idea.

The rest of their group was looking through the food and supplies.

"Someone should stand on the landing, listen for them coming."

"I'll go first. We'll switch off every half hour or so." Milo said, and went to the door. He held the .45 at his side. It wouldn't do him much good, but Laura wasn't about to tell him. He gave the panic bar a shove and disappeared into the darkness.

Milo stood on the landing in the dimly lit hallway. Shadows seemed to lengthen and shrink on the concrete walls. It was cool and damp. He sat listening, straining to hear the slightest sound. It brought him back to his days in the jungle, listening for a branch to snap, a noise that would give away the enemy's position. He found himself gripping the railing in front of him tight enough to make his knuckles white.

From below, a door opened and slammed. He took the .45 out of his belt. He cocked his ear but heard nothing else. Best tell the others, he thought.

He went back into the hallway, where Laura, Mike, and Sara sat against the wall. Mike was eating a granola bar and Laura had opened a bottle of spring water. Sara sat with legs crossed. Head down, she was fidgeting with her hands. Debbie stood near the window at the end of the hallway.

"I heard a door slam. Just be ready."

Milo went back out into the hallway and Sara watched Mike follow, taking out his gun. She would be their only real defense against the Dark Ones and contemplated going out in the hallway.

She got to her feet, as did Laura. She looked over and saw Debbie standing in the moonlight, watching out the window.

"I should go out there with them," Sara said.

"Stay here for now," Laura said. "It might be nothing."

"It's not nothing. It's them."

"Just stay with me."

Milo and Mike had decided to descend a few flights. They stood on the gray steps, listening. The sign on the doorway read 16. Milo figured they might be able to hear something if they moved down. So far, there had been no other noises. No footsteps, no voices speaking strange languages. Nothing.

"You sure you heard something?" Mike asked.

"Clear as day."

"Should we go down farther?"

"No. I don't want to have to haul ass up ten or twelve flights of stairs. Besides, what if they find some way around us?" Milo said.

"Maybe this wasn't such a good plan. Coming here."

"Gee, General Patton, maybe you should have thought of that sooner."

Mike scowled at him. "I didn't hear any better suggestions."

"Listen."

* * *

Sara watched Debbie at the window. She saw the shadow blot out the moonlight, then splash across Debbie, as if she were being marked. She started to tell her to get away from the window, but her voice caught in her throat and she felt herself move toward Debbie. A pair of glowing orange eyes appeared just before the glass shattered and a clawed hand came through and grabbed Debbie's arm. Debbie let out a gurgling scream as it drew her back toward the window.

Laura, looking desperate, said, "Sara!"

Sara ran for the window.

"I'm going down to have a look," Mike said, and brushed past Milo.

Mike was being a damned fool. Milo said, "Stay here."

"Be right back. I'll just go down a few flights."

"You'll give us away."

Mike didn't listen. He shuffled down the steps and turned onto the next landing. Milo squeezed the gun's handle harder.

Mike descended two more stories. He stood outside the door that led to the fourteenth floor, listening. He was pretty sure Milo was full of crap and had been hearing things. They would have heard a bunch of the freaks stomping up the stairs by now.

He went down one more flight, and when he saw the next landing, he realized why they had been silent: a thick black mist hung like a curtain in the stairway. They had entered the stairway and then turned into mist and traveled silently, much like the first attack on the city.

He turned and ran up the stairs, taking them two at a time.

CHAPTER 28

Sara watched the beast wrap its arm around Debbie's waist. Its form was visible through the window, winged and pale gray, as it hung on the exterior of the building. Debbie splayed her arms on either side of the window and dug her fingers in, trying to keep from being yanked outside.

It seemed, in Sara's mind, to take her several minutes to reach the end of the hallway. When she did, she grabbed Debbie's arm and pulled. Debbie didn't budge, but instead got pulled harder. She saw the drywall start to crumble where Debbie's fingers grabbed. The demon let loose a series of excited grunts, as if it knew its prey were getting weaker. There was no way she'd win a tug-of-war with the creature.

Now Laura joined them at the window and hunkered down and grabbed Debbie's legs to prevent her from being pulled from the building. Laura clamped on and pulled.

Sara looked for a place to aim a beam. She couldn't get off a shot without hitting Debbie.

The creature pulled. Debbie slammed against the window.

Sara saw her opportunity. The creature's arm, just above

the elbow. She raised her hand and light radiated from her fingertips. Bringing her hand down in a karate chop motion, she sliced the Light into the demon's arm. Its skin smoked but Sara had only partially severed its arm. She saw a mess of blackened muscle and bone where the blast had hit. Now Laura began to tug on Debbie's legs and Debbie tried surging backward. Sara saw the skin on the thing's arm start to stretch, the damaged bone being pulled apart as well. It howled and shrieked.

She gave it another chop and this time the arm severed. Debbie flew backward, barreling over Laura, and they both wound up on the floor. The demon's severed arm fell inside and landed on the carpet. Sara watched the muscles flex, the clawed hand grasping for something. After a moment it became still. The demon, now angry and wounded, flapped its wings and pulled away from the window.

"Move away," Sara said.

The other women listened, crawling rapidly away from the window. They weren't ten feet away when something struck the window frame hard enough to bend it in and nearly knock the frame out. Sara looked and saw the walls had buckled. For a split second she saw the now one-armed demon and then it disappeared from the window. It was going to come back for another run.

"The elevators. Get Mike and Milo. We're trapped," Laura said. "Debbie, you okay?"

She was slightly hunched over, rubbing her side. "My ribs are sore, but I'll make it."

The trip to Laura Pennington's apartment had turned up nothing, and Frank was beginning to lose hope of finding her. He and Jenny had knocked on doors of the neighboring apartments and found out nothing. Two people didn't answer, and an elderly woman named Margaret—who invited them in for gingersnaps—said she hadn't seen Laura in a few days. They declined the gingersnaps.

They had stopped at Buffalo General Hospital. Frank knew Laura worked there from his conversations with Charles. The hospital's emergency room was littered with people. The wounded and the dying were on gurneys in the halls, slumped against the walls, half conscious in waiting-room chairs. The nurses and doctors, pale and drawn and looking like the walking dead, rushed from patient to patient. They couldn't have stopped to talk if they wanted.

So now, they headed down Delaware Avenue, Frank watching the fingerlike extensions dip down from the mist to deposit their deadly passengers on Buffalo's streets. They reminded him of a tornado. He had only experienced one. He had been five and remembered hiding in his Aunt Carol's root cellar while the door shook and it sounded like God himself were trying to uproot the house.

They were headed back toward Laura's apartment, hoping to catch her, to find the girl and possibly Charles. Jenny was driving, Frank in the passenger seat rubbing his forehead, as if that would inspire him to find Laura. He looked up as they approached the apartment building.

He saw the flash in the sky, shooting from the upper floor of the old Statler Towers. It was a Guardian's beam, no mistaking it.

"Stop the truck, pull over," Frank said.

"It's getting dark. We need to get inside."

"Do it."

Jenny pulled the truck over in front of a coffee shop called Common Grounds. Frank peered at the Statler. On the wall he saw a winged shape. It clung to the side of the building and appeared to be reaching in the window.

"What is it?" Jenny asked.

"Look," he said, pointing. "That building. There's a Guardian in there, I saw the beam."

"Maybe David's up there," she said, sounding hopeful.

"Only one way to find out."

Jenny checked her rearview mirror, pulled away from the curb, and headed toward the Statler.

Milo heard quick footsteps slapping on the stairs. He tensed up, got into a shooter's stance, just in case it wasn't Mike. It was Mike, and he was coming so fast he tripped and fell forward on the stairs, putting his hands out to catch himself. He quickly regained his balance and looked wild-eyed at Milo.

"Back inside! Elevators!"

"They're coming?"

Mike grabbed him by the arm and urged him up the stairs. "They came up the stairway as mist. That's why we didn't hear them after the door opened."

Now Milo's heart thudded. He found himself bounding up the stairs, trying to keep pace with Mike, wanting to look back and see if anything was gaining but terrified of what he might see.

They reached the eighteenth floor and he heard them coming. *No need for them to be stealthy anymore*, he thought.

He followed Mike through the door and they slammed it behind them. It opened out into the stairwell, so there was no way to bar it. No way to stop them.

He turned around and found that the stairway wasn't the only problem: something slammed into the outside wall hard enough to buckle the drywall. Laura, Sara, and Debbie were on the ground, crawling away from the window. Debbie held her ribs and Milo's heart sank a little.

She's been hurt. My girl's been hurt.

Sara and Laura grabbed Debbie's arms and hoisted her up. Sara saw Milo and Mike at the other end of the hallway. They looked like two men who had just discovered the stairs were on fire. Or worse. The winged demon outside had just hit the wall hard enough to buckle it. A few more shots and it might find its way through.

Sara and the other women went to where Mike and Milo stood near the stairway door. Milo's face was red and sweaty; Mike's skin looked pale against his dark hair.

"What is it?" Sara asked.

"They came up the stairs in a mist. They'll be through the door any minute," Milo said.

"The elevators," Laura said. "Go."

They headed for the elevators, Sara in the lead, Milo and Laura helping Debbie along. Sara got there first and hit the down arrow. She heard the stairway door open. The grunts and growls of the Dark Ones followed and she looked and saw them reach the junction near the elevators. There were at least a dozen, all armed with jagged knives and spears.

The elevator doors opened with a ding. Sara, Laura, Debbie, and Milo piled inside. Mike hesitated. He was raising the pistol, a futile effort in Sara's eyes, but there he stood, like a sheriff facing a gang of outlaws. He fired, the blast sounding like a howitzer in the small space. She heard an awful shriek and saw Mike duck toward the elevator. The doors began to close. He managed to slip through, but one of them, a gaunt-looking thing with the skin peeled from half its face, jammed its clawed hands inside and pressed the doors open.

Sara stepped forward to blast it, but two more of them appeared, one of them holding a spear with a barbed tip. It thrust the spear ahead and she was sure it would run her through, but someone shoved her aside and she caught a blur before realizing it was Milo. The spear caught him in the side and he fell half out of the elevator. Sara managed to gain her balance and whip a beam at one of the Dark Ones. The light ripped into its throat and it fell back into the hallway.

Now more Dark Ones appeared outside the elevator and she realized with dread that they had grabbed Milo and were dragging him away. She heard Debbie yell, "Dad!" and was aware of hands trying to pull her back into the elevator. Milo was almost out.

Not if I can do something about it, she thought. She wrenched away from her friends and ducked past the demon and into the hallway. Milo moaned as two of them dragged him across the floor. She looked down the hall and saw the corridor was now packed with them. It looked like a convention for freaks.

More of them jammed into the elevator and dragged Mike, Debbie, and Laura into the hallway. Laura backed against the wall. She stood alone. The demons stood a few feet away. They clutched and grabbed at their captives. Two of them jerked Milo to his feet and he let out a groan. Sara saw the spreading blood on his flannel shirt. He'd been stabbed by one of their blades. Milo would suffer the same fate as David.

She fired off two quick beams and fried two of them. There were too many, maybe thirty crammed into the hallway. And she heard the winged creature thumping into the wall, determined to get inside.

The Dark Ones began to shove the captives toward the rear of the crowd. She saw Laura look back, attempting to reach for her. She had to do something.

A short, squat demon with a chest full of wormlike scars started toward her. Its eyes were milky white and devoid of pupils. She got a whiff of it, a scent of rot that seemed to settle in the back of her throat.

Laura and the others were almost out of sight, swallowed up by the horde, perhaps meant to be taken away and killed.

She looked at the milky-eyed creature and said, "Leave them. I'm the one he wants."

It stopped, bared its yellowed teeth, and said, "What did you say, girl?"

"I'm the one Engel wants. Take me instead of them."

The demon was on her in a flash, turning her around and lifting up her shirt. Its hands were cold and rough against her skin, and she felt a wave of nausea ripple through her stomach as its skin came in contact with hers. It pressed her against the wall, and she half expected to be run through, but instead it spun her back around. "You bear the mark."

It shoved her forward, into the crowd of them, and rough hands pulled her into the group.

She heard a gruff voice say, "Take them all to him. Let him judge." She thought she might have spared them, but for how long she didn't know. They shoved her along, prodding with the hilts of their weapons, and with each jab a sickening little ripple danced over her skin. She saw Laura and the others being pushed toward the stairway door.

They were all still alive, for now.

Sara reached the bottom flight out of breath and dripping sweat. She saw Milo being dragged along by two gray-skinned demons. Up ahead, Laura tried to turn and mouth something to her, but one of them placed a clawed hand on her head and wrenched her back around.

The horde moved them into the lobby, where more of them waited. She guessed the hotel never expected to have guests like this.

They were shoved forward, toward the doors, the hands clawing, grabbing, scratching at her the whole way, as if they enjoyed inflicting even small amounts of pain. Now she was at the front of the crowd, standing at the doors that led to Delaware Avenue. Laura and Mike were to her left, each of them with a demon wrapping its arm around their throats. Milo had been thrown on the floor like a sack of laundry. Debbie started to go to him, but they pulled her back and held her arms.

What were they waiting for?

* * *

Jenny had stopped the truck a hundred yards from the building and Frank saw the Dark Ones on the sidewalk and in the street outside the Statler. They lifted their black weapons in the air and pumped their arms. He was about to ask Jenny what the hell she thought was going on when someone—a girl—was shoved through the front doors. It might have been Sara, but between the distance and the darkness, he couldn't tell. A demon came out from the building and poked her forward and she staggered. The crowd around her gave her a wide berth. Frank soon saw why.

From above, a winged demon swooped in low and he saw Sara raise her arm to fire a beam, but the demon was too quick and it swooped in on her.

Sara felt the clawed feet grip her shoulders. There was a whipping of wings, and its foul smell washed over her. She felt terrified, thinking it was going to pick her up and carry her. They would stay alive for a few more moments, anyway. The demon squeezed harder and she was afraid the claws would dig in her shoulder, but instead there was hard pressure and she found her feet leaving the sidewalk. The beast gained momentum and it pulled her free of the ground and she felt her stomach get woopsy. She was looking down at the crowd of demons and then she shut her eyes as it carried her higher.

She felt her legs dangle and dared a look and saw the asphalt roof and the air-conditioning units of the Statler's roof, then the white monument in the traffic circle, all looking like a railroad miniature. They soared higher, the cold air rushing over her skin, and she peeked again and now the city was a mess of pinprick-size lights, like jewels on a black blanket.

They came to the black cloud and she wondered what would happen if it dragged her in there. She screwed her eyes shut and held her breath but there was a *whoosh*, the cloud parting before them, and they were up and over, looking down at the black fog that covered the city.

CHAPTER 29

Frank watched five people being carried up into the sky. He thought of using the Everlight to drive off the carrying demons, but by the time they were close enough, he would've been in danger of causing them to drop their passengers.

He saw the cloud part as the last captive was carried up and out. "Go, follow them."

"What about them?" Jenny asked, referring to the host of Dark Ones massed in front of the Statler.

"We have this," he said, and took the stone from his pocket. It glowed in Frank's palm and he instructed Jenny to speed up. She did, and he rolled down the window and, grasping the stone tightly, held his fist out the window. The beams shot out like rays of the sun, knifing along Delaware Avenue toward the Dark Ones. They covered their eyes, some of them running for cover. Others fell to their knees, wailing and howling.

Jenny drove the truck to Niagara Square, the demons parting before them. Frank instructed her to go around Niagara Square to South Elmwood, and get on the Skyway.

"We'll have to go through the cloud."

"That's what the stone is for?"

"It won't work in a vehicle."

"It will."

"It'd better," she said.

Jenny passed City Hall, checked the upcoming intersection, where the light was stuck on red, and got on the Skyway, an elevated highway whose future was currently in doubt. Some wanted it torn down. From what Charles had told Frank, the city shut the thing down whenever the snow got heavy, sticking a Buffalo cop car at the entrance.

They accelerated, Jenny weaving the van in and out of abandoned vehicles, a few times nearly getting wedged between a car and the concrete barrier. They passed the brown and gray Memorial Auditorium, now occupied only by flooded basements and mold. Charles had taken him to a Sabres game on a visit to Buffalo back in the eighties and all he remembered was how the blue wooden seat had made his ass hurt.

They came to the bottom of the Skyway, which led to Route 5. The wall of mist was a couple hundred yards away. Frank held the stone, and it began to glow stronger. Jenny accelerated and the truck lurched forward. Frank looked up, trying to spot the winged ones and their captives, but saw only the mist.

They got within fifty feet of the mist. The Light's beams cut white hot holes in the fog, and soon the truck was shrouded in light and Jenny drove it through the fog, her head bent forward as she squinted over the steering wheel to see.

They came out on the other side, Jenny steadying the truck's wobbly front end. She braked a little and slowed it down.

Now Frank looked up and saw the winged creatures, each of them with a captive dangling from its talons. They flew out over the gray slate sheet of Lake Erie and toward the abandoned steel mill. Its dirty gray roofs broke up a nice view of the open water.

That was where he was holed up, then. Frank suppressed a stitch of fear in his belly, telling himself they had the girl and the stone on their side. But they had to get into the mill and find Engel first.

He urged Jenny onward.

The Dark Ones began to descend. The air knifed into Sara, and the demon's grip sent pains down her arms. They went lower and her feet just cleared the chain-link fence that surrounded the mill. It set her down on the concrete, Sara lunging forward but catching herself as the demon rose back toward the sky and went into a circling pattern. It stayed there for a moment and then dipped and flew toward a long, narrow building on the other side of the concrete tarmac.

Laura looked around, examined her surroundings. She was near a guard shack and wondered if the man who had been killed at the mill worked at this one.

She looked out over an endless sea of concrete. Beyond the concrete were the remaining buildings, all painted in hues of gray and black. There were furnaces with black pipes and stacks raising toward heaven, and a skeletal structure that she thought did something with loading ore. She waited, heart hammering, for the others to arrive, and they did, their escorts dropping them off next to her, all of them landing smoothly except for Milo, who hit with a grunt. The demons climbed high in the air and flew in a circling pattern overhead.

Debbie went to him, got on her knees, and cradled him against her. He was holding his side.

"God, my side hurts. Wish I had a drink of water."

Laura didn't want to tell him what was really wrong, that he would be dead soon and would die horribly.

Laura joined Debbie, kneeling on the blacktop. She asked if she could examine him and he nodded. Then she lifted up his flannel coat and shirt underneath, exposing a pale, hairy belly. Then she got to it, the wound, like an open mouth, and the hot orange of the spreading infection. Or whatever it was.

"What is it?"

"It's caused by their weapons. We need to get you to a hospital."

Milo moaned and buried his head against Debbie's arm. "It hurts," he said in a muffled voice.

"What is it?" Debbie asked.

"It's more than I can help him with now," Laura said. "He needs to be on painkillers."

Sara noticed she didn't say they could cure him, or that he would be just fine. Giving him false hope would be a sin, and Laura didn't do that. Sara admired her for it.

Mike was growing impatient, pacing along the fence. "What are we waiting for? Let's hop the fence."

"And get torn to pieces?" Sara asked.

"What do you mean?"

She pointed to the sky. "Look."

He looked up, eyed the fence, and said, "They're probably too quick, anyway."

It wouldn't matter, because Sara saw someone emerge from the long, narrow building. He was heading toward them, and now more figures, perhaps a dozen, followed him. She could make out his silhouette and saw long hair and lanky limbs. The ones that fell in behind him carried the exotic weapons of the Dark Ones, long spears on poles this time.

"Looks like we're getting a welcome,"

They watched the man approach. She got a better look at him and found he looked like central casting's version of a nightmare. His long, stringy hair hung in hanks over his pale face. The open trench coat he wore bore greasy brown stains, and she saw his ribs and sternum protruding under the skin.

He frowned, eyes glinting like newly minted coins. The other Dark Ones fell in line to either side of him. That meant

Sara and the group had their backs to the fence and the Dark Ones were in front of them.

"So this is the little girl who is supposed to destroy me?"

"Engel," Sara said.

"That is I. You know what awaits you, don't you?"

Laura came up next to her and put an arm around her shoulders, a move that she appreciated, because she had begun to tremble. "No, what?"

"Why, pain, what else?" he said and grinned, the pale, thin lips stretching open.

"Let the rest of them go. I'll go with you."

Laura squeezed her tight, whispered, "Sara, no."

"And you"—Engel said, pointing an impossibly long finger at Laura—"are Charles's little bitch, aren't you? How nice to get mother and daughter here together. Your father will be glad to see you."

Laura let her arm slip off Sara's shoulders. "You've seen him?"

Engel threw his head back and laughed. "Poor little fool, I've done more than *see* him. I saw to his personal suffering. After what he did to me, it's only fair, yes?"

"You should have rotted in that grave."

"Oh, but I didn't," he said in a mocking singsong voice. He then turned to the creature to his right, an eyeless thing with sharp, bony hooks where its hands should have been. "Bring them."

Mike moved first. He still had his pistol and brought it out from in his coat and fired at Engel, catching him in the chest. The bullets struck Engel and he fell to one knee, holding his chest and whimpering. Head lowered, he continued to whimper until it eventually turned into a laugh. He stood up, and opening the coat, exposing the bloodless bullet hole. He stuck his finger in the hole and twisted. "You can't kill me."

Sara had to do something. "No, but I can." She fired a beam at Engel. It struck him and knocked him backward. With a quick slash of her arm, she created a white blade of

Light that sliced across the Dark Ones that had been to Engel's right. It cut their heads off and the corpses fell to the ground. There were five left, and as they started forward, Sara dispatched them with a quick succession of beams. The air took on the smell of burnt, dead flesh.

Engel began to rise.

Sara looked at Laura. "Get out. He wants me."

She ran, Laura trying to grip her arm, but Sara broke away, jumping over the bodies of the Dark Ones. She would run and hide in the mill, at least giving Laura and the others time to escape. Perhaps she could avoid him long enough to—to what?

CHAPTER 30

Engel rose to his feet. The girl had surprised him with that blast of light. He looked at the other pathetic wretches she had brought with her. They backed toward the fence, cowering. He didn't need them. They were an added bonus, and he had planned on using them for sport. It was the girl he wanted.

He turned and saw her running in the moonlight, toward the strange metal towers.

He turned to follow.

Laura watched her go for a moment. Sara's form got smaller and darker as she crossed the grounds of the mill. *Are you going to let her be hunted down by him? Can you lose her again and still keep your sanity?*

She couldn't.

As Engel turned, she charged him, catching up to him and leaping on his back and wrapping her arms around his throat. The smell of him made her stomach wrench. It smelled like something old and spoiled.

He broke her grip on his neck and she slid to the ground, landing on her butt. He turned around and she quickly got up. Now she'd pissed him off. Scowling, he cocked back his arm and flung it forward and something black and solid slammed into her stomach, exploding the air from her lungs and sending her down.

She tried to breathe, desperately tried to suck air, but it felt as if her lungs had locked up. She rolled on the ground, clutching her gut and staring at the thing he had thrown. It was round and smooth as a cannonball, solid black. God her gut hurt.

When her lungs unlocked and she was able to suck in some air, she noticed Mike at her side. She looked up and saw Engel taking quick strides toward the furnaces. Overhead the winged creatures circled.

She started to rise, and Mike stopped her by putting his hand on her arm. She didn't like that. "What are you doing? You'll get killed."

"I can't just sit here."

"You saw what he just did."

She had a dull ache in her gut from Engel's volley. "I'm going after her," she said, and shoved his arm away. She took a step and then the pain hit her again and she doubled over.

Frank and Jenny pulled up to the fence, stopping the van on the shoulder of Route 5. They got out, Frank looking up and seeing the winged creatures circling the mill. As they approached the fence, he saw a group of people standing near the guard shack. A college-age girl was holding a guy in a flannel shirt. Even in the darkness, Frank could see the guy's face had gone paper white. A younger guy holding a gun and a dark-haired woman who was bent over clutching her stomach completed the group.

"Hello!" Frank called.

They turned and looked at him and Jenny as if they were aliens stepping from the mother ship. "Reverend Frank Heatley and Jenny Chen, at your service."

"Is there a gate?" Jenny asked.

The young guy with the gun said, "Locked. You'll have to climb it."

Jenny scrambled up the fence and was over the top in an instant. Frank took a bit longer, nearly losing his balance when he swung his legs over the top bar. But he made it down.

They all introduced themselves. To Laura he said, "It's nice to finally meet Charles's daughter."

"He's here. Engel has him somewhere," Laura said.

That was the best news he had heard in a while. Providing he was still safe. "And the girl?"

Laura straightened herself up, but still kept a hand over her midsection. "She ran for the furnaces. Engel is after her. We found the stone, but it was dead."

"We figured it might be. I was able to recover the last one," he said and brought the Everlight from his pocket. "We have to find Sara. Jenny and I will go."

"You're not leaving me here," Laura said.

"You can't help. I know she's your daughter, but you'll have to trust us."

Laura looked as if she might cheerfully strangle Jenny. Frank intervened, saying, "I have the stone. We're both Guardians and we can fight them." He nodded toward Milo and said, "Stay here. Help this man. Get him inside."

Laura pondered it for a moment. "Time's wasting. Bring her back to me. Please?"

She had such a look of sorrow and fear on her face that if there were time Frank would have given her a hug and told her yes he would bring the girl back. Instead, he nodded. "Which way?"

"To those furnaces," Laura said, pointing. "What if we get attacked?"

"His army is occupied in the city. It's not you he wants right now anyway. Go inside and lock the door. You should be okay for a bit."

He realized those weren't the most comforting words, but it was all he had.

Laura watched Jenny and Frank run across the lot, Frank holding the strange, glowing stone over his head, the beams shining outward as if from a star. She helped Debbie get Milo to his feet and they went inside the guard shack. They laid Milo down, Laura letting him use her coat as a pillow. They found an old wool blanket in a supply closet, where it was stored with a cardboard box marked EMERGENCY SNOW-STORM SUPPLIES. She took a look in the box; there were candles, matches, canned soups, and a radio.

When Milo had been made reasonably comfortable, Debbie took Laura aside and said, "What is that stuff on him? Is it infected?"

She wanted to stop short of telling Debbie the truth. "It's something to do with their weapons. I saw a case of it at the hospital. It's not contagious, whatever it is. But it is serious."

"How serious?"

"He'll need medical care ASAP."

"Can I do anything for him?"

"Comfort him, hold his hand. That's about all for now."

Debbie took her advice, however flimsy, and knelt at her father's side and held his hand. He groaned every so often.

As bad as she felt for Milo, Laura had her own worries. She went to the window and looked out at the sea of concrete, and beyond that the mill buildings and furnaces. She hoped Sara was okay, hoped Frank and Jenny knew what they were talking about. She pondered what would happen if Sara didn't return, if Engel killed her. The thought of taking a nice handful of those sleeping pills and a tumbler of vodka occurred to her. She could slip away, maybe join the girl forever. Wherever that was.

But if Engel killed her and his monstrosities were loosed on the world, it wouldn't matter, would it?

Nothing would.

Sara came to a set of railroad tracks near the blast furnaces. There were a few rusted cars on the tracks, which she imagined had been used to transport ore pellets. Straight ahead was a black building and from that building the furnace rose for what looked like a mile. There were six of them, standing like alien sentinels in the darkness.

She saw the partially opened door and slipped inside. The building rose several stories, and one windowed wall admitted a small amount of moonlight. In front of her were a maze of stairs and catwalks and pipes that rose up to the ceiling. She went to the steps and began to climb, praying she wouldn't slip and break her neck.

As she climbed, she thought of Robbie and felt a pang of guilt that she hadn't called him. If she made it home, she intended to plant the longest, wettest kiss possible on him and tell him how much she loved him. Not like puppy love, when in the seventh grade she'd had a crush on Stevie Winchell, but maybe the real thing, like she could tell him anything, her deepest darkest secrets, and he wouldn't laugh or tell the guys on the lacrosse team. And maybe they'd go to college together, and beyond that, who knew? But first she had to get out of here.

Below her, the door opened and closed.

She turned down a catwalk, then turned again, trying to walk as softly as possible. She heard footsteps down below. Peering over the rail, she saw Engel, moving as if one with the shadows. He seemed to glide in the darkness.

She found a set of large pipes that went up to the ceiling. There was enough room between them and space behind for her to slip through. She slid between the pipes and ducked behind one.

Something brushed against her face. It was only a cobweb, but it still sent a shiver down her back. She brushed it away.

She heard footsteps on the metal stairs.

Sara peeked out from behind the pipes. On a catwalk parallel and higher than hers, Engel glided along, head scanning from side to side, looking for her.

He can't see me, can he? She didn't dare move.

He turned and looked in her direction. The moonlight caught his eyes, twin silver pinpricks in the dark. He appeared to be looking right at her. She could barely swallow and had to remind herself to take a breath. Remain totally still, she thought, feeling like an animal in the hunter's sights.

He moved along, and she took the opportunity to duck behind the pipe. That was foolish, looking out, but she had to at least give herself a chance to spot him. She plastered her back against the pipe and drew her arms in tight against her sides.

More footsteps echoing on the metal.

Was he getting closer?

She debated moving from her spot, hoping the darkness would hide her, but Engel operated in the darkness, didn't he?

This was bad. Worse than playing hide-and-seek with her friends as a young girl. She would always hide in the big walk-in closet in her house in Portland. Stuffed behind David's Carhartt gear and a stack of Christmas decorations, she would feel a delicious knot of fear in her belly until found. The difference now was that the seeker tortured and killed you.

Best stay put.

The footsteps got closer. He was approaching and she got a whiff of his rotted scent. He must have seen her.

She resigned herself to go, and slipped between the pipes and back on the catwalk. She looked left and there he was, grinning a black-gummed smile. Hand raised, he beckoned her with a finger. "Come, child, it is time."

Ahead was another set of steps. She whirled and fired a beam, but this time he raised his hand, palm up, and something black and shield-shaped rose in front of him and her beam bounced off it, showering sparks over the railing.

She made the stairs, and as she got to the top she felt his cold grip on her ankle. She kicked and thrashed, but his grip held firm. He dragged her down, the steps digging into her back.

She hit the bottom step and he loomed over her.

"Engel!" Frank shouted. "Let her go!" He held up the Everlight, and its glow filled the cast house, making the long abandoned place seem to come alive.

Engel put up his arm to shield his eyes. A grunt escaped him. He was perhaps thirty feet up and Frank saw Sara at his feet. He bent over and hoisted her up by the scruff of her neck. Her arms and legs flailed and she tried casting a beam at him, but it rocketed harmlessly into the darkness.

"I said let her go!"

"Put down the damned stone first. Then I'll talk. Otherwise she dies now."

Sara felt like a marionette. Engel had lifted her as if she'd weighed no more than a paper bag. Now she was pressed against the waist-high railing and it was cold and dug into her thighs. Reverend Frank and an Asian woman she had never seen stood below. The light from the stone felt comforting, warm somehow.

It went out as soon as it came. Frank lowered his arm. Engel still held her up.

"Now, let her go. I doused the light." Frank said.

"What do you have to offer me, should I spare her? Will you give up the stone, set it down?" Engel asked.

"Spare her. Let us all walk away from here. I'll leave the stone. She's no threat to you without it."

Engel lifted her higher. She felt her feet begin to leave the floor. "Let me go."

He leaned over and whispered in her ear, "It's of no importance, now."

"Engel?"

"Set down the stone. Back away from it. I'll let those of you that aren't Guardians go free. The rest I will promise a quick end. That is my final offer."

As if to prove his point, Sara felt herself hoisted higher. Now her feet weren't touching, and she felt her shirt rise up to her chest and tried to cover herself.

"I'll throw her over now."

Frank reluctantly set the stone on the ground, then backed up. The glow from it became muted and dim.

"Good," Engel said. "She dies anyway."

And with that, she felt herself thrust forward. Engel's hand let go of her shirt. Her pelvis smacked the railing, then she found herself flipping over in space and darkness and she saw the ceiling, then the floor, then felt a horrible thud in her ears. The last thing she saw as she lay on the mill floor, back broken, was Engel smiling down at her.

"You son of a bitch!" Frank said.

Beside him, in the darkness, he heard Jenny gasp, and then say, "Omigod, Frank." Then he was aware of Jenny winding her way around steps and the beams that held up the catwalks and he shook his head as if to clear away the shock. He bent down, picked up the stone, and followed Jenny, hoping that somehow the girl was still alive, but doubting it. He had heard the sickening crunch as her body hit the concrete.

He reached Sara. He was aware of Engel thudding his way down to them. It didn't matter. They might be doomed to die.

The girl stared glassily at the ceiling. A trickle of blood ran down the side of her face. Her arms and legs were splayed at her side. It made Frank want to weep, but he knew it would only give Engel reason to mock him. Jenny didn't feel that same reluctance. Fat tears dribbled down her cheeks and she wiped them away with her sleeve. More came.

From behind him, Engel said, "Put down the stone. You knew I couldn't let her live, didn't you?"

"I'll put down the stone," Frank said, and placed it on Sara's chest. "I'll put it right here for safekeeping."

"Come now. You waste my time."

Outside the cast house the group of demons that had been circling over the mill waited for them, perhaps three dozen in all. They surrounded Frank and Jenny and then two of them came forward and forced their hands behind their backs so no beams could be cast.

They shoved Frank along, Jenny at his side, until they reached the guard shack. Then one of them kicked in the door to the shed and Mike came out, helping Milo along. Debbie and Laura were last.

The demons parted as Engel stepped through. He looked paler than ever, his skin almost translucent. "Death awaits."

"Where is Sara?" Laura asked.

"I threw her from the catwalk," Engel said. "The sound her body made when hitting the ground was most delightful."

Frank looked at Laura. Very slowly, she closed her eyes and bowed her head. Then, as they were led away, he heard Laura begin to sob.

Laura saw darkness. Her nose ran and she could taste the salt of her own tears. There would be no need for a dinner of sleeping pills and vodka, after all. She cursed herself for letting Sara come here. They could have run and hid. Thousands of buildings in the city to hide out in, but she had followed Sara here, and now the girl was gone. Again.

They were led into a long, narrow mill building, and as they reached its end, she saw something against the wall, initially taking it for trash, but as she was pushed closer by her captor she saw it was a man. Curled up on his side, arms tied to a beam with thick rope.

Dad.

He was shirtless, and so thin she could count the vertebrae poking from his back. She was shoved to the ground and landed next to him. The others were given shoves and now sat on the concrete next to Laura.

Dad opened his eyes. She could see an array of cuts and bruises on his face. More bruises and lacerations covered his bare torso, from chest to waist. His breathing came in shallow gasps.

She felt her throat tighten up. He had been a kind and good man. Always taking time to put together her dollhouses as a girl. To teach her to ride a bike and get back on even though she had fallen and skinned her knees dozens of times and wanted no part of the bike. And the pregnancy. He didn't yell, didn't lecture, only took her face in his hands and kissed her forehead, telling her it was a blessing in disguise. Now the tears came. She couldn't bear to see him like this.

He opened his eyes and said, "Laura."

"How long have you been here?"

"Lost track of time. I came to fight him. He won," Dad said with a weak chuckle.

She moved closer, straining to examine his wounds in the dark. They were mostly lacerations and bruises. A few were infected, but it didn't appear he had been stabbed with one of their weapons.

"Did you find Sara?"

Her throat felt like it was closing on her. "We did."

"Where is she?"

A cold numbness seemed to seep through her limbs. "Engel killed her."

"Then it was meant to be," he said. "I'm sorry, Laura. I've caused you terrible pain."

"How?"

"I should have sent you both to safety all those years ago."

"How—how could you?"

Now she felt the tears come and she balled up her fists and tried hard to clamp down on her lower lip, but it trembled, and she put a hand over her mouth, letting out a choked sob. All these years, wondering where her baby went. The sleepless nights, the what-ifs. What if I hadn't left her? What if I had turned around faster? How could he do this to her? "Do you realize what you put me through?"

"I know."

"No, you don't."

"I only meant to protect her."

"Yeah, and it did a lot of good, didn't it? Why didn't you send us both away? Warn me, too. We could've stayed together!"

"You never would have believed me," he said, opening his eyes.

"You didn't even try. You just, just . . . took her."

"To save her," he said.

"How did you do it? Did you plan it? Did it cause you any guilt at all?"

He let out a tremendous sigh. "A group of Guardians from Routersville helped me. They tailed you to the pumpkin farm that day. Watched your every move, waited for you. When you went to get snacks from that table, they closed in around you. Another one of them grabbed the baby."

"Did you know her at all? Tell me you didn't get to see her, at least tell me that. If you got to be her grandfather—"

"Laura, I made a horrible mistake."

"Yeah," she said. "You did."

"I'm the worst father in the world."

"Really not the time for self-pity, trust me."

She couldn't look at him anymore. For the moment he wasn't her father, but a pathetic, miserable man who had destroyed her life in the name of what he thought was a good cause. She wiped the tears from her face. Then she turned her back on him and waited for what would probably be the end.

CHAPTER 31

Down in the Cobblestone district, flames crackled within the HSBC arena, and the windows that overlooked the lobby had blown out. The buffalo above the entrance had melted into a twisted lump. Outside the arena, it was worse. Piles of bodies, bodies in cars, bodies in the river, bodies impaled on spears and stakes. The cobblestones were slicked with blood.

On Chippewa, the college students that had gone out to the bar scene looking to hoist Guinness and drink Sex on the Beach were left hanging out of broken bar windows. Some still sat at pub tables, faces in pools of beer and spilled booze. At the Alligator, the rich-sweet smell of decay had begun to overpower the spilled beer and soaked-in odor of deep-fried wings and chicken fingers.

At Channel 7, the six o'clock news anchor, a petite brunette by the name of Mary Ford, had stayed on the air. If anyone had been watching, they would have seen the pale monster barge into the studio, and heard her frenzied screams as she was beaten to death with a spiked club.

At the Albright-Knox Gallery, when the first attack hit, a local artist named Phillip Russeau felt he had made it. There had been a reception with cheese and wine, his friends coming and marveling at his paintings. He was another Modigliani, they told him. Now, Phillip Russeau huddled in a darkened corridor of the art gallery, praying to Jesus and all the saints that the things didn't find him the way they had his friends. Their severed limbs now decorated the grass outside the Albright-Knox.

The Dark Ones moved across the city in hordes. Those that had remained in homes were dragged outside. In the Valley, whole families had been flayed, their skinless corpses left to hang from porches like meat in a butcher shop. In Niagara Square, a row of severed, eyeless heads lined the traffic circle, their mouths opened in permanent screams. On the Buffalo River, where grain had once been king and the long-abandoned silos and grain elevators stood watch, bloated corpses floated, turning the river red.

And the Dark Ones waited. Waited for the master to command them. Next would be another city, and another.

Laura huddled next to Debbie. On the other side of Debbie, Milo lay unconscious, which may have been a mercy. Frank and Jenny were farther down, both sitting, a demon holding their arms up and behind their heads. Only Mike remained standing, hands on hips, defiant. He seemed to be daring the winged creatures that guarded them to make a move.

Now, she heard footsteps, and in the darkness she saw

Engel's pale face. He removed his coat, revealing a hairless, muscular torso. "Which of you will be first? Hmmm?"

"Try me," Mike said, and lunged at him. Engel put an arm up, grabbed Mike's wrist, and twisted. The bone gave with a horrific crack. Mike went to his knees, letting out a scream. Engel's eyes grew wide. He twisted the wrist farther. Mike screamed again. Engel kicked him in the gut, but still held the broken wrist.

"Stop it!" Laura said.

The winged creatures surrounded Mike and Engel. One of them raised up its hand and a curved knife seemed to morph out of the darkness.

"Let's see what he looks like under that skin," Engel said.

Laura closed her eyes, stuck her fingers in her ears. She tried to block out the horror that was to come. She only hoped that when it was her turn, she would pass out. Mike let out a scream, a real lung buster that reverberated through the mill. Even with her fingers plugging her ears, it penetrated.

She had to do something. She got up and charged, grabbing one of the demons by its leathery wing and pulling. It turned around and backhanded her, catching her in the lip and sending her to the ground. The salty taste of blood filled her mouth.

She looked at Debbie, who had turned away. Soft sobs escaped her.

"Let him go!" Laura said.

From inside the circle, Engel said, "Would you take his place? Your turn will come soon enough."

She scrambled to her feet again, intent on stopping the torture, but one of the winged beasts turned. It had an extra eye in its forehead and a pair of horns that curled down around its face. It grabbed her in a bear hug and squeezed.

"Do not kill her, just hold her there."

If it wasn't trying to kill her, it disguised it well. Her ribs were pressed inward and she gasped for breath. Mike screamed some more. She smelled the thing's swampy breath and began to gag. It really was the end. She closed her eyes.

Despite that, there was Light. Coming through her lids, bright Light, the kind that if she looked into it would force her to shut her eyes. She opened them.

There was Light. Coming in the mill door in brilliant white streaks. The demons began to back away. Engel let out a groan of disgust.

She heard the voice but didn't believe it, "Let them go."

Sara remembered the final *thud-crack* she had heard after Engel threw her off the catwalk. There had been a sharp pain in her back, and she looked up and saw him looking down at her. Then things had gone dark.

She couldn't recall how long they had stayed that way, for part of the time had been erased. Then there had been the Light, dim yellow going to hot white, in front of her eyes, and then she felt warm, and it spread through her like oil through an engine. She opened her eyes and saw the catwalks and pipes. At first she couldn't move her limbs and had a horrific moment where she thought she had lived but was paralyzed. Then she could move her arms and legs. Soon after that, she sat up, and saw the Everlight fall from her chest.

Taking the stone with her, she left the cast house and wandered across the lot. She had heard the screams coming from the long narrow mill building and she took off running, the Light glowing in her palm with feverish intensity. She reached the mill door and found there was a neat halo of Light around her body, like an aura.

She went inside and saw the others. That was when she screamed to let them go.

Two winged demons immediately took flight. Without even thinking, she raised her arms and two beams the thickness of telephone poles erupted from her fingertips. They blasted the demons, reducing them to so much blackened flesh. The other winged ones came, and she cut them down, leaving Engel.

With a snarl, he charged at her, palms facing her, and something thick and black came at her with terrifying speed, but she put up her hands and a disk of light shielded her, sending his volley ricocheting to the side. It was enough to knock her off balance, and as she stumbled he whipped past her and ran from the mill.

She gave chase, hearing Laura yell, "Sara!" She kept going until she was outside. Engel waited, shirtless, hands clenched into fists at his sides.

"How is this possible?"

"Magic."

"You'll die anyway," he said, and raised his arms. A broadsword with a jagged blade materialized in his hands.

He began to move in. "Come back to me, my children! Now!"

Sara heard footsteps from behind, at the mill door. She took a quick glance and saw Laura in the doorway. "Sara."

"I can beat him," she said.

Now she saw fingers of mist, like funnel clouds in reverse, rising from the ground and traveling up into the mist that covered the city. When they joined with the larger mist, it twisted into a cone and shot down, heading toward the steel plant.

She'd been watching the spectacle of the mist and saw Engel at the last second, sword raised over his head. She moved aside as he swung it in a murderous arc and it struck the ground, spitting up concrete chips. She'd been lucky that time.

They circled one another. Stone in hand, she fired a beam, but he blocked it with the sword. They continued to circle, and this time she fired low, but he jumped over the beam. Now she heard something behind her, familiar strangled voices. A quick glance showed a small army of Dark Ones approaching. They stretched out along the fence, perhaps twenty deep, for as far as she could see.

"You see, you can't win."

From behind her, she heard another voice. "Finish him! You're strong." It was Reverend Frank. The Asian woman stood next to him. They didn't move to help, which told her this was her fight alone.

The Dark Ones grew closer. Engel charged again, swinging in a horizontal arc. Sara blocked it with a beam. His sword deflected upward.

One of these times he isn't going to miss.

He came back with a chopping blow, and again she blocked it, the light creating a shower of sparks. She immediately thrust upward, catching him in the shoulder, and he whirled around, shrieking. His back to her, she fired again, hitting him in the lower back. He fell to his knees and she moved in, eyeing the back of his neck, hoping to decapitate.

As she moved in, he remained on his knees, but when she raised her arm to deliver the blast, he spun around, faster than she thought possible, and thrust the sword up and through her middle. He let go of the hilt. She staggered backward. From the mill door, someone gasped.

She looked down and saw the sword jutting from her belly. It was heavy and nearly toppled her.

But there was no pain, and no blood, only a sense of *heaviness*. She gripped the blade, which felt sharp enough to slice paper, but her hands didn't bleed. She slowly removed it from her midsection and it fell to the ground with a clatter. The wound closed, her torn skin mending itself.

Engel looked dumbfounded.

She was aware of his army closing in around her.

Engel rose to his feet. "You little bitch."

Before he could conjure another weapon, she fired a beam. He attempted to block it, a circle of solid darkness forming around his arm, but her shot got past him. This one hit him in the chest and blew him backward. He lay on the ground, skin smoldering.

She fired again, and he twitched. He got to his hands and knees. She blasted him again, and again he fell to the ground.

Now, the Dark Ones around her had stopped. She looked at some of them and for the first time saw looks of fear in their eyes. *Good. You've caused enough of it yourself.*

Engel crawled, skin blackened in places, wisps of smoke rising from him. The air took on a burnt smell.

"Crawl like a snake, that's it!" she said, and ripped another blast. It caught him in the side of the head, opening up his skull. Thick black glop poured out. He raised his head one final time and screamed, a wail of anguish so terrible it made Sara shudder. Then he lowered his head and was still.

The Dark Ones began to wail. She saw them begin to burn up, bodies hissing, black smoke rising from them. Some fell to their knees. Others thrust spears into their own bellies, throats, and eyes. They were dissolving right before her.

Engel's body did the same, seeming to spontaneously combust, the skin bubbling and cracking, then turning charcoal black.

In a matter of minutes, all that remained on the ground were piles of ash, and after the last one had succumbed, a fierce wind blew, whipping through Sara's hair. It seemed to gather up the ashes, blowing them across the lot, then rising higher and higher, taking the remains to the sky, where they were scattered like snowflakes.

Laura ran to Sara. Above her, the ashes of the creatures were scattered until they were seen no more. She reached Sara and hugged her. The girl was crying, as was Laura. "You were dead."

"I thought so, too."

Reverend Frank had joined them.

"How?" Laura asked him, wiping tears.

"The stone has the power to resurrect the strongest Guardians. I tried it on a Guardian named McGivens in Routersville, but it didn't work. Sanborn—the one who originally slew Engel—was resurrected as well."

Sara said, "Dave never told us that."

"Charles and I were the only ones who knew. We didn't want him to fear for Sara's life any more than he already did."

Laura gave the girl another squeeze. "Let's check on the others."

In the mill, Milo was sitting up, shirt off, his pale saggy breasts resting on his belly. "Look at this!"

There was no evidence of the rot caused by the weapons. He put his shirt back on and got to his feet. "Jesus, I actually feel good."

Laura went to check on Mike. He was not so lucky. Engel and the others had torn off his shirt. Strips of flesh had been cut from his chest. They had tried to skin him and did a pretty good job on his chest. He was unconscious but breathing.

"He'll need medical care."

Frank came running inside. "There's an army convoy on 5. I'll go flag them down."

Help was on the way.